*I* am frequently asked if it has been a difficult proposition, being a butler extraordinaire. But I find that the most severe, the most powerful, even the most rakish master has a heart—and therein lies his salvation. And mine.

My name is Reeves, and I am a butler on a mission, sent by my now deceased employer to reclaim for the ton one of its finest members, a long-lost son who has gone without the civilizing effects money and position can provide.

I shall have to use all of my considerable persuasive powers, all of my most stealthy tricks, and perhaps even the unwitting assistance of a particularly lovely tutor, to civilize what may be the wildest member of the ton yet. Whimsical as it may be, I truly believe love can conquer even the most stubborn of hearts.

Fortunately, for all concerned, I relish a challenge, especially one of a romantic nature. As my late employer used to say, "If you want the impossible done, just ask Reeves."

### By Karen Hawkins

HER MASTER AND COMMANDER
LADY IN RED
AND THE BRIDE WORE PLAID
HOW TO TREAT A LADY
CONFESSIONS OF A SCOUNDREL
AN AFFAIR TO REMEMBER
THE SEDUCTION OF SARA
A BELATED BRIDE
THE ABDUCTION OF JULIA

*Coming Soon*

HER OFFICER AND GENTLEMAN

# Karen Hawkins

# Her Master And Commander

## AVON BOOKS

*An Imprint of HarperCollinsPublishers*

This is a work of fiction. Names, characters, places, and incidents are products of the author's imagination or are used fictitiously and are not to be construed as real. Any resemblance to actual events, locales, organizations, or persons, living or dead, is entirely coincidental.

AVON BOOKS
*An Imprint of* HarperCollins*Publishers*
10 East 53rd Street
New York, New York 10022-5299

Copyright © 2006 by Karen Hawkins
Excerpts from *Don't Look Down* copyright © 2006 by Suzanne Enoch; *Sex, Lies, and Online Dating* copyright © 2006 by Rachel Gibson; *Her Master and Commander* copyright © 2006 by Karen Hawkins; *Sword of Darkness* copyright © 2006 by Sherrilyn Kenyon
ISBN-13: 978-0-06-058408-5
ISBN:10: 0-06-058408-4
www.avonromance.com

First Avon Books paperback printing: March 2006

Avon Trademark Reg. U.S. Pat. Off. and in Other Countries, Marca Registrada, Hecho en U.S.A.
HarperCollins® is a registered trademark of HarperCollins Publishers Inc.

Printed in the U.S.A.

10  9  8  7  6  5  4  3  2  1

*To my son's dog, Duke—*

*Thank you for keeping my toes warm
and never giving me that you-are-so-stupid look
you save for the cat.*

*Everyone needs a dog like Duke.*

# A COMPLEAT GUIDE FOR
# BEING A MOST PROPER BUTLER
## by Richard Robert Reeves

*As I reach my thirtieth year of service as a butler in a gentleman's household, I find myself looking back. Between my secret recipe for boot blacking (an indispensable tool for a butler), and a vastly superior method to remove wine stains from velvet (which some will erroneously hold to be an impossibility), I find my memories salted with some faint wisdoms, a few tested experiences, and many, many interesting stories.*

*My only regret is that, due to my devotion to this profession, I have no children into whose hands I might deliver my wisdoms and memories. Therefore, in writing this book, I have decided to dedicate it to all the young men who are considering accepting a position in a well-bred establishment as a butler. In many ways, you are my sons, all of you.*

*Thus, I begin…*

# Prologue

A servant—any servant—should never overstep the boundaries of his profession unless required by the utmost necessity. Even then, he should do so with extreme caution. It has been my experience that when a servant haphazardly crosses the lines of propriety, society—or some force within—will often shove him right back.

*A Compleat Guide for*
*Being a Most Proper Butler*
by Richard Robert Reeves

*The White Thistle Inn*
*Yorkshire, England*
*1781*

"*H*e will come." Ten-year-old Tristan Llevanth leaned his forehead on the cool pane of glass. Below him, across the muddy inn yard, lay the road to London. Long and narrow, a brown ribbon threaded through the scraggly countryside, it stood heart-wrenchingly empty. "I know he will," he whispered, his breath fogging the damp glass. "Our father never lies."

"How do you know?" Christian said with a disgusted curl of his lip. "The earl never speaks to us. He doesn't even consider us his children."

Tristan turned to face his brother. "The earl of Rochester is a busy man. And he does, too, consider us his children for he gives Mother money to pay for our upkeep and the tutor."

Christian didn't look impressed. "He wouldn't be too busy to see us if we were his legitimate heirs. And he certainly wouldn't leave us here where it's cold and boring."

*Legitimate.* The word burned into Tristan's soul and he had to grit his teeth against the threat of tears. "He will come to save us. He must."

Christian met Tristan's gaze for a long moment, his expression skeptical. One would scarcely know they were twins to look at them. Whereas Tristan was blondish with broad shoulders and fists the size of ham hocks, Christian was black-haired and slender, though every bit as tall.

The only commonality the two shared was the color of their eyes, an oddly light and compelling green, like that of a newly bloomed leaf. An elfish color, one of the chambermaids had called it.

Tristan rather liked that. Perhaps he *was* magic and if he tried hard enough, their father would come riding through the fog and save them all. Especially Mother, who needed saving more than anyone else.

At the thought of Mother, locked away in a damp prison all alone, Tristan rubbed his chest where an ache lodged and grew. He knew what the ache was—fear. And it was the enemy. If he let the lump grow too large, he would not be able to make decisions, find a way out of their present difficulties. And Christian, for all his posturing otherwise, had to be as frightened as Tristan.

In the taproom below, the sound of raised voices echoed up the wooden stairwell, rising with Tristan's fears.

Christian glanced uneasily at the closed door. "We should leave. This place is not safe."

"We cannot," Tristan said sternly. "We wrote Father that we'd be here, waiting. And we will be."

"Tris... Brooks said the earl's men would not let him in. They just took the letter and sent him on his way."

"Father is an earl. He is a very important man. I am certain when he finally had time to read the letter—"

"He wouldn't even see Brooks. What makes you think he'll read our letter?"

Tristan shook his head desperately. "*No.* You are wrong. Father *will* come. He has to, Chris. He has to."

Christian's brows lowered. "You... you aren't going to cry, are you?"

Tristan pulled himself up, fighting the tears that choked him. After a moment, he rasped out, "I do not cry."

Christian met his gaze straight on. "Neither do I." Yet after a long moment, his shoulders sagged and he turned back to the window, staring sightlessly out at the graying evening.

Hands curled into fists stiffly held at his sides, Tristan said in a quiet voice, "If Father does not help, Mother could—" He swallowed.

Christian rubbed his forehead. "Brooks knows that. It is why he has been acting so strangely of late. He ... he is afraid."

Tristan knew that Mr. Brooks only stayed with him and Christian because the tutor believed that once Mother was freed, she'd reward him for his assistance in watching over her sons. At first, the tutor had been rather benign in taking care of them. But as each day passed and the likelihood of Mother returning seemed more remote, Brooks's temper had changed.

Last week, after he'd been turned away from the earl's house, Brooks had become more noticeably sullen and cross. He drank heavily and no longer pretended to be polite in speaking to his charges. There were times, in fact, when he was anything but. Tristan rolled his shoulders and winced where a bruise lingered there from the stick Brooks had applied to Tristan's shoulders for asking yet again if perhaps they should write another letter to Father.

"Does it still hurt?" Christian asked quietly.

"It's just a bit stiff. I almost forgot about it."

For a split second, emotion flashed hot and ready across Christian's eyes. Raw, bloody fury that made Tristan gape in surprise. But in the blink of an eye, the expression was gone and Christian had turned to look out the window once again.

Christian was like that; he hid his feelings well. Mother always said he was like a lake, calm on the surface though a powerful current rumbled beneath. Tristan, meanwhile, was the ocean—his feelings frothed and foamed on the surface, crashing like waves into every situation. Even this one. Especially this one.

The distinct roar of drunken laughter erupted from the taproom below. As one, Christian and Tristan turned to look at the closed door. The roar faded a bit, though the noise level was noticeably higher. Somewhere in the midst of that roar was Mr. Brooks, drinking and gambling away what precious little they had left.

Tristan leaned his forehead against the glass. "I hate this."

Christian turned and looked at his older brother. He loved Tristan and looked up to him, but there were times when his twin seemed to cling to hope when there was none. "We cannot stay here."

"We have to. For Father." Tristan sighed, his breath frosting the glass. "Maybe Mr. Brooks can write Father's man of business and find out why he hasn't replied—"

"Mr. Brooks has done enough," Christian said more harshly than he intended. Tristan's mouth thinned, a wounded look shone in his eyes. A surge of guilt made Christian clasp his hands behind his back. He squeezed his fingers so hard they burned. It wouldn't do for anyone to see how much his hands were shaking. When he'd sat at the top of the stairs last night, he'd heard far more than he'd shared with Tristan. Mr. Brooks had been talking to a man in a long coat. The tutor owed the man money—a lot of money. Brooks had already sold everything they had of value. All he had left was—

Christian pressed his lips together. He wouldn't think of it right now. Later tonight, when Tristan was asleep, Christian would think of a way to leave before the tutor decided to sell the only assets they had left. He and Tris would escape, perhaps go to London themselves and find one of Mother's friends. Perhaps they could even find someone to help her. Someone who cared more than their father.

The thought of the earl burned a hole in Christian's stomach. He hated his father. Hated him so much that seeing the old man dead wasn't nearly enough to satisfy the bile that flowed in Christian's veins. One day, he'd kill his father for what he'd done to him and Tristan. For what the old man hadn't done for Mother. There the old man sat, surrounded by his title, his lands, his fortune, yet he could not be bothered to keep watch over anyone who was not in his immediate favor. Not even Mother, who had once been wildly in love with the man.

The thought of Mother raised new shadows. It had been almost six months since she'd been dragged from her bed and arrested, thrown into gaol without a word of explanation. For weeks, no one would tell them why she'd been arrested. When Christian had finally overheard the butler telling the housekeeper that Mother had been imprisoned on charges of treason, he'd thought he'd misheard. But he hadn't.

Even now that day seemed a horrid dream. Mrs. Felts, the housekeeper, had cried, and Melton, the butler, had looked pale and grim. Neither of the boys had understood, of course. All they knew was what Mr. Brooks told them, that Mother was gone, but would come home any day. That the charges could be fought, refuted. But somehow, as the days passed, those words were spoken less and less often, until now, when they weren't spoken at all.

From the second Mother had been imprisoned, the funds from the earl had stopped. Not a single pence arrived. The servants had gone away, one by one, until only Mr. Brooks was left.

One day, a burly, unsmiling man had arrived at the house and nailed a sign on the front door saying the premises were reassigned back into the care of the bank because of arrears on the property.

Christian wasn't sure what "arrears" were, but within hours, Brooks had all of the silver in the house packed into a cart, and they were on their way. The family silver didn't last long. Slowly, as the weeks passed, the quality of their lives lowered. They no longer went to the inns in the center of town, but to the ones on the outskirts. Dirty and damp and vermin ridden, the feather mattresses gave way to hay ticking. And then to the hard floor.

Now, they were down to the last two candlesticks. Christian wondered what would happen when those were gone. What would they do then? More importantly, what would Brooks do?

A hand settled on his shoulder. "Don't look like that," Tristan said. "I will think of something."

Christian turned to look at his brother. "I hope so."

Tristan squeezed his brother's shoulder, suddenly filled with an aching determination to fix things. "We will manage. Wait and see if we don't."

Christian pushed his hair from his eyes. The light slanted over his face, touching the dirty lace at his throat and shining on the worn velvet of his coat. "Tristan, there is something you should know. The other day, on the steps... I heard Brooks talking to a man. About us."

Tristan's heart thudded an extra beat. "What did he say?"

"Brooks owes the man a lot of money. The man asked if we were strong. Tristan, he said—" Christian swallowed loudly, visibly collecting himself. "He said the last two recruits he'd pressed had died before they'd even made landfall."

Tristan's chest burned with the effort to breathe. Life at sea was difficult and deadly. Ships often sent gangs to capture able-bodied men and boys who were then dragged on board and pressed into service as sailors. It was perfectly legal to do so, even though many never returned to their homes.

Urgency tightened Tristan's throat. Surely they had a few more days to find a way out of this fix. Perhaps they could take the candlesticks and leave Brooks behind. Yes. That is what they should do—

Tristan stiffened. Over the noise of the crowd, he thought he heard—there it was again. Brooks was coming up the stairs, and he was not alone. There was no time. "Christian! Quick! Out the window."

"What—" His brother's eyes widened as Brooks's voice carried into the room. Christian whirled to the window and frantically began to work at the latch.

Tristan took the one chair that graced the room and rammed it under the doorknob. Pitifully wobbly, it was all he had.

The window latch gave with a loud snap. Christian pushed the window open and leaned out. "Tris, it's a long way down—"

The door rattled. Brooks's angry voice rose. "Damn it! Open up!"

Tristan ran to the bed and pulled a small red bundle from beneath it, the candlesticks clanking together. The door rattled louder. Brooks's voice rose with each word. "Open this bloody door or I'll beat the both of you!"

Another man's voice said something low and Brooks agreed. "I can do that."

Tristan grabbed up the bundle and ran to Christian. "Here." He thrust it into his brother's hands. "Take this."

"Tris, we're two stories up."

"We have no choice. I'll be right behind you—"

The door burst open. Mr. Brooks stood in the entry, his cravat mussed, his eyes wild. Behind him stood a large, cadaverous-looking man with eyes red-rimmed from drink.

Panic freed Tristan. He acted without thought, without direction. Whirling, he shoved his brother out the window. Christian clutched convulsively at the bundled candlesticks as he fell backward. A lone scream pierced the night.

"Good God!" Brooks said, leaping forward, his face pale.

Tristan made a mad dive for the window, but the man with Brooks was faster. "Ye bloody bugger!" the man yelled. He grabbed Tristan and jerked him back inside, the windowsill cruelly scraping his chest.

Tristan kicked, his boot landing solidly on the man's shin.

"Why you— Nobody treats Jack Danter like thet!" He tightened his grip even more, his strong arms pressing the air from Tristan's lungs.

"Careful, Danter!" Brooks said, looking ill. "You— you said they'd come to no harm."

"Stop yammerin' and fetch t'other!" Danter snapped,

his lips tight over yellowed teeth. "I'll deal with this one."

The tutor swallowed. "I don't believe I should—"

"Then pay what ye owe!" Danter's gaze narrowed, his arms tightening even more cruelly around Tristan.

Tristan gasped for breath. His chest burned, his eyes blurred and wet. *Run, Christian! Save yourself!* He thought it over and over, as if by repetition he might make it happen.

Brooks's gaze moved back to Tristan, something dismally sad in their depths. For a second, Tristan thought the tutor might save him after all. But instead, the man's shoulders slumped and he turned and went silently out the door.

Anger exploded behind Tristan's eyes. He sucked in a deep breath and lurched free from Danter's grasp. *"Christian! RUN!"*

Danter grabbed Tristan by the throat, his fist drawn back, his face twisted in anger.

As if in a dream, Tristan saw the fist coming toward him. There was nothing to be done. He was lost. All he could do was hope that Christian had made it, that Tristan hadn't killed his only brother by shoving him out the window.

It was the last thought he had before the fist met his temple and, with an explosion of white pain, blacked his mind to everything else.

# Chapter I

A butler's primary purpose is to serve his employer thoroughly and discreetly. Valor is the first part of discretion. It also helps to possess a large dose of tolerance and a very, very short memory.

*A Compleat Guide for*
*Being a Most Proper Butler*
by Richard Robert Reeves

*Rochester House*
*Somerset, England*
*1806*

*P*ristine and perfect, the river wound through carefully tended forests, flirting here and there with the stone-paved path before gently toppling into a wide, crystal clear pond. The deep blue waters reflected the flawless outline of a meticulously planned rotunda decorated with several columns and a pink marble fountain. Over the years, the rotunda had served as a trysting spot for lord, lady, prince, and pauper.

Over this astonishingly well orchestrated bit of idyllic beauty rose a nearby hillock. On it, set like a crown on a velvet pillow, sat a massive and stately manor house of lush gold brick, the mullioned windows sparkling enticingly in the late afternoon sun.

Rochester House was widely agreed to be the epitome of culture. The king himself had lauded the house and its furnishings as "the most exquisite in all of England."

The comment had been made almost two score years ago, and at the time, the sixth earl had merely bowed his head ever so slightly to acknowledge it. Privately, of course, he'd been quite pleased, but it would have been ill-bred to have appeared so. And a Rochester was never, ever ill-bred.

Still, the earl allowed himself a generous amount of time in private to savor the king's admiration. Each night, before closing his eyes, he remembered the words and the exact expression on the king's face as he uttered them. It helped Rochester fall asleep and often gave him the most delightful dreams.

Except now, of course. Now, he was far too busy with the irritating duty of dying with dignity.

The dying part was, he thought, rather simple. It was the "with dignity" portion that was a struggle. But then, anything worth doing was worth a good fight. The earl had learned that caveat long, long ago.

To be honest, Rochester should not have been surprised that he was dying. After all, he was well past his seventieth year of age, a fact he attempted to hide from his peers by keeping to powdered wigs for as long as fashion allowed, the liberal use of rouge, and a superb wardrobe that dazzled the eye and removed notice from his sagging skin and wrinkled brow.

To further add to the illusion of youth, he'd married a woman who was, by any count, more than half a century younger than he. Ostensibly, he'd married the lovely, vapid Miss Leticia Crowell for the express purpose of adding a beautiful woman to his household, much like purchasing a certain type of orchid to decorate one's dinner table.

The truth was, Rochester was desperate for a child. He'd thought to marry, produce a son, and thus secure his lands, fortune, and title. He winced even now at the crassness of it all. It was so tawdry, this breeding aspect. Sex for the purpose of pleasure was an art. Sex in an effort to bring forth a mewling child—Rochester curled his lip.

He'd never thought he'd have trouble fathering a child. After all, he'd managed to father brats *before* he was married, why would he have any difficulties *after*? Which was why he'd waited so long before tying himself to the demands of some silly chit who had to be told twice that one did not wear diamonds to a morning visit. Yet as much as he'd disliked the notion, he knew his duty and so, with the greatest reluctance, he'd married.

Unfortunately, fate had a cruel sense of humor. Now, here he was, gasping his last breath, married to a chit with more hair than wit, and not a single legitimate son to inherit either his wealth or the Rochester name. The name he'd worked so hard to build into something unique, something memorable, much like this house, was destined to die with him.

His fingers curled over the single sheet of paper resting in his hand, the noise drawing his gaze. Ah, yes, the list. He smiled a little, relieved. There was hope, after all.

He would make right all the things he'd done wrong. Even from the grave, he would maintain the quality of the Rochester name and keep the house in the family. It was a bold plan. But then...he was a bold man.

He smiled, wincing when a sharp pain rattled through his shoulder, the pressure on his chest increasing. Damn it, he had so little time left. Why had he waited so long?

The huge mahogany door that led into the earl's chamber opened and a tall, perfectly groomed individual entered. The man was dressed in the deep black of a butler, his air stately and calm. He carried a silver tray covered with a linen cloth.

Rochester never allowed any but the most elegant of servants in his employ. Yet even he had to admit that his butler, the indispensable Reeves, was a gem among gems. There was something startlingly commanding about Reeves. Dark and slender, his hair traced over each ear with a distinguished stroke of gray. And his wicked way of putting a shine on boots had caught even Beau Brummel's attention.

Rochester had the world's best butler and the entire ton was aware of it. Four times in the last two months alone, other members of the nobility had attempted to hire Reeves away, but Rochester knew the man's worth and he paid the butler a fortune.

Reeves set the tray on the table beside the bed. He removed a silver cover to reveal an amber-filled glass.

Rochester's hopes rose even more. "Bourbon?"

"Indeed, my lord."

"But Letty said she'd poured my bourbon out the window!"

"Had I realized what my lady was about, I might have been able to talk her into a more rational act, such as sending the bourbon to your summer estate. Alas, I was too late."

"Blasted interfering chit!"

"Lady Rochester was distressed you refused to listen to the doctor's good advice and continued to imbibe."

"I may be ill, but I am not yet dead!"

"No, indeed, my lord. Fortunately for all concerned, I just this moment recalled I had hidden a stray bottle of bourbon in the cellar in case the troubles with France worsened and our supply dwindled."

"Reeves, you are a godsend," Rochester said fervently, wetting his dry lips and struggling to sit upright.

Reeves assisted him, plumping the earl's pillow and smoothing the sheets, all the little touches that made Reeves so indispensable.

It took Rochester a few moments to catch his breath after such an effort, during which time Reeves discreetly pulled a small vial from his pocket and held it over the coveted bourbon. A few drops plopped into the glass.

"Hold!" gasped Rochester, appalled. "What are you doing?"

"Putting your tonic in your bourbon, my lord."

"I don't want that damn stuff!"

Reeves calmly picked up a waiting spoon and gently stirred, the silver clinking against the fine glass. "No bourbon, my lord? None at all?"

"I want the bourbon, damn you! But not that vile tonic."

"I realize that, my lord. So did the doctor when you had him ejected from the house by the footman."

That had been a bit rude of him, Rochester realized, though the charlatan had deserved it. "I don't need tonic."

Reeves looked at the earl's hand.

Rochester became aware that he was rubbing his chest with his palm, trying to erase the constant pressure. He dropped his hand. "Take that poison away! I won't have it now."

Reeves put the spoon back on the tray and replaced the silver cover over the glass. "Very well, my lord." He picked up the tray. "Will there be anything more? Some sherry, perhaps?"

Rochester sent his butler a sour glare. "Sherry is horse piss and water! Just leave. My valet, Miller, will fetch me a fresh glass of bourbon."

"Your valet would indeed fetch you a glass of bourbon...*if* he knew where to find it." Reeves walked sedately to the door. "Which, of course, he does not."

"You said you found the bottle in the wine cellar, so I shall have him look for it there," the earl said testily.

Reeves paused at the door. "Was, my lord. The bottle *was* in the wine cellar. Now however, it is *not*."

Rochester cursed, loud and long.

The butler's bland expression never changed. But as soon as the earl's outburst subsided, Reeves said, "I shall tell Miller to bring some tepid milk, to help with your bilious stomach."

"I don't have a bilious stomach and you know it! Oh

blast you to hell, bring me that damn bourbon. I only hope you have not completely ruined it with your poison."

The glass of bourbon was in Rochester's hand in a remarkably quick space of time. He sniffed it suspiciously, then took a sip. A warm tingle settled in his chest as the flavor flooded across his tongue. "Ah!"

Reeves smiled. "The tonic did not alter the taste too much?"

There was hardly any trace of the bitter tonic in the bourbon at all. Still, it would not do to let Reeves become too self-important. Rochester needed the butler's services too badly for that. Now more than ever. So instead of agreeing, the earl said testily, "It will do."

Rochester took another sip, then lowered the glass and looked at his butler. "I'm glad you're here, Reeves, for I've something to ask."

Reeves picked up his lordship's robe and placed it neatly in a large, gold leaf wardrobe. "Yes, my lord?"

"You are paid better than any butler in England."

"Yes, my lord. And I am worth every pence."

He had a point, Rochester thought grumpily. "I am not suggesting that *you* are not valuable. I only stated that you were *paid* well."

"How good of you to differentiate those two items, my lord," Reeves intoned.

Rochester eyed him narrowly. "That sounded like sarcasm."

Reeves gave a faint smile. "Sarcasm has a certain value, does it not? Perhaps I should ask for more wages for possessing such a sense of humor."

Rochester stared. "I should pay you for sarcasm?"

"I would rather think of it as compensation for putting up with yours, my lord."

Despite the ache that set on Rochester's chest, a laugh burst from him. "Damn you, Reeves! I should horsewhip you for being so cheeky."

"Ah, but I know where the last and only bottle of bourbon is hidden."

The medicine and bourbon was beginning to have an effect; the pressure in the earl's chest lessened a little and a gentle glow enveloped him as he set the empty glass on the table beside the bed. "Reeves, I must speak to you. It's about all of this—" He waved a hand to the room, indicating the entire property. "—when I die."

"Shall I fetch her ladyship—"

"Good God, no! Why would I want to do that? All that caterwauling—Reeves, I wish I hadn't married. Not that I've anything against Letty, mind you. It's just that, without an heir, there's really no reason for me to have been married at all." The earl attempted to smile. "But that is neither here nor there. Reeves, you have gone above and beyond your duty since the day you arrived."

"Thank you, my lord. It has been a privilege."

"That is why I want you to find my successor."

Reeves paused in folding the sheet to a more comfortable length beneath his lordship's pale hands. "My lord?"

"I am dying, damn it! I don't have time for quibbling."

Reeves's lips twitched. "My lord, whether you have time to quibble or not, I do believe I shall need more information than what you've offered thus far."

For some reason, the gentle tone made Rochester's throat tighten. "It's quite simple. I want you to find my heir and see to it that he does not embarrass the Rochester name."

"Your heir, my lord?"

The earl reached for the folded sheet of paper he'd set aside. He opened it now and consulted the scrawled list. "While I was unable to have a child in wedlock, I have been more than blessed without."

Reeves's brows rose. "My lord?"

"The eldest of my bastards—though he won't be one forever—will be the next earl."

"But… Pardon me, my lord. I am somewhat confused."

The earl took a deep breath. "Reeves, I just remembered I was once wed."

Rochester watched the butler closely, looking for some expression of surprise, but all Reeves said was, "Ah!"

The earl waved a hand rather lamely. "It was a … a rather secret marriage, but my man of business has the details well in hand. The priest who performed the marriage has been found and has been made to *recollect* the event. We've even found the register it was recorded in—but you don't need the details. Just know that it has all been taken care of."

"I see. How, er, fortuitous for your son. Do you think society will accept this story?"

"They have to. The priest is now the archbishop of Canterbury." Rochester chuckled. "He's a hot-tempered man, too. If one of my distant relatives comes crawling out of the woodwork and attempts to nay-say him, he'll toss them right out of the church and onto their arse."

The earl grinned. "Damn! I'd like to see that! I almost wish I wasn't dying so I could watch!"

"Perhaps your son will enjoy the sight for you, my lord."

"Not 'son.' Sons. They were twins. The oldest has been going by the name of Tristan Paul Llevanth."

"Llevanth." Reeves said the name quietly, thoughtfully. "That name is familiar."

The earl grimaced. "I know, damn it. The blasted fool had to go out and make a name for himself, which was extremely ill-bred. But I cannot do anything about it now."

"No, my lord," Reeves said, his brow drawn as he tried to remember where he'd heard the name before.

Rochester frowned peevishly. "I did love Pauline and if I could have saved her—she was unjustly charged with treason. That is what comes of such an unconventional upbringing. Her father had untenable political beliefs and encouraged her to read all sorts of rubbish."

"Rubbish, my lord?"

"All sorts of political foolery. He died well before I was around, which was a damned good thing. She had very strong opinions that did not always do her beauty justice."

"Yes," Reeves said. "Strong opinions are *so* unbecoming."

Rochester shot a hard look at the butler. "What does that mean?"

"Nothing, my lord. Nothing at all."

"Humph. Pauline and I eventually parted, though I sent her funds for the boys." The earl frowned. "Damn it, why couldn't Letty—but no. That does not matter now."

He sent a faintly regretful glance at Reeves. "I perhaps did not visit my by-blows quite as I should have." The earl fretted over this a moment, then sighed. "I cannot fix that now. Anyway, as I was saying, all was well until Pauline was accused of treason. It was a very nasty business."

Reeves adjusted his lordship's pillow. "I am certain you did all you should have, my lord."

"I wasn't here to assist her. If I hadn't been out of the country—" Rochester didn't speak, emotion tight in his chest.

"My lord?" Concern etched Reeves's voice.

"I was in Italy. It took me weeks to get back. As soon as I landed, I went to see the king, but... I was too late. She had died in prison the previous week and the boys were gone. Vanished! I tried to find them, but there was no trace to be had. Until—" Rochester pressed his lips together.

"Until?" Reeves prompted gently.

"I read Tristan's name in the blasted paper. I cannot tell you how horrified I was, to see someone of my own blood, his name bantered about as if he were a commoner!"

"Yes, my lord."

The earl tried to remember his sons, but could only dredge up the faintest picture. "I seem to remember that they were handsome youths, though quite different in coloring."

"If they had the Rochester looks, I am certain they were *very* handsome indeed."

"All of my children are extraordinarily well-looking," Rochester said sternly, hoping it was so.

"All of them, my lord?"

Rochester looked at the list in his hands, a faint flush coloring his pale cheeks. "Dying is so damned unfair! Here I am, a leader of society, known to all, an intimate of the prince's, and what happens but—" He gestured angrily at his thin and wasted frame. "—*this*! I never thought things would come to such a pass."

"Yes, my lord. Dying is wasted upon the well dressed."

Rochester's eyes narrowed. "Are you mocking me?"

"Never, my lord. It's just that I find it somewhat disturbing that you thought you'd never die. We *all* die, my lord. It would be unnatural, otherwise."

The earl's shoulders slumped. "I know, I know. I just— Damn it, I'm not finished yet! I was also going to hold a ball for Letty's birthday, and the prince had promised to attend, which would make it quite the event of the season— But it is too late for all of that, damn it." The earl handed the list to Reeves. "Here. These are my children. I was going to find them myself, but— Well, it is not to be."

"One of the ironies of this business of living is that we never really finish. Whatever time we have, we fill it, and when it empties, we fill it yet again." Reeves unfolded the paper. "I do not believe there is such a thing as enough time, my lord. For anyone."

"No, there's not."

"Although…" Reeves looked at the list. "Perhaps some things should have taken more priority. You had children out of wedlock and yet you've never mentioned them once in all the time I've served you."

Rochester's face heated. "The duke of Richmond is said to have more than twelve illegitimate children. Nine is not such a high number."

"Hmmm. Is this the same duke that you refer to as the 'Prince of Chicanery'?"

Rochester eyed his butler glumly. "You have a damnable memory, did you know that?"

"A moment ago, you were lauding my memory even as you drank your bourbon."

The earl fought a smile. "Pray do not attempt to divert me. I have requested my solicitor, Mr. Dunstead, locate the children. I am leaving them each something from my will, providing, of course, they prove themselves worthy of the Rochester name." The earl took a steadying breath, wincing when a pain shot up his arm. "That is where I have need of your services. Dunstead is to find them, but *you* are to civilize them."

"Civilize? But my lord, I don't—"

"Reeves, this is important." Rochester moved restlessly. "My children must be brought to heel. You see, Tristan Paul Llevanth, the next Earl of Rochester, was once a pirate."

Reeves blinked and the earl had the felicity of shocking his butler for the first time in twenty years' service. "A pirate?"

"Well, not anymore. He is naught but a sea captain now."

Reeves's brows rose. "Llevanth! I do indeed know that name; all of England knows it. Captain Tristan Llevanth sailed the *Victory* with Nelson at Trafalgar but a year ago. His name has been in the *Morning Post* and—"

"Do not remind me that he has become a public figure. It was excessively ill-bred of him."

"My lord, he is a hero. I know it has been said he was once a privateer—"

"Pirate. Don't sugarcoat it."

"Pirate, then, my lord. But Nelson won Llevanth a pardon so he could fight with the admiral at Trafalgar. That says quite a bit about his character."

"The fool is a sea captain," the earl said in a waspish tone, "which isn't much better than a common pirate in my book. It would not surprise me if the next earl picks his teeth at the table and rarely bathes."

"Have you met many sea captains, my lord?"

"That fellow, Nelson. He was at a soiree. A small, rude man, if I remember rightly. With no sense of style, as well."

"I daresay your sea captain is better favored. The Rochester family is notoriously well formed."

"Yes, but if what Dunstead has discovered is true, the next earl is also injured." Blast it, was he to have no luck at all? A sea captain with some sort of unfavorable injury. The earl could only hope his son was not badly scarred as well. That would be too much indeed.

"I read about that, too," Reeves said, still looking somewhat startled. "I don't know the severity of the injury, but it was enough that he was forced to resign his commission. I heard that Admiral Nelson himself would have been saddened by that, for he thought quite highly of Captain Llevanth."

"Humph. Well, I can only hope he comes to his senses and accepts my conditions for the inheritance."

"My lord, pardon me, but you say that as if you'd spoken to him rather recently?"

The earl plucked at the coverlet.

"My lord?"

"Yes, yes! I heard you! I wrote to the fellow. I thought

it was the least I could do, seeing as how I'm not getting over this illness and I haven't had much commerce with him."

"May I inquire as to his response?"

"No."

"I see. What, exactly, *did* you write to him?"

"I told him I hoped he knew what was expected of him once the title was his. His answer was most rude."

Reeves sighed. "My lord, this is quite a large task."

"I don't see what is so difficult," Rochester said testily, suddenly feeling quite tired. "Just find Llevanth and convince him to take on the mantle of earl. Then teach him what he needs to know that he may do it with the taste and breeding I have worked so hard to attach to the name."

"But...if he is a sea captain—"

"If you do not prevail, he is lost. The title and lands will be his, but his sibling will get the fortune *if,* of course, he becomes more civilized as well. He *must* be made to accept his duties. I refuse to have all my work undone in one generation."

"Yes, my lord."

The earl leaned back, his chest easing somewhat. "Thank you, Reeves. I knew you would not let me down. Once I have died, your salary will be doubled. When you finish turning the oldest into a true Rochester, you are to go to Christian, the younger one, and do the same for him. It should not be too difficult. None of my children can have anything less than a superior understanding."

Reeves folded the list neatly. "Has Mr. Dunstead found them?"

"Not yet." The earl yawned. "I fear my second son might be in hiding. There is some indication he might be something more—shall we say, 'memorable' than his brother."

"More memorable? Than a hero of a naval battle?"

"Unfortunately, yes." The earl pressed his lips together. "I will leave Dunstead to explain it to you."

"My lord, I hate to ask this, but, ah...has either of your sons shown any violent tendencies? I mean no disrespect; it's merely a matter of personal safety."

"If they did, you may be assured they had good reason. My sons may not know how to dress, but they are *still* my sons. No Rochester has ever been involved in anything truly unsavory."

"Thank you for your reassurance," Reeves said dryly.

The earl yawned again, his lids sliding half closed. "Blood will always tell."

"Yes, my lord." Reeves tucked the list into his pocket and began drawing the heavy draperies about the huge gold bed. "You need your rest, my lord."

"Thank you, Reeves. I shall sleep well knowing you will be working to reclaim the lost Rochester heritage." The earl forced his heavy lids open. "Oh, yes. I almost forgot. In addition to your wages, I will supply you with a generous allowance that you might take whatever supplies you deem necessary. You may wish to take a few of the others with you, as well."

"Others, my lord?"

"I can't imagine a sea captain will have either a decent cook or valet."

"Perhaps he has both." Reeves dimmed the lamp.

Rochester was barely aware of it. The tonic combined with the bourbon had taken hold and he was already drifting off to sleep. He'd set things as much to rights as he could and he was confident that his man Reeves would take care of the rest.

Reeves always did.

# Chapter 2

Resist the urge to overstarch your employer's cravats or muddy his boots in retaliation for some real or imagined slight. If you feel you must make a statement, it is most expedient to do so when the gentleman is eating. He will be in a more temperate mood and, at times, his mouth well-filled. For an astute butler, that could well be a Very Good Thing.

*A Compleat Guide for*
*Being a Most Proper Butler*
by Richard Robert Reeves

*T*he blue waves hurled themselves against the jagged cliff face, thundering with fury across encrusted rocks. High on the cliff top, far above the ocean, sat a large cottage. Built of the same black rock that decorated the shoreline, it was almost invisible except for the thick curls of smoke that puffed from all three chimneys.

Captain Tristan Paul Llevanth stood before the cottage, staring into the wild black water below, fascinated as ever by the swirling, foaming madness. The wind flapped his cape, tangled and damp, about his legs. A dull ache lifted from his heel through his knee and his fingers tightened over the brass knob of the hated cane. "Blast it, even standing pains me," he growled, cursing his wounded leg to the deep blue and back.

He took a deep breath, lifting the damp scent of the ocean into his lungs, releasing the pain into the air even as he allowed the coolness to replenish his spirits. The breeze tussled the one lone tree that stood on the cliff, sending a smattering of brown leaves swirling to the ground.

Behind him, the familiar slam of the door rang out. In a moment, one of the men would be there, pretending to ask an innocuous question. Ever since he'd been wounded, his own bloody crew—the ones who'd remained with him—had taken to treating him like a scabby, new to ship and wet behind the ears.

It was galling. It also reminded him of the early days, when he'd been naught but a soft landlubber with no calluses and less understanding of what it meant to be at sea. At first, he'd fought. Fought his destiny with his entire being. He'd been sad and frightened and sick with worry about Christian—

*No.* He wouldn't remember those days. He'd remember the later ones. When he'd finally made his peace with the sea and life on board.

Though he grew to hate his first captain, a harsh, unjust man given to beating his men for the slightest offense, Tristan loved life at sea and reveled in the wildness of the crashing ocean that had once terrified him.

Though Captain Reynolds had no place in Tristan's heart, the crew had been beyond compare. Many of the men from that first assignment were with Tristan still, having weathered storms, faced raging seas, and fought the fright of being becalmed hundreds of miles from shore with too little water. They were stalwart of heart and generous of spirit and had stood with him against marauders of all sorts and sizes.

A faint smile touched his lips. There were those who cursed pirates and he was certain some of them were unworthy men indeed. But to Tristan, stolen from the safety of shore and forced to the sea under a harsh captain given to regular beatings and worse, pirating wasn't as horrid and undesirable as it might have been under different circumstances.

Indeed, when his first ship had been overrun in a bloody battle, the captain killed and Tristan's crewmates taken prisoner, he met with more generous behavior than he had when serving Captain Reynolds.

The captain of the pirate ship, Captain Ballaliet, a former French naval officer reduced to pirating to pay his gaming debts, had invited the English crew to join his own. With the promise of plunder, better food than Tristan could remember, and a benign master, the invitation was too good to miss. Thus Tristan made the painless transition from English sailor to roving pirate.

Tristan looked out over the roaring ocean with unseeing eyes. He was no saint and he'd done things he now regretted. Though it had been an amoral life, he'd prospered and eventually Captain Ballaliet had captured a ship and given it to Tristan. Together, they'd sailed and had been nigh unstoppable. Had a stray bullet during a particularly difficult boarding not caught Captain Ballaliet in the chest, Tristan might even now be sailing the seas, looking for a tempting frigate to capture.

But once Ballaliet had died, the fight had left Tristan and he'd drifted aimlessly. The crew had not been happy, for they were paid only when they captured a juicy prize. Had he not overtaken a certain ship off the Rock of Gibraltar and met Admiral Nelson, Tristan's life would have been different. Nelson had seen something in Tristan worth saving. To repay the Admiral, Tristan had pledged his ship and men to the Battle of Trafalgar. It had been a stunning victory, but at what cost? Nelson was gone, taken by a sniper's bullet while countless others had died or been left maimed, wounded beyond salvage.

The wind whipped through Tristan's hair and tried to pull it from the ribbon. He closed his eyes and let the damp air brush over him. If he held very still, it almost felt as if the ground were moving like a ship in a near calm sea. He could almost hear the creak and groan of the rigging, smell the pitch and tar of a newly scrubbed deck. Reflexively, Tristan rolled back on his heels—

A red-hot pain lanced through his leg. "Bloody damn!"

"Cap'n!" First Mate Stevens grasped Tristan's arm.

Tristan shook off the first mate. "Blast you to hell, Stevens! I don't need a nursemaid."

"I know, Cap'n. I just didn't want ye tossed overboard like an empty barrel. 'Tis a far drop off'n this cliff."

Teeth clenched, Tristan lowered his foot back to the ground, leaning heavily on his cane as he did so. "I am not in any danger of falling off the cliff, you blasted ass. I may not be able to keep my crippled foot solidly on the deck of a seaworthy ship, but I damned well can navigate dry land by myself."

Silence met this outburst. Tristan knew without looking that his one-time first mate's face would be as long as the sea was wide. Damn it, he hadn't meant to wound the man's feelings. He silently cursed his uneven temper; every little incident was a burning swab to a primed cannon.

"Sorry to disturb ye, Cap'n," Stevens said in a miserable voice. "I didn't mean to—"

"You didn't," Tristan said abruptly, willing the pain in his leg to subside. "'Tis me and naught else. I've a bit of a temper. This weather—" He pressed a hand to his thigh.

Stevens nodded. "Indeed, Cap'n! Master Gunner Thurwell was sayin' his arm was painin' him jus' this mornin'."

"Thurwell spends a lot of time complaining of his injured arm even though the doctor found nothing amiss."

"So I've noticed." Stevens looked out over the ocean, his face easing a bit at the sight of the swells. He sniffed the air. "A nor'wester is comin'."

"Aye. A fierce one unless I miss my guess." Tristan looked down at the small man and gave him a twisted smile. "I miss the sea on days like these. She'd have roiled beneath us and given us a merry ride."

"Aye, so she would have, Cap'n," Stevens said

wistfully. "The men and I don't feel the same as we used to, back when we were sailors." Stevens leaned against the tree and tugged a bit on the knit hat that covered his wispy white hair, a sad look in his eyes. "I never knew how much stock I took in bein' a first mate until it was gone. One day ye're a sailor, the next day"—he spread his hands, a faint shake visible in his callused fingers—"ye're nothing. Nothing at all, it don't feel like."

Tristan clenched his jaw. Something happened to a man once he was forced from the sea and left to hobble about land like a commoner. It left one feeling empty. Useless. Like flotsam tossed upon the shore and left to rot. Which was why he never slept. Or rarely, anymore. He knew with an odd certainty that he was going to die wrapped in loneliness.

The only place he felt at peace was here, on this ledge, the wind and spray buffeting his body. If he closed his eyes and let the feel and sound carry him away, he could almost pretend he was back at sea.

His leg twinged when he accidentally put his weight on it. For a moment, he welcomed the familiar ache. It filled the emptiness of his soul, pulled his thoughts from the hollow days that spread ahead of him.

"Lor' Cap'n!" Stevens exclaimed. "Batten the hatches. There's a Lady O' War headed this way and she looks ready to fire in our direction."

Tristan looked in the direction of Stevens's stare. There, marching down the ragged path that led into the garden, was a familiar figure. Smallish in size, shorter by a head than even Stevens, was a woman. She marched along without even looking at the path before her, attesting to the number of times she'd made the trip.

She reached the garden gate, flicked the latch to one side, entered the garden, and shut the gate smartly behind her. The wind tickled the bottom of her blue cloak, swirling it about her booted ankles and tugging at her tightly pulled hair.

Tristan glanced at Stevens. "I thought we were going to put a lock on that gate."

"It's on me list, Cap'n."

Tristan sent the first mate a flat stare.

"I mean t'say," Stevens added hastily, "that I'll see to it first thing this afternoon."

Tristan nodded. When he'd first bought the cottage on the cliff, he and his men had been the only occupants for miles. In fact, other than an abandoned house that was almost hidden by brambles just a half mile down the rim of the cliff, his house was the only structure in sight.

Tristan had liked the solitude and it had been with a sense of foreboding that one day, while looking out over the sea, he'd noticed that someone had cleaned away the brambles from the front of the empty house. His paradise was about to be invaded. Three months ago, a heavily laden cart had pulled up to the cottage and two women and their servants had alighted. Tristan's life had taken a decided turn for the worse. "I don't know why she insists on coming here."

Stevens pursed his lips. "Perhaps she fancies ye."

"And has decided to attract me hither by stealing my sheep and then hurling accusations at my head? I scarcely think it."

"Ye're probably right," Stevens agreed, watching their visitor's progression up the path with obvious interest. "'Tis said the young doctor is wishin' to sail into that port."

Stevens lifted up on his toes as their visitor tramped up the path and out of sight a moment behind a large yew bush. "They say the doctor is smitten and wishes to marry the widow—the younger widow, not her mother, that is."

Tristan flicked a hard glance at Stevens. "You have an uncanny ability to ferret out inane gossip. It's a pity we were never sent to spy on the French. I'm certain the war would have been shorter simply by your efforts."

"'Tis one of me many good qualities," Stevens said serenely. "Ah, here she is. Full sail over the hillock, right on course."

Stevens shook his head. "Gor' help ye, Cap'n, but looks as if a bee has gotten up Mrs. Thistlewaite's bonnet all the way to the foremast. Must be that blasted sheep again."

Tristan looked back over his shoulder at the woman now struggling against the wind as she climbed the last leg of the path. For all her forceful movements, she appeared rather waiflike, with a heart-shaped face beneath a tightly pulled bun of brown hair that still managed to spring forth with a curious curl or two at the brow.

Of her shape he knew nothing, for he'd never seen her without her voluminous cloak, though he suspected from the delicate lines of her face and throat and the slender shape of her hands that she was as trim a ship to ever sail the seas.

Not that he cared, of course. He was perfectly happy

alone, slacking his lust with an occasional trip to the small town located at the base of the cliff. The inn there sported two exuberant maids, either or both for the taking, had one enough coin.

Besides, he recognized the cut of this woman's jib. She was a stern, strict sort, the type of woman one might marry if one prized well-beaten carpets and hot food all for the mere price of listening to an endless line of chatter over the dinner table. Tristan liked eating his dinners in silence. As for his carpets, they were underfoot, so who cared of their cleanliness?

She reached the end of the path and planted herself before him. Every line of her body, every nuance of her expression bespoke acute irritation.

Stevens nodded merrily, his sharp blue eyes watering a little in the blustery wind. "Ahoy there, Mrs. Thistlewaite! And what brings ye forth on such a day?"

"I came to speak with the captain."

Tristan looked at Stevens. "You may handle this."

"No, he may not!" Their visitor crossed her arms, her gloved hands gripping her elbows. "Captain Llevanth, I came to speak to you and no one else."

"I was afraid of that."

Her gaze narrowed, and despite his irritation, Tristan found himself noticing her eyes. They were wide and slightly uptipped at the corners, and of a remarkably rich brown color, rather like the darkest swells of a storm-lashed sea and lined by the thickest of lashes overset by a lilting slash of brows. The lady's frown grew. "You know why I wish to speak to you."

Stevens leaned forward to say in what he probably

considered a conspiratorial whisper, but was fairly close to a normal voice. "Cap'n, I daresay 'tis the sheep once't again. One of 'em has a likin' fer the lady's garden, he does."

Tristan shrugged. "What does she expect me to do about that? You cannot tie up a sheep. A wolf would get it."

Stevens pondered this. "That's true. There's no real way to tether them that they'd stand fer. If ye used a rope, they'd just eat it. And ye can't chain 'em fer fear of rubbin' sores on their little legs. We'll have to tell her we can't—"

"Oh!" The lady threw up her hands. "Please do not talk about me as if I were not here!"

Stevens looked from the lady and then back at the captain. "Cap'n, did ye think we were talking to Mrs. Thistlewaite as if she wasn't there?"

Tristan pretended to consider this, aware the lady's temper was rising by the moment. Just to irk her further, he let his gaze wander up and down her, lingering on certain areas as if he could detect her shape beneath the voluminous cape. "No," he said finally, "I do not think we were talking to her as if she were not here since, if she were not here, we would not be talking about her—or to her—at all."

*"Oh!"* She planted her hands on her hips. "Captain, if you wish me to take this matter to the constable, I will!"

Tristan sighed. "Very well, Mrs. Thistlewaite." He reached into a pocket and found his pipe. "Tell me the sins of my unruly livestock. I hope they are not partaking of spirits. I will not stand for public drunkenness in my sheep."

"Oh, stop being so absurd." She eyed his pipe with disapprobation. "Must you do that?"

"Yes." He packed the bowl with tobacco and tucked the leather pouch back into his pocket.

Her lips thinned. "Captain Llevanth, I moved to this location to establish a teaching seminary for young ladies. My mother and I are working hard to have things readied, including the placement of some tiles in the garden to make a walkway. We cannot do that when that sheep traipses in over and over, eats our herbs and sends our housekeeper into hysterics."

Tristan lit his pipe, shielding the tinderbox from the wind with one hand. Fragrant smoke drifted from the embers, and was immediately whipped away in the stiff breeze. "Do you know what I'd do if a sheep was causing my housekeeper to have hysterics? I would rid myself of the housekeeper. She is obviously unfit for duty. Pity you're not on a ship, you could just have her keel-hauled and stop her caterwauling that way."

"Captain Llevanth, this is not a matter for levity."

He raised his brows. "Mrs. Thistlewaite, I did not, nor do I now, wish you to be here. Which is why I also have no desire to see you successful in your endeavors to bring even more feminine distractions to this peaceful corner of the world."

The widow lifted her chin. "Is that why you've been placing your sheep in our garden? To make us leave?"

"I don't want you here, true. But I don't care enough to go to such trouble as transporting a sheep anywhere. My sheep are marked and well within the free-range law of the borough. They may go wherever they wish."

The woman's back stiffened. "*Someone* is putting

them in our garden. They cannot be opening the gate themselves."

He flicked a gaze over her face, noting the proud curves and pure line. It really was a pity his sheep weren't behaving. He'd only purchased them to give the men an occupation.

Tristan hadn't expected to be responsible for his crew once he'd left his ship. But somehow, after moving to the house on the cliff with only Stevens for assistance, the men had shown up, one and two at a time. At first all was well, but every sea captain knew the dangers of idle hands. To head off any potential trouble, Tristan set his men to the occupations available, including caring for the sheep, cleaning the galley, scrubbing the little cottage top to bottom, and anything else he and Stevens could come up with.

Tristan took a calming draw on his pipe, the warm glow of the ashes stirred by the wind. "Madam, perhaps you aren't aware of this, but I am a captain. Captains do not concern themselves with sheep."

"Who does, then?"

"Stevens!"

The first mate stepped forward eagerly. "Aye, sir?"

"Listen to the woman for me. Pray let her think you are paying her the strictest attention. Meanwhile, I am going inside, where it's warmer." Tristan turned and walked back toward the house, leaning slightly on his cane.

The flash of a blue cloak halted him in his tracks. Mrs. Thistlewaite once again stood before him, only now she spread her arms to either side as if to block his way. Tristan shook his head at the futile gesture. Really, the woman had more tenacity than…well, just about any-one he knew. She was also rather pleasant to look upon if one ignored the fact she always seemed to be frowning.

She fixed those great brown eyes upon him once again and he noted that they sparkled angrily. Oddly, some of his own distemper melted at the sight.

"Captain Llevanth, I do not wish to speak to your butler. I always speak to Mr. Stevens and nothing is ever fixed."

"Fixed? Is something broken?"

"My patience."

"Your patience is not my concern."

"Oh! You—you—you—"

"Brilliant return volley. Almost as good as shooting pea shot in retaliation for twenty-pound cannon fire. Surely you can do better than that?" Tristan wasn't sure why he was goading the lively widow but…a faint smile edged onto his face. It was an enjoyable pastime for all that. Surely it said something about the sorry state of his affairs that he both enjoyed and loathed arguing with his nearest neighbor.

Her arms dropped to her sides, though her posture remained charged with acrimony. "I did not come to exchange pleasantries with your first mate or to discuss cannon fodder."

"Shot. Cannon shot."

"Whatever you wish to call it."

"Madam, I've said it before and again; this is not my problem. Shut your blasted gate—*firmly*. There. Your problem is now solved."

She stamped her foot, her boot landing in a puddle and splashing mud upon the edges of the moss green skirts barely visible beneath the voluminous blue cloak. "Captain, the gate *was* shut. *Firmly.*"

"So my sheep are *jumping* the fence into your garden?"

"Yes. The white one with the black face."

Tristan looked over his shoulder. "Stevens, do I have a white sheep with a black face?"

Stevens scratched his chin, his brow furrowed. "Hm. Seems I seen one of that cut not too long ago."

"Is it possible that this particular sheep can jump a fence the height of the one surrounding Mrs. Thistlewaite's garden?"

"By Peter's watery grave, no!" the first mate said, chuckling at the thought.

She frowned, her flyaway brows looking even more elfin. Before she could say anything, Tristan continued. "Stevens, is it possible for a sheep to fly?"

Stevens snorted.

"What about crawl? Could they crawl *beneath* a gate?"

"Lord, no! They're too puffed up. Why they can barely fit through the gate upright and with it open as it is."

Mrs. Thistlewaite's full lips pursed into a scowl. "Captain, I do not know how your sheep manages to creep past my fence, but he does. And then he grazes through my spice bed like a great scythe, eating all of my herbs and—"

"Stevens?"

"Aye, Cap'n?"

"Do *we* have a garden?"

Stevens looked around them and blinked. "Why yes. Ye're standin' in the middle of it."

Tristan took a draw on his pipe as he eyed the foliage that lined the path. "Are these herbs?"

"Aye, sir. Some of them."

"Do any of our sheep cross the fence to eat these herbs?"

"Why no, Cap'n. Not once, that I can remember."

"Hmm." Tristan noted the rising color in the widow's face. Perhaps he enjoyed teasing her so much because she looked so very prim and perfect, her hair so severely bound, her cloak buttoned to her throat, her mouth a determined line that almost dared to be invaded. Plundered. *Tasted.*

He found himself staring at her mouth. The bottom lip was fuller than the top and gently rounded. He wondered if it was as sensitive as it looked, how she would react if he kissed her, and then gently—

Startled at the direction his thoughts were taking, he pulled himself back into the present. "Mrs. Thistlewaite, sheep do not jump good fences, nor do they crawl beneath closed gates, nor do they fly through the air to land in the midst of a garden. I, myself, have a garden, and the sheep never bother it, so I feel there are no grounds for your complaints. You will have to deal with the sheep issue on your own."

"Captain," Mrs. Thistlewaite said, her voice frigidly perfect, "I see I wasted my time coming here."

"You not only wasted it, but you have made yourself unwelcome. If you keep pestering me, I shall train my dogs to herd all of those silly sheep onto your land every blasted morning. Then you shall have *real* cause for complaint."

"Oh! I cannot believe you'd—How dare you?" She

drew herself up, her eyes flashing fire, her mouth set. "You, sir, are no gentleman."

*No gentleman.* The words flamed across his mind. His father had been a gentleman. "I've never wished to be a gentleman. Not now. Not ever. From my experience, *gentlemen* are not worth knowing."

"I daresay you know so many."

"I know more than I wish I did," he snapped, his temper rushing to the fore. "But what about you? If I am no gentleman, are you so much a lady? Where *is* your sense of propriety, coming to visit a single man, no chaperone in sight?"

Something flashed through her eyes, a spark of... was it hurt? Tristan instantly regretted his hasty words, for he'd meant to spar, not wound. But before he could say anything, she'd turned and sailed away. Her skirts swished around her ankles, the wind tugging on her hair as she rapidly made her way down the path, back to the gate and the safety of her own home.

The first mate watched her march away. "That is a fiery wench, that is. Stormy like the sea and just as unpredictable."

There was admiration in the man's voice. Tristan had to admit that he rather admired the spirit the young lady displayed as well. And that mouth of hers... so sweetly curved and gently plumped. He wondered what she'd feel like, beneath the voluminous folds of her ever-present cloak. She might be fat.

He didn't realize he'd said the words aloud until Stevens shook his head. "Lud, Cap'n. Indeed she is not! She's a trim rig and full-sailed like a proper woman should be. Not a bit of extra leeway to her. In fact, she's—" Stevens caught Tristan's incredulous look and colored deeply.

"When have you seen Mrs. Thistlewaite without her cape? I've never once seen her without the blasted thing."

"'Twas when ye asked me to fetch the physician fer Mr. Thurwell. The doctor was at the widow's house."

Damn that doctor. Still...Tristan wondered why the widow had reacted so strongly to his barb. Something had definitely caused the wind to fall from the widow's oh-so-righteously filled sails. He frowned, still perplexed. There was a mystery there. One that needed solving.

"Cap'n?" Stevens was now leaning far out over the rock, looking down to where the road wended up the cliff face from the village.

"Aye?" Tristan answered absently, his mind still on the lovely widow. What secrets were hidden behind her eyes? he wondered.

"Ye'd best come and see this."

Tristan sighed and limped over to join the first mate, pausing to knock the dying embers from his pipe against a rock. "What is it?"

"There, sir. Two coaches and three wagons, full of things, all climbin' up the path to here."

Tristan's frown grew. Who the hell would be coming to visit him on such a day as this? Indeed, who would come to visit with such an entourage? The front coach was huge, tied to six lumbering horses as they struggled to make it up the winding road. It was a fine equipage, he noted, much strapped with trunks and bags.

The cumbersome coach was even now slowly

clambering up the steep, curvy road that traced the face of a treacherous cliff. As he wondered who it might belong to, the crest on the side panel flashed dully in the overcast gray sky.

Tristan's heart turned icy. He knew only one person who possessed such fine coaches and horses. Only one person who would show up unannounced and bring an entire household of servants with him, to oversee his every want and need. And that was the last person who *would* come and see Tristan.

Or was it? Heart thundering an odd beat, Tristan straightened and turned back to the cottage. "Whoever it is, they will be an hour, perhaps more before they make landfall. Long enough for us to bite off the edge of this chill with something substantial."

Stevens grinned, displaying a row of missing teeth. "A pint of the house's best?"

"Or two." Tristan hurried his step as much as his limp would allow, the wind ruffling the capes of his cape. The cold was beginning to affect his leg, making it ache even more. Whoever was coming to visit would be met with the same reception he gave everyone—nothing.

He had no need for people, other than the ones the sea had already thrown upon his shores. Those, he understood. Those, he would help. But for everyone else . . . he just wanted to be left alone.

He only hoped that the occupant of the coach did not expect a welcome of any sort, for the bastard would not get it, earl or no. Not from Tristan, anyway. Not ever.

## Chapter 3

It is your duty to make certain your master and everything about him are presented to his peers with care and style. A good butler never ceases his efforts until the last spoon is in place, the table linen pressed and starched, the floors polished and the brandy dispensed. "Steadfast to the last" will win the day.

*A Compleat Guide for*
*Being a Most Proper Butler*
*by Richard Robert Reeves*

*P*rudence marched home, her heavy boots thumping loudly on the stone-strewn pathway. Blast that man! He was impossible, rude, arrogant, irritating, and worse. All she'd asked was that he keep his silly sheep on his own land. Why couldn't he just do that one small thing?

Worse, he'd seemed supremely unimpressed she'd made such a request. Perhaps he wasn't teasing when he said penning sheep was not required. Which was, of course, the silliest thing she'd ever heard. Of course, there'd been many things living in the country had taught her, one of them being the rather narrow nature of some of the laws.

She turned off the road and onto the garden path, the fragrant scent of mint lifting in the fresh air. The breeze danced about, rifling through the crisp brown leaves.

Prudence made her way to the front door. Painted red, it mirrored her temper. Scowling, she grasped the chilled brass handle and gave it a firm twist. It creaked open. Just as she entered, the wind grabbed the door from her hand and slammed it shut behind her, the sharp sound echoing through the house.

"Prudence?" Mother hurried out of the sitting room, her brow drawn, her gentle green eyes troubled. At fifty-two, she was still an attractive woman, her soft brown hair carrying only a touch of gray at her temples. "Prudence! Why did you slam the door?"

Prudence undid her bonnet and set it on the small table beneath the peg where she hung her muffler. "The wind caught the door. I hope it didn't frighten you."

Mother smiled, smoothing her skirts a bit, some of the tension leaving her face. "Oh no! I just thought you might be agitated about something."

"Me? Agitated? Perish the thought!" Not that she didn't *feel* like slamming the door—she had. But she refused to give in to base anger. The captain's rude behavior called for something far more planned and cunning. A grand scheme, perhaps, one that would reduce him to a quiver.

Feeling somewhat placated by such an image, Prudence hung her cape over her muffler on the peg and managed a smile. "How was your morning, Mother?" Prudence went past her mother and into the sitting room. "Did you finish darning the tear—"

A man turned from where he'd been standing in the middle of the room. Of average height with brown hair and blue eyes, he was attractive in a rather quiet way.

Prudence dipped a reluctant curtsy. "Dr. Barrow. What a pleasant surprise." She sent a hard look at Mother who colored but kept a determinedly innocent look on her face.

"Mrs. Thistlewaite," the doctor said, gulping loudly. "H—How nice to see you. I just came by to, ah—I came to see if perhaps—that is to say, I was wondering if—" He shot a panicked glance at Mother.

"Prudence," Mother said a little too brightly. "Dr. Barrow came to see if you were available for a ride in his new carriage!"

The last thing Prudence wanted was to ride in a carriage with a man who could not string two sentences together without blushing. While it was true the doctor was a very kind, gentle sort of man, there was none of the deep connection she'd felt with Phillip.

*Phillip.* She looked down at her hands, clasped before her. She missed her husband even now, three entire years after his death. Not as much as she once had—there had been weeks, even months, when she'd wondered if she'd ever smile again. She had, of course. It had just taken time. A long time. But now, she was able not only to remember Phillip, but be glad for the time she'd had with him.

They'd met and married in six mad months when she'd been but eighteen. Phillip hadn't been much older, so they'd practically grown up together. Perhaps that had been part of their friendship, their love. Whatever it had been, she missed that closeness. The pure loveliness of looking across the breakfast table at the person on the other side and knowing she was exactly where she was supposed to be.

Mother gestured to the tea tray sitting by the fire. "Prudence, you returned just in time. Mrs. Fieldings just brought tea."

Mrs. Fieldings was their housekeeper, and a sterner, more dour woman did not exist. Still, she had a magical touch when it came to pastries, which was evinced by the plate sitting with the teapot. Every pastry was golden and fluffy, glistening with honey coating, the room rich with the scent of warm butter and mouth-watering freshness.

Prudence finally found a smile. "Tea will be just the thing! I am famished." She raised her brows at the doctor. "Will you be staying?"

He turned even redder, glancing wildly at Mother, then back at Prudence. "I—ah—I really must be on my way."

Prudence wondered if the captain cared enough about anyone to blush. She tried to imagine him stuttering and could not. But then, she couldn't imagine the captain being polite, either.

The man was a complete behemoth. Part of it was his size; he towered over everyone, his shoulders so broad they looked as if he could carry a ship as easily as command one. He wore his profession with every barked order, every impolite utterance.

What really bothered her was that he didn't seem to

care. He was perfectly happy being boorish. She remembered the way he'd looked at her when she'd first walked up to him in the garden—he'd stared at her head to foot, his gaze lingering in a very disturbing way. She shifted uncomfortably at the thought, her skin tingling as if he'd actually touched her.

"Um, Mrs. Thistlewaite, may I say you look well today?"

Usually Prudence found the doctor's disjointed and milquetoast utterances rather irksome, but after spending twenty minutes with an oaf like the captain, she decided she rather liked the doctor's nonthreatening presence. "You are too kind! I hope you are staying for tea. It's so cold outside."

He glanced regretfully at the clock on the mantel and shook his head. "Was just telling your mother I couldn't remain a moment longer. I wish I could, but— patients, you know."

Mother rushed forward. "Surely they would understand! I thought you'd stay long enough to have tea. At least *one* cup."

"Perhaps next time." He bowed to Prudence, meeting her gaze with a look of entreaty.

She immediately smiled. "Of course you must be on your way. Perhaps you will return another time and visit longer."

His smile was blinding. "That would be lovely. Mrs. Crumpton. Mrs. Thistlewaite." He bowed to both of them. "It was a pleasure."

"And you." Prudence dipped a curtsy, her gaze sliding to the tea tray. Her stomach rumbled so loudly she was certain the doctor had to have heard it.

He didn't seem to notice, though, for he bowed again to her, then took Mother's hand for a brief moment before leaving.

"Well!" Mother said as the door closed behind him.

"Well, indeed." Prudence was already at the tea tray. "Mrs. Fieldings outdid herself yet again." She carried the tray to the small table before the settee and poured two cups of tea. "I wonder what brought the doctor."

"I'm sure I don't know," Mother said, placing pastries on two plates and handing one to Prudence. Mother's bright green gaze fixed steadily on Prudence. "You could at least have asked the doctor to dinner."

Prudence took a bite of pastry. "I didn't want Dr. Barrow to come to dinner. He is always ill at ease and it makes conversation so difficult."

"He's a doctor. Surely that has some merit."

"Indeed it does. If I feel ill for eating too many of these delicious pastries, I shall call on him immediately."

Mother sighed. "I don't know what I am to do with you."

"Nothing." Prudence finished her pastry and wiped her hands on her napkin. "I can take care of myself, thank you."

"So I see." Mother took a sip of tea. "How was your visit with the captain?"

"It was horrid. The captain did everything but toss me out onto my ear." Had the man had his way, Prudence had no doubt she'd have been tossed out on something far more ignominious than her ear.

Mother's face fell. "That is too bad. I had hoped—" She frowned at Prudence. "Were you polite?"

"Of course I was! How can you ask that?"

"Sometimes—just sometimes, mind you—I've noticed you have a tendency to let your temper override your good sense."

"Mother!"

"I'm sorry but it's true."

"I was very polite. It was the captain who displayed such a ferocious temper. In fact, he has such ill feelings about females in general that he said he wished our attempt to establish a seminary may fail. The man is a horrid, selfish person."

"Perhaps you just caught him at a bad time," Mother said cautiously. "He is a war hero, you know. Lucy has been talking to one of his men."

"Mother, you should not gossip with the upstairs maid."

"But she knows all about the captain! How else would we have discovered he is a war hero?"

"We still don't know if he is a war hero. All we know is that one of the captain's men told Lucy the man was a war hero. That is not quite the same thing."

Mother sighed. "You are far too young to be so jaded."

"And you are far too old to be so naive, though I must say you don't look a year over forty. I hope I shall age so gracefully."

Mother's smile broke forth like the sun over the ocean. "You really think I look but forty?"

"I begin to think perhaps Dr. Barrow is coming to visit you and not me."

That won a full chuckle and Mother settled in to enjoy her tea.

Prudence finished her second pastry. She had been furious when she'd left the captain, but sitting here now, before the fire, sipping a nice cup of tea with lots of sugar and extra cream, made her irritation disappear like smoke before a gentle breeze.

She glanced around their cottage with a deep feeling of satisfaction. It was warm and cozy here in the sitting room, the settee and drapes a delightful red color. Flowered pillows and a thick Aubusson carpet on which sat a matching set of cherrywood chairs filled the room with warmth and color. "Phillip would have liked this room."

Mother paused in taking a sip of tea, her eyes darkening momentarily. "Oh, Prudence. I'm so sorry. What made you think of him?"

"I always think of him," Prudence said with a sigh.

"I know." Mother's eyes filled as she reached over and patted Prudence's hand. "Prudence, I wish sometimes that— Well, it doesn't matter."

"What? You wish I didn't remember Phillip?"

"Oh no, dear! I would never wish that. I just wish you'd find someone else. You deserve to be happy."

Prudence took a satisfying sip of tea. "I am happy. Very. Except for the sheep problem."

"It is most vexing," Mother replied, sending a side glance at Prudence. "I wonder how they are getting past the gate."

"However they are doing it, the captain flatly refuses to pen up his sheep. The man is a nuisance."

"Do you really think so?"

Prudence put down her cup, the bowl rattling against the saucer. "Mother, the man not only refused to pen up his sheep, but he threatened to train his dogs to *herd* those infernal animals onto our land unless we stopped *pestering* him about it!"

"Goodness," Mother said, looking rather miserable. "Your interview did not go well at all."

"No, it did not. But I am not finished with the captain."

Mother brightened. "Oh?"

"No. I will find a way to *make* him listen to us. See if I don't."

Mother waved her pastry in the air, her eyes sparkling indignantly. "That foolish sheep, trudging through the new hedgerow and eating all the mint! The nerve of it!"

Prudence toyed with the handle of her cup. "How *do* those sheep get over that fence?"

"That is the question, isn't it? I wonder if they have found a way to undo the latch."

"And latch it back? I don't think so." Perhaps she'd go to the village in the morning and make some inquiries of the herding laws. She knew the perfect depth to curtsy to a princess, a duchess, a countess, and a viscountess. But she knew absolutely nothing about livestock.

"If you keep scowling like that, you will get lines in your brow." Mother's gentle voice held a touch of exasperation. "What *did* that man say to so upset you?"

Prudence picked up her teacup, absently staring into it. The captain had not said anything she hadn't expected. Not really. It was more the way he'd *looked* at her; in a way that had made her feel painfully aware of herself. In the same way Phillip had looked at her, only . . . the captain's look had burned, simmered inside of her. She'd never felt that with Phillip.

"Prudence?"

She looked up to find Mother staring at her, brows raised. Heat touched Prudence's cheeks. "I'm sorry, Mother. I was just thinking about the captain. He was rude and it made me angry." Which was true. Perhaps that was what she needed to focus on—how mad the man had made her. Yes, that was good. Prudence set her cup back on the tray. "Mother, I have had it with the captain's lackadaisical manner of watching after his livestock. If he will not tend to them, then I will. Only I will use a spit over a hot fire and mint sauce."

"Prudence! You cannot go about threatening to cook another person's sheep."

"Mother, we are now in the wilds of Devon. London rules do not apply. Let me deal with the sheep; you tend to starting our school." Prudence straightened her shoulders. Yes. She'd deal with the captain in her own fashion. "Mother, have you heard anything from your friend, Lady Margaret? She promised her daughter would be our first student."

Mother's expression darkened. "I meant to tell you . . ."

Prudence's heart sank. "She said no."

"I'm certain she didn't mean to make promises she didn't intend to keep. Something very grave must have prompted her to— Well, here. Read it for yourself." She pushed her hand into the pocket hidden in her morning dress and handed a very small note to Prudence.

"My, how Lady Margaret does go on and on," Prudence said dryly as she opened the painfully short note. "She never meant to send Julia, did she?"

"I'm sure she did! But Lady Chisworth's Academy is quite selective, and I'm sure if I was in the same position and you had been accepted there that I—"

"You would not have disappointed a friend you'd known since you were six, no matter how select Lady Chisworth's Academy might be."

Mother sighed, a wistful expression on her face. "No. I don't suppose I would."

"Nor would you disappoint a friend who had come to your aid every time one of your numerous children caught the slightest complaint. Why, when I think of all the times you've rushed to Lady Margaret's side to help her nurse those brats of hers through God knows how many illnesses—"

"Prudence! You shouldn't say such things."

Prudence sighed. "You're right and I am sorry. It just makes me angry when people take advantage of you. We bought this cottage so you could make a seminary. All we need are a few well-placed students and you would be set. I really thought your friends meant their promises to assist you."

Mother's shoulders sagged dispiritedly. "I did, too. Not only has Lady Margaret led me astray, but Lady Caroline has, as well. It seems as if none of them was ever truly my friend."

Prudence reached over the small table and took Mother's hand in her own. "I am sorry things are not turning out as we'd hoped."

Mother managed a smile. "Yes, well, I refuse to let it bother me. We'll find a way to launch our school."

"I know we will. We simply must think. Who else of our acquaintance has a seminary-aged daughter?"

They were silent for a long time, both mentally going through their various acquaintances. It wasn't easy, as they'd lost so many supposed friends when Phillip's business had fallen and the scandal had occurred. Prudence's throat tightened at the memory of those dark weeks.

Mother straightened. "Prudence! I know just the thing! I believe I shall write a letter to my old friend, Lady Boswell."

"Lady Boswell? From Scotland? The one who sends us those horrid, hard Christmas cakes every year? I didn't think she had any children."

"No, but she has more than twenty nieces. Last year at the Daringham breakfast I distinctly remember hearing her lament how she'd determined to pay for all of their educations since her brothers had no funds to speak of. Whatever you might say about Lady Boswell's rather irregular way of doing things, she is a strong proponent of women having an education."

"Twenty nieces. Mother, do you think . . . ? Perhaps if we gave her a special price—"

"Exactly! She's as thrifty as she is tall. I believe we might fill our five slots almost immediately."

Prudence clasped Mother's hands. "That is marvelous! I do hope— We must make certain the repairs on the cottage are done quickly. You can teach the girls comportment and dancing and all sorts of accomplished things, and I can teach them gardening and drawing and philosophy and Greek and—"

"But *first* we must resolve the sheep issue. We simply cannot have those animals wandering all over our garden. What if one bit a student? Perhaps you should speak to the captain again, only this time, pray use a more gentle tone."

"He leaves me with no choice. I've asked him repeatedly to do something about those blasted sheep—"

"Prudence!" Mother's voice edged with soft disapproval.

"I'm sorry. It's just that I have asked him and asked him and he does nothing more than shoo me away like some sort of buzzing insect."

"That's no reason to lower your standards of speaking. As I've told you often enough, a woman is judged as much by—"

"—her speech as by her deeds. I know, I know. I don't mean to be so indiscreet, but that man raises my ire."

"Hm. You know, Prudence... perhaps there is something to your irritation."

Prudence looked suspiciously at her mother. "Oh?"

"There must be something about the captain that attracts you if he's able to raise your temper so."

"Nonsense. I am often angry with men I don't know."

"When?"

"Whenever I read the *Morning Post*. There are several contributors—all male, I might add—whom I do not care one snap of my fingers for. Every time they dip their pen into the ink pot, steam begins to rise from my ears. They express no one's opinion but their own, yet presuppose they are speaking for the masses. I have no time for such worthless conceit."

Mother's lips quirked into a smile. "That's not anger. That's irritation."

"Well, it feels like anger to me."

Mother gave Prudence's hand another squeeze, and picked up her own teacup. Her eyes smiled over the rim at Prudence. "Don't look so grim, dear. Everything will work out. And if it doesn't, you can always marry the doctor."

*That would be just lovely,* Prudence thought glumly. Marriage to the doctor would be about as thrilling as napping during an opera.

Whatever happened, she'd win this war with the captain. Win it and help Mother establish a successful school, too. Then she'd see who had the last laugh. The captain would see that she'd not yet begun to fight.

# Chapter 4

The First Meeting with your employer is vastly important. Here, you must set the tone of your future relationship. This is a delicate maneuver as too much familiarity breeds contempt while too little begets a disturbing tendency for said employer to run roughshod over one. Take a stand on important issues, but do so in a discreet manner that allows your master to retain his pride. And you, yours.

*A Compleat Guide for*
*Being a Most Proper Butler*
by Richard Robert Reeves

*T*ristan leaned his head against the high back of his favorite chair, savoring the burning warmth of his brandy. He shifted slightly, wincing as he did so. His damned leg ached deeply, as if the very bones were grinding against one another.

He forced his mind elsewhere, away from the pain, to the carriages even now climbing the cliff road. His first thought had been that it might be his father. But that simply could not be. The man had never made the slightest attempt to contact him; why would the bloody fool do so now?

Not that it mattered. There would be no welcome for the earl in Tristan's life. Not now. Not anymore.

He was through with wishing. The time to believe in knights in shining armor and happily ever after had died years ago when Tristan had been forced aboard that damned ship. It was the one home truth life had taught him—if he wanted something good in his life, it was up to him and no one else to make it happen.

His gaze drifted to the terrace doors that lined one wall. He loved this room, had had it built to look as much like his cabin aboard the *Victory* as possible. It held the same furnishings with the exception of his bunk. At night, when he could sleep, he occupied the large corner room upstairs, the only chamber not filled to overflowing with his past shipmates.

He sighed, looking into his glass. When he'd been injured and had finally realized that he was no more for the sea, he'd come here to hide. To lick his wounds and wait for death. He'd had no greater purpose than that.

But something had happened. After he'd arrived, Stevens had come. The first mate had been wounded at Trafalgar as well. Given a tiny pension and set on land, he'd had nowhere to go.

So, Stevens had gone to his former captain. He'd sent no word of his imminent arrival, and indeed, Tristan, sunk in a three-month drunk, had been vaguely surprised, but also relieved. At least he wouldn't die alone.

Stevens was but the first arrival at the cottage by the

sea. One by one, the wounded came to visit... and then stay. Now, almost every room in the cottage housed three or four, and sometimes more, men. Stevens ran it all like a ship, even setting rotating dinner bells so the galley wasn't overrun at any time.

For Tristan, the nearness of his former shipmates was a blessing. They gave him a purpose. The only problem was, his rather meager pension was not enough to put food on the table and pay the doctor's bills. He'd been fortunate in his service and had put away some small amounts for investments. Those had paid and paid well. But with the constant drain, Tristan knew it was only a matter of time before he had to close the doors of his little house.

His sprightly neighbor would certainly like that. Especially if he took his sheep with him. Tristan almost chuckled at the memory of the lady's outraged expression when he'd smoked his pipe in front of her. She was hot at hand, that one. Sparkling and fiery, like tinder to a match. He'd rather enjoyed this morning's little exercise. It had momentarily chased away the cobwebs of his existence. He wondered what she'd do if he removed her cloak the next time she visited.

A sharp rap sounded and Stevens stuck his head into the room. "Cap'n?"

Tristan, deprived of such a pleasant daydream as his neighbor unfurling her charms, cast a surly eye toward his first mate. "Aye?"

Stevens entered the room, his cap clasped between his hands. "Sorry t'bother ye, but do ye remember that coach and t'other carts we saw humpin' up the cliff road?"

The coach. He'd allowed himself to forget it, but all of

his earlier thoughts returned. Tristan's heart chilled, and every last vestige of brandy evaporated from his mind, leaving him with crystalline clarity. "They've arrived."

"Aye. There's a crew of them, but only two come to the door. A tall, slender fellow and a short, dumpy one. 'Tis the tall one as gives me the shivers." Stevens glanced over his shoulder, then lowered his voice to say, "He's a mite bossy."

"Tell him to go the hell away," Tristan said harshly.

Stevens kneaded his cap. "I would, Cap'n. In fact, I done tol' them ye were not here, but the one man looked down his nose at me and...well..." The cap was so twisted that Tristan wondered if it could ever be used again. "I hates to say this," Stevens finally burst out, "perhaps ye should see this bloke."

"No."

Stevens didn't look very convinced. "But—"

"I know these men. They work for the earl of Rochester, don't they?"

"Well, yes. In a manner of speakin', they do. But—"

"I want nothing to do with them."

"But—"

"That is an order, Stevens. Do you understand?"

"Aye, sir." The first mate sighed heavily. "I tol' them ye'd not see them, I did."

"Then tell them again."

"Aye, aye, Cap'n." With a shake of his head, Stevens left.

Tristan was afforded an entire two minutes of peace before a knock once again sounded at the door. It opened, only this time it was not Stevens but a stranger who walked in.

Tall and thin, with a patrician face and dark hair touched with white, the man carried himself like a peer to the realm. His blue eyes surveyed Tristan from head to toe.

Tristan scowled, refusing to rise. "Who the hell are you?"

Another man peered around the first one, this one short and squat with wrinkled clothing and clutching a satchel as if afraid someone might attack him and remove it from his arms by force.

The thin man bowed. "My lord, allow me to introduce myself. I am Reeves. The butler for—"

"Let me save you some trouble; I want nothing to do with Rochester. To me, the earl is dead."

The plump man cleared his throat. "I'm sorry, but— my lord, I am Mr. Dunstead, the solicitor, and—"

"I am not a lord."

"Ah," the man called Reeves interjected smoothly. "But you are. I am indeed the butler for the *late* earl of Rochester. My lord, I regret to inform you that your father is dead."

Tristan's heart froze. The earl. Dead. Gone forever.

He found his gaze fixed on the tumbler in his hand, noting in a detached manner how the fire flickered through the heavy cut glass. He'd always known that this day would come, had always imagined the relief he'd feel when it finally arrived. He'd told himself that he was looking forward to it, that with his father's death, he would find some of the peace that had been denied him, the life that had been stolen from him. Perhaps even the brother he'd lost.

The thought of Christian made his hand tighten

painfully about the glass. He forced himself to loosen his grip. *Don't think about it.*

Instead, he'd think about the loss of the man he'd never known. The man who'd left him without recourse. Some emotion sifted deep within him. It took him a moment to recognize it—it was grief. A deep, inalienable sadness. Not for the man himself, of course; Tristan had barely known him. But a sense of loss for what would never, ever be. It was as if some small part of him was still the child in that tavern room, waiting for his father to come. Waiting for some sign he was loved.

"My lord?" The words were spoken low, with respect. "We are very sorry."

Tristan looked up to find both men regarding him with something akin to pity on their faces. Tristan slammed the glass down on the table by his elbow. "Do not look at me like that! Why did you come to tell me such a worthless piece of information? I cannot be the new earl. The bastard did not so much as acknowledge me. How could I have inherited the title?"

The little man, Dunstead, blinked behind his spectacles. "Because...oh dear. This is quite complicated, but your father—"

"Do *not* call that arrogant ass my father. He was not before, nor will he ever be."

Reeves cleared his throat. "My lord, I understand why you are upset. But you should know that I was with his lordship at the end. He was adamant you were to be the next earl."

"Why? Because he had no other sons?"

A pained look crossed Reeves's face. "That is neither

here nor there. You are the earl. He went to quite a bit of trouble to make certain you would be."

Tristan sat back in his chair. "You don't seem to understand. My brother and I were born on the wrong side of the blanket. Much as I loved my mother, she was sometimes too generous in her trust. She thought he would marry her, but he did not. So... I cannot become the new earl."

"Ah, but apparently the earl had an epiphany on his deathbed. He suddenly remembered that he had, in fact, married your mother. He even has a member of the church willing to testify to that fact."

Tristan's smile was mirthless. "He did not go to all of this trouble because he loved me so much. If he wanted an heir so badly, why didn't he just marry and have his bloody heir?"

"He tried to," Reeves said. "He and the duchess had no children."

Dunstead nodded briskly. "You are his eldest child. It is only right that you take your father's place."

A bitter laugh broke from Tristan's throat. "My father's place—that is too amusing for words."

The butler and the solicitor exchanged glances. Mr. Dunstead set his satchel on the desk. "Perhaps if you saw the will yourself. I am supposed to read it to you but if you'd like—"

"Leave it there."

"My lord?"

"Put it on the desk and then leave," Tristan said, reaching for his cane and gaining his feet. "I don't want you here."

"B—but, my lord! I must explain the stipulations."

"Stipulations?"

"Yes. You have inherited the title. However, to gain the fortune, the trustees must approve you as..." The solicitor glanced helplessly at Reeves.

The butler met Tristan's gaze. "The late earl wished to make certain that the next occupant of Rochester House should be worthy of the name."

Worthy? That bloody bastard never once bothered to own up to Tristan's birthright, and then, on his deathbed, he had the gall to demand that Tristan be *worthy*? "I don't want the bloody fortune. Nor the damned title. And he can take his damned house to hell with him, too."

Reeves sighed. "He would have, my lord, had he been able. Trust me on that."

"I won't take a pence from that empty, shriveled old man."

Mr. Dunstead blinked, his eyes hideously large behind the thick glass of his spectacles. "Don't— My lord! Do you realize— Do you know— It would be unheard of to—"

"What Mr. Dunstead is saying," Reeves interjected smoothly, "is that it would be quite foolhardy to turn your back on twenty thousand pounds per annum."

Tristan turned his head. "Did you say twenty?"

"Thousand." Reeves raised his brows. "*And* Rochester House as well as the Rochester Townhouse in London, both of which are masterful edifices and fully furnished in a most elegant style."

Dunstead nodded. "They come with trained staff, too. All you'd need to do is"—he made a sweeping gesture with his arm—"move in. Once, of course, you've garnered the approval of the trustees."

Twenty thousand pounds. The things he could do with that sum. He could move away from the cottage—or better yet, build a number of them for the men. He could also hire a doctor just to stay here, and minister to them all. Then, when that was done, he could perhaps... What would he do? There were so many possibilities, so many things he had always wanted to accomplish that his mind would not settle on one.

Of course, that was if he gained the "approval" of the trustees. He glanced at the solicitor. "Who are these trustees?"

"Contemporaries of your father's. Well versed in comportment, manners, dress—everything a gentleman should know."

"Bloody hell, I am to become a popinjay and then let a group of warbling fools judge me?"

Dunstead pushed his glasses up on his nose, shifting uneasily from foot to foot. "Ah. Well. I suppose if you wish to look at it that way—"

"I will not do it!" It was inconceivable. Even from the grave, his father was trying to make Tristan feel like less. His jaw tightened. "No. I won't have it. None of it. Now be gone, both of you."

Dunstead huffed his astonishment and then began to collect his papers, but Reeves did not move. He merely sighed. "How sad. I suppose we shall just have to find Lord Westerville then."

"Who is that?"

"Your brother, Christian."

Tristan paused, his gaze riveted on the butler. "Christian?"

"If you fail to meet the criteria for the fortune, it goes to your brother, Viscount Westerville."

Dunstead locked his satchel. "The will is on your desk, should you decide to read it."

"You cannot find my brother," Tristan said, ignoring the solicitor all together. "I've tried for years and have been unable to discover even a trace of him."

"Perhaps you did not look in the right location."

Tristan took a hasty step forward, leaning heavily on his cane. "Do you know where he is?"

Reeves smiled. "We found you, did we not?"

Dunstead pushed his spectacles back in place. "We must leave, Mr. Reeves. It's getting dark and we have a long way to go."

Reeves glanced at the terrace doors. "It's already too late to take the coaches and wagons down that treacherous road. Besides, the horses are spent, and—" He looked at Tristan. "I wonder... My lord, would you allow us to stay for a day or two? We've traveled far and are a bit weary. Our horses need rest, especially after pulling so much weight up that horrid road."

If Reeves knew how to locate his brother, then Tristan would be foolish to let the man out of his sight. "Stay. I am afraid I don't have much room—"

"We will make do in the stables," Reeves said, as if anticipating just such a suggestion.

"The stables?" Mr. Dunstead blinked. "But...how—"

"We will do very well," Reeves said smoothly. He bowed to Tristan. "Thank you for your consideration. Once the horses are rested, we will, of course, be on our way."

"But—" Dunstead said.

Reeves took the solicitor by the shoulders and turned him toward the door. "Lord Rochester, thank you! I hope to speak to you again soon, once you've had time to digest the new things in your life." With that, the butler steered the solicitor into the hallway and closed the door softly behind him.

Tristan stood staring at the closed door for the longest time, scattered thoughts raging through him. His father, dead. His brother, perhaps found. A fortune to be won. And a title, all his. Lord Tristan Llevanth, Earl of Rochester.

What a horrible, horrible joke.

If he was to digest all of that, it would take an entire bottle of brandy. Or ten. Shaking his head, he sank back into his chair, reclaimed his glass and took a long gulp. He was an earl. For some reason, he wondered what his starched-skirted neighbor would think of that. Would she be impressed? Or merely demand yet again that he keep his sheep out of her garden?

Lifting his glass in her general direction, he silently toasted her. Not only was she delectable, but she was brimming with good sense—he could almost smell it on her. That was the kind of woman one avoided at all costs; the marrying kind.

Sighing, he laid his head against the back of the chair. Truthfully, he'd trade his earldom for one night in the lady's bed. One long, passion-filled night, filled with scented skin, and the silk of her hair . . .

The thought made him shift uneasily in his chair. Damnation. What the hell was he supposed to do now? He was an earl. A bloody earl. An earl with a bad leg and a cottage filled with broken sailors. What good was the title without the funds?

Even from the grave, his father still had the power to irk him. Teeth clenched, Tristan tried to focus on Christian. On hope. Thoughts swirled round and round as Tristan drank his way through the bottle, the hours slowly passing. The sun would be breaking over the horizon before he managed to calm his thoughts enough to stumble to bed. But even then, one distinct image lingered behind his alcohol-fogged eyelids; that of his lovely neighbor, curtsying low, displaying her bosom for his earl-like approval.

It left him with one thought before he sank into a deep sleep... Maybe being an earl wouldn't be such a hardship, after all.

# Chapter 5

A proper butler never, ever interferes with his master's Personal Matters. Unless, of course, his efforts will make his master's life better in some measure. For some, this can justify a large amount of interference, indeed.

*A Compleat Guide for*
*Being a Most Proper Butler*
*by Richard Robert Reeves*

"*You*, sir, will remove your sheep from my garden," Prudence demanded, her voice a bit shivery, as if she was cold. She found that odd, to be cold AND dreaming.

The captain turned, apparently unaware that he was but a figment of Prudence's slumber. He was standing on the bluff, as he'd been the other day, the wind whipping his cloak about him, his broad chest displayed by a thin white shirt open at the neck, his black breeches tight about his thick, muscled legs.

Prudence had to fight for breath. This was the best

*dream she'd ever had. His open shirt was scandalous enough, but the tight cut of his breeches was quite distracting. Very distracting. So distracting that—*

*He was suddenly before her, his warm hands on her shoulders. He looked deeply into her eyes. "I will do anything you desire, my sweet. So long as you give me one kiss."*

*"A kiss? I could not—" Well, she could, she supposed. When dreaming, one was allowed to do things one might not in Real Life. "Very well. One kiss. But only one, so—"*

*He clasped his arms about her, bent her back, and captured her mouth with his. Even in her dream, he was impatient, masculine, and forward. Prudence shuddered and shivered, moaning with the heat that blossomed at his touch, at the feel of his warm mouth on hers, at the sensual shiver of his tongue slipping past her lips.*

*How could she experience such feelings in a simple dream? How could she truly feel the texture of his skin, smell the freshness of his linen, taste the tang of salt on his lips? How was it that she—*

A harsh knock broke through her muddled slumber. Prudence scrunched her eyes more tightly closed and pulled her pillow closer, desperately hanging on to the image of the captain, his handsome face bent over hers, his mouth just inches from her own—

The harsh knock sounded again, but this time the door opened and Mrs. Fieldings said in her usual flat tone, "Rise, madam. The cock's done crowed."

Prudence groaned as the last image of the captain dissipated into wakefulness. She rolled onto her stomach, hugging her pillow even tighter.

Mrs. Fieldings threw open the curtains, the light streaming into the room.

"I wish you wouldn't do that," Prudence said, pulling the covers over her head, the air brisk with morning chill.

Mrs. Fieldings calmly peeled back the covers. "Slothfulness doth not put bread upon the table."

Prudence hated homilies, especially before breakfast. She opened her eyes to small slits. "Yes, well, not getting enough sleep can—it can, ah, make a fish grumpy." There. Not quite as pithy as Mrs. Fieldings's home truth, but it would do.

The housekeeper sniffed. "You made that up."

"I did not," Prudence said as loftily as she could while still hidden beneath the covers, her eyes barely open. "I heard it from, um, the captain's men."

"Those wastrels. 'Tis time you arose, madam. The early bird gets the worm."

Blast it! This was war. Forcing the last vestiges of sleep aside, Prudence sat up. "Last in, first out."

Mrs. Fieldings's sparse countenance tightened. "Lazy hands make merry mischief."

"Two in the hand are worth—oh bother!" Prudence swung her legs out of bed, stretching mightily. She mumbled, "I don't know why I even try. You beat me every time."

A faint smirk touched the dour housekeeper's mouth. "Breakfast is ready. Your mother is already in the dining room." She poured some fresh water into the china bowl on the washstand, placed a clean hand towel beside it, and left.

Prudence found her slippers and rammed her feet

into them, then made her way to the bowl. She washed her face and hands, scrubbing hard at her lips where they still tingled as if the kisses had been real. She looked in the mirror and found herself smiling. It had been a long time since she'd dreamed of anyone other than Phillip. "It's about time," she told herself.

Not, of course, that the captain was the sort of man for a romance. He was dark, dangerous, and unruly. Still, he was pleasant to dream about. That was all some men were good for.

Smiling at her own nonsense, she took off her night rail, unbraided her hair and ran a comb through it, then pinned the long locks up on her head. Her hair was unfashionably long, the thick strands brushing the tops of her hips. She supposed she should have it cut, but somehow, she never did.

The sun shone warmly into the room, belying the chilled wind that rattled the shutters. Prudence stood in the warming beam and pulled a round gown of pink muslin over her head and tied it securely.

Odd that she'd awoken, dreaming of the captain. And not just thinking about him, but dreaming about him...about his eyes, that odd green color and intense. About the shape of his lips when he'd flashed that one swift smile that had sent her senses reeling. About how those very lips had covered hers and delivered the most passionate, unique kiss she'd ever—

She covered her face and shivered. Before now, she'd always thought Phillip's kiss had been wonderful, gentle and tender, just like him. Her chest tightened at the thought. How could she compare a dream kiss from a man like the captain—a kiss that held less meaning than a scrap of torn paper—to a kiss from Phillip, who had been her husband and best friend?

Still...now that she thought about it, Phillip had never kissed her like the kiss in her dreams, with such passion and focus. Of course, that was probably because of the type of man the captain was. When she was with him, she felt as if his entire energy was directed at her and no one else. As if only she and he existed in that moment, even if he was irked with her about his sheep. Phillip had never made her feel that way, and yet...she had loved Phillip. Dearly.

It was a sign that the feelings she had for the captain were simple lust.

Heavens! She was losing her mind. Thinking was obviously not a good thing to engage in before breakfast. Hunger was warping her usual calm logic. Before she tackled weighty thoughts—or at least thoughts that had anything to do with one very masculine, very irritating sea captain and his wayward sheep, she'd have a nice breakfast and some tea. Yes, that was what she needed.

And after that...why, after that, she'd take care not to think about him again. Not even once. Yes, that was what she'd do. Besides, she had dozens of things to see to today as it was. She left her room and ran lightly down the stairs, trailing her fingertips on the smooth worn wood.

It was warmer downstairs. Mother was sitting at the head of the dining-room table, listlessly plucking at the edge of her napkin when Prudence came in.

"Good morning!" Prudence bent and kissed her mother's cheek, then took the seat beside her. "I'm sorry I'm so late. I couldn't wake up this morning."

Mrs. Fieldings entered the room and went to the sideboard, lifting the cover off two plates. "Time waits for no man."

Prudence sighed. "I think we've had enough homilies for one day."

Mrs. Fieldings sniffed. She brought the plates to the table and set them before Prudence and her mother with a decided thunk, then marched from the room.

"Oh dear!" Mother said, looking after the housekeeper. "She is certainly in a mood."

Prudence buttered her toast and spread a healthy amount of marmalade over it. "We have a lot to do today. We have to finish the curtains for the back two bedchambers, to get them ready for our boarders."

"That is going to take some time."

"We should be able to finish one set today if we both work on it. Once that's done, we must see to getting the barn in more presentable shape. We will eventually need to get another horse besides Elmira."

"I hope we will be able to afford one. I quite hate seeing poor old Elmira harnessed to the carriage. She tires so quickly."

"We will be able to afford it. I'm certain we will. Mother, I have been thinking. Perhaps our school should specialize in something."

Mother poured cream into her cup. "Goodness, you are full of ideas this morning! You must have slept very well indeed."

Somehow, Prudence's dream had revitalized her in some way. She shrugged. "I just want to help."

"Oh, you are, dear! I couldn't do anything without you. What is your idea?"

"The other seminaries for girls specialize in something. Mrs. Ashton's Select Seminary believes theatrical productions produce a becoming confidence and they perform several tasteful plays each term. Lady Barkstow's Academie for Ladies has its own horse trainer. Every girl is given a horse on arriving, and the school promises that they will all be capital horsewomen by the time they leave."

"Horses?" Mother put down her fork. "That sounds rather expensive."

"I wasn't suggesting we do the same thing as the other schools," Prudence said quickly. "But we must find our own specialty so we can convince good families to bring their daughters here and not elsewhere. We could provide a combination of the gentler arts and some good, healthy fresh air activities. We are in the countryside, so perhaps we can turn that to our advantage."

Mother sighed a little. "Prudence, I wish we weren't reduced to this. I love the idea of a school, but I hate that we *have* to do it. That takes so much of the enjoyment out of it."

Prudence pushed herself from the table. "Mother, I am sorry about Phillip's—"

Mother put her hand over Prudence's. "Stop. He didn't mean to leave things in such a state."

"It's not only the money, but the humiliation of—" Prudence pressed her lips together. "All those people trusted him. He should have realized he was in over his head and not made so many promises."

"He was overly optimistic, perhaps. But what he did was not criminal. There should have never been so many people pressing him for funds. And then, to cut us socially—" Mother looked down at her plate. "I know that was difficult for you."

"For both of us. I thought some of those women were my friends, but they weren't." No, her supposed "friends" had believed the lies published in the papers. That Phillip had stolen money from his investors, that she had enticed men to invest. It was horrid and tawdry, and still, after three years, left a horrid taste in her mouth. Worse had been the strain on Phillip of those ugly rumors. He'd grown pale and tense. And then ill. He'd just seemed to waste away before her very eyes.

She took a sip of tea to stop the tightness from building in her throat. "There is nothing to be gained in reliving the past. Besides—"

A loud bleating filled the air. Mother and Prudence looked at each other. The bleating came again, louder and much closer this time.

Mother jumped to her feet and ran to the window, almost pressing her nose to the pane of glass. "Prudence! It's that same sheep! Eating the tops off all of the winter kelp."

"Not the winter kelp!" Prudence tossed her knife and fork to the table. "That does it! I am going to the captain's cottage, only this time—" What could she do? Her mind raced, rejecting plan after plan. Finally, one clear thought danced before her. "I know what I'll do.

Mother, I will take that silly sheep to him! Let *him* put up with it!"

Mother blinked. "But—"

Prudence was already out the door. Mother rushed to follow. "Prudence, wait! Don't go while you are in a dither! You'll just say something foolish. Finish breakfast, at least." Mother caught Prudence's arm and halted her. "You'll be calmer. You might even have some time to do something with your hair. And while I like that gown, perhaps the blue one with the—"

"No." Prudence pulled free, yanked her cape from the hook by the front door and slung it about her shoulders. "It's time we spoke to the captain in his own language."

"Oh dear!"

Prudence wrapped the muffler about her neck. "I am going to take the captain's sheep right into *his* household for a change. See if he likes that!"

"Prudence, perhaps it would be better if you—"

But Prudence was already gone, her face set in determined lines. "Captain Llevanth," she muttered as she marched out the door and toward the sound of the bleating, "ready or not, you are in for a very sheepish morning."

# Chapter 6

It is important for your master to command the respect of his peers and neighbors. Anything you can do to assist in this process, however painful it might be, will be to your eventual benefit. Unfair as it is, your service will be judged on his appearance. One gravy spot on his new waistcoat could lead to the loss of a great deal of respect on your part.

*A Compleat Guide for*
*Being a Most Proper Butler*
*by Richard Robert Reeves*

*P*rudence rapped a sharp, staccato knock upon the weathered door, her knuckles smarting through her glove. Overhead a lone seagull cried, the sound tossed eerily through the air. The wind whipped a bit colder against the door, stirred her skirts, puffing cold air about her stockinged ankles. Prudence shivered and pulled the collar of her cloak more tightly about her neck.

Where was the blasted captain? No doubt he was

inside, toasty warm beside a fire, and drinking heavily. She'd heard that sailors were wont to do such things.

Behind her came a loud bleat. She looked over her shoulder to the sheep that was standing docilely enough behind her, tied to her waist by her bright red muffler. "Quiet, Mrs. Fieldings!" For some reason, she'd had to call the sheep something, and somehow the housekeeper's name had seemed appropriate. There was something about the sheep's unamused look that reminded her forcibly of Mrs. Fieldings's usual morning reproachful sternness.

The wind blew harder and Mrs. Fieldings reached out and nibbled on the edge of the muffler, showing her yellow teeth.

"Stop that!" Prudence told the animal. "Mother made that for me."

Mrs. Fieldings did not look impressed. If anything, she nibbled more.

"Save it for the captain's drapes." Only the morning chill answered this sally. Prudence shivered and knocked again, even harder this time. Still no answer came, though the icy wind played and swirled and she began to feel the cold even more seriously. "Tare and hounds," she muttered, reaching toward the door and this time, pounding her fist on the hard wood panel. "Where is everyone?"

The words had scarcely left her lips when the door burst open. But no tall and threatening sea captain glared down at her. Instead, Stevens peered out, blinking rapidly as if just waking. He was wearing a black broadcloth coat over a striped shirt, his hair covered by a kerchief.

He looked quite "piratley," pausing mid-yawn when he recognized her. "By the seas, Madam! I thought 'twas a dunner as come to demand the dibs, I did."

So, the captain was in bad repair financially, was he? She shouldn't have been surprised. "I am not a bill collector."

"No, indeed ye aren't, Mrs. Thistlewaite. Can I help ye?"

"I have come to see the captain."

"Oh ho, ye have, have ye? Well, be that as it may, I cannot let ye in. I'm not one as to let a female come havy-cavy into the house without an invite, I ain't."

"I was invited."

"By who, might I ask? Surely not the cap'n, for he'd no more let a female within the—" The round man's face lit up. "Oh now! I know who invited ye! 'Twas John Pewter, wasn't it?"

"John—no. I don't know who that is—"

Stevens held his hand well over his own head. "About this tall, and with yellow hair tied in a queue, bit of a gimp in his right leg?"

"I don't—"

"I daresay he thought not to leave his name, but 'tis no matter. I sent him to the tavern to find a wench, but if he found ye instead—"

"No one found me in a tavern!"

Stevens looked disappointed. "No?"

"No!"

"Oh well, then. Pity, though." He lowered his voice confidentially. "The lads and me thought the cap'n needed some cheerin' up and so we—" Something must have changed in her expression, for he suddenly reddened and stepped aside. "Never mind that! Just come in. 'Tis too cold to be quibbling over an invite."

Warmth beckoned. Prudence took an eager step forward when a sharp yank on the muffler stopped her in her tracks. "Oh, yes! Wait." She turned around, planted her heels, and pulled with all her might. Bit by bit, head bowed as she resisted every tug, Mrs. Fieldings the sheep walked through the door. The second she stepped over the threshold, some new panic hit her, for she looked around with wide eyes, bleated loudly, then turned, scrambling to get back outside.

Prudence held on with both hands.

Stevens yelped. "Gor!"

There was a loud clatter and two men came running around the corner. One was tall, with a gold ring through his ear, his head bald except for twin tufts of white hair over each ear. He was dressed in a dirty-looking coat over a long white night rail, boots on his feet. The other was short, round, and red-faced, his nose pierced with a gold hoop. He wore an improbably long black shirt over orange breeches.

The men saw the sheep attempting to escape and they immediately ran toward it. Footsteps sounded and three more men came running from another hallway, all of them as improbably pierced and dressed.

That was too much for Mrs. Fieldings. She bolted with renewed strength, yanking the muffler from Prudence's hands and galloping madly away, the red muffler flying behind her.

"After her, men!" shouted Stephens.

The men all looked at Prudence.

She took a hasty step backward. "Not me! The sheep!"

"Aye!" Stevens snapped. "The sheep! The one wearin' the muffler!"

Off they went, a jumble of clothing and effort, elbowing each other at the door and cursing loudly.

Prudence gasped when she saw one of them held a pistol, an evil-looking man with a scarred face and a worn blue coat.

Stevens must have seen it, too, for he yelled after the marauding herd, "Don't ye be hurting the poor thing, either! 'Tis the cap'n's, ye know, and he might be wantin' to save her for Michaelmas dinner!" He shut the door. "That was a lucky thing, bringin' that sheep! Thank you very much!"

Prudence paused. "What do you mean, 'thank you?' "

"Aye! 'Twill keep the men busy fer hours. They're always mopin' and complainin' how there's naught to do. Now they can chase that sheep 'til their noses fall off their faces."

Wonderful. She'd brought that blasted sheep all the way from her house and Stevens was *happy* about it. Blast it all. She could only hope the captain was not so sanguine. "Do you think the men will catch the sheep?"

"Those nabbers? Lord love ye, missus! O'course they won't catch it! They couldn't find a reef on a pure sunny day with a stick, those men. Not that they're not a good sort, fer they are. They just need a bit of direction, is all. And without me or the cap'n there to guide them, well... I daresay we won't see some of 'em fer hours. Maybe longer."

"I hope they do not hurt the poor thing, though she's stronger than you might think."

"'Tis a wonder ye got her here at all." He turned and began walking down a narrow corridor. "Come along this way, missus. I'll take ye to the cap'n."

Prudence paused. Should she go? If she did, what would she say? Without the sheep, her purpose was rather . . . lost. Had she any sense, she'd leave.

She blinked after Stevens, noting with mounting interest the inside of the cottage. Larger than the one she and Mother had rented, it had far fewer windows and was rather dark. There were two doors into the small hallway, both of which were tightly closed. From beneath one, a thin slice of light appeared. She took a step forward, her gaze glued to the light.

Stevens planted himself before her. "Ye don't want to go in there, madam."

"Oh. No. Of course not." She looked at the light. "What's in there?"

"That's where old Riley Neilson be laid up. He busted up his left hip, he did, during the last skirmish with the French. We've been tending him."

"In the front room?"

"He can't make it up the steps, he can't. We use both front rooms as berths. Riley is in the portside with Taggart, Lewis, and Jacobson, whilst me, Toggle, and Toots MacGrady be in the starboard."

"You *live* in the front rooms?"

"Aye."

Goodness, what sort of house was this that men actually lived in the front parlor and the dining room, using them as bedchambers? "Which room is the captain's?"

Stevens gestured down the dark hallway. "The library. He calls it his quarters, he does."

She'd already taken two short steps in that direction, but now she stopped. "Does he . . . does he sleep in there as well?"

"At times. But he still has his chambers upstairs. We haven't needed it yet, though if we get any more . . ." Stevens shook his head sadly. "We're up at topsail now. Filled to the quarterdeck and beyond."

"Filled . . . with sailors?"

"Aye, madam. All of us were at one time or another in His Majesty's Royal Navy. We all served under the cap'n at Trafalgar." Stevens beamed. "He's a war hero, ye know. The captain says we all are."

Prudence hadn't believed the upstairs maid's claims about the captain being a war hero of some sort, but now, looking at Stevens's proud expression, she thought perhaps it was the truth. "That must have been quite exciting for you all."

"Aye! Admiral Nelson was on our ship when—" A quiver passed over the old sailor's face. Though he suppressed it quickly, his eyes were suddenly wet.

Prudence felt like the lowest heel. She cleared her throat. "How many of you are here?"

Stevens poked his thumbs into the sleeves of his waistcoat and squinted up at the ceiling. "Twenty-seven."

"In this one house?"

"Well now, some come and some go." A sad look crossed Stevens's face. "'Tis hard fer a sailor to weigh anchor fer long. There's a restlessness that's hard on the soul."

"This is quite a large undertaking, then."

"Ye don't know the half of it. The cap'n feeds us and clothes us, he does. But he doesn't give it to us fer nothing, which is good, as a man has to have his pride. All the men work, whenever there's something as needs doin'."

There was much more to the captain than she'd thought. Much, much more. "That is quite generous of him."

"Indeed 'tis." The first mate scratched his chin, then gestured down the hallway. "This way if ye wish to speak to the cap'n."

"Yes, please." She was beginning to realize that behind the captain's gruff and grim exterior was a heart of some sort. Of course, it was possible the man was merely turning the men to his own purpose...though she couldn't really tell how.

Stevens wiped his nose on his sleeve. "Follow me, then. The cap'n is out walkin', but ye can wait on him in his quarters."

"Thank you," she said, following the man down the hallway.

He went to the last door and threw it open, then stepped aside. "In with ye!"

The sudden spill of gray light hurt her eyes as she entered the room. One wall was hung with long French doors, the silvered skies outside framed by deep green curtains. Light, such as there was, poured into the room. "Much better," she said approvingly. "This room is brighter."

"Aye. 'Tis like stepping onto the deck of a ship, isn't

it?" Stevens pointed to the large wingback chair that sat looking out over a small terrace and to the ocean cliff beyond. A book and a pipe rack told a tale of their own. "The cap'n likes to sit in here when the sun sets. I think he can pretend to be sailing the seas, meself." A wistful note crept into Stevens's voice. "I miss those days."

"He pretends?" Somehow, Prudence didn't think of the captain as a man given to make-believe.

A shadow crossed Stevens's face, his blue eyes darkening. "Sometimes that's all ye get, madam. Pretendin'."

Prudence thought of how much she missed Phillip and how, in the days right after his death, to get through the difficult times, she'd pretend—just for an hour— that he was really just gone on a visit or a trip. That he would be back. Of course, he never came, and sometimes it made her all the sadder.

She thought of the captain and how he limped. "Will the captain ever sail again?"

"Nay, missus. Because of his leg. Can't keep his footing on deck. Some captains, they would sail anyway, just tie themselves to the mast. But Cap'n says an unfit body in charge has led to many a failure and he'll not be one of them. Always thinking of his men, he is."

"I see. Where is he now?"

"I daresay he stopped by the barn." Stevens's face crinkled into a smile. "We've some visitors, we do. The cap'n sent them to the stables. I'll see if'n I can find him. Perhaps ye should drop an anchor here whilst I fetch him."

Prudence nodded. The man gave the room a last

look, as if expecting the captain to suddenly appear, and then left.

As soon as the door closed, Prudence looked around, her gaze sweeping the room. Large paintings of ships being tossed about rough seas adorned the walls. She walked from picture to picture, taking in the blue, green and salty grays of the ocean swells.

She wandered more slowly, noting a brass instrument on a table, a myriad of other intriguing objects with it. She removed her gloves, laid them over the back of a chair with her cloak, and picked up the instrument, the cool metal pressing into her palm.

She knew so little about the captain really, other than the fact that he had a sheep that was capable of climbing over her fence. A sheep now running unchecked through the countryside, wearing her red muffler, a boatload of men chasing it.

Her lips twitched. That could be quite amusing to see. She replaced the brass...thing, whatever it was, her gaze sweeping the room. There, on a shelf by the fireplace, and somewhat above her head, was a small engraved cup. From where she stood, it looked as if it said THE VICTORY. She squinted and stood up on her tiptoes, trying to make out the exact etching, but she couldn't. The light was too poor.

Could it be...The *Victory* had been the ship from which Admiral Nelson had led the Battle of Trafalgar. Surely Captain Llevanth had not been in charge of *that* ship.

The answer to a good many of her questions might well be on that cup. She stepped closer to the shelf and reached up on tiptoe, but her fingers barely grazed the outer edge. It was far too high. Glancing around, she found a chair. She would stand on it and then she could not only reach the shelf, but she would be able to see the cup up close and read the engraving completely.

She cast a cautious eye toward the doorway. No sound emanated from the darkened hallway. There'd been no rug lining the wood floor and the captain was unlikely to walk about on tiptoe, especially not with his limp, so she was certain she'd hear anyone approach.

Prudence dragged a straight-backed chair to below the shelf, grimacing a bit when the legs scraped the floor. Once she had the chair in place, she tiptoed to the hallway and peeked out the door. Nothing. A bit of breathlessness left her. She returned and nimbly hopped on the chair, reached up to the shelf and found the cup.

*To commemorate the bravery of the* Victory *and the final stand of Admiral Nelson, to Captain Tristan Llevanth, who stood true, fast, and brave even while wounded.*

*With admiration, from His Majesty, King George III.*

That was certainly something! She traced the lettering, the etching rough against her fingers. Had King George himself presented the award to the captain? How odd to think that the king had once had his fingers right where hers now were.

She replaced the award and, reaching even further back, teetering on her tiptoes, her fingers grazed the next award in line. This one was a large gold cross, outlined with blue enamel and set with a single jewel. A huge blue ribbon threaded through the large loop at the head of the cross, so it was apparently to be worn over a uniform of some type.

She frowned. She'd heard of the St. Christopher's Cross, given to seamen and soldiers who'd exhibited unusual bravery in battle. Could this be one? Whatever it was, it was a beautiful piece and quite impressive. She smoothed her fingers over the cool metal, admiring the color even as she glanced at the remaining awards and medals.

The captain had been no coward when it came to wartime activities. That could be very useful information, she decided. She'd have to be careful not to appear too confrontational in her manner; he would take it as a challenge, something he apparently enjoyed.

She pursed her lips. She supposed she didn't blame him. She rather enjoyed a good row now and again herself. She lifted up on her tiptoes to replace the cross—

"What are you doing?"

The words snapped through the dead silence, so deeply spoken and so close, that Prudence took a startled step back—a dangerous move for someone balanced on their toes on the seat of a wobbly chair. The cross gripped in her hands, she gasped deeply, wobbling a second on the edge of the chair.

And then she fell, tumbling back, back, back...right into the arms of the man she'd come to conquer.

# Chapter 7

It is a delicate thing, to always be right, especially when dealing with a man of breeding and, one would hope, some pride. A proper butler will know how to make it appear that all decisions are made by one's master. Or at least, heartily approved by him even when they are not.

*A Compleat Guide for
Being a Most Proper Butler*
by Richard Robert Reeves

*M*oments before Prudence's fall from the chair, Tristan had been standing in the courtyard, glaring at the barn. His father's servants were in there and it felt wrong somehow. He wanted no reminders of that dark part of his life.

Something brushed his leg and he glanced down. "Ah, Winchester." The cat purred loudly, pressing its orange-and-white face against Tristan's boot. He leaned a bit more heavily against the gate, his cane resting against his thigh as he scooped up the waiting cat and absently scratched one of its rather ragged ears. "Easy," Tristan murmured to the cat. "It's uncharted territory to be certain. But we've been in worse weather. We'll come about. See if we don't."

Winchester flicked a nervous ear, so Tristan gave the cat's head a brisk scratch before setting him back on the ground.

"There ye be, Cap'n!" Stevens said, coming up at a run.

"Aye, here am I," Tristan said, his gaze fastened on the wide oak barn doors. From behind the doors came a myriad of sounds, hammering and sawing and all sorts of noises. What the hell was that man Reeves up to?

"Cap'n, ye won't believe this, but—" An especially loud racket made Stevens turn toward the barn. "What's that?"

"God only knows, although I am about to find out." He grasped the handle of his cane and pulled himself from his leaning position against the gate. "Stevens, I am beginning to believe that allowing Master Reeves and his entourage to rest in our barn for a day or two was an error."

"I am thinkin' the same thing meself, Cap'n. What do ye think he's doin' in there?"

"I don't know. Other than request permission to clean it up a bit, he's asked for nothing more. However, I think it's time to find out." Tristan made his way to the door. Just as he placed his hand on the large, rusty iron ring, a shift in the wind produced a most amazing smell.

Stevens lifted his nose to the air, inhaling noisily. "Gor, Cap'n," he said in a reverent voice, his eyes half closing. "What's that?"

"I don't know," Tristan said, puzzled. He swung open the door and stepped inside, halting in amazement.

The entire barn had been cleaned out; scrubbed from floor to rafter. All of the hay stores—what few there were—were neatly stacked against the far wall. The tackle and tack had been moved there as well, neatly hung on newly placed hooks. That left the majority of the barn empty. Or it would have been empty had someone not placed barrels at regular intervals with meticulously cut boards laid across them, end to end. The effect was a huge, table-like structure that ran the entire length of the edifice.

Reeves had turned the barn into a dining hall. Worse was the bustle of what seemed to be an army of liveried servants.

"Bloody hell," Tristan said. What could Reeves possibly hope to gain with such a ridiculous thing as a dining table large enough to fit thirty or forty persons?

Stevens stiffened. "Cap'n, cock an eye starboard! 'Tis Toggle, the lazy shifter!"

Sitting at a barrel, plate before him, napkin tucked under his chin, was a large man with a round, roly-poly face. He wore a dirty white shirt that stretched over his paunch, which was only partially hidden by a long coat that draped down past his knees. His ensemble was only slightly less nattered than he, for his graying hair was roughly chopped about his melon head, a good bit of it standing straight up in the back, sorely in need of a good brushing.

His eyes widened when he saw Tristan and he stumbled to his feet, fork and knife still clutched in his fists, a shiny stain on his chin. "Cap'n! I didn't think—I mean, what're ye doin' out here?"

Tristan clasped his cane tighter, but Stevens interjected, "Toggle, ye fool. Just whose barn do ye think this is?"

The former bo'sun's mate looked around, his eyes wide. "It belongs to the cap'n, I'd think, seein' as how 'tis in his own yard."

"It *is* the cap'n's, ye ninny!" Stevens shouted, face red. "Now put down yer fork 'n stand to like a real sailor, or I'll have ye keelhauled and whipped within a day of yer life!"

"Master Stevens, sir! I—I—I was just—" Toggle realized he was gesturing with his fork and hurriedly returned it to the table. "I was just helpin' Master Reeves test the cook's new recipe fer—" He looked past Tristan and Stevens, a hopeful expression on his face. "Master Reeves, what's this called again?"

"Beef polonaise." Reeves walked past Tristan and Stevens to the barrel. He lifted the cover on the dish in the center, a mouthwatering scent rising through the air. "My lord. Master Stevens. Perhaps you'd like to test the recipe as well. It's a wonderful wine sauce mixed with—"

"No, we would not." Tristan glowered at the butler. "How many servants did you bring with you?"

"Twenty-one, my lord. It will take that many to set up a new household, although had I known you already had such a retinue, I might have left one or two of the footmen behind."

"I did not give you permission to make a dining hall out of my stables."

"No, my lord. You did not. However, seeing as how you are now the earl of Rochester, it seemed only fitting—"

*"What?"* Stevens gaped. "The cap'n is an earl?"

Reeves nodded wisely. "Indeed. He has just become the *seventh* earl of Rochester. He stands to inherit a great fortune, as well."

Stevens stepped back a pace, hand to his heart. "An *earl!*"

"Keep it down!" Tristan growled, glancing around, though only Toggle and Stevens were within hearing.

Toggle tucked his napkin more securely beneath his chin. "Master Reeves has been telling me all about the cap'n's good fortune and how he's one o' the top peers in the land and how he can have this sauce fer every meal if he wishes it and—"

"That's enough!" Tristan caught Toggle's rather vapid gaze. "I don't want anyone to know of this. Am I understood?"

Toggle nodded obediently, his attention already drifting back to his plate. "I won't tell no one, Cap'n. Not a soul. Jus'...may I finish me rations?"

Bloody hell, was his entire crew to be won over by nothing more than a tasty sauce? What kind of men were they, anyway? "Reeves! I will not have this."

The butler raised his brows. "Not have what, my lord? The sauce? Very well. I will tell the chef you do not care for beef polonaise, however I do think you might enjoy it if you had the correct wine and—"

"I don't want any sauce, beef polonaise or not. Reeves,

I want you and your men out of my barn." Tristan sent a glare toward Toggle. "You! You may finish your rations, but that's it. After that, it's back to work with you!"

"Aye, Cap'n!" Toggle sank gratefully back into his seat and began shoveling food into his mouth as fast as he could.

Reeves sighed. "My lord, I fear you mistake my intentions. I just thought to bring your men a little taste of what could be."

"You wished to win them over and thus win me." Tristan thought to embarrass the butler, but all Reeves did was smile.

"Perhaps. I suppose it's not to be, though. I shall have the men pack our things."

Toggle made a sound of distress, but Tristan ignored him. "See to it that they do." He looked around, frowning. "Where are your horses?"

"We made use of the sheds." Reeves spread his hands wide as if to indicate he'd had no other choice. "It was better to keep the animals away from the kitchen area."

"This is a *barn,* Reeves. A *barn*. Do you understand that?"

"Of course, my lord. It is whatever you say it is. After all, you *are* the earl."

Damnation! "Look, Reeves—"

Toggle cleared his throat. "Pardon me, Cap'n, but Master Reeves and his men made the sheds as shipshape as they've ever been. He's bloody good at organizing. He'd make a helluva first mate."

Stevens gaped. "*What* did ye say?"

Toggle blinked. "Not better than ye, of course! I didn't mean it that way, indeed I didn't!"

Reeves bowed to Stevens. "From what Toggle has let fall, I know you to be my superior." He fixed his calm blue gaze on Tristan. "Before I leave, I shall write down what I know so far of Master Christian's whereabouts."

Christian. How had Tristan allowed himself to forget that? He nodded shortly, a flush of guilt washing away his irritation. "That is most generous of you. I am sorry I cannot allow you to stay in my barn. I cannot have such upheaval—"

"My lord, please! There is no need for an apology."

"Yes, well...you may take an extra day to pack, if you need it."

"There ye go, Cap'n," Stevens said, nodding as if he'd solved their difficulties for them. "We're back on course!"

Reeves smiled at the first mate. "Master Stevens, I hesitate to ask, but would you like a bit of supper before we pack our belongings?"

Stevens looked at Tristan. "Would ye mind, Cap'n? I mean—me lord?"

"Stop that! I won't have that 'my lord' balderdash spoken in my own home."

Stevens's brow lowered. "I don't know that I can call ye Cap'n anymore. 'Tis an insult to the king, not to respect the gentry."

Reeves nodded thoughtfully. "Rules have a place in our lives, do they not, Master Stevens?"

"Indeed they do." Stevens opened his mouth to say something else when he froze, then slapped a hand to his forehead. "Gor, Cap'n! I almost forgot! Mrs. Thistlewaite is in yer study."

Tristan straightened. "More sheep troubles?"

"She brought one of yer sheep with her; says 'tis the very one as has been breakin' into her garden."

The news transfixed Tristan for a moment. "She brought a sheep?"

"Aye, Cap'n. Tied her muffler about it and dragged it all the way from her house."

Despite himself, Tristan chuckled.

"Goodness," Reeves said, his eyes bright with interest. "Who is Mrs. Thistlewaite? She sounds like a lady of great resources."

"Lud, Master Reeves! 'Tis the smoothest little schooner ye ever saw, smart as they come and trim as a gull! She and her mum wish to start a school for comportment near here, and we've all been waitin' to see what happens. They're widows, the both of 'em, but I've yet to hear a bad word spoke about either."

"A widow, hm?"

Tristan shot a hard glance at Reeves. He didn't like the way the butler said the word "widow," as if it opened up a whole new avenue of hope.

But Reeves met his look blandly enough, so Tristan asked Stevens, "Where is that blasted sheep now? I hope it is not also residing in my library."

"Lord, no! Although, I do think that's what Mrs. Thistlewaite wished to do. But as soon as she crossed the front doorway, it took off for deeper water. Some of the men are chasin' it now."

"Good. I hope they may catch it so we can have it for dinner. Reeves, we shall speak more later of your use of my barn."

"Yes, my lord."

Tristan turned and limped his way back toward the

house. He reached the terrace and opened one of the doors into the study, then halted. There, balancing on a chair seat, was his neighbor and chief irritant. She stood on the edge, raising up on her tiptoes. One hand rested on the shelf above her, the other held something that glittered. But what interested him the most was that she was, for once, devoid of her cloak.

Tristan quietly closed the door. Stevens was right—the little widow was indeed a sight to behold. She reached up on the shelf, her gown pulled tightly over her generous chest, outlining the full swell in a way that made his body hum.

More tantalizing still was the way the light from the fire backlit her skirts until he could just make out the length of her legs and the seductive hint of her back-side curve. His body tightened with need and he was assailed with a strong sense of vexation. "What are you doing?"

His guest took an instant and startled step backward, her foot coming precariously close to the edge of the chair. Tristan was there in a trice, dropping the cane and striding forward regardless of the pain, arms out-stretched. He caught her just as she fell, collapsing into his arms, flailing wildly.

One of her elbows caught him in the chin. He blinked as white spots danced before his eyes, even as he pulled her tight against him, pinning her arms. For a heart-splitting second, he wobbled in place, struggling to gain purchase on his stiff leg as she squirmed against him. "Hold still, you fool!"

His harsh tone must have cut through her panic, for she stilled and looked up at him, her eyes wide. She had the most beautiful brown eyes, Tristan decided, fascinated once again with the slant of her brows. She was almost exotic in her features, and he liked the faint laugh lines that danced from the edges of her lashes, tempting him to try and win a laugh for himself.

Her gaze narrowed. "Why are you smiling?"

"Was I smiling?" he asked, turning on his good heel and sitting in the chair she'd fallen from. He nestled her in his lap, her scent tickling his nose. She smelled of fresh cut lemon and something else... Was it pastries?

"Captain Llevanth, you may release me now."

"I could," he agreed, noting how her hair shone in the light streaming from the windows. She was a trim piece, but rounded for all of that. He rather enjoyed the feel of her in his arms.

"Captain Llevanth!"

He raised his brows.

"You will release me at once, or—"

He waited.

"Or—"

Her expression went from outrage to irritation in the space of a half of a second. "Put me down this instant!"

He was well aware that he should do as she asked. But she felt so damned good, warming his lap, her lily-fresh scent tickling his nose, that he simply could not. Could not put her down. Could not even loosen his hold, not for a thousand pounds and ten earldoms. "I will put you down when I want and not a second sooner."

Her mouth dropped open, all prim astonishment. "I beg your pardon?"

Tristan couldn't help himself; there was something irresistibly tempting about Mrs. Thistlewaite. "You may beg all you wish, sweetness. I won't stop you."

Her gaze narrowed. "Captain Llevanth, I will not be treated in such a—"

Tristan kissed her. He hadn't *planned* on kissing her, but somehow, it seemed the logical way to stop her ranting. He was prepared for her anger. What he was not prepared for, was his own reaction to such a basic, simple touch.

The moment his lips covered hers, something changed. The amused attraction he'd been fighting exploded into a million raging fires. He paused, his eyes opening. He found her looking back, her gaze clouded by the same shocked passion.

Tristan didn't give her time to think; he kissed her again, more forcefully this time, splaying his hands along her back, molding her to him.

After a second's hesitation, she gave herself to the kiss. Her arms crept about his neck and her lips parted beneath his. Time held still as Tristan mingled his breath with hers, shared the tumultuous beat of his own heart, her low moan spurring him on.

Tristan heard the noise first, the unmistakable creak of the front door somewhere far down the hallway. Somewhere in the back of his lust-emblazoned mind he knew what that meant, that someone would soon be entering this room. Unfortunately, the part of his mind that was able to reason through what this interruption meant was unable to penetrate the deep, tightly closed, and far more sensually occupied recesses of the rest of his mind. Thus it was that when Stevens walked into the library after a brief knock, Tristan was not surprised to see him. He was, rather, surprised he hadn't done anything to stop kissing his delectable neighbor.

Prudence, on the other hand, apparently hadn't heard the door, for she gasped when Stevens's rather shocked, "Gor!" rang through the room.

"Oh my goodness!" She immediately tried to gain her release from Tristan's arms by wiggling madly, but he wouldn't have anything to do with such an inane idea. He liked her there. Wanted her there. Wanted it more than anything he'd wanted in a long, long time.

"Captain Llevanth!" she hissed under her breath.

He noted how a long strand of her hair had been released from the knot of hair at the base of her neck. "I believe you should call me Tristan."

"I will do no such thing."

"And I will call you—" He frowned. "I don't know your name."

Stevens cleared his throat. "Her name is Prudence, me lord."

Prudence cast a baleful gaze at the first mate, who reddened and shuffled his feet, though that in no way diminished the huge smile on his face. "Sorry, missus," Stevens said. "Yer upstairs maid is a bit of a talker."

"And your employer is rude. Captain, release me."

Tristan supposed he really didn't have a choice. He couldn't hold her forever. "As you wish, madam." He sighed and set her on her feet.

The instant he loosened his hold, she whisked herself as far away from him as the room would allow, moving so quickly her skirts hung on the small tea table and pulled it with her.

Stevens looked at the crooked table, his brows high, his face red. His smile widened. "Well, now. I didn't mean to interrupt ye, Cap'n. I mean, me lord."

Prudence's face was about the same shade as she reached down and unhooked the hem of her skirt from the edge of the table. "Dratted table!" she muttered.

Her heart was still thundering in her ears and blocking all coherent thought. Somehow, she feared she was making a horrid mull of things, though she didn't know how. "I—I will leave now."

"Nonsense," the captain said calmly, not looking in the least put out at being found in such a—Prudence didn't know what she would call the embrace, other than "most improper." "Mrs. Thistlewaite, I have some questions for you. You just arrived, and yet here you are, poking through my things. Tell me, is this the way they do things in London? Wait until a man is out of the room, then feel free to look at all manner of personal items?"

Prudence's cheeks heated. "No! Of course not. I didn't mean to pry, it's just that Stevens mentioned Trafalgar and I was curious, so—" She bit her lip. "I am sorry. There is no excuse for my curiosity."

"Hmm." The captain crossed his arms over his chest and flicked a lazy glance at Stevens. "What's toward?"

"'Tis about Reeves, Cap'n."

Prudence paused in straightening her gown. "Reeves?" She hadn't meant to ask the question aloud, but something about the way the first mate said the name sparked her curiosity.

Stevens nodded. "He's a butler. From London! He came to serve the cap'n."

Prudence looked at the captain. "*You* have a *real* butler?"

Stevens nodded even more vigorously. "He does now! Reeves was the old earl's butler and now—" He broke off when the captain sent his first mate a glare guaranteed to burn the man's socks.

"The old earl?" Prudence blinked. Heavens, what was this? "I am confused. Which earl?"

"The earl of Rochester," Stevens said, turning his shoulder a bit so he couldn't actually see the captain. "The old earl was the cap'n's father."

Prudence turned to the captain, her mouth agape. "Your father was an earl?"

The captain's expression darkened and he said in a heavy tone, "My father was a lazy, worthless jackanapes. Anything more than that is left for question." He glared at Stevens. "What did you have to report about Reeves? I hope he is taking down that mess he made in the barn."

"Actually, me lord, he decided that since ye gave him one more night and he had all of that sauce readied, he might as well make use of it. So he's invited the lot of us to join him fer dinner. Ye are included, o' course!"

"What?"

"Aye, Cap'n! He's havin' them put white cloths over the table his men made and they set out the china as was packed in the barrels on that last cart that he lugged up the cliff. The lot of them is in there now, making a horrid noise and scaring poor Winchester to death."

"Winchester?" Prudence asked. Her breath still came rapidly and it was all she could do to distract herself from what had just happened.

"Winchester is a cat," the captain said quietly, his curiously green gaze flickering toward her a moment.

His eyes were so unusual, she thought, so...beautiful. He raised his brows, his lips curving in a self-satisfied smile.

Prudence blushed, realizing she'd been staring. She hurriedly said, "I really must be going."

"You only just arrived," the captain replied.

"Aye, missus! Ye'd like Winchester. He's an orange tabby and the best mouser we ever had." Stevens chuckled a bit. "We kept Winchester aboard the *Victory* right up to the very end. We never so much as saw one rat the whole time we was at sea."

Prudence managed a smile. "Indeed. Winchester sounds like a prime cat." Somehow, she could not see the captain...no, the *earl* caring about such things as a cat.

She tried to reconcile herself with the fact that her neighbor was not all he seemed. Still, she didn't think she quite believed the earl story. Not that the captain seemed to, either. "Captain, about this earl question—"

"There is no question," the man said quietly.

Stevens rocked back on his heels. "I remember one rat was so big as could lift the mainsail by hisself, he could."

Distracted, Prudence's gaze narrowed. "Oh?"

"Why yes, madam," Stevens said, warming to his audience. "'Twas a huge rat, the size of a dog."

To Tristan's delight, Prudence plopped her hands on her hips. "And how could a rat raise a sail? Did you tie his tiny paws to a rope?"

"Of course not! Ye couldn't make that work, 'deed

you couldn't. But we did make a little rope harness for the beastie. And off she went, pullin' that blasted sail, even against the wind! 'Twas the damnedest—oh, sorry, madam. 'Twas the most twiddlepated thing I ever saw."

Prudence looked Stevens up and down. "Have you been drinking?"

He blinked. "Why...no, madam! 'Tis scarce on ten. Now had it been noon, ye might have got me on that one."

"If you have not been drinking, then what on earth possessed you to think I'd believe such a tale as that?" She puffed out her cheeks in an exasperated sigh. "Rats hoisting sails. Next you'll be telling me you used one to navigate with, too."

"Actually, madam," Stevens said earnestly, "there was one rat as swallowed Johnny Barn's silver pocket watch and—"

"Oh! Not another word!" She rounded on Tristan well before he had time to hide his grin. "And you!"

His smile faded of its own accord. "What about me?"

"It seems that lying is a natural attribute of all sailors."

"Here now," he protested. "I didn't lie to you and neither did Stevens. We were merely telling you a yarn."

"Which time, *my lord*?" Her voice scoffed across the last words.

Tristan shrugged. "I don't like the title myself."

"Pull about there, madam!" Stevens said. "The cap'n is indeed a real live earl."

Prudence cocked a disbelieving brow at the first mate. "Of course. He is an earl. And I am the duchess of Devonshire."

Stevens gaped. "No! And right here, in our own little corner of the world! If that don't beat all. I suppose 'tis a good thing then that ye've become cozy with the cap'n. He could use a duchess or two on his frigate, 'deed he could. Especially now he is gentry."

Prudence drew herself up to her full height, what there was of it, and flashed a distempered look at Tristan. "You've trained them well. They lie with authority, the lot of them."

Tristan crossed his arms over his chest and leaned back in his chair. "That particular bit of information happens to be the truth. I am an earl."

"Of course you are."

"I am not saying it's deserved. My father held the title, though he refused to acknowledge me." He managed a faint smile. "I was born on the wrong side of the blankets, you know."

Her cheeks pinkened. "I didn't know, but it does not matter."

"It eventually did to my father. When he discovered he was dying without legitimate issue, he did what he is best known for—blatant chicanery—and made things work to his favor, as ever. Thus, here I am, possessor of a proud title."

Her brows lowered and she frowned, as if mulling this over.

Tristan didn't enjoy telling her this. He wasn't really sure why he had bothered, except that he didn't wish her to think him a braggart, holding a title that wasn't his. "It's all quite confusing. I won't inherit the fortune, land or houses unless I comply with the late earl's notions of behavior."

"Which would be?"

"Bowing and scraping and kissing the arses of half the nobility."

"Goodness. You sound disenchanted."

Tristan scowled. "I'll not dress in velvets just to win some blunt, no matter the amount."

Prudence sniffed. "That is quite noble of you, turning your back on a fortune in an effort to keep to your values of slovenly dress and rude behavior."

Tristan burst into laughter. "A man must have his principles."

"Indeed. I've often heard it stated that a man without principles is like a ship without a rudder. What would you be without your surly disposition and unmannerly outbursts? Certainly not the rough sea captain we've all come to know and ... recognize."

"Please don't hold back on my account."

She smiled sweetly. "Ah, but you are an injured man. I would so hate to insult you when you're not at your full capacities."

Stevens threw his hands in the air. "Heads down! I think perhaps I'd best be going, I should. Mayhap I'll bring back some tea, if there's any to be had." He scurried from the room, sending Prudence a warning glance before he disappeared.

The woman had the audacity to smile. "Your man seems to think I am in some danger."

Tristan's eyes narrowed. "So you are, sweetheart." He leaned forward. "Allow me to assure you that I am at my full capacity, injured leg or not. The musket ball did not come anywhere near the Important Part."

Her cheeks bloomed. "That will be enough of that, thank you."

"You were the one who suggested I was not able to take the seas at full sail."

"Yes, but I did not mean—oh, never mind. I can see that you are merely teasing me."

"Perhaps," he agreed. He admired the delicious way her lips quivered as she tried not to return his smile. Her eyes met his, and suddenly, everything felt right. Right in a way they had not for a very, very long time. Perhaps ever.

He wondered if perhaps, in accepting the title, he might not find many more such moments—with a woman such as this.

"I wonder..." She regarded him steadily, her head tilted to one side. "What exactly do you have to—" She colored suddenly. "I'm sorry. It is none of my concern."

No it wasn't. Still... Tristan watched her from beneath his lashes. Mrs. Thistlewaite may not be titled, but her every movement bespoke breeding and elegance. She seemed out of place in the simplicity of his library. She moved like a countess, he decided. And since he was now an earl—

Good God, where had *that* thought come from? He needed to focus on the funds, not daydream about such wasted silliness.

Yes, he told himself. Think of the funds. Never again would an injured sailor go hungry or without wages. The house could be enlarged. Perhaps some berths added in a wing that would keep him from turning away the newly arrived. He was at capacity as it was now.

To win the funds, he'd have to pass muster with the trustees, and something in Reeves's expression had led Tristan to think that that might not be an easy task. What if he couldn't do it?

He suddenly became aware of Prudence standing before him. She gave a sharp curtsy and said, "I really must go. I've errands to run this afternoon, though I've yet to complete the task I set out to do in coming here."

"Ah, yes. My sheep."

"The next time one finds itself in my garden, I shall make soup of it."

He raised his brows. "You can cook? Had I known that I should have sent you a more tender ewe."

Her eyes narrowed, her full lips pursed in an accusing scowl.

Tristan threw up his hand, laughing. "Hold fire, woman! I am teasing you! I vow on my mother's grave I did not know my sheep had climbed your gate yet again. I am as mystified as ever as to how that keeps occurring."

Her shoulders straightened, though some of the suspicion left her eyes. "However that may be, they are still *your* sheep. It is time you took responsibility for them."

"I'm a sailor, not a shepherd. But for you..." Tristan eyed his neighbor from the top of her glossy brown curls to the tantalizing glimpse of her slippered toes before saying in a voice heavily laced with appreciation, "for you, I could be."

Her face flushed a delightful pink and she made a hurried curtsy. "Th-thank you. I—I—You—you—

you—" She grimaced. "Oh blast it! Just keep your blasted sheep on your own property!" and with that ringing announcement, she spun and almost ran from the room.

# Chapter 8

It is a delicate thing, to always be right. An intelligent butler will know how to make this difficult fact palatable. At least, for the moment it counts.

*A Compleat Guide for*
*Being a Most Proper Butler*
by Richard Robert Reeves

*T*ristan leaned his hand on the frame above his head and looked out of the terrace window. The wind stirred the greenery, waves of hedgerow brushing the quickly darkening sky over the cliff beyond. At the corner of the view, the edge of the barn was just visible.

The barn...

Tristan scowled at it. If he had any magic to him at all, the bloody edifice would disappear from sight and with it, the dilemma he now faced. He wanted those damn funds. The more he thought of what he could do with them, the more impossible it seemed to walk away from the "opportunity" offered.

How like his wondrous father to make life so miserably unfair. The man must even now be laughing in his grave.

The thought simmered in his stomach like molten lead. "Damn his bones." Tristan turned on his heel, away from the window. "I'd rather shovel coal than kowtow to a bunch of mealy-mouthed members of the blue-blood set." They were of the same ilk as the old earl, who had not helped Mother so many years ago, and left her to die of the ague in a chilled, damp prison. He remembered discovering his mother's fate almost two years after the fact, the wound still fresh, the pain still real.

Anger surged through him. He'd lost so much over the years. His brother. Then his mother. And now, the father he'd never had.

Tristan curled his hand into a fist against the glass and rested his forehead on it. Damn the earl to hell. Tristan would spend no more time thinking about him. There were more weighty issues at hand; like Christian. Tristan had looked for his brother for so many years. Now, he had the opportunity to find him. All he needed was Reeves's information and some time.

He rubbed a hand along his jaw, the scratch of his overgrown whiskers sounding loud to his own ears. As the haughty Prudence had left, he'd glimpsed a bit of redness to her chin that had nothing to do with embarrassment and everything to do with his whiskers. He'd have to shave more often if the tempting lady was to be about.

*Prudence*. Despite the weight on his chest, he smiled. The name suited her well. The memory of the kiss lingered, his bottom lip tingling as if he could still feel it. She'd been quite troubled by that embrace. Very troubled. He had to admit he rather enjoyed seeing the little wren flustered.

She looked far more appealing when she was mussed by his kisses. Appealing and...he pursed his lips, considering how she'd appeared when he'd finally allowed her to regain her feet. She'd looked rather wanton, truth be told. There was fire in that woman's heart. Fire and a sensual nature that was fighting for release.

It was a pity she was what she was—the type of woman one married. Had she been a more free-and-willing type, he might have made an effort to establish himself in her good graces. Or at least in her bed.

Prudence was lovely, spirited, intelligent and honest. In a word, exactly the sort of woman he avoided like the plague. The thought of settling was unpalatable. He was a wandering man now, a man of the sea. The thought of staying in one place was a hardship, the thing that made his injury so desperately unbearable.

The very thought of being chained to a house—a home—was painful for him, which was why he didn't mind the men invading his cottage. He might have purchased the blasted place, but it was no more his home than any other place he'd slept since he'd first taken to the sea.

That was why a relationship with a woman like Prudence could lead to nothing but heartache. She was a woman who made her home wherever she went. She would not be satisfied wandering from continent to continent, which Tristan fully intended on doing once the men were more secure. She would want a house with curtains and a garden, and a husband who enjoyed sitting by the fire night after night.

He was not the last interested in being nailed to the parson's cross. Not in this lifetime, anyway. He had too much to do as it was, his crew to care for, his brother to find. Besides, he'd been alone almost his whole life and it was not such a bad fate. He really hadn't had anyone to call his own since... *Christian.*

An odd ache twisted Tristan's heart. How was his brother? Had the years been kind? Or not? These were the questions that had plagued him until, tortured by the lack of answers, he'd stopped asking them. Stopped wondering. Stopped hoping.

Until Reeves.

Tristan looked down and realized he was clutching the cane knob so tightly that his fingers ached. It was difficult, thinking about this.

But here lay a new challenge. A new sea to navigate, as it were. And navigate it, he would. He would find Christian. He would also win the funds from the trustees for his men. Life sometimes demanded compromises that were difficult and demanding.

He glanced over his shoulder at the desk. The will sat there, silently mocking him. He'd read it all, every blasted word, and still could not believe what it said. Nor how much wealth the old earl had left, not just to him, but to Christian.

"Bloody hell, where is Reeves?" Tristan looked back out the window. He needed the butler. Needed him to find Christian, and also to help find a way to appease the trustees.

Unlike other naval figures, Tristan had eschewed public life. He hated the falseness of it all, the silks and velvets that covered black hearts and selfish souls. Knowing his father, he could almost guess at the cut of the cloth of these "trustees." Tristan would have bet the *Victory* that they were all soft, overblown, pretentious arses, the lot of them.

Tristan looked at the barn, noting the warm-looking beams of light shining through the cracks in the door and spilling across the quickly darkening yard. It was tempting to cross the short distance and see which of the men had decided to join Reeves's troupe for dinner. Certainly Toggle would still be there; the man was led by his stomach. And perhaps one or two of the others. Tristan supposed he couldn't blame them; it wasn't often they were met with such succulent fare.

The rations were getting more meager, the living quarters more cramped. Like a ship at sea with no land in sight, they were running short on supplies. Even now, piled neatly on the corner of Tristan's desk, was a stack of bills that would soon be pressing. His funds had been stretched to their limits and yet there always seemed to be another lost sailor in need of a home.

Tristan shook his head. He'd think about that another time. For now, he'd try to remember the name of the sauce that had so caught the bo'sun's mate's fancy. That was something worth remembering, he decided as his stomach rumbled. He glanced at the clock on the mantel.

Bloody hell, it was almost six bells. Where was his dinner, dammit? Usually Cook had rations on the table well before now.

Tristan limped to the door and opened it. "Stevens!" A strange emptiness echoed without. To Tristan's ears, it sounded as if he was alone in the house.

That was odd. In the last year, he could not count upon one hand the number of times that had happened. Tristan walked down the hallway, the eerie silence growing. Were all of the men in the barn? Surely not every last one of them. What of *his* supper?

Growling to himself, he grabbed his coat off the hook and pulled it on before making his way outside. Within moments, he was at the barn, amidst the loud din of voices.

Tristan opened the wide door, halting stock still at the scene. If the place had seemed different before, now it was positively transformed. The entire barn was spotless, the long narrow table down the center covered with crisp white linens and set with sparkling silver and china. Large silver candelabra decorated the centers, carefully placed tureens set here and there.

What astounded him beyond the magnificence of the place settings was that every last one of Tristan's men was present. Even Stevens, who sat at the head of the table looking almost kingly, a beatific expression on his face as he contemplated the food before him.

Bloody hell. His entire crew had jumped ship. The sight sent a pang through him.

"My lord?"

The quietly spoken words came from behind Tristan. He turned to find Reeves standing a short distance away, a smallish man at his side sporting a very large, very black moustache.

Reeves bowed. "My lord, allow me to introduce you to the chef, Signore Pietra."

"Pietra? That's Italian."

"Indeed, my lord. Your father—"

"I have asked you not to call him that."

Reeves hesitated. "As you wish, my lord. As I was saying, the late earl brought a French chef into his house years ago. Soon everyone was following suit. So, last year, he imported Pietra. The man is a genius."

The diminutive chef looked amazingly like a frog in a white hat. He bulged with pleasure. "Ah, thank you, Signore Reeves! My lord, Reeves is a genius. When I first come, I say I cannot cook in the barn! It is unheard of. But Reeves, he brings out his cart and there it is, a cookstove like no cookstove I have ever seen! Tables where I need them! And all of my favorite pans! So, it was not so hard, after all."

Reeves looked pleased. He glanced at Tristan and said in an undertone, "It is a new Gunner and Albertson cookstove. One of the latest."

"I see," Tristan said, though he plainly did not.

The chef nodded. "I will cook for you, my lord!" He turned on his heel and yelled, "Nico! Set another plate for his lordship."

Tristan reached out to stop the man, but it was too late. Already two liveried servants scurried to the table carrying glassware.

Reeves smiled gently. "The hand of God cannot be stilled."

"I am not trying to still God's hand. Just yours. Speaking of which," Tristan eyed the butler severely, "you were to give me all of the information you'd collected on my brother."

Reeves's expression sobered instantly. "Indeed I was. However, Mr. Dunstead suggested I wait. Just this afternoon he received some information that may well lead him directly to your brother. The solicitor left this afternoon to pursue it. He thinks to return within a day or two."

Tristan's heart leapt. "Two days? Then my brother is nearby?"

"It is possible, my lord. I do not know what Dunstead heard exactly, but he was quite adamant it was necessary to pursue it forthwith. And so he did."

Tristan didn't know what to say. He just looked blankly at the butler, struggling against an onslaught of emotion.

Reeves cleared his throat and discreetly looked away. "I think you will be pleased with the meal. Already the duke of Cumberland and the duchess of Berkley have announced their intentions of garnering the services of your chef. There is no greater compliment than having that which others covet."

"So I've been told." Tristan took a deep breath, the rich scents making his mouth water. Certainly he'd never seen his men so quietly intent. He looked at them more closely. There was something different...and it was more than their actions, though they were unaccountably quieter. "My men..."

"Yes?"

Tristan straightened. He wouldn't have believed it if he hadn't seen it with his own eyes; every one of his men was wearing a new coat. Even Stevens, who sat lording it over the others at the head of the long table, was resplendent in a black coat with red and gold braid.

Reeves beamed. "Not knowing the full capacity of your household staff and realizing there was little time to have uniforms made, I brought an odd assortment of old liveries. I informed your men that in order for them to be served, they had to choose a coat from the selection."

"Bloody hell." It was all Tristan could think to say. He could not help but notice the quiet good cheer that permeated the men gathered before him. Despite his misgivings, he had to smile a little himself. The men knew so little happiness of late. It was yet another reason for him to pursue and win the funds from his inheritance.

Tristan crossed his arms over his chest, knowing what he had to say, yet the words stuck in his throat as thick as a morning fog. "Reeves?"

"Yes, my lord?"

"I have reconsidered my position on my inheritance. A matter has arisen that requires funds. If I do this thing—manage to convince the trustees that I'm worthy of the title—then I'll have access to all those funds, will I not?"

"Yes."

Tristan looked out at his men, a spontaneous rumble of laughter making him more resolute. "Then I shall do it." His mouth twisted in a grimace. "I had no idea that sorry bastard was so wealthy. I knew he was well set, but the amounts put forth in the will—I was astounded. You'd think he could have spared a pence or two when asked for assistance." Like when Tristan's own mother had languished in gaol.

Understanding flickered across Reeves's face. "Your father—I'm sorry, my lord. The late earl. He was many things, oddly generous with those who worked for him and yet quite closed to those within his own family."

"He was a selfish bastard."

"Yes. He was. He also lived to regret that he was not able to come to your assistance when requested."

"Not able?"

"He was out of the country and thus did not receive notification of your mother's plight until it was too late. The earl was quite saddened by events."

Tristan's jaw tightened. "I will not tell you what I suffered because of what transpired with my mother, nor do I fully know what Christian suffered, but none of it had to happen." Tristan hated the bitterness in his voice, but he could not help it any more than he could stop breathing. "My father paid no heed to either of us. Had he done so, he would have known when something went awry."

Fortunately, Reeves didn't try to convince him that he felt otherwise. The butler merely nodded, understanding on his face.

"I shall not let that interfere with my pursuit of the funds," Tristan said finally. He clasped his hand tighter about his cane, leaning against it a bit as a twinge ran up his leg. He was standing far too much and he would pay dearly for it tomorrow. "Where do we begin? What exactly do I need to do to garner the favor of the fops my father put in place as trustees?"

A reluctant smile touched the butler's mouth. "How do you know they are fops?"

Tristan leveled a gaze at Reeves. "From what little I do know about my father, he thought fashion far more important than anything else."

"I can see why you would think that and, indeed, you are correct; they are not men of superior intelligence. They will be concerned with comportment rather than character."

"Just as I thought."

The butler pursed his lips. "Perhaps you might see your way to taking a few lessons in comportment, and then a new wardrobe. The usual things a man might need when setting up a fashionable establishment."

What an ill-gotten waste of time. "It's a pity I can't enroll in that damn academy Mrs. Thistlewaite wishes to begin. I daresay she knows all that sort of nonsense."

Reeves's brows slowly rose. "I beg your pardon, my lord?"

"I said it was a pity I couldn't enroll in—" Tristan caught the gleam in the butler's eyes. "No, do not even think it. I was merely funning."

"My lord, perhaps you do not understand. We have only one month before the trustees come to inspect you. Stevens has been telling me about Mrs. Thistlewaite and her plans. It might serve well— very well indeed."

The entire idea was preposterous. "Engaging Mrs. Thistlewaite as a tutor is—"

"A tutor! Yes, that would do very well. A capital idea!" Reeves said, nodding, his expression more and more animated. "Mrs. Thistlewaite might indeed be of service, for a small fee, of course. It would serve you well, and free my time so that I may oversee the training of your staff. A man is known by the quality of his servants."

Tristan opened his mouth to protest when a small, interesting thought flickered through his mind. If he agreed to set his course just so, then the delectable Prudence would be in his house.

With him.

For hours on end.

He found himself grinning. Perhaps learning to be an earl wouldn't be so painful a process with such a distracting armful within reach. Thus he was able to say with real feeling, "Reeves, you are indeed a genius."

Reeves was already smiling. "Thank you, my lord. I do my best."

Prudence put her sewing basket in her lap and began digging for some red thread. One day, she was going to organize her basket. Place all of the threads about cards by color, and tuck all of the scraps into a neat pouch. She might even place the straight pins in one cushion instead of having them stuck in the edges of the trim work left over from last year's unsuccessful attempt to make a chemise.

She pulled out a pair of woolen stockings and examined the hole in the toe of one. "Blasted stocking," she muttered, wondering if perhaps magenta thread would blend well enough to mend it. The red thread seemed to have vanished.

It was sad to be remending an already mended stocking, but she had little choice. They were reaching the last of their funds. If they did not gain some pupils soon, they'd be reduced to selling some of their precious furnishings.

Sighing, Prudence bent her head and began mending the stocking as best she could.

The door opened and Mother scurried in, her hand plopped on her lace cap, holding it in place. Her eyes lit on seeing her daughter. "Prudence! There is a man to see you!"

*The captain.* Prudence flew to her feet, her sewing basket falling to the floor. "The captain is here? Now?"

"No, no! It's not him. This gentleman is somewhat older. Very distinguished, too." Mother leaned out the doorway and peeked down the hall, adding in a faux undertone, "I wonder if he's a member of the peerage. He has such an air, but I don't remember seeing him before."

A member of the peerage? Prudence's stomach tightened. She remembered all the days when one after another, men who'd invested in Phillip's program had arrived at the house. Some had been angry. Some sad. But the worst had been desperate. They'd put their entire fortunes in Phillip's hands and wanted someone—anyone—to tell them they would earn it back.

At the time, Prudence had still been reeling from Phillip's illness. She hadn't known where to turn and the interviews had been painful, though not as painful as Phillip's eventual death and then the scandal following. She pushed away the unwanted thoughts, smoothing her skirts nervously.

Mother dashed to stand by the settee across from Prudence's chair.

Mrs. Fieldings entered, the gentleman behind her. The housekeeper looked properly impressed. "Mr. Reeves, madam."

The gentleman was tall and slender and dressed in an impeccable black coat, his cravat simply tied. He bowed, his blue eyes bright, his black hair tipped with white. "Madam, I am Reeves, butler to the earl of Rochester."

Prudence paused in mid-curtsy. "Earl?"

"Indeed, madam."

Prudence didn't know quite what to say. After a belated moment, she gestured to her mother. "This is my mother, Mrs. Crumpton."

Mother curtsied. "Mr. Reeves! From the earl of Rochester's! How exciting! I didn't even know there was an earl within distance—"

"Mother, I believe Mr. Reeves is referring to the captain."

Mother's eyes widened. "The captain? Is an earl? A real live *earl*?"

Reeves gave a stately nod. "Indeed, madam. He has but this week inherited the title. Which is why I am here." The man turned to Prudence, his gaze lingering at her feet. "I trust I am not disturbing your sewing."

"My—" Her sewing basket laid at her feet. Oh yes. She'd forgotten about that. "I was just finishing." She bent and retrieved the basket, scooping the contents into it as quickly as she could.

As she did so, he bent as well and calmly assisted her. "Madam, I have come on a matter of business." He sat back on his heels and met her gaze squarely. "The earl is in a quandary. To gain control of his fortune, he must be approved by a set board of trustees. They will expect to see a man of distinction and manner or they will not approve the release of the funds. You have met the captain. While he has the distinction necessary, his manner could use some gentle polishing. I believe that is where we need you."

"You want me to tutor that—the captain?"

He stood, helping her to her feet and placing the basket on a nearby table. "Yes, madam."

Mother clapped her hands.

Prudence sent her a quelling glance. Really, the captain didn't even like Prudence. Well, he liked to kiss her, that much had been evident. If Prudence was truthful, she'd rather enjoyed it herself. Quite a bit, in fact. Her cheeks heated. Spending time with the captain—the earl, that is—was not a good idea. "Mr. Reeves, I am afraid I cannot do as you request. I am quite busy and—"

"Nonsense," Mother said firmly. She looked at the butler. "Prudence would be delighted to assist."

"But Mother—"

"Prudence, the man is an *earl*, for heaven's sakes! How can you refuse him?"

"Easily. Mr. Reeves, I am afraid it is impossible. I don't think I could—"

"Of course, there will be a handsome compensation."

Mother's eyes brightened. "How much?"

"Mother!"

"You should not sell your services for a pence less than they are worth," Mother said calmly. She lifted her brows at the butler. "Should she?"

"Indeed she should not," he agreed, implacable as ever. "The earl is prepared to be generous."

"He knows of this?" Prudence asked suspiciously.

"It was his idea," Reeves returned in a gentle voice.

"Oh."

"He is willing to go as high as a hundred pounds for the month."

It was a fortune. Prudence cleared her throat. "Well. That is certainly generous. However, there is a small issue of—Reeves, the captain does not like me." He desired her and any other woman who might tumble into his arms. But he certainly had never expressed any other emotion—like concern or respect. Which was, she thought a bit tartly, a great pity.

Reeves's smile turned wry. "I haven't found many people the captain does hold in affection."

"He must hold his crew in some affection; he lets them live with him."

"You are right; he does care for them. Deeply, I believe. But he is not affectionate toward them. He is, in fact, rather short tempered. However, they know him and love him and thus everyone seems quite happy with the arrangement."

"I wouldn't be."

"No, madam. Fortunately, what I am asking of you has nothing to do with affection. I merely wish to hire you to tutor his lordship."

Prudence pressed two fingers to her forehead. Tutor.

The captain. The man who, by simply brushing his fingertips over her arms, could send shivers over her bared skin. "I—I am not sure I—"

"Without your help, he will lose the fortune and his men will suffer greatly," Reeves said in a quiet, earnest tone.

Prudence thought of the men she'd seen, many of them battle scarred and unfit to make it on their own. "What exactly would I have to do?"

"Within one month's time, you will need to teach the new earl the rudiments of polite society."

"One month?"

"Yes. The trustees will come then to make their decision. He will need instruction in dancing, conversation, rules of behavior..." Reeves shrugged. "Just think of the captain as a rather large and gauche debutante."

Despite her misgivings, Prudence had to chuckle. "I don't believe he'd like anyone to think of him in those terms."

"No, madam. Which is why we won't tell him."

She looked at the butler for a moment. "You believe secrets are sometimes necessary things?"

"Indeed, my lady. Don't you?"

"Sometimes. But not with the captain. If I think of him as an overgrown debutante, then I will tell him. Personally, I believe his arrogance has caused quite a few of the problems in his life."

"Indeed, my lady. It is also one of the things that has kept him alive. His life has not been as easy as he would have you believe."

Prudence's interest flared yet higher. The captain did

have a limp, but other than that, he seemed so strong, so capable, so assured.

Reeves added, "It is also possible that that very arrogance will make his transition to earl all the easier. Members of the peerage are not known for their humble manners."

She smiled a little at that. "Reeves, in your experience, have you found all earls to be as arrogant?"

"Every last one."

"Heredity?"

"And a firm belief they are favored by God. Which is something only they and the Creator truly know."

Prudence looked down at her hands, clasped before her. "I don't know. I just—"

"He needs your help, madam. Unless I greatly mistake the matter, the men in his employ are all he cares about. Yet there are so many, he cannot keep up with the costs."

Mother sighed. "That's true. Why, the doctor was just telling me how some of those poor men were wounded and had been improperly cared for. He is over there at least once a week and says he should go more often, but dares not as the burden on the captain's purse would be too much."

"That is too kind of the doctor," Prudence said dryly. She looked at the butler. "You believe the captain will use the money for his men?"

"I am certain of it."

She squeezed her fingers together, mulling this through. She would make a healthy wage, which would ease Mother's mind a good bit. She would also be assisting those poor sailors who lived with the captain—

or rather, the *earl*. She needed to remember his title, if nothing else.

Perhaps the best part was that she would have the chance to mold the earl to a more acceptable form, teach him the rudiments of society and have the benefit of watching him bloom under her tutelage.

For an instant, she had an image of the earl on his knees before her as he thanked her for showing him the error of his ways.

It was purely imaginary, of course, but still... the scene held a lot of appeal.

She nodded once. "I will do it."

Reeves smiled. "Thank you, madam!"

"Tell him I will come tomorrow by noon. If the trustees have given us naught but a month, we will have our work cut out for us."

# Chapter 9

To remove wine stains from velvet, immerse the garment in cold water softened with a touch of vinegar. Do not fear that the harshness of the vinegar might harm the velvet. Though soft to the touch, there is a sturdiness to the fabric that many do not realize.

*A Compleat Guide for*
*Being a Most Proper Butler*
by Richard Robert Reeves

The next morning, Prudence slowly made her way toward the captain's cottage. After a fitful night filled with uncomfortable dreams and restless feelings that would not go away despite the teaspoon of laudanum she stirred into her nightly cup of tea, Prudence had awoken heavy-eyed and irritable.

She'd exchanged halfhearted homilies with Mrs. Fieldings, dressed in her second-best morning gown of pink muslin, and then joined Mother for breakfast.

While Prudence was dreading the coming day, Mother was annoyingly cheery. She chattered about how exciting it was to know a real earl until Prudence could stand it no more. She'd abruptly finished her breakfast, made her goodbyes and, wrapped in her blue wool cloak, left home for the captain's.

No, she told herself. Not the captain's. The earl's. She sighed, her breath frosty white in the chill of the morning. It would take some time adjusting to that.

She was a bit late and she knew it. Still, she could not seem to hurry. Since late last night, an odd sort of dread had begun to settle in her stomach. She could not forget the captain's heated kiss, nor her impassioned response. That was what really made her feet drag along the path despite the freezing wind; that she wondered at her reaction to a mere embrace.

Perhaps it was just the length of time since she'd been with a man. Certainly she'd enjoyed the physical aspects of being with Phillip. He had been a tender and gentle lover, something she now treasured. He'd loved her reactions to him, as well, and had encouraged her in every way.

Growing close to Phillip had been easy, relaxed; she'd done it almost without thinking. From their first meeting to the day of his death, being with Phillip had been...simple. With the captain, nothing was simple. Every moment quivered with tension and awkward awareness.

That sort of thing was not love, Prudence told herself firmly. She was not some green girl to confuse tension with true emotion.

She'd already experienced love, had lived in the

warmth of Phillip's adoration for their brief time together. What she felt for the captain was nothing more than simple physical attraction that would fade all too soon.

She straightened her shoulders. Enough of that. Time to face forward. Today she would find out what she could about the earl's abilities and, perhaps, a little of his past history. Reeves's words from yesterday had piqued her curiosity.

A blast of icy wind sliced through her cloak and gown. She put her head down and pressed on. The wind was wild and unruly, growing more furious with each step. By the time she reached the cottage she could no longer feel her feet. Blast it, was even nature against her today? She needed all her wits to deal with the captain.

He was an odd mixture of gruff ill temper and subdued humor. Beneath it all lay a heavy and seductive sensuality that sent her senses humming. Still...little as she knew him, she didn't fear him at all; for all his harsh talk, the man couldn't bear to fence his own sheep or turn away a single wounded sailor. She rather suspected the captain's bluster and brawn hid a heart much softer than he wished.

She really should think of him as "the earl" or even as "Rochester," difficult as it was. "The captain" he'd been when she'd first met him, and the captain she'd always secretly think of him.

Prudence reached the house just as a skittering of wind swirled against it, chilling her to her woolen chemise. "Lud! I am going to mull myself into a block of ice." Without another thought, she knocked briskly on the door.

The wind blew again, whistling up the face of the cliff before spilling over the garden and slapping against the house, whipping her skirts forward. Prudence shivered, knocking once more. Where was Stevens? Surely even if he was out, someone would be home—

The door swung open. But it wasn't Stephens. Instead, a huge form filled the entire door frame, an oddly light-colored green gaze pinned upon her. "You," the captain said, his voice more a growl than anything else.

"Yes, me," she said, forcing her frozen lips to make the words. "Didn't Reeves inform you I was to be here?"

The capt—no, the *earl*—leaned on his cane, the muscles in his arm bulging slightly. "Reeves said you would be here at noon. It is now"—the earl took a watch from his pocket and flicked it open with his thumb—"twenty minutes past."

"I had urgent things to attend to this morning." Goodness but she was cold. Her lips were numb and her teeth beginning to chatter ever so slightly. "Where is Reeves?"

"In the barn. He has decided to teach Stevens the manner of a real butler."

Prudence thought that humorous, though her attention was fastened on the wind as it whipped harder than ever, almost roaring. It blew Prudence's skirts forward and made her ankles ache with cold, plastering the earl's white shirt over his chest.

He was dressed very inappropriately, she decided, shivering and huddling deeper in her cloak. He wore black breeches and boots, his white shirt open at the neck and revealing the strong column of his throat. He placed a hand on the door frame, and looked down at her, his expression inscrutable.

Prudence clenched her jaw. "It would be p—polite of you to invite me inside."

His brows lifted. "And have you berate me under my own roof?"

"I didn't come to b—berate you at all." She pressed her lips over teeth just beginning to chatter.

His gaze traced her up and down, disbelief plain upon his face. "No?"

"Why d—d—don' t you invite me inside and s—s—see?" she managed to gasp.

He gave a muffled curse, reached out and unceremoniously plucked her from the stoop and set her inside. "You little fool." He slammed the door closed.

"I am n—n—not a f—f—f—" It was too cold to finish the word. She sunk her chin to her chest and tried to grit her clacking teeth.

He took her by the elbow and led her down the hallway, his cane thunking softly on the hall runner. "So you say, my little ice maiden. Come inside and thaw."

It was hardly a hospitable offer. But she knew it was all she was going to get and, frankly, as cold as she felt, she'd have been tempted by an invitation from Beelzebub to warm by the grates of hell. Gritting her teeth against the urge to refuse, she allowed him to guide her into his library.

To her chagrin, more than her teeth were chattering now. Her whole body trembled with cold.

He glanced down at where his hand closed over her

elbow. "Good lord, woman! Why are you so cold? Surely you weren't on the stoop that long?"

"I—i—it was a l—l—long w—w—way here," she managed, the shaking deepening.

"You walked? The entire way?"

"I w—w—walk that far all of the t—t—time."

His face darkened. "Not in this weather, you don't. Blast it! I thought you'd bring a carriage."

"We d—d—don't have one."

"Then I shall send one for you from now on. Bloody hell, do you want to catch your death? No doubt you'd blame that on me, too."

"Y—y—you didn't invite m—m—me in and—"

Large hands grasped her shoulders and marched her across the room to where a warming fire crackled. "Stand here and stop talking. I cannot stand to hear all of that stammering."

Once they reached the hearth, he turned her to face him. "Don't move."

She looked up at him, unable to speak for her chattering teeth, and nodded.

He paused, and to her surprise, the faintest hint of a grin touched his mouth, momentarily softening his face. Prudence blinked. He was always a handsome man. But when he smiled, his entire face changed. He looked approachable and gentle, his handsomeness compounded. He appeared so handsome, in fact, that her chest tightened in a most distressing way.

*Stop that!* she told herself, forcing her gaze downward. But all that did was put the earl's broad chest directly in line with her eyes. He was built on massive lines, a giant, in a way.

She shivered, hugging herself, the warmth from the fire slowly seeping through her skirts. "Th—thank you."

He grunted. "You need something more to warm you." He turned away and limped to the small table by the terrace doors.

An odd sense of loss filled Prudence at his absence, which was completely silly for he was only across the room. The cold was truly affecting her. She put her hands behind her, blessed warmth soaking through her, stilling her trembling a good bit.

He returned then, a small brass pot in his free hand. "You're damned lucky I was about to make some rum punch. I already had it mixed and on the fire. I had to remove it to answer the blasted door."

Prudence started to tell him that she didn't drink rum, but her lips wouldn't form the words.

The captain sent her a wry grimace. "Don't even try. I'm fixing it whether you want it or not." He set his cane to one side and took up an iron hook. He slid this into the pot handle and used it to hang the pot on a metal peg over the fire. "It won't take long. I had the fire stoked a few moments before you arrived, just for this purpose."

Even more of the shivers receded. Prudence turned to face the fire. The orange and blue crackle of the flames chased the chill from her body, a faint lassitude seeping through her.

The earl stirred the contents of the pot. The tantalizing scent of lemon and cloves and cinnamon filled the air, spiced with something more pungent.

He replaced the lid and regained his cane, then limped back to the table to collect some glasses.

Prudence was left by the fire. She held her hands to the dancing flames, soaking in the heat.

"Warm yet?"

The voice was so close to her that she jumped.

A deep chuckle met this and he passed her to set the glasses on a table. Then he lifted the cover off the small brass pot.

"That smells w—wonderful."

"It is. It'll warm you up, too."

She squinted her eyes at him, but his attention was back on the brass pot. He took the ladle and poured a goodly amount into a glass mug, then turned and pressed it into her hand. "Here. Drink this."

The amber liquid sparkled in the half-filled glass. Light from the fireplace reflected in the depths and the mouthwatering scent engulfed her. "I don't think I sh—"

"Yes well, I think you should. I'm master and commander of this rig, and a bloody earl to boot, so drink up." He came to stand near her, leaning an arm against the mantel and glinting down at her. He held a glass himself, this one filled almost to the rim.

He was so close. And so...large. The heat from the fire was slowly melting her frozen skin and she lifted the glass and took a delicate sip. Warmed liquid drenched her mouth, filled her senses, heated her stomach...and sent a swirl of rum-soaked pleasure through her. She gasped, staring at the glass with surprise.

He grinned, taking a deep drink himself. "Good, isn't it?"

She pressed a hand to her throat.

"Take another drink."

She eyed the glass with misgiving. It was as potent as the man who'd made it, and as dangerous. "No, thank you."

He chuckled, his green eyes sparkling. He took another drink, as if in challenge. "I daresay you've never before had spirits."

"I've had wine. And sherry."

"Water, both of them. This is premium rum punch."

She looked at the glass. "It's quite strong."

"Yes, it is. Which is why you should drink some. Try it again, only this time, go a little slower. After that, we shall begin the lessons." An amused twinkle lit his eyes. "I promise to be a very apt pupil."

She supposed it wouldn't hurt to take one drink. Besides, her chest was pleasantly warm where she'd tasted the beverage before. She lifted the glass and took another slow sip. This time the liquid slid down her throat and tickled her palate, caressing her chilled bones.

"Better?" He watched her from over the rim of his own glass.

"Much," she murmured, drinking a bit more. A curious warmth trickled through her, heating her from heels to shoulders. She was suddenly very aware of everything around her—the man before her, the warm red of the room, the coziness of the roaring fire, the delicious scent of the rum punch. "What a pleasant room."

He paused, his glass halfway to his lips, his gaze never leaving her. "Yes, it is. I like it better than all of the others."

"I know that. Stevens told me." Prudence smiled and finished off her rum punch. "He likes to talk about you."

"Odd," the earl said, giving Prudence a lopsided smile that quite stole her breath. "He rather likes to talk to me about you."

"What does he say?"

"Ask him yourself. He is but down the hallway. All you'd have to do is open the door and yell."

She lifted her chin. "I do not yell for servants. Perhaps that is a good place to begin our lessons—how to address servants."

He reached over and took her empty glass from her resistless hands. "Why not?"

"A true gentleman never raises his voice."

"That is a hard rule for a man of the sea." He refilled her glass with fragrant punch and placed it back in her hands.

Prudence curled her fingers over the warmed glass. She wouldn't drink this one; she'd just hold it. She was already the tiniest bit tipsy from the first glass. A second glass would be dangerous. "It isn't what you know of manners, it's what you wish to know."

"I don't want to be fettered to such nonsense, though it seems I have no choice."

"I don't consider using manners being fettered."

"That depends on what your objectives are, my dear," the captain said, his voice deep with meaning.

She eyed him narrowly. "What do you mean by that?"

He grinned. "Nothing, my love. Pray have another sip of punch. It will make things all the clearer."

"I think you're trying to get me drunk."

"Trying? Does one *try* to walk? *Try* to breathe? No, one does it or dies."

"Ah ha! You *are*, then!"

He chuckled softly. "You are too swift for me."

She smiled triumphantly, holding her glass before her. "I didn't drink any of the second glass. I knew what you were trying to do."

"Oh, you did, did you?"

"Yes. Which is a good deal too bad because I really like the punch and I would like to drink it."

"Then drink it."

"I can't. You will take advantage of me."

His brows lowered. "I do not take advantage of women, tipsy or no."

"Ah, but you said you didn't like being fettered by manners."

"And?"

"A true gentleman would not attempt to take advantage of a lady. I think *that* is why you don't want to learn any manners." She waved her hand grandly. "It all seems very simple to me."

He chuckled. "I am rather glad you aren't drinking that second glass of punch. Madam, let me assure you that I shall not take advantage of you."

For some reason, a small flicker of disappointment settled in her heart. "Not at all?"

"No."

"Oh." She stared into the fire, mulling this over. "Wait! What about a *seduction*? That is quite different from taking advantage, *and* it is something gentlemen do with frequency."

His laugh enveloped her. "Very true. A seduction is not necessarily a bad thing. It could, in fact, be quite pleasurable."

Prudence found the thought fascinating. What would it be like to be seduced by a man like this? He was unabashedly male and did not follow the normal dictates of society. Whatever he did, it would be exciting. Beyond exciting. She cleared her throat. "This is not a proper topic of conversation for us."

His eyes laughed at her. "No?"

"No." It was all such a pity. Not only could they not pursue interesting topics of conversation, but they could not allude to the improper things they'd already done. She sighed and, to ease the pressure in her throat at the memory of their passionate kiss, took a sip of the punch. Just a very, very tiny sip.

It sent a flash of warmth through her. "Oh, who cares for propriety. My lord, I owe you an apology."

"What for?"

"For kissing you. You must understand, it has been quite a long time since my husband died, and I miss—" Embarrassment scorched her cheeks. Good God, what was she doing? That was not something she'd meant to admit. She glared at her glass and set it down with a decided thunk. "Never mind. I don't know what I am saying."

"I do. You miss 'kissing.' " He shrugged, though his gaze remained riveted on her with an intensity that belied his casual stance. "I imagine that is quite normal."

It didn't sound quite so bad when he said it that way.

He waved his glass. "Sometimes, I miss 'kissing,' too."

Her gaze drifted to his leg, her thoughts fixed on him. "Ah," she said softly, wondering at the stab of disappointment that met this revelation. "Your wound prevents you from . . . relationships."

The captain's brows snapped down. "What? Relatio— *no!* No indeed! I can assure you that I can—that is not an issue here!"

She blinked, rather astonished at the harshness of his voice. "I am sorry to have offended you, I just thought you might have hurt yourself and that was why—"

"I am well aware what you thought, madam. Let me assure you that your fears are unfounded. I only injured my leg from the knee down. As I mentioned yesterday, I am fully functional."

"Then why do you miss 'kissing'?"

"It is sometimes difficult to focus on enjoyment when people have died." His gaze dropped to his glass. "I cannot tell you what that is like."

The somberness of his voice caught her. "I'm sorry. You—Reeves was right."

"Reeves?"

"He said you had been through some very difficult situations."

The captain finished his drink, and then used the ladle to dip some more punch into his glass. "We must all run through a storm or two before we reach our destinations."

She considered this a moment. "Well I, for one, have no intentions of running through anything. I shall go around the bad weather in my life, thank you."

A deep chuckle met this. He had such a lovely lopsided grin; it made her heart flutter.

He took a drink, then set his glass aside. "Mrs. Thistlewaite, you are a soft night wind, the kind that blows from the east and gently sets you down in the port of your choosing. I am glad you will be here to help me navigate the shoals set out by my bastard father."

Well! That was certainly poetic! And not at all like the harsh and rather unpleasant man she'd thought the earl to be. She started to take a step forward, when she realized that her foot seemed to be fixed in place. She glanced down to find that her skirt had caught on the bracket of a small table that held her glass of punch. "Oh bother. I am anchored."

He chuckled and picked up his cane to limp to her. There he set the cane aside, leaning it against the settee, then knelt down, his bad leg straight to one side. She couldn't help but admire the muscles in his thighs. With large hands warmed by the punch, he untangled her skirts from the table. As they swung free, he leaned back and grinned up at her.

Something happened then... Later on, she'd wonder if it was a memory of their previous kiss or a flare from the rum punch, but the earl looked so very... *dear*, sitting there before her, his green eyes sparkling. Somehow, her fingers found their way to his thick, black hair. It was amazingly soft, springing beneath her fingers and clinging as if it had a life of its own.

His smile faded, his eyes darkening ever so slightly.

From somewhere deep inside her, Prudence knew she should stop. Knew she was breaking every bond of polite behavior, the very thing she'd come to teach him.

But there was something about this man, some untamed wildness that drew her to the line of propriety and over.

She knew she'd regret every action she was about to commit. But somehow that didn't matter. What did matter was that she was here, with him, now. That her fingers were threaded through his wonderful hair, that he was looking up at her as if she was the only woman in the world.

It was a madly impossible moment. Prudence felt herself slipping over the side of desire, sinking into a wildly improbable sea of passion, and it was then that she knew she was lost.

# Chapter 10

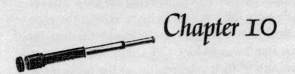

In your estimation of your fellow man, be sure to allow for the foibles of basic human nature. No matter the circumstances, the effects of passion, greed, and gluttony cannot be denied.

*A Compleat Guide for*
*Being a Most Proper Butler*
*by Richard Robert Reeves*

*S*he wanted him. The thought trembled on her lips, never quite escaping. It left her with a taste of longing so strong that her heart thundered in her ears and quickened her breath.

The moment lengthened, tantalized. The captain's eyes darkened even more. "Prudence..." He captured her wrist in his large, warm hand and pulled her fingers to his lips.

A deep shiver raced through Prudence at the touch of his lips to her bare skin. There was something achingly intimate about this moment; him kneeling at her feet, her fingers in his hair, his lips touching her. Fire licked between them, drawing her closer, closer.

She fought the swell of feelings. Fought the ache of emptiness that struggled for release. She had loved Phillip. But it was so long ago. Oddly, the memories of the warmth of their relationship, of the passion they'd shared, seemed to push her forward. Her fingers slipped from his hair, to his collar. And then she was pulling him up, to his feet...and into her arms.

He was so tall she had to bend her head back to lift her face to his. It was unique, this disparity of heights, but she liked it, especially when he gently held her in his massive arms and captured her to his chest, the scent of soap and sandalwood engulfing her.

Prudence wanted this kiss so badly. The last kiss seemed to have ignited the desire for even more. And it had been so long since a man had truly held her. So long since a man had touched her in this way. With Phillip, she'd tasted quiet passion, but this was something more...hotter, more desperate.

The captain's lips touched hers. Prudence gave herself completely to the moment, lost in the daze of pleasure and rum that soaked through her. She clutched at his shirt, pulling him closer, the linen crisp under her fingers. His skin warmed the cloth until she was certain he burned as much as she. It was with a faint sense of despair that she finally gave in to the nameless pull that emanated from him and released her grip on all coherent thought. Within seconds she had slipped into the heated waters of desire and submerged fully into his embrace.

The kiss deepened and lengthened. The captain

moaned against her mouth, plundering her deeper, more fully, as his hands ran up and down her sides, his thumbs brushing the fullness of her breasts and causing her to arch against him.

The front door slammed. Reason returned, a slash of icy water after a warm, deep slumber. Prudence broke free from the earl's embrace and quickly whisked herself around the settee. She didn't worry that he might follow her; the furniture boundary was to keep *her* from reaching back out to *him*.

"Well," the earl said, raking a hand through his hair, "That was...interesting."

Despite the wry smile he attached to the words, his breathing was as rapid as Prudence's own.

He found his cane and moved beside the settee, one hand resting on the back. "I am afraid I have had too much punch to kiss you without wanting more. I should not have attempted it."

She nodded, touching trembling fingers to her mouth where his kiss still seared a heated imprint. "Nor I. I don't know what I was thinking—"

"It wasn't you. And it wasn't me. It was the rum punch." He took a deep breath, and shook his head as if to clear it. "You came today to discuss the lessons, I believe."

"Yes. Of course." Prudence bit her lip, aware of the awkwardness of the moment. "Well!" She smoothed her gown and struggled to collect her thoughts. "I have some idea, but we need a solid plan if we're to meet the expectations of the trustees within a mere month."

His mouth twisted in a self-deriding smile. "I am so lacking in polish?"

Her cheeks heated. "No! I didn't mean—"

"Yes, you did. And I agree. It will take all of our combined efforts to gain that blasted fortune."

"I do not think that true. As a whole, your manners are perfectly acceptable. If you would but learn a few rules of comportment...that is all you need."

He smiled. "Like...do not kiss your tutor?"

*"Exactly."* She ignored the heat rising up her neck to her cheeks. She'd never been one to flush so quickly, but it happened every time the earl cast his pale green gaze her way. She wondered if perhaps she was taking the ague. Yes. That was the problem—she was developing an illness of some sort, one that would end the moment she was no longer in close contact with the man who was watching her even now.

It was a pity he was so ineligible. She almost grimaced at the word— "ineligible" didn't begin to describe the earl. He was handsome and attractive and capable of caring, as evidenced by the way he worried about his men. But he was also forceful and rough and possessed a restless spirit. He was a man who would take his pleasure when and where he found it, then leave. She knew instinctively that if he hadn't been injured in battle, he would not now be standing beside her.

The thought was sobering. She pressed the uncomfortable thoughts away and managed a smile. "Shall we begin?"

"Do your worst, madam."

Prudence thought a moment. From the corner of her eye, she caught him shifting heavily from one foot to the other. "It cannot be good for you to stand so long. Why don't you take the chair and I'll sit here." She moved as she spoke and perched on the edge of the settee. There. That was a nice, safe distance.

He hesitated, then made his way to the chair. "I am not an invalid, you know."

"I didn't say you were. I merely said you might be more comfortable sitting. I know I will be."

He glowered a bit, but sat. He stretched his stiff leg before him and placed his cane to one side.

Prudence watched him from beneath her lashes. "Let us begin with something simple. Titles are very simple, once you learn their order. At dinner parties, guests are seated by rank and—"

"Why did you agree to tutor me?"

She paused. "Does it matter?"

"Yes. You know why I am here; it is only fair that I ask the same question."

He was right, blast it. "It is a sad fact of life that food and shelter costs money."

"Money is a satisfying reason for many things."

"At times, yes. I am glad you and I are able to assist each other. Perhaps soon, both of our wishes may come true and we'll gain our fortunes."

His look of complacency disappeared behind a scowl. "I never wished for the fortune or the title. I didn't wish for a damn thing but to be left alone."

"Come now! You have been given a wonderful opportunity—a fortune, in fact, and all you have to do is learn a little polish. Yet you are far from happy about such a fortuitous happenstance."

"Aye, I receive a fortune. A fortune from a man who was never the father he should have been. A man who never once, in all the days of my childhood, bothered to visit either me or my brother one single time. A man who did everything he could to have legitimate heirs so that I wouldn't see a farthing of his, not to mention the title and lands."

Prudence bit her lip. "I didn't know."

He shrugged, though his gaze remained hard. "My father abandoned me and my brother when we were born and was nowhere to be found when Mother was taken to prison falsely charged with treason."

Prudence didn't know what to say.

"My mother died in a dank cell. Only later was she cleared of all wrongdoing." His smile was mirthless. "A classic case of too little, too late."

Prudence's throat tightened at the thought of how dear her own mother was to her. "I am sorry. How... how did you end up being a sea captain?"

"I was impressed upon a ship and I found the sea."

"How old were you?"

"Ten."

Good God. He'd been but a child.

His hand curled about the knob of his cane and he regarded his outstretched foot with unseeing eyes. "I came to love the sea, but only after we were captured by pirates."

Prudence's eyes widened. "Pirates? Goodness! That must have been frightening."

"There is very little about the sea that is not frightening." He watched her narrowly, as if judging the effect his words were having on her. "Pirates or no, they were good to us. Better, in fact, than my captain had been. So, when they asked us to join their crew, I did so."

Prudence choked. "I beg your pardon! Did you say that you *joined* the pirate crew?"

"I did. If you are to do this thing for me—the tutoring—you shall know all. I attacked ships and stole their cargo." His expression darkened. "Do not look so shocked. The work was not so different from what we were doing under the king's flag when we were scouring the seas for French frigates for the very same reason— overtake them and empty their holds, lives be damned."

"I—I see."

"I doubt it. The difference between being in the Royal Navy and being a pirate is not as far apart as you might think. One is fueled by the desire for power, the other fueled by the desire for gold."

"Did you have to kill anyone?"

"I killed far fewer men when I was a pirate. The pay was better, too, as was the treatment—But there was a cost." He shifted in his seat, stretching his legs before him. "I became a wanted man. I could not come home. I didn't think that would bother me, but I was wrong."

The words were softly spoken, the earl's voice deep. Prudence had to blink tears from her eyes. "That is horrid."

"It was. For eight years I never touched foot on English soil. Then I met Admiral Nelson. I captured his ship during a horrid squall. He was so impressed with my abilities that he offered to secure a pardon if I would but sail with him. I agreed. He secured my pardon and I came home." The earl lifted his cane and tapped the end of his boot. "I can still remember how lovely it felt, that first moment I put my foot back on English soil."

"I daresay it was." Prudence found herself looking at the captain's foot. "How did—"

He shrugged. "I took a ball at Trafalgar, fighting beside Lord Nelson."

"He was killed during the battle."

The earl's jaw set. "I saw it. Held him as—"

Prudence saw the wetness of his eyes. Her heart ached, but she wisely did not say a word.

After a long moment, the earl took a breath. His eyes had darkened a bit, his mouth lined with tension. An indefinable air of sadness enveloped him, reminding Prudence of the heavy fog that shrouded the sea each morning. "I can no longer sail," he said. "My life is over."

"Nonsense," Prudence said briskly, though she wanted nothing more than to stand and hug the man before her. It seemed he'd had so little care in his life. So little gentleness. "You have been very successful so far, despite the troubles you've faced."

He slanted her a hard look, his green eyes shadowed and distant. "More than anything, I miss being at sea, being free." Her gaze dropped to his leg and he grimaced. "And now, this. I'd rather be shot in my good leg than take anything my father touched, but I have no choice."

"Then do not take the money. Find another way."

His gaze locked on hers. "There is no demand for crippled sea captains. And that, my dear, little, meddlesome but tasty neighbor, is all I know how to do."

"If you are committed to helping your men, you will find a way. Even if your father's money is not it."

He looked at her a moment, his lids lowered over his eyes, his expression intent. "Perhaps."

Prudence bit back a sigh. He would not accept solace of any kind, that much was obvious. "Well, Captain— or rather, I should say Rochester. We should begin with some basic tenets on manners."

"Do your worst, my love." He sprawled in his chair, one arm now slung over the back.

Prudence ignored him. "Captain—I mean, Lord Rochester—"

"Tristan."

"Lord Rochester," she continued. "From now on, you must watch your language for vulgar phrases—"

His eyes gleamed with humor. "What vulgar phrases?"

"I am not going to say them, if that's what you wish. Instead, every time you use a vulgar phrase, I shall cough, like this." She coughed gently against her fingers. "That way you will know you are using a potentially lowering phrase."

He crossed his arms, his booted legs thrust before him, looking dangerous and all too masculine. "Anything else, my beautiful tutor?"

"We will also have to work on your air. You are a bit surly at times."

He opened his eyes wide. "Me?"

"Yes, you," she said, hard-pressed not to grin.

The earl gave a crack of laughter. "Do not hide your light in the fog. Say what you really mean."

"There are times you act like a complete jacka-napes."

He did laugh then, long and loud, his eyes crinkled in the most engaging manner. "I cannot see the problem with that. I've known plenty of supposed gentlemen who were jackanapes."

"So have I. But none of them came under the scrutiny of a board of trustees." She paused, thinking. "Do you happen to know who the gentlemen are? Perhaps I might recognize their names, or at least might have heard of their character enough to give us a small advantage."

He stood and took up his cane, then limped to the desk and found some papers. He carried them back to his chair and flipped through the heavily written sheets. "Here it is. *The trustees will consist of Viscount Southland, the duke of Eddington, Mr. Poole-Biddly, and the earl of Ware.*"

Prudence pressed a hand to her temple as the names rang through her mind. Southland and Ware. Southland had been furious at what he thought was Phillip's deception. And Ware . . . she closed her eyes.

Ware had been the one who'd insisted she'd been a conspirator with Phillip. That she'd used her "wiles" to attract new investors in a scheme destined for failure. His last conversation with her had been horrid and he'd barely stopped short of calling her a common prostitute. It had been one of the most humiliating and horrid moments of her life.

"Prudence?"

The earl's deep voice broke in on her thoughts. She took a steadying breath. "I am sorry. I was just thinking. I know some of those men. They are leaders of fashion, quite haughty in their ways."

"Then we will be just as haughty in return."

If only it was that easy. Memory of her humiliation rose and she hastily stood. "We should plan how we are to spend our time. We've none to waste." She walked past him and to his desk. There, she sat down, pulled forward a piece of foolscap, and uncapped his inkwell.

He turned slightly so that he was facing her once again. "I feel I am not going to like this."

She selected a pen, examined the nib and, satisfied it was sharpened enough to write without blotting, she dipped it in ink. "I am setting a schedule. It will keep us on task."

No list, no matter how well thought out or executed, would reduce the attraction she felt for the man across from her. Yet she harbored the vague hope that a paper and ink reminder of her purpose for being in the earl's lair might give her the strength to hang onto the last vestiges of her pride. That was the one thing she could count on—her pride. And she intended to cling to it with both hands no matter what passionate storms or furious waves he might send her way.

"Tell me the truth, my lovely Prudence—"

She coughed gently.

"I cannot say 'lovely?'"

"No. Nor can you call me by my Christian name."

"Not even here, in the privacy of my own library?"

"You would be wise to practice good habits at all times."

"Prudence—" he ignored her cough "—do you truly believe you can turn a sea captain into a gentleman in only four short weeks?"

"Why not?" she asked, smiling a little. "I am only glad my task is not the reverse."

He seemed amused at that. "You could perhaps teach a man to sail in such a short time. Not well, of course. But it could be done."

"But not to lead. Not to command. Not to understand the seas. That is something that would take much more practice."

He chuckled a little. He gained his feet and found his cane, then made his way to the desk.

She tried not to watch. And failed miserably. He was dressed in smooth well-fitted breeches, his white shirt tight across his chest and shoulders. His clothes hugged him with a closeness that left little to the imagination and certainly sent hers spinning wildly out of control.

He came to her side and leaned a hip against the desk, resting the cane head against his thigh. He was now positioned to read over her shoulder, his hip just brushing her arm.

If she leaned to her right…her gaze slid in that direction and found his muscular thigh, right at eye level. The thought of her fingers on his leg sent a flash of heat through her so strong that it sucked the breath from her.

Her stomach tightened, her skin heated. With fingers that trembled ever so slightly, she smoothed the paper and collected her thoughts. "First, we must ascertain what you already know. And what you do not."

"Know? About being a gentleman?"

"About general comportment. Gentlemen have perfected the art of politeness, but all people use some rules of comportment in some form or another. I daresay you know more than you realize."

His lip curled slightly, not a smile, but almost. "Oh I know all sorts of things about comportment, my love."

*My love.* She coughed against her fingers, sending him a warning glance that only earned her a smug, masculine smile. She quickly returned her gaze to the paper, curling her fingers tighter about the pen. "What areas of comportment are you already versed in?"

He leaned forward and she suddenly realized that not only was he within reach of her fingers, but she was within reach of his.

The earl placed his hands flat on the desk, looming above her. "My dearest Prudence—"

She coughed again, sending him a determined stare.

He grinned. "My dear—"

She coughed a little louder.

"Pru—"

She coughed so loudly she thought she might lose a lung.

The earl laughed and threw up a hand. "Pray do not hurt yourself on my account!"

Prudence wrote *Proper address.* "Do you know how to greet an earl?"

"If it was my father, I would just call him—"

"Don't!"

He shrugged. "I shall not burn your tender ears."

She wrote *Titles of nobility.* "What about dinner conversation?"

"Here? Now?"

"What topics would you consider of merit if you were having dinner with the trustees?" At the earl's raised brows, she said, "What do you and your men discuss when you eat together?"

"Ah! Many things. The tides and fish we've seen. Last week, Little Petey told us about his first wife and how she dropped children like a dog whelps a pup—"

*Dinner conversation.*

He scowled at the phrase, his humor evaporating. "I know how to make dinner conversation."

"Not if you're talking about whelping, you don't." She nibbled on the end of the pen for a moment. "We don't have any reason to worry about dancing. But what about escorting a lady into a room? Or a carriage. How do you do that?"

The earl looked down at her a moment. He set his cane against the desk. Leaning down, he scooped her out of her chair and into his arms.

"What are you doing?" she demanded, swinging her feet. She still held the pen, though she'd left the paper on the desk. His skin felt warm through the thinness of his shirt. "Put me down!"

"I'm holding you. Very gently. Isn't that gentlemanly?"

"No! Now release me!"

He put her back in her seat, smiling at her as he did so.

"Oh dear, oh dear, oh dear!" *Companionable skills.* She hoped he didn't notice how her hand trembled over the letters.

He placed the back of his hand against her cheek. His skin warmed her own. A slow, sensual shiver traveled down her spine at the simple contact. Prudence closed her eyes, pressing against his large warm palm. The air about them grew thick.

"Prudence."

His voice rose smoky and pure. Prudence stared up at Tristan, at his mouth. He had gorgeous lips, firm and masculine. A heated flush crept through her, prickling across her skin in the most sensual fashion.

Tristan saw every emotion, every thought as it flickered over Prudence's expressive face. He could see the desire growing in her wide brown eyes, could read the rising passion that softened her mouth and made her lips part ever so sweetly. God, but she was a beauty, this fiery neighbor of his.

His body heated yet more and he found himself leaning down, toward her mouth, ever closer, their lips drawn to each other as a compass needle to the north.

Tristan knew he should stop this madness. Prudence was not the sort of woman to partake in an empty dalliance. He knew it, knew the danger of pursuing this storm-strewn course. Yet all of the raw emotion he'd carried inside of him since being wounded, pressed him forward. Prudence was an uncharted course, an unpredictable adventure on her own. And his adventure-starved soul longed to touch her, to quench his thirst for excitement on the uncharted shores of her lushness. But more than that, there was something wanton about the woman before him, something untamed and untrammeled, that spoke directly to his own restless soul.

A faint sigh slipped from her lips, her eyes half closing as she lifted her face to his. He sank a hand into her hair and he covered her lips with his—

"There you are, my lord." Reeves's smooth voice ripped the silence like a storm wind in a too tightly drawn sail.

Prudence whirled away. Tristan straightened, ready to order the butler out of the room, but one look at Prudence's pink face made him pause. Perhaps it was a good thing Reeves had entered the room when he did. To give her time to recover her composure, Tristan moved so that he blocked her from the butler's view. "Reeves. Did you need something?"

It was difficult to tell what the butler had seen, for not the slightest expression crossed the man's face. "My lord, would you and the young lady like a luncheon served here, in your library?"

Paper suddenly rustled as Prudence stepped out from behind the desk, holding the pen and foolscap. "Thank you, Reeves, but I must return home. I—I just remembered something I must immediately see to. I will establish a schedule and then the earl and I can begin fresh in the morning."

"Very good, madam."

Prudence waved the paper in the air. To Tristan's amusement, she still sounded a bit breathy, speaking so quickly it was difficult to understand her words. "I was just making a list of the earl's abilities. There is much to be done."

Reeves's brows lifted. "Abilities, madam?"

Tristan crossed his arms and grinned. "Abilities, Reeves. Mrs. Thistlewaite thought perhaps I might already know some things that would be of use in meeting the trustees, though upon questioning, she has changed her mind."

"Nonsense," Prudence said. "Though you *do* need to work on your general comportment. Perhaps we should begin with something simple tomorrow morning. Like breakfast."

Tristan leaned forward until his face was mere inches from hers. "Mrs. Thistlewaite, I am not a child to be reminded to wipe my mouth with my napkin."

Her gaze dropped to his mouth, her lips parting again. Only this time, her tongue slipped out and dampened the pink slope of her bottom lip.

Startling heat flashed through him. Damn, but this woman made him feel like the first time he'd set foot on a ship—hot and uncertain and...excited.

Unaware of her effect, she glanced at Reeves, her slanted brows slightly lowered. "I will test his knowledge when I come tomorrow. Playact a few society scenarios."

Reeves bowed. "An excellent idea, madam."

"I don't like it," Tristan said, feeling as if the world was oddly out of control. "This is so much foolishness. To hell with the damn trustees, every bedeviled one of them."

"Madam," Reeves said in his soft voice, "perhaps we should add 'expletive training' to the list."

She waved the list. "It is already on it."

Tristan glowered. "I don't need any training in that area, thank you. I know my expletives well."

She sniffed. "You know them *too* well."

Reeves nodded. "Perhaps we will find some more acceptable alternative expressions for you to use, my lord."

"Like what?" he demanded.

"Like 'Egads!' or 'By Zeus!' " Prudence replied. "I should think either of those would be acceptable."

"Not to me."

The butler raised his brows. "Perhaps something more colorful, like 'Green cravats!' or 'Blessed spoons!' "

Prudence's rich chuckle was the only thing that kept Tristan from leaving. "That," he said sternly, "is the silliest thing I have ever heard."

She flashed him a grin that made his body tighten. "It is your decision—the funds or your horrid words. Pick one."

"I refuse to give up every vice I possess at the whim of a pack of froth-laced fools."

"No indeed, my lord," Reeves said soothingly. "There would be nothing left of you if we were to demand you give up *every* vice."

Prudence tried to choke back a laugh and failed. "You should see your face."

Tristan merely glared.

"Lord Rochester," Reeves said, "may I point out that any transformation you make is only temporary? After you've won the funds, you may return to whatever form of behavior you wish."

"Just think," Prudence said smoothly, "you can be as boorish as you wish once you have the funds. People will just think you eccentric."

Reeves nodded. "Madam, while you work on your list, I shall see to his clothing."

Tristan looked down at his shirt. "What's wrong with my clothing?"

"Nothing," Prudence said, still writing, "so long as you confine it to your study when no one else is about."

She finished writing and read through the list, then glanced at Reeves. "Table etiquette?"

"His table skills are surprisingly excellent."

"Surprisingly?" Tristan growled. "I do not like being talked about as if I were a child."

Prudence folded the list in half. She replaced the pen, then walked to the door. "My lord, Reeves and I were not speaking of you as if you were a child, but as a project."

She paused beside Reeves and looked back at Tristan, her eyes dark with meaning. "Which is what you are; a project."

Tristan didn't like that one bit. But with Reeves there, he could hardly protest. So instead, Tristan offered the lady a mock bow and said in his grandest manner, "I may have a project of my own, madam. Until tomorrow."

She looked him up. Then down. She turned to Reeves. "You will need to help him with his bow, as well. It's almost as poor as his vocabulary."

"Wait one moment—" Tristan began.

But she was already gone, the flash of her blue skirt disappearing out the door.

Reeves bowed to Tristan. "I shall see Mrs. Thistlewaite to the door."

"A lovely idea. Please make certain she does not jerk the handle from the door."

"I shall endeavor to prevent that." With a final bow, Reeves quit the room as well, leaving Tristan with a half-empty bowl of rum punch, a settee that looked oddly empty, and the uneasy feeling that nothing in his life would ever be the same.

\* \* \*

The cottage lay in utter darkness, a steady rain drumming a thorough tattoo against the windows and roof. A lone rider astride a large gelding rounded the last turn of the treacherous cliff road and pulled up hard at the gate. Water sluiced over the man's hat and cloak, cascading in sheets down the sides of his horse.

The rider, long since wetted through and through, ignored the downpour, jumped down from his mount and tied the horse to the gate. Hat pulled low to keep the rain from completely blinding him, the man strode to the front door.

Despite the unlikely hour of the night, the door was answered on the first knock by a distinguished-looking gent in a black suit.

The traveler shook the water from his cloak and removed his wet hat, then stepped inside. "Me name is—"

"Please lower your voice," admonished the gent, his startlingly blue eyes shaded with disapproval. "Everyone is asleep."

"Oh. Of course. Sorry, guv'nor." Tommy Becket was no fool. He'd agreed to do this errand for a gold coin. He'd originally thought that the man who had sent him was the one with the heavy purse. Now that Tommy had a chance to set his blinkers on the partner, he wasn't so sure. The man before him had the shine one only finds on the very rich. "I've come from Witlow. I've a missive from Mr. Dunstead fer a Mr. Reeves. Would that be ye?"

"That would be me. Did Mr. Dunstead say when he would be returning?"

Tommy shook his head, water dripping from the

brim of his hat. "No, he didn't. He jus' said, 'Tommy Becket, I've a mission fer ye. A very, very important mission.'"

"Mr. Dunstead has become something of a dramatist. Odd how travel will do that to a person."

Tommy didn't think he liked the man's tone, but he wasn't sure. "He is an important man, too. He says to me, 'Here, Tommy, take this secret missive to Master Reeves. It's a dangerous trip, but don't ye fear! He'll make it worth yer while.'"

"He didn't ask that you return for the coin?"

Tommy blinked. "Oh. Well, he did say something about payin' when I comed back with a letter from ye. But I thought since it was a-rainin', that ye might see yer way to givin' up a bit o' the gold yerself."

"We shall see. Where is this missive?"

Tommy glanced right, and then left, then reached into a pocket and pulled out a crumpled, damp letter. He handed it to Reeves, who took it and immediately carried it to the lamp that stood on the small table by the front door. Reeves quickly read the missive. He frowned and read it again, only this time, his brows rose slowly.

After a moment, he refolded the letter and tucked it into a pocket, then turned to his visitor, who was now looking at the coats hung on the rack in the front hall as if evaluating their worth.

"Good news, guv'nor?" Tommy asked.

"Good enough." Reeves withdrew his own missive from an inner pocket along with a gold piece and handed them to the man. "Please see to it that Mr. Dunstead gets this missive. He is expecting it." The butler opened the door. "Thank you for your efforts. I believe that will be all."

"Aye, guv'nor." Tommy glanced outside at the pouring rain. "Do ye think I might stay a while, at least until the rain has let up a bit?"

The door remained open. "No. I don't think that would be wise. You did a marvelous job. I shall tell Mr. Dunstead what a service you did him." With that, Reeves politely but firmly escorted the messenger out of the house and shut the door.

Long after the hoof clatter of Tommy's horse had faded away, Reeves stood in the front hallway, leaning against the door, a pensive look on his face. Twice, he pulled out the missive and reread it before replacing it in his pocket.

Finally, he pushed himself from the doorway and collected the lamp, then made his way to the small room he'd commandeered for himself.

Thank God the old earl was already dead. If he hadn't been, Reeves was fairly sure this letter might have done it.

# Chapter II

Boot blacking should be done in two layers.
The purpose of the first layer is to smooth over
places where the leather might be scuffed or
worn. The purpose of the second layer is to add
a shine that will both protect and endure. Both
layers should be administered by someone with
a thorough and firm hand.

*A Compleat Guide for
Being a Most Proper Butler*
by Richard Robert Reeves

*M*orning arrived. Tristan made it to the library at
a quarter to eight. Reeves was already there, arranging
covered salvers that brightened a newly installed table.

Tristan looked at the table. The sparkle of silver
mingled with the sheen from delicate china. It was
quite different from the pewter service he usually used.
"What the hell is this?"

"Breakfast, my lord. It is the meal one eats first

thing in the morning. The term is from 'break fast,' which came about in ancient times when people did not eat after dark and thus their morning meal was the time to break their fast."

Tristan crossed his arms over his chest. "You know damn well I was not asking where the word 'breakfast' came from. I was merely wondering why in the hell this table and those"—he gestured to the silver and the china and the rest of the silly things in a vague way—"*things* are in my study."

"Ah. Well. I found this small table in the front sitting room, being used as a footrest for Master James's berth." Reeves pursed his lips. "We will have to do something about the men being housed in the common areas."

"I don't have room for them elsewhere."

"Indeed, my lord. But for the trustees' visit, we may move them to the barn. Since Signore Pietra has taken such a liking to the new cookstove, most of the men are in the barn for a good part of the day, anyway. I don't think it would take much to convince a few of them to sleep there as well."

Tristan nodded. "That can be arranged." He leaned his hip against the settee, resting the cane on his knee. "Why am I having breakfast in my study?"

"I thought it would allow you and Mrs. Thistlewaite some privacy as you begin your instruction."

"How do you know she hasn't already eaten?"

"Because I sent a note over with the carriage you'd ordered. I hope you do not mind but I left the wording so that she may assume you were the one who invited her."

Tristan sighed. "I should have; I didn't think of it." He'd thought of *her* of course, all night long. But he hadn't thought to invite her to breakfast. He'd never felt so inept in his life as when dealing with the widow. Damn it, as much as he hated to admit it, perhaps these lessons would be good for him. Perhaps he had been too long at sea.

"You *did* think to send the carriage." Reeves adjusted the flowers. "That was a *very* handsome gesture."

"She arrived yesterday looking like an iceberg. I couldn't do anything less." Tristan made his way to the red chair that sat beside the settee. He looked at the chair, then nudged it just a bit closer to the settee.

Reeves lifted a cover from a salver. "Signore Pietra outdid himself once again."

Tristan's stomach was already growling, but the scent that arose from the table made it worse. "I am famished."

"The lady will arrive in but a few moments. Would you like some hot tea while you are waiting?"

"Bloody hell, no! I shall have ale with my breakfast."

Reeves made no move to fetch a mug. Instead, he quietly stared at the ceiling.

Tristan sighed. "I don't like being an earl."

"Yes, my lord." Reeves neatly folded two napkins and placed them by each plate. "May I say that Mrs. Thistlewaite is a delightful woman. The men respect her." The butler added one last touch to the table, straightening a fork that was slightly askew. "I hope she never regrets accepting our offer to serve as a tutor."

Tristan could not mistake the quiet suggestion. "I have no intention of making her regret anything."

He remembered her admission yesterday afternoon while she was in the thrall of his rum punch, that she missed "kissing." Though he'd been amused at the time, her honesty had touched him. Beneath her rather prickly exterior lay a flesh-and-blood woman with healthy wants and needs. Before he'd met Prudence, he'd never considered such things. Most of the women he'd known were more concerned with the amount of coin he had to offer or—after Trafalgar—the prestige of being associated with a war hero. There was more to Prudence than such shallow reasoning. Far more. She was a woman driven but not owned by her own desires and passions. A person capable of so much, if life would but allow it. That was something Tristan could understand.

The door opened and Stevens bounded into the room, wearing a new black coat, his face scrubbed, his cheeks shining as if polished. "Mornin', Cap—I mean, mornin', me lord!" He winked at Reeves. "How was that, Master Reeves?"

"Much better, Master Stevens. Much better, indeed."

Stevens grinned. "I ordered another pot o' tea and asked the men to keep mum as the cap—I mean, the earl has work to do."

Reeves smiled benignly. "Thank you, Stevens."

Tristan eyed the first mate's new coat. Several sizes too large, the sleeves hung over the man's hands, the hem resting at the back of his calves instead of his knees as it was meant to.

Stevens held out his arms and turned, glancing back over his shoulder. "Do ye like it, Cap'n?"

Reeves sent Tristan a pained smile. "Master Stevens believes the coat makes his er, posterior appear large. I hastened to tell him that it did no such thing and was, in fact, quite slimming."

"What do ye think, Cap'n? Does it make me arse look big?"

"I don't know and I am not going to look at your arse to see."

Stevens's face fell and he twisted his head, trying to see for himself. "Master Reeves said he would get it tailored before the trustees come to visit."

"How kind of him."

"Thank you," Reeves said, as if unaware of the sarcasm in Tristan's voice. "As butler, Master Stevens should have the best of the liveries."

Stevens tucked his thumbs into the buttonholes of his coat. "I'm the butler, so I get the *very* best of the liveries. Mrs. Thistlewaite won't know me when she sees me!"

A knock was heard on the front door. "There she be!" Stevens said. He bounded from the room.

Tristan pulled a chair from the table so he could sit, only to be halted when Reeves cleared his throat.

"My lord, a true gentleman always stands whenever a lady enters the room."

"What does a lady do when a gentleman enters the room?"

Reeves gave Tristan the ghost of a smile. "In my experience—and I admit it is rather limited—they complain about the lack of heat or fresh air and sometimes both."

"This system is not a fair one."

"No, my lord. I wouldn't call it fair in any sense of the word. But it is all we have."

Bloody hell, there were so many rules. Tristan gave a disgruntled shrug before pinning his glare on the butler. "By the way, have you heard from Dunstead about my brother?"

"Dunstead should return today. As soon as he arrives, I will send him to you."

"Good. I wish to—"

The door opened. Stevens stood at attention by the door, beaming as if he'd magically produced Prudence from his own pocket. She walked past him into the room, saying over her shoulder as she did so, "No, no! It doesn't make your posterior look large at all—"

Tristan laughed, immediately drawing her attention.

She flushed as she curtsied. Today she was gowned in lovely blue that made her brown hair and eyes look darker.

Reeves cleared his throat.

Tristan hurried to return Prudence's curtsy with a stiff bow. What a horrid waste of time, all this bowing and scraping. If his father were alive, damned if Tristan wouldn't kill the old man for making his life so miserable.

Prudence nodded to Reeves. "How are you today, Reeves?"

"I am well, thank you, madam." Reeves went to the chair opposite Tristan's and held it out. "My lady, we are pleased to have you with us. His lordship has been impatiently awaiting your arrival."

It amazed Tristan how well Reeves could lie. It was a bit frightening.

She slanted a covert glance at Tristan, her gaze meeting his a long moment before a faint smile touched her lips. She knew Reeves was telling a whopper, but like Tristan, she was going to play right along with it. "How kind of him," she murmured, then crossed the room to take her place at the table.

Tristan waited until she was sitting before taking his own chair. Reeves poured tea into their cups and filled the juice glasses. He also placed some marmalade and honey on the table in small containers. Tristan tried to still his impatience; he just wanted to eat. All of this fussing was interfering with his efficient ways of doing things.

Finally, just as Tristan thought he could stand it no more, Reeves removed the covers from each plate to reveal some more of Signore Pietra's magic. A variety of deep, rich scents wafted up to Tristan's nose. His stomach, already rumbling, pinched in expectation. Tristan took his fork and knife and began to cut his ham.

Prudence cleared her throat.

In addition to the ham, there were eggs stirred with cream and cooked to perfection, links of spicy sausage, a rich bit of kidney pie, and several pieces of gently browned toast. Tristan reached for the marmalade.

Prudence coughed. Loudly.

Tristan spared her a glance. "You may have some, too." He opened the marmalade jar and reached for his knife when—*thunk*. A blinding pain wracked his good shin. He dropped the knife with a clatter. "Bloody hell, woman! Why did you do that?"

She looked from him to Reeves, who stood patiently by, his gaze now fixed on the ceiling.

Tristan rubbed his shin and glared from one to the other. "What?"

"Reeves asked if you required anything else and you did not answer."

"I was eating! Besides, he could just look and bloody well tell I didn't need anything."

"Before he leaves the room, you should let him know if you need anything else, and then, if not, thank him for his services."

"Couldn't you have just told me that instead of kicking me to death?"

Her cheeks flushed. "I tried to give you a hint, but you would not take it."

"Is there no middle ground between a hint and a kick? Next time, say what you want and say it out loud."

"I am sorry if you think my actions excessive, although the way you were looking at your plate, I didn't think you would have heard a word."

To be honest, Tristan didn't think he would have, either. The eggs were damn good. "I suppose I should thank you for not kicking my injured leg."

She sniffed. "I thought about it."

"Why am I not surprised? You are incorrigible."

She flashed him a look from beneath her lashes that warned him that his other leg was still within reach of her pointed-toed boot.

"Don't even think about it," he murmured.

She tried to look haughty but failed to look anything other than adorable. Tristan decided that one of the most delectable things about his prickly Prudence was the quality of her beauty. She was elegant in a quiet sort of way. She had lovely shoulders, softly rounded arms, and a graceful neck. But it was her face that caught his attention. From her stubborn chin to the sweep of her brow, every feature echoed intelligence and humor and...passion, perhaps. But what made her so different was the way she thought.

Reeves cleared his throat. "Is there nothing else, my lord?"

Tristan waved him away. "No, Reeves."

Prudence coughed.

Tristan added quickly, "But ah, thank you for your efforts." He raised his brows at Prudence.

She gave a tiny nod.

Reeves's smile blossomed. He bowed. "Thank you, my lord. Pray ring if you need anything." With that, he withdrew.

As the door closed behind the butler, Tristan leaned back in his chair. "Well? Was that better?"

"Much," she said, almost glowing in approval.

To Tristan's surprise, a full grin broke from him in the warmth of her smile. Startled by his own reaction, he quickly turned his gaze to his plate. Bloody hell, when had Prudence's opinion come to mean so much to him?

It would not do to grow too used to having Prudence in his life. She was a temporary passenger on his frigate and nothing more. Which was a good thing, he decided, the glow from her warm smile wearing off completely. Unless he decided to retire forever on this rocky cliff and spend his remaining days contemplating the dust growing on his soul, he'd best steer clear of all women like Prudence; women who captured a man with the silken nets of companionship and home.

That was not for him. He would enjoy what benefits he could from these next few weeks, and then return to his old way of life, free and unfettered. Meanwhile, a little flirtation would not be amiss...providing he was cautious.

As he cut his ham, he decided that perhaps he'd been on his own a bit too long, for he'd forgotten how pleasant it was, looking across the table and into such beautiful brown eyes.

He was just finishing his last bite of ham when he caught Prudence regarding him consideringly. "Is something amiss?"

"Your table manners. Reeves was right; they are excellent."

"Except when I forget to compliment the help?"

"Except then." She took a sip of tea. "Well, my lord? Shall we begin? We have much to discuss."

He put down his fork. "Do your worst. Subject me to whatever plaguey notion you have of comportment."

"Comportment is not a plaguey notion at all. It is what makes us civilized."

"And here I thought it was fear of being beheaded, transported, or sent to rot in gaol that made us such upright citizens."

She sniffed. "That may be your reason for being civilized, but it is not mine. Manners set us apart from animals."

"Animals have manners, too. They just do not take them to such extremes."

She frowned. "What animals have manners?"

"Ants. They walk in a single line, do they not?"

"Frequently."

"Ever see an ant shove another out of the way?"

"Well. No."

"Exactly. They are polite to one another. Always. Meanwhile men bind themselves up in ridiculous fashion and rules, then do not pay one another the commonest of courtesies, like respect or kindness."

Her dark eyes twinkled with a reluctant flare of mirth. "That is a very good point."

Tristan wiped his mouth with his napkin, then leaned back in his chair. "Now you know why I find this entire situation lamentable. But it matters not; I must have that fortune. So go ahead, ruin me with rules. Keelhaul me on your idea of etiquette. Confine me to perdition with politeness. Do your worst. I am yours to do with as you will."

Prudence's eyes narrowed. "Don't tempt me with words like 'keelhaul.'"

He pretended amazement. "My lovely Prudence, I am astounded to hear such uncharitable words fall from your lips."

"Yes, well, if you were privy to my thoughts at times, you'd be far less astounded by my words."

That made him laugh. "You *look* like a soft wind in an easy port, but I fear you're more of a typhoon on a very rocky and inhospitable shore."

"What I am is determined to earn the money Mr. Reeves has promised me. Now, if you don't mind, the trustees will be here in a few short weeks, and one of the most important lessons of all will be how you comport yourself over the table."

"Desultory dinner talk is one of the most important lessons? Surely you jest."

"I'm afraid not. You will be expected to know how to converse intelligently and without hesitation or rudeness, plus address all manner of persons."

"I already know how to speak like a member of the nobility. Here. I'll show you. Talk to me."

She raised her brows. "I beg your pardon?"

"Talk to me. I'll show you that I know how to speak like a member born."

Prudence had to stifle a sigh. She wasn't sure where he was going with this, but it couldn't be anywhere good. Still, the quicker she played along and proved him wrong, the faster they could get to their lesson. She finished her tea and stood. "Shall we move closer to the fireplace? We can take up this conversation there."

Tristan stood as well, leaning on his cane. "Of course." He watched as she walked to the red chair that was now positioned next to the settee. Her gown was full, tied beneath her breasts with a wide pink ribbon, the skirts scarcely touching where they swept down to her feet. Tristan found that he could just make out the curve of her hips as she walked, a fact he found quite absorbing.

She sat in the chair. "Pray have a seat, my lord."

He took the settee, legs stretched before him, cane leaning against his knee. Prudence noted that his hair fell over his brow, shadowing his eyes until they appeared a more muted color. He really did have the most gorgeous eyes, surrounded by thick lashes and—

Good heavens. *Do your job and nothing more.* "The

best way to show you how to have a genteel conversation is to have one."

"Very well," he said, his eyes gently mocking her. "What do you want me to do?"

"Pretend I am the duchess of Devonshire—"

He almost choked.

"What?" said Prudence.

"Have you met the duchess?"

"Unfortunately, yes," Prudence confessed. "The woman is a sad flirt and talks in a very affected manner."

"Then why do you want to be her?"

Prudence made an impatient sound. "I don't want to be her! I just wish to give you some opportunity to practice using titles and the proper forms of address. So I said I was the duchess."

He smiled at her, a glint in his eyes. To her chagrin, he slid down the end of the settee until his knee was almost touching hers. Prudence gathered her skirts. They were brushing against Tristan's legs and for some reason, that drew her attention to such an extent that it made speaking sensibly very difficult.

Bother it all, but she'd thought she'd come prepared to deal with the earl's flirting manner. She'd spent the better part of yesterday evening telling herself over and over that she *had* to maintain a nice, safe distance and keep the topic on the issue at hand. That was all she had to do.

She'd even carefully planned on sitting in the chair and not the settee, as that would make certain the earl would not traverse too closely. She glanced down to where his foot was now pressed against hers. Apparently not.

She moved her foot and plastered a determined smile on her lips. "Please stop that. Let us pretend I am the duchess and we're sitting together at a soiree and—"

"A soiree?"

"Yes. It is a party held in the evening hours."

He leaned forward and rested his arms on his knees. Now his hand was only an inch from where hers rested on the arm of her chair. "If you wish to be at a soiree, then we will be at one. But before we go any further, I have one question."

"What?"

"What are you wearing to this soiree?"

She blinked. "Wearing?"

"Yes. I want the full experience. What would you, the sensual duchess of Devonshire, be wearing to this event?"

"I never said she was sensual."

"Oh, but she is."

"That is a matter of opinion," Prudence said stiffly. For some reason, it irked her to hear the captain call the duchess a "sensual" woman. Just what did he mean by that?

He put his hand on hers where it rested on the arm of her chair.

Prudence pulled free. "No, thank you."

Chuckling, he dipped his head so that his eyes were level with hers. "If the duchess is anything like you, then she's *very* sensual."

Her irritation fled before an onslaught of heat and...something else. Good God, but the man was a master at making her skin heat, her heart gallop, her mind flutter like the edge of a curtain in a hot summer breeze. She tried to swallow and failed. "Lord Rochester, pray do not make this so..."

"Amusing? Interesting?" He brushed the back of his hand over her cheek. "Enjoyable?"

She jerked her head away. "My lord, please!"

"Now *that* is a word I love hearing from a woman's lips: 'please.'" He leaned on the arm of the settee, his fingers hanging over the edge and near her hand. "So...what are you wearing, my dear Lady Devonshire?"

She sighed. "You are impossible."

He looked hurt. "I just asked what you were wearing so I could picture it more accurately. If that is a problem, then—"

"No," she muttered. "If that's what it takes to win your cooperation, so be it." She thought a quick moment. "I am wearing a white and blue silk gown covered with pink and blue rosettes."

He leaned back a little, his gaze traveling slowly up and down her as if he could actually see the gown. After a moment, he leaned a little closer. "Lady Devonshire, may I say you look lovely this evening?"

Prudence nodded approvingly. "That is quite an unexceptional comment."

"Thank you," he said gravely. "But ah...is that you speaking? Or the duchess?"

"Oh. That was me. The duchess would probably say something like, 'What a compliment, my lord. Thank you.'"

"It is naught but the truth." He captured her hand

and pulled it to his lips. He kissed her fingers, his mouth warm on her bare skin. "You are the most beautiful duchess in the room. And the way your gown is so low cut..." He leaned forward, his gaze staring at her bosom.

Prudence yanked her hand from his.

He gave her an innocent stare. "What?"

"That is *not* a proper statement and you know it."

"It's what I'd say to the duchess, if she were here. In fact, it's almost exactly what I *did* say to her when she supped with me aboard my ship. And she enjoyed it very much."

Prudence's brow snapped low. "I don't want to hear about the time you met the duchess. Let us return to our playacting and ascertain what is correct behavior and what isn't. Commenting on the cut of a woman's gown is *not* correct."

He sighed. "So many rules."

"My Lord Rochester," she said, once again the duchess, "what brings you here to this delightful rout?"

He took her hand, turned it over, and pressed a warm kiss on her palm. "You, my love."

She sprang up from the settee. "Oh for the love of— Will you please stop that!"

He sighed. "How am I to pretend you are the duchess of Devonshire if you will not stay in character?"

"How am I to play the duchess if you keep saying such things?"

"It's what the duchess would expect."

She glowered at him, then sat down and arranged her skirts. "Let us forget about the duchess of Devonshire for the moment. Let's pretend instead that I'm the duchess of Richmond."

"Richmond? I don't know her."

"She's all of eighty years old and a termagant. She is also something of a prude, so you'd best watch what you say. I once saw her slap a man across the cheek with her fan for merely looking at his watch while she was speaking."

Tristan eyed Prudence morosely. "You are determined to take all of the fun out of this, aren't you?"

"I want you to be successful in your bid to win the fortune. Now, let us begin once again. Lord Rochester, don't you think it is rather warm today?"

His brows rose. He looked past her to the terrace window. Prudence's gaze followed his. A frigid blustery wind blew, ruffling the thin trees and round shrubs in waves.

Prudence forced herself to meet Tristan's gaze. "It's quite, *quite* hot here in *London*."

Tristan grinned, his teeth flashing, his eyes crinkling at the corners. "I suppose if you can pretend you're a duchess, I can pretend the sun is shining in London. So yes, it is a warm day."

They continued on for several more moments, bantering back and forth in a most unexceptional way. Finally, Prudence sat back, smiling widely. "You do very well once you are not talking to someone with whom you might flirt."

"As the trustees are all men, we'll hope it doesn't become an issue."

She chuckled. "That is a very good point." Tristan

would not have to learn so many of the ton's useless posturing and manners if some of the trustees had been women. A woman would forgive much in a man who was so disturbingly attractive.

A sudden thought occurred to Prudence. What had Tristan said about the duchess of Devonshire? Something about the duchess being such a sensual woman.

A jumble of heated thoughts rushed through Prudence's head, an unfamiliar pang tightening her heart. She'd met the duchess once and the woman's overt sensuality had made Prudence quite uncomfortable. Was it possible that the duchess and Tristan had met and—

Prudence bit back the thought. It didn't matter though it would not surprise her one little bit. Tristan was the sort of man to enjoy such dalliances; he'd probably had hundreds. Prudence shifted in her chair, wondering why the thought was so unpalatable. She didn't care what the earl liked or didn't like. She was here to assist him in gaining a little polish and nothing more.

He must have noticed Prudence's reticence, for he asked, "What is it?"

"When did you meet the duchess of Devonshire?"

"She and her retinue traveled on my ship to France."

"And?" Prudence's heart pounded in her throat. She didn't want to know any more. And yet . . . she couldn't seem to stop asking. "You spoke to her?"

He leaned back against the settee. "Yes."

"I see." She clamped a hand about the arm of the chair. "And what did you think of her?"

He took longer to answer this time, his brow lowering. "A lowly sea captain is an acceptable companion when a lady of fashion is traversing the seas, away from her usual friends and family. Such a captain might, if he was willing, even be a candidate for a discreet dalliance. But for anything else..."

He shrugged, though there was a tension across his face that hadn't been there before.

Every word hurt. Prudence hated that she'd asked. Now she was left feeling oddly empty. "Society can be cruel." And harsh. And lonely.

"You don't know," he returned, his voice sharp.

"Perhaps I do, though that is not important. My lord, we should practice your dinner conversation a bit more. The trustees will expect to be invited for that, as well."

The earl crossed his arms. "Not until you explain what you meant."

"Oh for heaven's sake! I just—" She sighed. "You are no longer a lowly sea captain, as you put it, but an earl. A handsome, wealthy earl. Any duchess in London or elsewhere would be thrilled to be seen with you." The words did little to make Prudence feel better for she suddenly realized they were true. Quite true. With or without polish, the earl's startling good looks, piercing green gaze and seductive charm would have the female half of the ton falling right into his lap— literally.

Tristan saw the flash of a thousand thoughts flicker over Prudence's face. Her face was so quick to respond to her thoughts, yet he did not know her well enough to understand all of her expressions. "If I am so highly placed, then I suppose that means you are beneath me, then." He grinned. "I rather like you there."

She did not smile.

Tristan's own humor faded. "Prudence, I didn't mean—"

"Oh, I wasn't thinking of you. I just... I am not fond of the way society lines people up, worthy to unworthy, all at the whim of a few."

"Why are you so bitter toward society? Several times now, I've seen a look in your eyes."

A little of the tension seemed to leave her shoulders, though her hands were pressed into fists. "You do not want to hear my story."

"Try me."

Her gaze met his, questioning, seeking. Whatever she saw must have reassured her, for she said, "Very well. I will tell you why I do not trust society." Her gaze dropped to her hands, which were clasped in her lap. "My late husband was very good at investing. He made our fortune and established us well. Phillip had a gift for making money. He gained notice for both that and his generosity. I don't remember him ever refusing to help anyone."

"That could be a gift, or a curse."

"So I have learned. He began to manage the money of others, as well. Eventually, his services were in demand by various members of the ton. He made thousands of pounds for some very important people."

"He must have been very talented."

"He was. Phillip was a very personable and handsome man; he loved people and always thought the best of everyone. And people naturally liked him. We were soon invited everywhere."

"That must have been a heady experience."

She flashed him a painful smile. "You have no idea. I was enthralled. Me, Prudence Crumpton Thistlewaite, sitting down to dinner with two duchesses, an earl and his countess, a viscount and two of the patronesses for Almack's. They were so nice to me." Her lips quivered, then she pressed them into a straight line. "Or so I thought."

"What happened?"

"One of Phillip's largest investments didn't come through. Then another. Finally, a third. He'd had failures before, but nothing like this, and never three in a row. In the space of three months, he lost all of the money entrusted to him. He thought things would come about if he could convince the investors to wait a while, ride out the downturn. But they would not. They wanted their money back right away. Phillip did what he could, giving away most of our fortune in the process and desperately trying to talk the investors into believing in him just a bit longer." She paused, closing her eyes as if to ward off a horrible apparition. "They would not."

"Patience is not one of the better qualities of the ton."

She managed a wan smile. "No, it is not. Between the investments turning and the demands of the men Phillip had been attempting to help, we lost everything we owned as well as, according to the *Morning Post*, the fortunes of several highly positioned men. But it was not enough that he was also ruined; the men wanted revenge. Whenever they spoke of what happened, they made it sound as if Phillip had cheated them in some way. The papers repeated their comments and rumors began to look like facts."

"Damn them!"

"I cannot stand to even see one now." She looked down at her hands and uncurled them. "They said he'd broken the law, but he hadn't. He was just unfortunate. Our own fortune was lost as well. An inquiry was called and it went on for a year. Phillip was cleared, but the weight of it devastated him, especially when *I* became the object of gossip."

Tristan noted that her back was ramrod straight. He captured her hand and lifted it to his lips, then kissed each of her fingers. "People can be complete nod cocks. Do not allow the dross of human experience make you feel poorly."

A grateful look flashed across her brown eyes. "I try not to, but it is difficult."

Tristan made certain she could not see where his right hand was clenched about his cane. "If you do not mind telling me, what was said about you?"

Her cheeks flushed. "Ugly things. That I had enticed men to invest in Phillip's projects. That I had—" She sent a glance his way, then shook her head. "It is not worth repeating. We were completely ruined, financially and socially. We lost our house, our horses, all of it, and our new 'friends' abandoned us. I think perhaps that hurt the most."

"Prudence, I am sorry." He knew what it was to be left behind. Alone. And without. "I wish I could change things for you."

That was all he said. But it was enough. She looked at him, her heart in her amazing brown eyes. He could see the hurt, the pain. And the flash of warmth at his words.

She lifted a hand to his cheek. "Thank you."

He caught her hand and turned it so that he could place a kiss in her palm. "Thank *you*," he said simply.

Color high, she smiled, then pulled her hand free. "The ton is an odd and cruel world, but it is what we have to deal with now." She smoothed her skirts, visibly gathering herself. "This is not helping your cause at all."

"No? I was just thinking of a compliment about your eyes, how lovely they are. Surely that sort of neat phrase twist is worth something."

"I'm here to tutor you in the art of graces, not the art of flirtation. We really must distinguish one from the other." She flashed him a smile and he had the distinct impression her confidences were now at an end.

He didn't want to continue with their foray into "correct" behavior. He wanted to hear more about her, more about who she was and why. But he knew if he protested, she might leave and he was unwilling to risk losing her attention, even for one day.

So to amuse himself and to keep her within arm's reach, he resumed his place on the settee and said with a falsely solemn air, "I shall do my best to distinguish between flirtation and 'graces' as you call them, if *you* will attempt to smile more. It soothes the savage beast in me."

She laughed, the pure sound sending a heated vibration all the way to his toes. "Lord Rochester, nothing can soothe the savage beast in you. Perhaps that is a good thing, too."

Tristan looked at Prudence for a moment, admiring the silky curve of her cheeks. She was a beautiful woman. Not startlingly so, but quietly, with a certain amount of elegance. "I think I know what we should do. Let us cease this pretending. We'll just be who we are. You will be Prudence Thistlewaite, a lovely widow from an obviously genteel family while I am who I am, a bastard earl sadly inept at social interaction."

Her eyes met his. There was a faint hesitation, then she smiled. "That would be lovely."

"I think so, too."

For a long moment, they looked at one another, only the crackling of the fire rising between them. Then Prudence ducked her head in a nod, her cheeks flushed a pretty pink. "Where should we begin?"

"I will do my best not to embarrass you and you will do your best to correct me without making me puff up with irritated pride."

Humor shimmered in her eyes. "You do puff up."

"So Reeves has been at pains to inform me. It's annoying how he can couch an obvious insult in such a way that you find yourself agreeing as if he'd just given you the grandest of compliments."

"Do you think it's an insult to correct someone?"

"Only when it is done to me," he replied dryly, rewarded for this piece of deprecating honesty when she bubbled with laughter.

He grinned in return, feeling absurdly relaxed and at ease. "Shall we return to our discussion of the weather,

Mrs. Thistlewaite? I have thought of no less than *three* perfectly acceptable comments I could make."

Her smile was almost blinding. "My lord, it would be my pleasure."

# Chapter 12

It is widely believed by many members of the ton that, for servants, the greatest rewards in our honored profession come from praise. That is a very noble concept, though a blatant falsehood. Whether servant or master, saint or supplicant, nothing motivates more thoroughly than the sight of a freshly minted gold coin.

*A Compleat Guide for*
*Being a Most Proper Butler*
*by Richard Robert Reeves*

*S*ome ten miles east, on a particularly rocky stretch of coast, sat the New Inn. A solid stone structure with glass windows so thick as to make peering through them nigh impossible, the building squatted on a narrow line of beachhead, facing the sea.

The inn and its adjacent stables were locked from the mainland for two hours during each high tide. That, and the charms of its two buxom serving maids, made the tavern immensely popular with the men from the village. Providing that their screeching, fuming wives did not arrive to fetch them home before high tide, the inn afforded the perfect excuse to stay an extra few hours.

Tonight, just as the waters of high tide receded enough to make crossing the sandy bridge possible, a lone rider trotted his horse into the inn yard and dismounted. The link boy, Lukie, knew right away this was no ordinary cove, not only by the quality of horse, but by the shiny shilling that was pressed into his hand. Copper pennies were what the boy usually saw, except when Gentleman Jack was about.

Then the riches flowed, not just to Lukie, but to his sister, who was one of the serving maids, and his aunt, who cooked meat pies and thick stews for the patrons. In Lukie's world, only highwaymen could afford such largesse. One day, the world willing, Lukie planned to take to the high toby himself.

Lukie stole a look at the gent. Oddly, the man didn't appear to be a highwayman; he was too soberly attired. Lukie wondered if the gent was a servant, or perhaps a vicar. It had to be one or t'other.

Smiling at the thought, Lukie pocketed the shilling and led the horse to a nearby trough so it could drink its fill.

The gent took off his gloves and tucked them away. "Pardon me, but I am looking for a certain gentleman."

Lukie's smile almost slipped, but he managed to keep it in place. "Oh? An' who might thet be?"

"A man. He's quite tall, six feet and perhaps a bit more, slender build but athletic, black hair, and eyes of a very unusual shade of green." The gent's blue eyes seemed to see through Lukie. "Do you know him?"

Heart pounding in his ears, Lukie's gaze flew to the door of the inn and then back. "No, guv'nor! I ain't never heard of a man like ye're describin'."

"Hmmm." A faint smile touched the gent's face as he, too, looked at the door. "I see. Well, thank you all the same." With that, he turned and walked toward the inn, pausing outside the door to reach inside his coat for a moment.

In the light from the lantern hanging by the door, Lukie could just make out the curve of a pistol tucked securely into the man's waistband.

Eyes wide, he watched the man straighten his coat and then enter the inn. The need to call a warning grew in Lukie, but somehow, he knew such a commotion would not be welcome. No, it was better to sit quietly and be ready in case he was needed.

Besides, Gentleman Jack could handle the man, if need be. No one was bigger, faster, or more daring. And no one had a way with a sword like Jack. Reassured, Lukie led the gent's horse into the stables.

Reeves, meanwhile, took a step through the doorway of the tavern. Had he any hope for a quiet entry, it was quite dashed. The boisterous inhabitants stopped their conversations to regard him with far from friendly glances.

Reeves slipped his hand beneath his coat, the cold metal of his pistol reassuring. He was not a man given to violence, but it never paid to be less than prepared. "Pardon me," he said quietly. "I am Reeves and I am looking for a gentleman."

One of the bar wenches chuckled. "Ye've come to the wrong place then, luv, fer we've no gents here."

This caused a general burst of laughter and one or two good-humored protests. Reeves let it all pass, taking advantage of the mayhem to get his bearings.

The New Inn was not new at all, but rather an ancient establishment several centuries old. The ceilings were low with large wooden beams smudged with more nights of smoke than any living creature had seen. Smooth rocks taken from the shoreline surrounded the huge fireplace where a stack of logs burned merrily. The floor showed the most wear, dipping in a rut along the bar where countless feet had marched on their way to fetch refreshment. To one side, over the serving area, a single narrow staircase disappeared upstairs.

The occupants of the inn looked to be a mixture of farmer and laborer, with a few unsavory elements mixed in. Reeves waited for the laughter to die down before he amended his request. "I am looking for a particular man, one Christian Llevanth."

There was no answer to this, just blank stares and shrugs. Two men by the door—one a small, slender fellow with an oddly round face and small, narrow eyes, the other a huge redheaded giant of a man with a fierce expression—seemed especially resentful of his presence.

Reeves cleared his throat. "If Christian Llevanth is not here, could I perhaps inquire after Gentleman Jack?"

Silence, cold and tense, filled the taproom.

A thick-necked man with brown hair glared at Reeves. "Not a constable, are ye?"

"No. I wish him no harm."

The man chuckled, though there was no smile in his eyes. "So they all say."

His companion, a black-haired man with a patch over one eye, snarled a smile. "I'd be careful who I'd be askin' about. There are some as might take offense at ye suggestin' they're consortin' with a known highwayman."

"I mean no disrespect, but I bring news of the gentleman's father."

That caused a fresh set of murmurs. The red-haired giant lumbered to his feet and immediately silence reigned again. "I think ye'd best be leavin'. We don't want no strangers here."

"I must find Christian Llevanth. If you happen to see him, would you please tell him that I bring word of his father?"

"No," the giant said with a tenacious tilt of his chin. "I won't tell him nothin' fer ye, ye bas—"

"Willie!" came a low, masculine voice from the stairs. "Shut it!"

Reeves turned as a gentleman made his way down the stairs. As tall as his brother, Christian did not have the sheer size, but was built on leaner, more elegant lines. His clothing was notable for the quality. His cloak had the sheen of the finest wool. His breeches fit perfectly, the crisp lay of his shirt bespoke the finest Spanish linen, and the tight line of his coat was unmistakably French in design. But every piece, even his cravat, was as unrelentingly black as his hair. The only color was the sparkle of a ruby at his cravat and the flash of silver from an elaborately hilted rapier.

He looked exactly like what he was—a thief, though a stylish one. Christian crossed the room toward Reeves, moving with a fluid grace.

The giant eyed Reeves up and down. "He looks like a bloody steepler to me."

"Steepler?" Reeves asked.

The giant snorted in disgust. "Ye know, a nambler. A torcher."

"My friend Willie thinks you look like a constable." Christian smiled, curiosity burning in his bright green gaze as he sauntered toward them. "I believe Willie has the right of it."

"I am not a member of the constabulary."

Willie considered him again, then smirked. "Aye. Ye don't have the nellies fer it."

"What Willie means," said Christian, taking a chair at an empty table by the fire, "is that he doesn't believe you have the—"

"I gathered what Mr. William meant, my lord."

"My lord?" Christian's smile broadened, his teeth white in the dim tavern. "You are sadly out there, my friend, whoever you are."

"I am not mistaken at all," Reeves said softly. "I have some news. Some rather distressing news, I am afraid."

Christian froze. The giant opened his mouth but Christian raised a hand.

The giant shifted uneasily. "Jack?" he asked. "Whot's toward?"

Christian turned a face carved of stone toward his companion. "My father."

"*This* gent is your father?"

"No. My father was an earl. And now, it appears he is dead." He looked toward Reeves for verification, his face pale in the smoky light.

Reeves nodded. "I am afraid so, my lord."

Christian shook his head as if to clear it. "It is so odd. For some reason I had it in my head he would live forever. Why would I have thought that?" He was silent a moment, staring into the fire as if searching among the flames for something.

Suddenly, he roused himself and sent a quick glance at Reeves. "I am sorry. I forget myself. Won't you have a seat?" He winked at the serving wench, who giggled and brought two ales to the table. Christian tossed a coin in her direction, watching absently when she tucked the gold piece in the low top of her corset in a suggestive manner.

"You are quite well known here," Reeves said politely, taking his seat across from Christian.

Christian turned an empty chair his way and placed his booted feet on the seat. "It is good policy to be friendly with the locals."

Willie sent a warning glare at Reeves. "Sam and I will be right here, by the door."

Christian nodded absently. He waited until his servant was out of earshot before he asked, "Who are you?"

"Your father's butler."

"How did you find me?"

"It wasn't easy. I assumed, as did everyone else, that upon escaping being pressed like your brother, you would go to London to be close to your mother."

"She died before I arrived. I knew she was sick, but I didn't realize how serious it was."

"It must have been a shock."

Christian took a drink from his tankard. "You have no idea."

"No, my lord. When we first began our search, we inspected the records of every orphanage, every dockside industry, and every inn along the quay. Then it dawned on me that perhaps we were looking too low."

Christian's lips quivered. "I was the son of an earl. And not just any earl, either."

"Exactly, my lord. Your father's very attitude. Once I realized that, it didn't take long to find a trace. First one here, then one there." Reeves met Christian's gaze. "You kept using variations of your father's name and titles. In Bainbridge you were Viscount Westerville. In Bath, you were Lord Rochester Stuart."

"A common device. When assuming an identity, one should always use a name one can remember when under duress."

"A very good piece of advice, my lord. I shall endeavor to remember it. Mr. Dunstead, the old earl's solicitor, found a positive physical description of you in London."

"London?"

"Yes, my lord. From the daughter of the French ambassador. He says you stole his daughter's heart, although he seems more upset over the loss of her jewelry."

A dreamy smile crossed Christian's face. "Michelle was—" He kissed his fingers to the air. "*Magnifique.*"

Reeves allowed himself a small smile. "I am glad to hear it. Gentleman Jack seems to be doing quite well."

"The benefits far outweigh the dangers." Christian took another drink. "So my father died, hm. I cannot be sorry."

"He left you the title of Viscount Westerville while your brother, Tristan, inherited the earldom."

Christian froze. "Tristan?"

"Yes. He is alive and well. Though I rather think you know that."

A shuttered look entered Christian's eyes. "Perhaps. It is rather easy to follow a war hero."

"You were watching him longer than that. When your father's solicitor made inquiries at the shipyards in London during the search to locate your brother, someone had been there before him."

Christian took a drink, his long lashes hiding his expression. "Perhaps. Tell me, Reeves, how did my father leave us with his titles? Our mother never wed Rochester."

"Your father set everything to rights before he died."

"How?"

A faint smile touched Reeves's mouth. "Does that matter?"

"I suppose not." Christian shook his head. "I still cannot believe this. Where is Tristan now? I know he has been injured. I went to London to look for him, but he'd already left by the time I arrived."

"Oddly enough, he settled not far from here."

Christian gave a short laugh. "Here? You cannot be telling the truth."

Reeves smiled. "You were destined to meet, whether

I arrived or not, only it might have been under less fe-
licitous circumstances." Reeves tilted his head to one
side. "You may look like your mother, but your air of
fashion is definitely your father's."

Christian gave a bitter smile, lifting his tankard.
"Here's to my father's air. May it hold me in good
stead."

Reeves lifted his tankard and toasted before taking a
tentative sip.

"Welcome to my world, Reeves. Plump, willing
wenches and bitter ale, all warmed by the excitement
of the road."

"Excitement...and danger. Master Christian, I hesitate to suggest this, but I believe the time has come for
you to find another profession."

Christian gave a twisted smile. "A war hero earl has
no need of a highwayman for a brother."

"I don't believe the earl would agree with you."

"He always was pigheaded." Christian flicked a serious glance at Reeves. "He is well, otherwise?"

"I believe so. He still has a limp, you know, from his
wounds. I do not think that will ever leave him. But his
men are still with him; they drive him to distraction."

"His men? Then he still sails."

"No," Reeves said. "They came to him. He has a
house on the cliff in Devon."

"He lives there with his crew?"

"The ones who can no longer sail. They dote on
him."

A faint smile touched Christian's mouth. "They are
his family. When you have no family, you adopt the
lost souls who wander through your life."

Reeves glanced at Willie, who stood by the door, glowering at the entire room.

Christian's gaze followed Reeves's. "Yes, he is one." The fire flickered a little as a gust of wind chased down the flue, puffing smoke into the room.

"I believe your father regretted his inactivity in your life.

"And I regret not having slit his gullet with my rapier."

"I am surprised you did not."

"I had no right to deprive Tristan of his father." Christian shrugged. "Besides, I have been busy."

"Yes, my lord. Being a highwayman must be an enormous drain on one's free time."

Humor flickered in Christian's green eyes. "I am not just a highwayman. I am also a gentleman farmer. I have lands, you know. Quite a respectable holding, in fact."

"I am not surprised, my lord. You are very resourceful. As was your father." The butler paused. "He was a wise manager of his funds and a good master. Unfortunately, he was also rather free with his affections. A wide pond, but not very deep."

A reluctant smile tugged at Christian's mouth. "The old man was a reprobate on every level."

"Yes, my lord. Though he most certainly had a way with his cravats."

"I'm sure God is impressed. Tell me of Tristan. Does he enjoy being the earl? Has he purchased half of London with the funds?"

"He does not yet have the funds. The trustees will be arriving in four short weeks to ascertain his worthiness for the title. If he gains their approval, then a very large sum will pass into his hands. If he does not, then the funds will be added to the rather generous amount the late earl named for you. Providing, of course, that *you* meet the trustees' approval at that time."

"An earl without money. My father's sense of humor did not change, even upon the deathbed." Christian found his hand curling tightly about his tankard. He loosened it and said in a flat voice, "So I am now Viscount Westerville in reality."

"Your father left you the title of Viscount Westerville and ten thousand pounds per annum."

Christian whistled.

"Will you accept it?"

"Are you mad? Of course I will take it, and gladly!"

Reeves sighed. "Finally, a sane one."

Christian laughed. "I take it Tristan has not been so accommodating?"

"He says he would rather...how did he word it? It had something to do with his nether regions being burned off."

"That is Tristan for you. He sees things in black and white. All pride, that one. I, however, will enjoy spending the late earl's funds whilst he is merrily burning in the pits of hell."

"I am glad to see you are not bitter," Reeves said dryly.

Christian's expression hardened as quickly as he'd grinned before. "Do you know what he did to my mother? How he left her to rot in prison? Accused of a treason she did not commit?"

"My lord, perhaps he had a reason—"

Christian slammed down his mug, ignoring the startled glance of those around. "My mother died in a damp prison, accused of a crime she did not commit, alone and afraid. He knew it and did nothing to help her."

"My lord—"

"Don't. Not another word. I made it my business to discover what I could of her circumstances. I cannot change her fate now, but one day, I will find who caused her such pain."

Reeves looked into Christian's burning green eyes. "I am sorry." It was all he could say.

"My father was a bastard, through and through. A gentleman by birth, but not by heart." Christian finished his tankard and replaced it on the table, nodding to the hovering barmaid that he wished for another. "I am a viscount." He smiled bitterly. "How amusing."

"I am certain your brother will be glad to share his thoughts with you on the vagaries of holding a title."

Christian took the new tankard from the maid, winking at her as she sashayed away. After she left, he turned his attention back to Reeves. "Do not tell my brother you have found me."

"But, my lord! Why?"

"There are things I must do if I wish to re-introduce myself into his life. From the sound of things, he does not need more problems than he has now." Christian pushed his tankard aside. "Give me a week. Perhaps a little more. I will contact you then."

Reeves sighed. "As you wish, my lord."

"In the meantime, if you or my brother have need of me, leave word for me here."

"Very well. One day, we must speak more about your father, though now is obviously not the time." Reeves stood and bowed. "I am pleased to have finally found you. I promised the late earl I would do so."

"You are very loyal to a man who did not deserve such consideration."

Reeves smiled. "Certainly his behavior to you warrants no feelings at all. But his behavior to me was not the same. I owe him. And I am a man who always pays his debts." Reeves drew on his muffler and gloves. "I shall leave you, my lord. But hopefully, not for long."

"I will not wear that."

Reeves looked at the waistcoat. "May I ask why not?"

Tristan grimaced. "I don't like waistcoats, and I especially don't like that one."

"My lord, it will be easier for us to convince the trustees you are worthy of the fortune if you look the part as well as act it. Mrs. Thistlewaite seems to believe you've made great improvement this last week, so the addition of some new clothing is essential at this juncture."

"I don't mind looking a gentleman. But I do mind wearing a blasted pink waistcoat."

"It isn't pink. It's puce."

Tristan took the waistcoat to the window and held back the curtain. He stared hard at the material. "No. It is pink."

"It is puce," Reeves said in a voice of utmost patience, "however, I don't suppose it's a shade you've often seen. I daresay they do not make sails this color."

"You'd bloody well better believe they don't."

Reeves cleared his throat.

Tristan sighed. "I'm sorry. I meant to say, 'You'd better believe they don't.' The 'bloody' part just slipped in there."

"You are doing much better, my lord. But I know it will take time."

If there was one thing Tristan wasn't sure he had, it was time. Although he'd spent most of every day of this past week with the delectable Prudence and had learned far more about the manners of the ton than he ever wished, the creep of the days weighed on him with a heavy certainty. Worse, his financial situation seemed to be getting more difficult. Just this morning he'd had to call the doctor in to look at Old John Marley's bad leg. The news was not good; it would take weeks, perhaps months of recovery, and a good bit of medicine as well.

Tristan sighed. He needed the fortune. Now.

To that end, he'd tried to be a willing and apt pupil when Prudence came to visit. Even that event was difficult. He could not seem to keep from crossing the boundaries of propriety whenever she was in the room. He was learning a good deal from her, and knew what he could and could not do. But with her, the rules just seemed so . . . wasted. Irrelevant.

Their lessons had become a sort of sweet torture. The air between them grew thicker every day. But what was more significant was that he thought of her all of the time and was beginning to suspect he might miss her once their time was over.

Perhaps he'd hire her to continue serving as his tutor anyway, only this time he'd insist she not wear quite so many clothes. He imagined her expression should he mention such a notion. The thought made him chuckle.

Reeves's voice broke in on Tristan's reverie. "My lord, what are you smiling about?"

"Nothing. I was just remembering something Prudence said."

Reeves pursed his lips. "You mean Mrs. Thistlewaite?"

"I mean Prudence."

"It would be more correct—"

"I may wear your bloody waistcoat, but I'll be damned if I will call Prudence anything other than her given name."

Reeves bowed. "As you wish, my lord."

"Good," Tristan said, feeling like a heel for yelling at the butler. Truly life had improved with Reeves about. Not only was the food better, but every morning the most winsome of companions came to dine with him.

Tristan fingered the waistcoat. "If I wore this at sea, I'd be laughed off my own ship."

"By other, equally fashion-conscious sailors, no doubt." Reeves cocked a challenging eyebrow. "Since you do not favor puce—"

"Pink."

"—puce, then perhaps I can find another that might suit." Reeves carefully placed the waistcoat over his arm and returned to the trunk at the foot of the bed. He folded the garment, wrapped it back in its paper and gently laid it in the trunk. Then he began to shuffle through the clothing that was still packed, pausing to cast a rather caustic glance at Tristan. "Before I begin, is there any other color you won't wear besides pink? Blue? Violet?"

"Yellow."

"Why won't you wear yellow?"

Tristan grinned. "It makes my skin look sallow."

For an instant, a hint of a smile flickered over Reeves's mouth, but he managed to repress it. "I shall endeavor to remember that, my lord." He bent back into the trunk, emerging a moment or so later with yet another waistcoat.

Tristan took a step back. "Good God!"

Reeves blinked down at the waistcoat. "What?"

"It *shines*."

"Oh. Well, yes. It's a silver etched waistcoat trimmed with blue lacing and black edgework. Quite the thing, actually. It came all the way from France and—"

"Bloody hell, I'll look like a walking coin in that thing. Or some woman's necklace."

"It is only for evening wear, my lord. Quite unsuitable for day. I didn't hold it up to suggest you wear it right this moment, but merely to see if it was more to your liking."

"I'd look like a fish marching about on land." Tristan shook his head. "That's what you get for allowing the French to determine fashion."

Reeves carefully refolded the waistcoat and replaced it in the trunk. He then emerged with another, far simpler one. This one was red, with narrow black trim.

Tristan took the waistcoat and eyed it with disgust. "What happened to plain black for a waistcoat?"

"They went out of style in 1763, my lord, and are now only worn by obsequious country squires, arrogant highwaymen, and other Notorious Persons."

"I don't know about country squires, but you are right about highwaymen. They do wear a lot of black."

Reeves's blue eyes suddenly fixed on Tristan. "May I ask how you would know that, my lord?"

Tristan turned to the mirror and began putting on the waistcoat. "I was held up on the road to Bath not a year ago. The man was dressed in black head to toe, which made it damnably difficult to pin him."

"Pin, my lord?"

"Shoot."

Reeves paused. "You *shot* at him?"

"I tried, but he managed to run away. I didn't find any blood, so I must assume I missed, which was a damned shame."

Reeves gave a strained smile. "Of course, my lord. Here. Let me help you with your coat."

Tristan slid his arms into the sleeves. It felt odd, wearing such a tight-fitting garment. Indeed, all of the clothing Reeves had had made for Tristan were unusually close, from the knitted breeches to the cravat, he felt like a sail tangled in rigging.

He took up his cane. "I am now trussed like a goose. If you don't mind, I wish to take my morning walk."

"You should have a half hour before Mrs. Thistlewaite arrives. Just be careful of the puddles." Reeves nodded toward Tristan's glossy boots.

"What good are boots if you cannot get them muddy?"

Reeves opened his mouth to reply when the door

flew open and Stevens stuck his head in, his eyes widening when he saw Tristan. "Coo'ee, Cap'n—I mean, yer lordship! If ye don't look like a gent now, I don't know who would!"

"Master Stevens," Reeves said calmly, "it is customary to knock before entering a room."

"Ye don't say. Well then, here." Stevens turned and knocked on the door behind him before smiling at Reeves. "How was that?"

"Excellent except that you should wait *outside* the door, knock, and *then* wait to be bidden to enter."

"Lord, what a long time that would take! Cap'n—yer lordship, did ye ever hear the like? Knockin' and then waitin' to be tol' to come in?"

"Rules, Stevens. I am strangled by them. Before the month is out we won't recognize ourselves."

"Master Stevens," Reeves said. "Did you bring the shears as I requested?"

Stevens nodded, reaching inside his voluminous coat to remove a wicked pair of shears from his waistband.

Tristan eyed them uneasily. "What's that for? Cutting up that pink waistcoat to make a set of sails?"

Stevens snickered. "Cap'n, surely ye know! The shears are for yer hair."

*"What?"* Tristan took a step back, looking aghast at the shears. "Reeves, you are not cutting my hair."

Reeves sent a stern glare at Stevens. "That was not the way I wished the earl to learn of my suggestion."

Tristan scowled. "That does not look like a suggestion."

"That's all it was to be. Your hair needs to be trimmed. Current styles do not allow it to be the length of yours."

Tristan scowled, touching the neat queue at the nape of his neck. It hung just below his shoulders, which was an acceptable length; indeed most other captains wore theirs longer. But he'd had his hair this way since he'd first sailed, and he'd be damned if he'd give it up now. "I'm not cutting my hair. The trustees can be damned."

Reeves sighed. "Perhaps Mrs. Thistlewaite can make you see reason." With that, the butler dismissed a rather subdued Stevens, and went about the remaining morning preparations.

Tristan found himself glancing at the clock, counting down the minutes until Prudence came to visit. His time with her was quickly becoming the highlight of his day. The thought made him pause as he buttoned his coat. He *did* think about her quite a bit. In fact, if he coursed out his morning, he'd been thinking of her off and on since he'd awakened. But his awake thoughts were not as disturbing as his last dream.

In his dream, she'd been in his bed, just waking up as the morning sun broke over the horizon. She'd been deep in slumber, her long, silky brown hair wrapped about her naked shoulders—

Not that he knew if she slept naked. He didn't, of course. If she didn't, he wondered what it would take to convince her to do so.

He smiled a little, allowing Reeves to settle the new coat about his shoulders. Most women were so concerned with the way they appeared that they didn't seem to care how they actually were. But Prudence was deliciously herself, a fact he appreciated. He'd sailed the seas alone for too many years to withstand the gale force of a petulant, self-absorbed woman.

Prudence was different. She filled him, tantalized him, challenged him, and more.

"My lord?"

Tristan blinked. "I'm sorry, Reeves. You were speaking?"

"Yes, my lord. Several times, in fact."

"I apologize. I was thinking of...a ship." A ship with lovely topsails indeed.

"Of course, my lord," Reeves said, taking up the lint brush and smoothing it over Tristan's shoulders. "I didn't realize you had a ship called the *Prudence*."

"Th—what are you talking about?"

"Only that you murmured the name as I was smoothing your sleeves."

"Oh."

Reeves replaced the silver-handled brush on the tray on the dresser. "An odd coincidence, that, to be certain. To have both a ship and a neighbor named Prudence. It must make conversation difficult at times."

Tristan met Reeves's gaze directly. "Are we done dressing now?"

"Yes, my lord. We are. Permit me to say that you look quite dashing."

"Thank you, Reeves." Tristan turned to leave, but paused, a thought holding him in place. "Oh. I meant to ask this morning and almost forgot."

"Yes, my lord?"

"Any word from Dunstead?"

There was a moment's pause. Not much, but telling all the same. "Not yet," Reeves said.

"Hm." Tristan eyed the butler narrowly. "One night last week, a stranger came to visit. Very late. You met him and spoke with him. I know because Toggle was up to use the privy and he overheard. You received a missive from Dunstead."

A faint frown rested on Reeves's forehead. "Master Toggle is very good at being where he is not wanted."

"It's his gift."

"Yes, my lord."

"Well?"

Reeves did not answer.

"I see. The second odd happening was three nights ago. You left after dinner and did not return for two hours."

"Yes, my lord. I did at that." The butler met Tristan's gaze, then sighed. "I was not going to say anything until the issue had resolved itself, but...perhaps this is better. My lord, Dunstead did indeed locate Master Christian."

Tristan's heart skipped a beat.

Reeves held up a hand. "I cannot say more now, my lord. Not yet. It is a matter of honor. He has not given me permission to reveal his location to you."

Tristan clenched his teeth. "Is he well?"

"Yes, my lord. Quite well."

The tightness in Tristan's throat eased. "Reeves, I *will* see him."

"I think it is what he hopes, too."

"I doubt it or he would already be here. Did he say why he does not wish for us to meet?"

"I believe he has some decisions to make first. About his chosen occupation."

"And what is that?"

"I fear I am not at liberty to tell you that either."

"Reeves, I am not a patient man."

"No, my lord. I will make certain Master Christian is reminded of that fact, as well." Reeves made his way to the door. "Enjoy your morning walk, my lord. I will have the breakfast table readied for your return."

Tristan gave a short nod, struggling to maintain his temper. To be so close to Christian and yet so far. He closed his eyes and took a deep breath. But he could not force Christian to come forward if he was not yet ready. Finally, he said, "Thank you, Reeves. For everything."

The butler smiled. "It was my pleasure." With a final bow, he was gone.

Tristan stood staring at the closed door. *Christian. What in the hell are you doing?*

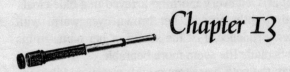

# Chapter 13

To remove stains from furniture, mix a powder
from black rose oil, alkaline soap, and bullock's
gall. Be sure to use only in a room with an open
window. It is quite difficult to scrub whilst unconscious.

*A Compleat Guide for
Being a Most Proper Butler*
by Richard Robert Reeves

*T*ristan strode down the path, still mulling over
Reeves and his secrets. The morning sun was just breaking over the sea, a brisk wind lifting over the cliff. The
last week, he'd gotten up earlier than necessary in order
to walk the cliff. It cleared his head and gave him a certain peace of mind. Today, it gave him no peace at all.
All he could do was think about Christian.

Waiting was hell on earth. Tristan would give Reeves
one week to produce his brother. One week and no
more.

He wondered what Christian would think of Prudence. The thought brought to mind the tempting armful that arrived every morning arrayed in a blue cloak, her hair tightly pinned, her brown eyes warm with laughter. Prudence. Just the sound of her name in his thoughts made life seem more bearable.

Today the path was strewn with glassy puddles, the stones covered with a slick moss. He tramped his foot onto the hard path, fire shooting up his leg. He winced, grinding his teeth against the pain. He would not let this wound beat him. Nothing would beat him. If Prudence had taught him anything, it was that even the irksome in life could be dealt with if approached with patience and diligence.

It was a fact he'd known, but had somehow in the weeks and months of his convalescence, allowed to slip away.

He rounded the corner, and the cottage came into view, sturdy and strong against the thrashing winds. Tristan forced himself to walk the remaining steps down the path to the garden gate at an even brisker pace, keeping the bruising pace with each step, his breath harsh in his own ears.

Perhaps if he walked more forcibly, *made* the muscles in his leg stretch and reach...perhaps he would get better. He clenched his teeth and forced himself onward. Only the steady crunch of the cane and the thud of his boots mattered. Only that.

He would reach the gate.

He would not falter, no matter the cost.

No matter the pain.

Just the gate...

He made it. Tristan grabbed the top board and leaned on it, lifting his burning leg and bowing his head. Pain coursed through him, but he welcomed it. It didn't pay to fight the pain. Instead, he let it ripple through his leg, following the course of the lead ball that had almost killed him.

It had always been that way for him—first he fought and then he accepted. Fate had never sat on his shoulder but had mocked him from afar, showing him what he could have, but did not. It did that with his father, with the injury that ground him from the sea, and now it was happening with Prudence.

He wanted her. Wanted her in his life even after this farce with the trustees was over. But it would never work. She was cultured, educated, and from a world he'd only viewed from a distance. Yet every day he ached for her in a new way. He'd been right about Prudence from the first; she was the sort of woman one married *if* one was also cultured, educated, and from that world.

He was not. His father had seen to that.

Tristan placed a hand on his leg and scowled down at it, the pain in his heart fresh and new. He wasn't even whole. Had his life been different, he might have been able to provide for her, offer her something more than a sea-less captain.

The truth was he had nothing to offer. Nothing to give her. Unless he won the fortune.

But... would that be enough? He thought of her face when she mentioned her late husband, Phillip. She'd loved the man; that much was obvious. Tristan's jaw ached. How much had she loved Phillip, and did she still?

A crunch sounded on the path behind him. "Good morning."

The warm voice was at odds with the chilled wind, which tried to whip away the round, mellowed tones. Tristan turned to see Prudence coming down the path toward him, the wind tugging strands of her dark hair free and whipping them across her face. She caught his gaze and paused, leaning against the yew tree, her eyes dark with some indiscernible emotion.

Was it pity? Bile rose in his throat, burning him, burning his thoughts. "You are early," he said, his voice harsh even to his own ears.

She raised her brows. In most women, the gesture would seem somewhat imperious, or at least questioning. But on Prudence, with her flyaway brows, the effect was different. On her, a quick lift of the brows made her look mischievous.

He swallowed his irritation. "You shouldn't be out in this weather. It is damp."

She shrugged. "It is not as cold as it was last week." Her gaze drifted past him to the sea. "It is beautiful from here."

"Indeed it is." He glanced up at the gray sky and frowned, unable to tell the hour because the sun was hidden. "Is it time for breakfast?"

"Reeves sent me to find you."

Tristan took the cane firmly in his hand and strode toward her, his teeth clenched against his limp. He paused when he reached her side and silently held out his arm.

She smiled and curtsied before placing her hand on his arm, her fingers resting lightly on his sleeve. "Very prettily done," she said with a blinding smile that made his body react in a most inappropriate way.

Taking his lustful thoughts firmly in hand and tamping down any emotion he might feel, he returned her smile, realizing with a sinking feeling that one day soon, she would no longer be here. No longer come out onto the path looking for him.

But at least he had her for today.

He placed a hand over hers. "Let the lessons begin." With that, he escorted her through the terrace doors and inside.

Prudence undid her cloak. Tristan took it and laid it across a chair. She watched him, wondering if his hands were indeed lingering on the soft wool or if it just appeared that way. She frowned. There was something different about him this morning. Something...uncertain.

The table was set as it always was, everything just so. Prudence stood beside her chair and waited for the earl to approach the table.

To her surprise, she found that she rather enjoyed breakfast in such a high fashion. It was especially nice seeing Tristan each morning, his large, brown hand cupped about the delicate china, a ready smile in his green eyes.

This last week had proven difficult on many levels, not the least of which was the way Mother waited at home at the end of each day, her eyes full of hope.

It had become painfully obvious Mother harbored some ill-founded hopes for Prudence and the earl far beyond that of tutor and pupil. Her incessant questioning was beginning to grate on Prudence's temper. The earl might well be attracted to Prudence, but it was nothing more than a physical spark, a connection of a rather earthy nature. One she was well aware of and, to be honest, very tempted to sample.

And why not? she asked herself rather determinedly. She might be a widow, but she was not dead. She missed being with a man, and seeing the earl in such close proximity was stirring her passions anew. And all too soon their time would be over.

The earl walked toward her, his hand clasped about the cane. She frowned when she noticed his limp was a bit more pronounced today. "Are you feeling well?"

"I am fine. But you…" His gaze raked her from head to toe. "You look lovely."

His green eyes seemed darker this morning, too, as if he'd been carrying some weighty thoughts. She tilted her head to one side and regarded him. There was concern in his gaze…and something else that sent her heart thudding against her ribs.

Their eyes met and the air closed in. He walked closer, then slowly circled her. Like an animal on the hunt, his attention was completely on her. Prudence's skin heated, and it was all she could do not to turn and watch him as he closed in behind her, his legs brushing against her shirt. She held her breath as he reached past her, his chest touching her back lightly, his breath brushing her neck as he reached out…

And pulled a chair from the table. He murmured in her ear, "Pray have a seat, Mrs. Thistlewaite."

*The jackanapes,* she thought even while fighting to still her pounding heart. She took the seat reluctantly, waiting for him to find his own chair.

He took his seat and lifted his brows. "Well?"

"That was nicely done. Except the touching part."

"Oh. Did I touch you?" He was all masculine innocence...if there was such a thing.

"Yes, you did. You were a bit close."

"You don't like close?"

"Not *that* close. Our aim is to practice politeness."

"I thought I was polite, pulling your chair from the table." He watched her pour the tea, then said in a thoughtful tone, "However, now that I think about it, I suppose your sentiments explain why you don't have any children."

She almost choked. "I beg your pardon?"

"I said—"

"I know what you said! It's just that—" She took a deep breath. "It is not correct to mention such topics."

"Such topics?"

"As having children and—and being touched."

"I didn't bring up the touching. You did."

She had, hadn't she? She sighed. "If this was a real breakfast, then you should not mention either of those topics."

"Never?"

"Well, not directly, of course."

He paused in placing his napkin across his lap. "What do you mean 'not directly?'"

"I have heard women talk about another woman they said was 'increasing.'"

He chortled. "If she was going to have a child, I daresay she *was* increasing."

"Yes, well, it's not a topic a gentleman should mention, so please do not," she said stiffly. Goodness, but her cheeks felt hot. She cleared her throat. "Now, let us talk about dinners. When the trustees arrive, you may want to—"

"Wait. This is not a 'real breakfast,' as you said." He leaned forward, his elbows coming to rest on the table before him. "Tell me, Prudence, why *didn't* you have any children?"

Her jaw tightened and a low, almost forgotten ache arose in the region of her heart. She lifted her cup to her lips and took a sip, more to still their trembling as to give her time to regain control. "As I said, that is not a topic for polite conversation."

"Ah, but we aren't polite society, are we?" he answered softly, leaning back in his chair. "Not yet. For now, you and I are the outcasts from society. The expatriates."

"I am. But you will not be for long." It was true, with the title and the fortune, he would be accepted in any home in London, while she... She put down her cup. She would be left behind.

Something was happening here. She was slowly beginning to feel something for the earl. *Lust*, she told herself firmly. *It is just lust.* Unfortunately for her, it was a *lot* of lust.

"...and it happens every time."

She blinked, realizing he was speaking. "I'm sorry. I did not hear you."

"I said that women often forget I am present. One moment they are speaking to me, the next they are staring at their teacups in a trance-like state."

She had to smile. "Was I staring at my teacup?"

"Yes. I tried not to take it personally, but I failed." A reluctant smile lurked in his green eyes.

He really was a handsome man, especially when he grinned at her like that. She cleared her throat. "Well. This is certainly a lovely repast."

Every day she did this to him. He'd get a little too close, a little too emotionally intriguing for her comfort, and out came her teaching face. He'd be forced to make impersonal small talk until he could turn the topic back into more interesting lines.

She buttered her toast. "Orange marmalade is the best thing on earth."

"No."

She paused, knife hovering over her toast, her brown eyes questioning. " 'No' is not an acceptable answer to a comment. You should agree or expound on your reasons for not agreeing. You do not just say 'no.' "

"I wasn't talking about the marmalade. I was saying I don't want to make inane small talk today. I've had my fill."

Prudence put down the knife. "We have done quite a bit of social banter. Perhaps we should discuss something Reeves mentioned to me. He has suggested that in the days before the trustees arrive, we should attend a local gathering, a country dinner of some sort to test your new skills."

"I would rather talk about you."

Tristan saw her rejection before she uttered it. She shook her head almost vehemently. "Let us instead talk about the coming visit from the trustees."

He sighed. She was not going to make this easy.

"Very well. I will give you three minutes to talk about the trustees, and then I do not want them mentioned over the table again today."

"Three minutes? That won't do." She bit her lip, her dark eyes assessing him. "Ten minutes will be better."

"Four minutes."

Her gaze narrowed. "Seven."

"Five minutes and that is my final offer."

"Done! When the trustees first arrive, what will you do?"

He leaned back in his chair. "Stevens will admit them. Reeves is working with Stevens right now so he will know what to do and say. Two of my men—MacGrady and Toggle—serve as footmen. Reeves is training them as well. They will take our guests' coats and hats and hang them in the front room. Then, Stevens will escort the trustees in here, to the study. That is where I will dazzle them with my lack of wit and stiff manner of speaking."

"How will you dazzle them?"

"I will greet them, shake their hands or bow as they indicate, and then seat them. Depending on the time they arrive, I may or may not offer them a drink." He sent her a dark look. "That is a fact that offends me greatly."

"You cannot offer them brandy before noon."

"I daresay some, if not all, have drunk much stronger libations and much earlier than noon. I personally believe we will all want a nice large drink, perhaps two. I daresay they are looking forward to our meeting as much as I am, if not less."

"You could be right. Still, you want them to think of

you as genteel, and you never know when someone might have a prudish streak."

"I suppose," he said, completely unconvinced.

"You are coming along nicely," she said, blinding him with her smile.

The problem was, he didn't want to "come along nicely." He wanted to come along in a way that wasn't nice at all. In a way that was heated and sensual and decadent. One that took him beneath her skirts and between her thighs.

She took a sip of tea, her lips touching the edge of her cup in a damnably attractive way. "Very well, my lord. After you've seated the trustees, what will you do?"

"Make mind-numbingly inane conversation. At some point, I will ask them about the will, but during this earlier time, I am to establish myself in their eyes as a gentleman of the world."

"Excellent! You will do marvelously well."

"Oh yes. This week has been a great success. I can now bow like a boot-licker of the worst kind, listen to frivolous coxcombs as if they had something of value to say, and speak a full half hour without saying anything at all."

She laughed then, a gurgle of a laugh that made him smile in return. "I am sorry the skills seem so useless."

"They *are* useless."

"Not to the trustees." Her lashes dropped down over her cheeks. "My lord—"

"Tristan."

"I cannot—"

"I am the earl here, not you. I want you to call me

Tristan. Please," he added softly. "We have spent enough time together that I thought you might consider me more than a neighbor, but a friend."

Her brows rose. "That was very prettily said! My lord, may I ask you a question? It is something—well, you might not wish to answer."

"Ask anything. Just know that I shall return the favor."

Her eyes sparkled. "I have nothing to hide."

"Neither do I. So what do you wish to know?"

"About...when you became a sailor. You were pressed into service at such a young age. Was it very difficult? You certainly seem to have grown to love it."

"I did grow to love it. However, the first year was very difficult. I was homesick and angry and would learn nothing unless it was at the tip of a cat-o'-nine-tails."

She glanced at his shoulders.

"Yes. There are scars. Many of them. I was as stubborn as a child as I am now, if you can imagine."

"You said you were but ten! Surely they would not whip a ten-year-old."

"They did and do. It's a hard life."

"That is barbaric!"

"I agree. For that reason, I did not use impressed men on my ships."

"Good for you!"

"Oh don't make me into a saint. It is a safety issue. I had no desire to wake up with a knife in my back."

"I can see how that might happen!" She frowned a bit. "Tristan, if you didn't press your men into service, then how did you keep your crew?"

She'd used his name. He hid his triumph only by moving his aching foot a little and wiping his smile off his face before it fully came to rest. "The sea is a hard life, but a profitable one if you have a good captain, as I was." *Was.* That was certainly hard to say. He swallowed and continued, "I believe that only poorly qualified captains must press their crews."

"When you were pressed, was your father aware of what happened?"

"Reeves said my father was out of the country at the time. I don't think he knew what happened to either me or my brother—"

"Brother?"

"I have a twin. He and I were separated when I was pressed." Tristan gave a mirthless smile. "I told myself for years that my father really cared and would have prevented my mother's arrest as well as my own fate had he been aware. But now I rather doubt it. I daresay in his way, he was glad enough to see my brother and me out of the way. He certainly made no effort to find either of us. Not until recently, that is."

Tristan looked down at the dinner setting, at the sparkling silver and delicate china. "My brother escaped. I looked for him, but was unable to locate him. This morning, Reeves told me he has found my brother. I haven't seen him in so long—" Tristan could not continue.

Silence filled the air between them. Tristan wondered about Christian, where he was, what he was doing. Why hadn't he come to see him? What "business" did he have to attend to before he came? It was possible that—

A small, warm hand covered over his. Tristan did not know what to do. It was a simple gesture, one that probably happened hundreds or thousands of times each day. Yet he could not remember a single time someone had done such a thing—reached out to him with nothing more than the spirit of human kindness. Touched him for no other reason than to reassure him.

For a moment, Tristan could only stare at the delicate fingers that slipped over his. He followed the line of that hand to the narrow wrist and on to the sweetly curved arm. From there, he found Prudence's well-defined shoulders, graceful neck, and finally, her sensually velvety brown eyes.

He turned his hand and laced his fingers with hers. A flash of heat exploded through him, so strong and so sharp that he almost gasped aloud. Good God, but he wanted this woman. But it wasn't just lust. He'd felt that before. This was different, lust and...possession. He didn't simply want to taste her; this time, he wanted more. He wanted to devour her, possess her, take her and mark her as his. He wanted to languish in her arms, savor her feel and the scent of her skin.

His body tightened with need, with desire, and he fought it with all of his strength.

She squeezed his fingers in apparent sympathy. "I am sorry about your brother. I am sure you will find him." She withdrew her hand. "I feel I have asked so many questions—I didn't mean to pry." She suddenly brightened. "Well! Now you may ask me a question or two."

Still bemused, he leaned back, struggling to regain his thoughts. Everything seemed far away, like waves crossing a storm-washed deck. She'd held his hand, touched him with the most innocent of intentions and he'd exploded into a sea of lust. He fought for breath. "Yes. I—I—ah, there *is* one thing I've wanted to know for the longest time. Mrs. Thistlewaite... Prudence." He lifted his brows in earnest inquiry. "What *is* your favorite color?"

She opened her mouth. Then closed it. She'd asked him such a personal question, she'd been certain he'd do the same to her. But... "My favorite color? It is red."

"I thought as much," he said, a sense of satisfaction sitting about him.

She pursed her lips, feeling a bit let down. "Is that all?"

"I may ask another?"

She nodded.

"Well then..." His voice deepened, strengthened. Slow and silvery his words slipped about her, an actual touch. "Why did you choose to come to Devon, of all places?"

Despite herself, her gaze flickered toward the window, toward the sea where it crashed and flashed below.

"Ah," he said, his voice warm and appreciative.

"Since I was a child, I have loved the sea. It pulls me somehow." She wrinkled her nose. "But I cannot sail for I get deathly ill."

"You haven't been on the right ship."

"I've been on three. They were all different and they all made me ill."

"You were never on the *Victory*."

"The *Victory*? Nelson's flagship?"

"*My* ship." His voice rang with simple pride.

She smiled. "Your ship, then. Was that the ship—" She glanced at his leg.

His gaze followed hers, a shadow crossing his face. "Yes." With an abrupt movement, he placed his napkin on the table and stood. "Come. Have a look at her."

"Look? She's here?"

"In a manner of speaking, yes." He took Prudence's hand and pulled her to her feet, then led her to the furthest wall. On it hung a large picture of a neat little rig fighting storm-sized swells.

She remembered looking at it the first day she'd come. "So this is the *Victory*."

He nodded, his hand still clasped about hers. "Nelson himself gave me that picture when I first received command of her."

Prudence tried to admire the painting, but she was too aware of where Tristan's hand engulfed hers. He had very masculine hands, she decided with approval. Large and brown and curiously callused, one of his easily encompassed hers. For some reason, the sight sent a tremor through her, a faint quiver of excitement.

How silly. She pushed the ridiculous thoughts aside just as he turned to face her, pivoting a little on his cane as he did so. He was so close...so very close. If she tilted her head back and lifted her lips to his, he would be within reach. She wanted to kiss him. If she was honest, she wanted much more, too.

Prudence closed her eyes and stepped away from the temptation that so beckoned her. But as she did so, her heel hit the earl's cane and she wavered an instant. His arm instantly shot out to catch her. In the space of a second, Prudence found herself held against the earl's broad chest, her breasts pressed against his coat, her face upturned to his.

He looked down at her, his eyes on her mouth, his own lips parted. His skin was sun browned, his cheeks and chin covered with rough stubble that begged to be touched. She was aware of the warmth of his arm about her waist, of his strength as he held her so effortlessly, of the fact that by the simple expediency of lifting her face to his, she could touch her lips to his...

He slowly released her, allowing her to slide down the length of his body with the utmost slowness. Prudence's heart pounded noisily in her ears. Her whole body ached with unspoken desire. God, but she wanted him. Wanted him so badly that she could almost taste his tea-scented kiss, feel the roughness of his scruffed chin on her bared skin.

Though he'd allowed her feet to rest once more on the ground, he made no effort to release her. Prudence knew she should move out of reach, but the feel of a man's arm about her was so comforting, so *right,* that she did not do anything at all but stand in place and savor the moment. A moment certain to pass swiftly.

"I suppose I should release you," he murmured, his voice low and hot.

She closed her eyes, soaking in the feelings, the scents. The fresh sea smell of his coat, the starch scent of his white shirt. "I—I suppose you should."

"A gentleman would."

She had to lick dry lips before she could respond. "A gentleman would," she agreed.

Neither moved. The moment stretched, the air thickening with each breath. She could feel his chest moving in and out, slowly and inexorably, and she found herself breathing to match his. Her skin prickled with awareness, her breasts tightened and peaked. How she wanted him. It was like being swept along in a tidal force, drawn resistlessly into the dark of a whirlpool. But she had to resist. She had to.

"Prudence..." The word stirred her hair. His lips brushed her temple. "Prudence, we should—"

She kissed him. With one gesture, she poured out the burning want and aching desire she'd been fighting since she and the earl had first crossed paths. It had been so long since she'd given in to passion, so long since she'd allowed herself to feel anything at all that it threatened to overwhelm her.

Tristan reacted instantly. His mouth moved possessively over hers, and he clutched her to him. Somehow— she was never certain how—he managed to maneuver them into the nearby chair without the slightest of staggers.

Prudence wanted to ask him if he'd hurt himself but forgot the words when Tristan's mouth grazed her ear, his heated breath sending a cascade of shivers through her.

She burrowed her face in his neck, then wrapped her arms about him tighter. His hands slid from her waist, down her hips to her thighs. She could feel every nuance of his touch through her morning gown, the sound of their erratic breathing filling the air. Prudence gasped when his hand found the bottom of her skirt and he brushed it aside and cupped her calf, pulling her deeper into his lap. He was already erect, hard and straining, and she could taste the passion in his kisses, in the urgency of his touch.

Her own body answered, and emboldened by him and his wandering hands, she ran her fingers over his chest, pulling at his cravat to reach his skin.

He lifted his head and muttered a curse. "Too much damn clothing."

For a moment, Prudence could only stare at him. Then a quivering smile tickled her lips. He was so dear just then, tousled and frustrated, his eyes dark with passion, his erection firm beneath her. Prudence would never know what possessed her. Indeed, later that very night, she would stare up at the ceiling of her own bed and wonder what wanton spirit overtook her.

Somehow, she found herself straightening, her gaze locked with Tristan's as she slowly undid the tie at the neck of her gown.

She paused as the tie fell loose at her neck. This was it—the last moment she could turn away. Yet she knew in her heart that this was right—that being with Tristan right now, this instant was where she belonged. They might not be destined to be together for all time— indeed circumstances and their own personal paths made such a thing an impossibility—yet there was no denying she belonged in his arms at this moment. And right now, nothing else mattered.

Before her bemused eyes, his breathing quickened, his lips parted. He could not look away and she knew she held him in her thrall. It was a heady experience. It had been a long time since she'd excited just such a look in a man's eyes and she drank it in now. It fueled her desire for the moment even more.

He watched as she pulled the neck of her gown open, then pushed it over her shoulders and to her waist.

Tristan groaned, his chest moving rapidly as he seemed to struggle for breath. His gaze brushed over her, lingering on the shadows of her breasts, clearly visible beneath the sheerness of her chemise.

Tristan didn't think he'd ever seen anything so beautiful. She sat on his lap, proudly bared except for a bit of lace and silk. The chemise might cover her breasts, but they did so with a clinging touch that left little to his fevered imagination. The lace at her throat emphasized the delicate lines of her throat and shoulders. A tiny silk rosebud rested between her breasts, anchoring the center seam of the chemise.

It was all he could do not to lean her back and take her right there. Yet as anxious as he was for her, a part of him savored her, savored the moment. She was offering herself freely, without reservation. Yet, he knew he should not accept her gift. A real gentleman would stop now. A real gentleman—

She ran the tip of her tongue over her bottom lip.

Tristan groaned. "I cannot—"

She leaned forward, and the chemise dropped away from her breasts. He could see the rounded swells, almost taste the tempting tautness of her nipples.

Prudence placed a hand on his cheek and looked directly in his eyes. "Please."

It was the only word she uttered. A true gentleman did not leave a lady wanting.

Breathing her name, Tristan swept her to him, kissing

her madly, savoring the softness of her inside his arms. He worshipped her mouth, tasted her sweetness. Suddenly, she stood, untangling from his clasp, her gown falling to the floor. Only her chemise and stockings separated them, her slippers apparently having been kicked off when he wasn't paying attention.

He took a shuddering breath, his gaze devouring her. The silky scrap of lace and seductive silk drove his ready excitement ever higher.

As quickly as she'd stood, she now knelt before him, her arms over her head as she slowly withdrew the pins. Within seconds, her hair tumbled down about her, curling and frothing like the waves of the ocean.

Tristan's heart thundered so hard he thought it would stop. For weeks he'd dreamed of her just like this. Never had he wanted anything more. She was wild and fresh, a rain-kissed sea after a hard storm. And for the moment, she was his. His and no one else's.

She reached for his foot. "You need to undress, too."

He grabbed her wrist. "Let me."

She set back on her heels, watching as he carefully pulled his boot free, then the other. He stood and somehow, in moments he would never recall, he undressed, Prudence's eager hands assisting him.

As soon as he was bared, he stood before her. Her dark brown gaze traveled over him, lingering with appreciation hither and yon. He did not move when she reached out and gently traced the thick white scar that ran from his knee to his ankle.

She looked up at him. "I'm sorry."

He wasn't. At this moment, he wasn't sorry about one damn thing. He took her hands and hauled her to her feet, swooping her against him, the silk of her chemise sliding against his bare skin. "I don't give a damn about anything except you."

She was so beautiful, standing before him, the firelight flickering across her hair, lining it with streaks of gold. He plunged his hand into that silken mass and pulled her mouth to his.

His hands never stilled. Her chemise soon dropped to the floor. Somehow, they were no longer standing, but on the settee, the cushions lifting her hips to his. They came together with a breathless joining that sent a million spirals of pleasure through Tristan's body. He sunk into her as if he'd never before had a woman. As if his life to this second had not existed. As if all the exultant days at sea had collided into this one, perfect moment.

Beneath him, Prudence shivered and moaned, grasping his shoulders urgently. She moved with the passion and ardor of a woman who loved loving, her hips pressing against his, her lips parted as she gasped with each thrust.

The pace increased and all too soon, Prudence rasped out his name, her legs clenching tightly about him as she rode the waves of pleasure. Her passionate cry undid Tristan. He grit his teeth against the onslaught, but the hot passion tore through him as he slid into her one last time.

For a long moment, they lay there, spent and exhausted. Their harsh breaths mingling. Tristan wasn't sure how long they held one another, but eventually, Prudence stirred a bit beneath him. Tristan immediately lifted on his arms.

She smiled, a sleepy sort of smile. "I would call that brilliant."

He grinned. "It wasn't very gentlemanly of me."

Her smile faded only slightly before she said with perfect seriousness, "There are times when it is good to be a gentleman, and times when it pays to be a pirate."

A laugh broke from him and he kissed her swiftly. "You, my lady, are a delight."

A shadow passed over her eyes. She shifted in his arms and he rolled upright to give her more room. He hadn't meant for her to leave his embrace, only to lift his weight from her, but she did just that. She stood and collected her clothes, her movements jerky and hurried.

Tristan raised up on one elbow. "What's wrong, sweet?"

Prudence used her chemise to wipe her thighs. Her mind was a welter of confused thoughts. She hadn't meant for this to happen, but she could not in all honesty say she was sorry. It had been every bit as fulfilling as she'd imagined it would be. All she regretted was that this was all they had—this moment of closeness—and then it would be back to their usual arrangement. It had to be that way.

Whatever the earl may be now, he would always be a bit of a pirate. She saw it in everything he did and said. Even when learning the rudiments of comportment, there was a barely controlled wildness to him. He was not the sort of man one should marry. He was the sort of man one loved and then, as quickly as possible, left. The thoughts pained her more than she could say.

She finished dressing. He watched, making no move

to dress himself. After a moment, she sighed. "Tristan, please. You must dress; someone might come."

"I don't care. Prudence, did I hurt you?"

The concern in his gaze was palpable. Prudence had to fight to swallow. "Of course not! It's just—this cannot happen again. I am supposed to teach you manners, not...this."

His laughter silenced her. For an instant, she stiffened, outraged that he could take her concerns so lightly.

"Prudence, don't look at me like that! I have been thinking about you for days now—weeks! Dreaming of this." His lips quirked into an adorably lopsided smile. "It was even better than my dreams, and that says quite a bit."

She bit her lip, wishing she could banish the sinking feeling in her stomach. Was that all it had been? A fulfillment of a dream? She busied herself pinning up her hair, all the while wondering at the disappointment that weighed her spirits. She'd wanted their lovemaking to mean—what? What *could* it mean? Tristan had never led her to believe their attainment of pleasure was anything more, but somehow—to her and only her—it meant more. A lot more.

She turned on her heel and walked to the other side of the room, each step a feat of will over want. Each click of her boot heels rang like a nail in the coffin of what-could-be. She reached the window overlooking the garden and pretended to peer out at the bay. "I do so love the sea," she said rather inanely, struggling to find something to fill the silence.

Behind her, she heard his sigh and then the rustle of

clothing as he dressed. It took every ounce of strength she possessed not to turn and run back to him, to throw herself in his arms. She knew he was affected by her as much as she was affected by him; she'd seen it in his gaze, in the way his breath had quickened, in the ardor in his eyes.

They could not give in to this flare of passion. Of all the things they had, a future was not one of them. He was not the sort of man one fell in love with and married. No, Phillip had been that. Calm, logical, practical—none of those were adjectives she'd attach to the earl. She and Tristan didn't even have a commonality of interests or beliefs or—anything. All they had was passion.

She took a steadying breath and turned. "My lord— Tristan—I am sorry, but we must not—"

The door opened and Stevens bounded in, a silver tray in one hand, a letter in the center. "Aye there, Cap'n—I mean, me lord! Ye've a letter!"

Tristan's expression darkened. He met Prudence's gaze for a long moment, and then turned away and held out his hand.

Stevens bustled up with the tray, the letter sliding side to side. "It just came this very minute!"

Tristan caught the letter as it flipped over the side of the tray. He held it out at arm's length, water dripping from one corner.

"I'm not the best with the trays yet, me lord," Stevens said in a confidential tone. "I spilled a lot of tea on it this morning when I brought in the pot."

"Next time, dry the tray before you use it again."

"And dirty a towel?" Stevens looked outraged.

Tristan shook his head and opened the letter carefully. He held it up to the light. "The ink has smudged. I can't quite read..." His gaze narrowed. "Damn."

Stevens leaned around the earl's arm to read the letter himself.

Reeves entered the room, pausing when he saw Stevens.

"'Tis a letter," the butler/first mate said proudly. "I carried it all the way from the front door on the silver salver like ye told me to!"

"That is very good, Master Stevens. However, it is very rude of you to read his lordship's mail over his shoulder. The missive could be an issue of a personal nature."

Stevens's face fell. "I can't read *any* of his mail?"

"No. That is one of the sad facts of being a good butler. We never get to read the good mail."

Stevens sighed. "'Tis a lot more fun bein' a bad butler."

Tristan gave a muffled curse. "Blast it to hell. It is from the trustees. They are coming to visit next week."

Prudence caught her hands together. "So soon?"

Tristan nodded grimly. "I daresay they are anxious to make an end of this. They will be here a week from Thursday."

"Thursday!" Prudence pressed a hand to her forehead. "That's too early!"

Reeves pursed his lips. "We will just get ready a bit quicker than we anticipated." He looked at Tristan. "My lord, I hope you don't mind, but I ran into Squire Thomas in town. I believe you are acquainted with him."

"Aye. He's invited me to his house on many occasions, though I've never attended. I don't need that sort of foolishness."

"Actually, that is just the sort of foolishness we do need. I made certain the squire knew of your change in circumstances and he immediately requested your presence at his house for a small dinner party early next week." Reeves glanced at Prudence. "We spoke of perhaps attempting an event of some type, though I had no notion of doing it so soon."

Prudence nodded, trying her best to look assured when all of her thoughts were jangled by her own impropriety. "Yes. The dinner party would be excellent practice for the earl."

"I don't need practice," Tristan said, his brow lowering.

Reeves sighed. "My lord, the more at ease you feel with your new situation, the more in command you will be with the trustees. I strongly recommend that you go."

Tristan sent a hard glance at Prudence. "And you?"

"What about me?" she returned, frowning.

"Will you be going as well?"

Reeves cleared his throat. "The invitation did not involve Mrs. Thistlewaite."

"If she is not going, then neither am I," Tristan said in a distinct voice.

Prudence blinked. "But—"

"You have been with me through this entire charade. I won't go without you there. I will need your advice if I run aground."

"But I was not invited! Reeves, explain things to him!"

Reeves was looking at Tristan, a considering look on the butler's face. "Perhaps his lordship is correct. Let me see what I can do to rectify this oversight." He met Prudence's amazed gaze. "It _would_ be good if you were at his side, madam."

Tristan crossed his arms and leaned back against his desk, looking far handsomer and far more masculine than was necessary. "There. We go to the dinner party together, you and I." His gaze met hers, a promise lurking there. A promise of mischief and seduction. "We shall both have a fine time. A very fine time indeed."

That was, Prudence decided, exactly what she was afraid of.

# Chapter 14

Social functions are the tests of your effectiveness. Is your employer well turned out? Are there any smudges on his leathers? Any stains on his velvets? Any wrinkles in his linens? These are the things by which we are judged.

*A Compleat Guide for*
*Being a Most Proper Butler*
by Richard Robert Reeves

*O*n the day of the dinner party, Prudence arrived at the captain's house at exactly seven. It was already dark, with faint thunder rumbling and lightning flashing in the distance. She paused on the step and glanced behind her at the vivid display, the long forks of brilliant gold streaking over the black sea.

She loved the wild weather. When she'd first arrived in Devon, exhausted after dealing with all of the weighty difficulties surrounding Phillip's death and subsequent burial, she'd found the weather oppressive. The skies were as dark and gray as her spirits. But little by little that had changed.

Now she welcomed the testy wind and the arrogant thrash of the rain. The wildness of it reminded her that she was alive. As did the earl. Smiling at her own non-sense, she pulled her cloak more tightly about her neck as she lifted her face to the wind and soaked in the frosty breeze.

It was freeing and exhilarating, but it was also cold. She was glad the earl had sent his carriage or she would have been too uncomfortable to enjoy the scen-ery. Sighing a little, she turned and knocked on the door.

Stevens opened it almost immediately. "There ye are, madam! I've been waitin' on ye!"

Without being asked, he assisted her with her cloak, falling back a step when her gown was re-vealed. "Coo'ee, madam! Ye look as fine as nine nails, ye do!"

Prudence's cheeks heated, her hands unconsciously smoothing the blue silk. It was actually one of Mother's gowns, her best in fact. Prudence had been surprised when Mother had brought it to her room.

It was of shiny blue silk under white netting, and had tiny blue and pink rosettes sporting the tiniest of green leaves. The skirt was deeply set, the white netting split to reveal the sheen of the blue silk at the front. The sleeves went to the elbows, a white ribbon tied at each.

It was a beautiful gown, although the neckline was lower than Prudence had ever worn, the deeply cut edge decorated with a hint of white lace, which drew the eye rather than disguised the lowness.

She'd argued with Mother about perhaps sewing a bit more lace in the opening, but Mother had waved aside such suggestions by pointing out that Prudence was a widow, and no longer "in the first blush of youth."

Prudence frowned, catching sight of herself in the lone mirror in the front hall. Perhaps Mother was right, even though Prudence was only thirty-one. It *was* far beyond the expected age for missish airs and false modesty. She might as well enjoy that small positive notion any way she could.

"Ye look like a frigate in a full moon on a glassy sea, madam," Stevens said, looking her up and down, frankly admiring. "The cap'n will be glad to see ye lookin' so fine." The butler turned to the hooks by the door and carefully hung up her cloak.

"Thank you, Stevens. Where is the earl?"

"In his room. Reeves is helpin' him dress. The cap'n—I mean, the earl—looks fine as a galley himself." He led the way down the hallway. "The cap'n—I mean, the earl—was feeling a bit low about this evenin's entertainment and I thought perhaps ye were feelin' the same, so I set some sherry on the sideboard in case ye might want a fair drab to tide ye over."

"Thank you, Stevens! Sherry would be just the thing."

Stevens laid a finger beside his nose and nodded wisely. "I can tell these things, ye know. 'Tis me gift. Me mum could do the same thing, she could."

"Well, whatever spirits whispered in your ears, I am glad they did."

Stevens puffed up mightily and opened the door to the library, standing to one side.

Prudence noted all of the new and improved touches in Stevens's manner compared to the first day she'd come to see the earl about the sheep. Funny, she hadn't thought about it, but the sheep had stopped jumping the gate the second she'd begun tutoring the earl. That was certainly odd—

"Here's the sherry! I took a swig of it meself, but 'tis a wee bit too sweet." Stevens went to pour her a glass. "The cap'n—I mean, the *earl*—will be down as soon as Master Reeves convinces him to wear that pink waistcoat."

Prudence took the glass from the erstwhile butler. "Pink?"

"It looked pink to me and the cap'n—I mean, the earl—but Reeves insisted it was not. He called it 'puke,' which is a horrid name to call anything, though in this case it do seem appropriate."

She choked a bit on the sherry. "I'm sorry. But do you think perhaps the name of the color is 'puce'?"

"Aye! That be it! Still, call it what ye will, pink is pink and that's not the proper color fer a man to wear, especially one like the captain. 'Tis rather like seein' them geld a fine stallion." Stevens straightened his shoulders. "Speakin' of which, I had best be goin' to see if Reeves needs any help. Will there be anything else afore I leaves ye?"

Prudence shook her head, smiling. "Stevens, you have become quite the butler. You sound just like Reeves."

Stephens brightened, his cheeks glowing with pleasure. "Do ye think so? He's been teachin' me how to do things proper, though it has been a horrible burden to bear, puttin' up with always bein' wrong."

"I'm sure it is," Prudence murmured. She glanced at the clock on the mantle. "I hope the earl won't be long, or we'll be late."

Stevens held up a hand. "Never fear! I'll light a fire beneath him. Just wait 'til ye see the captain in his new clothes; he will have all the ladies a-twitter." Stephens appeared much arrested by this thought. "Perhaps the cap'n will find a woman at the squire's to marry."

A stab of irritation flashed through Prudence, melting her previous good humor. "We are not going to the squire's dinner for his lordship to find a wife."

"Why not? He has a title now, don't he? And money, if he can pull the wool over the eyes of those trustees. Why shouldn't he also get a wife? He will need someone to help him spend it."

Prudence could think of a thousand hazy reasons, but none she could express. Fortunately, Stevens suddenly remembered he'd been on his way to fetch a pin for Reeves when she'd arrived. Bowing quickly, he skittered from the room and left her alone with her thoughts.

Prudence took another sip of sherry. Stevens was right; perhaps Tristan should be thinking of finding a good woman to marry. Once she was finished smoothing out his rough edges… She paused, thinking of the earl smiling at another woman. Of the earl holding another woman. Of the earl kissing another woman the same way he'd kissed her—

"Oh bother," she snapped, spinning on her heel and facing the door. Her temples suddenly pounded. Which of the local women would want anything to do with the earl? The thought held her. Good God, every blessed one.

"The *earl*," she reminded herself. Tristan was indeed an earl, a soon-to-be-wealthy earl. A soon-to-be-wealthy earl with startling green eyes and a lopsided smile that could make one's heart leap. It wasn't who would be interested in the earl, but rather, who wouldn't be?

She rapidly reviewed all of the women who would be at the party. Mrs. Reed, of course. The young widow had been pursuing Reverend Olglethorpe diligently, though he had been adamant in his refusal to countenance her interest.

Prudence was certain the vile widow would willingly reset her sights on Tristan. Prudence sniffed. It was a pity the woman was so puffed up with her own consequence or she'd know that her nose was several sizes larger than it should have been.

Then there was Miss Simpson, whose father was the local magistrate. She was reportedly a handsome girl, though Prudence found her unforgivably overbearing. Surely Tristan wouldn't be interested in such a girl, even if her father was the richest man in the area.

Other names of eligible women flittered through Prudence's mind. Oh damn. Damn. Damn. Frowning mightily, she poured herself yet another glass of sherry.

Reeves stepped back and surveyed his handiwork from head to toe. "My lord, you look a gentleman."

Tristan gritted his teeth, enduring the inspection. He felt like a ship with a broken top rudder, adrift in an oily sea, left to the fickle winds and the hands of fate.

Reeves nodded. "You look well, my lord. Very well."

"I will not wear the pink waistcoat."

"You are wearing it," Reeves pointed out gently. "And it is not pink, but puce."

"Putrid is more like." Tristan turned to pick up his watch fob when he caught a glimpse of himself in the mirror. Tall and broad shouldered, his hair was neatly tied back, and his shoulders were outlined by the black evening coat, the only colors he wore were the pale puce waistcoat and the sparkle of a ruby in his cravat.

Reeves came to stand behind him. "You look just like him."

Tristan's hands curled into fists. "It is not a likeness I treasure."

"Perhaps you should. I've often thought it a pity we do not celebrate the good that sometimes comes out of the bad."

Tristan met Reeves's gaze in the mirror. "It is a greater pity when there is no good."

Reeves pursed his lips. "I am afraid I would have to disagree with that, my lord. The old earl left you his title and funds, though he did have other options. He could have legitimized one of his other unfortunate relatives and named another heir."

"You are right. I should be thankful. And I am. Only . . . not to him." Tristan looked once again into the mirror, into his own green eyes. "Still no word from Christian?"

"No, my lord. We can only hope he is getting his affairs in order so that he may assume his position without—" Reeves bit his lip.

Tristan turned to face the butler. "Without what?"

"There are times one should leave one's past in the past."

"What the hell does that mean?"

"I shall leave it to Master Christian to tell you."

Tristan regarded the butler with frustration. "You are damned cryptic at times."

"So I've been told."

"That wasn't a compliment."

"I am aware of that, my lord." The butler sighed. "I wonder...how old was Master Christian when you last laid eyes on him?"

"We were ten."

"It has been over twenty years. He might be greatly changed."

"I would know him anywhere."

"Given the right lighting and the correct circumstances, I think you would, too."

"What the hell does that mean?"

"Nothing. Only...it would be well to acknowledge that the brother you think you knew might no longer exist."

The thought was unsettling, to say the least. Tristan picked up his cane. "No matter what, I want him back in my life."

Reeves bowed. "I shall let you know as soon as I hear from him, my lord."

A knock sounded on the door. Reeves went to open it and Stevens stood there. He brightened on seeing Reeves. "What do ye know! Someone did open the door when I knocked."

"Amazing, is it not?" Reeves said, shutting the door.

"Sails and oars, Cap'n!" Stevens shook his head. "Next ye'll be wearing skirts and a bow in yer hair."

Tristan raised his brows.

The first mate flushed. "I didn't mean that, me lord! It just slipped out fer I know ye'd never wear no skirt or bow. I just meant—"

"I know what you meant," Tristan growled.

Stevens sighed. "I was just a mite out of breath from seein' Mrs. Thistlewaite to the library. She looks a picture, she do."

"Mrs. Thistlewaite always looks a picture." Which was annoyingly true. Even red nosed from the cold, her hair wind tossed, her clothes a bit wrinkled from the walk to his house, she managed to look delectable.

"Indeed, she's a fine woman," Stevens agreed. "But tonight, she looks a lady born. Ye'll have yer hands full keeping the beaus from overcoming her on the dance floor, mark me words!"

Tristan frowned. "Beaus?" He looked at Reeves.

The butler nodded. "That is, after all, one of the purposes of a country party. To provide some social opportunities for those looking for a wife...or a husband."

Tristan didn't like the sound of that at all. He wondered if the doctor would be there, ready to pant over Prudence and annoy the hell out of Tristan. "Whoever is there, they had better leave Prudence alone."

Reeves seemed to contemplate this. "Unless she wishes it, of course. Then you cannot, in all honesty, interfere."

"Interfere? I will be there to protect her."

"Mrs. Thistlewaite is not a child, my lord. Unless she requests your assistance, you cannot do anything. I only hope she might find someone who will make her happy. She is such a lovely woman."

To Tristan's irritation, Stevens nodded. "She's a trim rig, make no doubt about it. Daresay there are any number of gents willin' to—"

"Enough!" Tristan glared at Stevens and then Reeves. "I don't wish to hear another word."

Reeves bowed. "As you wish, my lord."

Scowling, Tristan walked out the door and made his way downstairs.

Bloody hell, what did Stevens mean by suggesting that Prudence would have the ill thought of flirting? She was not that sort of woman. He remembered her in his library, of her hair unbound and her mouth swollen from his kisses—well. Perhaps she *was* the type, but only with him, damn it! He glanced down, annoyed to find that he'd hardened at the mere memory of touching her.

She was his. His until he was through with her or she him. And he would allow no one else to broach the subject. If some drunken coxswain thought to jump Prudence's deck, Tristan would be ready to discourage the jackanapes with a pistol if need be.

He scowled to himself as he reached the bottom of the stairs. It was a good thing Stevens had mentioned such a happenstance or Tristan might have been caught asleep at the helm.

He made his way down the narrow hallway, the light from the library shining into the gloomy passage, a beacon from a dark shore. Less than a month ago, he'd been peaceful here, watching his life drift by, only the concern for his men giving him a reason to rise from bed. Now, things were more clear...more hopeful, somehow.

Tristan paused outside of the library and looked down at his clothing. The cloth was softer than he was used to, though it bound him tighter. He adjusted his cravat for the umpteenth time, using a finger to loosen it a bit about the neck, certain he was creasing it in some way that would horrify Reeves.

It seemed as if his father was reaching from beyond the grave to irk him, to punish him further for the ignominious fact of his existence. But Tristan was made of sterner stuff.

He would not allow this inconvenience to interrupt his plans. He would help his men, establish a real home for the sailors, and then forget about everything else.

All he needed was the funds and he would be free of this silly playacting. Then he could be who he really was. And Prudence would be his for the taking.

With that thought, he walked into the library—and came to a stunned halt. Standing before the fire was Prudence. She was dressed in a blue-and-white gown of some sort, though that was not what he really noticed.

What he did notice was that the bright blaze from the fire backlit Prudence's entire body through the thin silk that draped over her. He could see the enticing curve of her hips and the long, supple length of her legs. There wasn't a curve out of place. She was breathtakingly perfect and she set his loins afire without even knowing it.

"Ah! My lord, there you are."

Her soft voice shook him from his reverie. He stepped

forward, fighting the urge to grab her up and carry her to his room. Had he been able to be himself and not this shell of an earl, that was what he would do.

A sudden thought shook him. What if Prudence unknowingly stood before the fireplace at the party at the squire's? Every bloody man there would be enthralled. They would all see her as he did now. A low roar began to sound in his ears.

"You look very well," she said, a shy note in her voice.

Tristan gathered himself with some effort. "As do you." He forced his gaze to move up from her outlined form, his heart jumping when he realized the charms of her bodice. Bloody hell, who had allowed her to wear such a daring gown? He could keep her from standing before the fire, but how was he to cover her shoulders and chest?

She smiled, blithely unaware of his growing consternation as she walked to the sideboard to replace an empty glass she held in her hand. He noted that she wobbled just the slightest bit as she did so.

He looked at the near-empty decanter and he almost groaned aloud. Good God, he was escorting the world's most beautiful woman and not only was she underdressed, but she was tipply. "I don't want to go to this dinner."

"You must. It's our last chance to practice." She came to his side, leaning against him until her breasts pressed the back of his arm, her smile warm and inviting. "Don't worry. I will be with you all evening."

He looked down at where her hand rested on his sleeve, right beside the enticing swell of her bosom.

His hand closed over hers. If he stayed here, he would end up making love to her. He knew it as clearly as if it were written in ink on a piece of blinding white paper. Perhaps it would be better to be around others. At least until one of them was of a cooler, more composed mind.

Tristan pressed his lips to her fingers. "I will not let you out of my sight."

"Then let us go." With that, she half pulled him to the door, looking entrancing and exciting and thoroughly sensual. "'Tis an adventure!"

Tristan followed her, feeling very grim indeed. He would go to this blasted dinner party and, at the first possible moment, take his leave, making certain Prudence went with him.

God, but he hoped it would be a short night. He didn't think he could make it through a long one.

# Chapter 15

Always be willing to share your knowledge with common man and nobleman alike. The seeds of wisdom can survive on the rockiest of soil.

*A Compleat Guide for*
*Being a Most Proper Butler*
by Richard Robert Reeves

*T*he dinner party was doomed the second they arrived. Not only did the kindly country squire turn out to be far younger than Tristan remembered, but the lout was unmarried as well. Feeling betrayed by Reeves, Tristan had tried to accept the situation as best he could. Unfortunately, it quickly became apparent fate was against him, especially when the handsome young squire had the audacity to practically leer down the front of Prudence's gown when Tristan helped her remove her cloak.

That had not gone well at all. Though Tristan couldn't

blame the man on a purely masculine basis, it had infuriated him nonetheless. Fortunately, the squire caught Tristan's warning glare and hastily beat a retreat across the room, though not without sending more than one admiring glance Prudence's way. Tristan thought about dragging the lout outside right then and there and blacking both of the man's clocks, but there was worse waiting.

He'd no more navigated Prudence through what seemed a gauntlet of lecherous men than they found their pathway blocked by Dr. Barrow. The young doctor was obviously surprised at Prudence's appearance and spent a good ten minutes doing what he could to monopolize her precious time. The doctor was a more serious threat than the squire, for try as he would, Tristan could not hint the man off.

Well, Tristan would just stand here, at her elbow, and never leave her side. The blasted fool *had* to eventually catch one of Tristan's "Black Looks." Damn it to hell, his glares had frightened Barbary pirates nigh to death! How could a simple-minded doctor not be affected?

Tristan began to wonder if perhaps the doctor possessed poor eyesight. Perhaps the weak-kneed fool couldn't see well enough to realize he was in dire danger. If that was so, it might take a word or two to get Tristan's message through to the sapskull. But how to do it without Prudence hearing?

He spent the next fifteen minutes mulling over a plan and by the time the announcement came for dinner, he knew what he was going to do. Unfortunately, he didn't realize that seating was by social standing. And an earl outranked a mere widow by several degrees, which meant he was captured by a horse-faced woman who had the audacity to practically toss Prudence at the doctor before she yanked Tristan out of the room, her fingers curled into claws on his elbow.

Tristan did not like this bit of maneuvering. No wonder the nobility were always challenging each other to duels and whatnot. The rules that bound society were barbaric, to say the least, especially when they forced a man to sit at the furthest end of the table and watch his woman surrounded by a pack of hungry he-wolves.

It was too much to bear. Every time Prudence laughed, he was torn with jealousy and longing. By the time the men excused themselves to the library for port, Tristan was ready to slit throats, prisoners be damned. However, thanks to the fact he was now unhampered by Prudence's presence, he was able to do what he'd wanted to from the first.

Tristan made his way to the doctor's side. That unworthy gentleman stood by the fire, sipping from a large brandy snifter in what Tristan thought was a deplorably effeminate manner.

Deep in thought, the doctor didn't hear Tristan approach. Tristan leaned forward, near the doctor's ear, and said in a booming voice, "Doctor!"

Doctor Barrow jumped, the snifter flying from his hand and crashing to the hearth.

Tristan looked down at the shattered glass, moving slightly when a servant rushed up and began to clean the mess.

The doctor's face blazed red. He shot an embarrassed glare about the room before looking back at Tristan. "Lord Rochester. You surprised me."

"I shouldn't have," Tristan murmured. "Surely you knew I would look you up. You have been quite particular in your attention to Mrs. Thistlewaite. I believe it would be good for you to desist."

The doctor blinked. "Desist? B—b—but—I never—"

"Never is a lovely word. Let us keep it at that, shall we?" Tristan finished his drink and set it on the mantel.

"My lord! I must protest! My relationship with Mrs. Thistlewaite is—"

"Over." Tristan leaned closer, his voice low with menace. "I once slit the throat of a rival pirate captain who stole a cargo that was mine. Slit it from here—" Tristan pressed a finger to the doctor's jaw right below his left ear. "—to here." He slid his finger across the buffoon's throat to the same spot on the opposite corner of his jaw.

The doctor's mouth opened, then closed.

The story wasn't true, of course. But the oaf seemed to believe it easily enough.

Even now the doctor was blenching as if he might faint. "You—you—you—I—I—I—Must go."

Tristan shrugged. "You don't need to leave now. You may wait until after—"

He spoke to empty air; the doctor was already across the room, speaking in an animated voice to the squire, who was looking at Tristan with something akin to astonishment.

Tristan was actually smiling when the gentlemen rejoined the ladies, but his triumph was short lived.

"What have you been doing?" Prudence hissed, not five minutes later.

"Me?"

Her brows lowered even more, her arms crossed beneath her breasts.

"I did nothing but tell the truth."

"You told Dr. Barrow you would slit him from his throat to his—" Her eyes snapped. "What were you thinking?"

Tristan scowled. He hadn't really been thinking. Just reacting. Of course, now that he thought about it, perhaps he had overstated his case a tad. But only a tad, and he'd be damned if he'd admit as much to Prudence. Not with her looking at him as if she'd have him split and gutted for a pence.

"He was rude to you."

She blinked. "Whatever gave you that idea?"

"No one did. I saw it for myself."

She crossed her arms, which was an unfortunate thing to do as it pressed her breasts upward, even more prominent in the low-cut gown. "You saw it for yourself? When?"

"Before dinner and then during. He was monopolizing your attention. Why, I could barely get a word in edgewise, the lout."

She closed her eyes and pinched her nose, breathing deeply.

Tristan became concerned. "Prudence? Are you well?"

"No. I am not. I have a headache and I want to go home."

"Good!" At her outraged look, he added hastily, "I'll get your cloak."

They made their excuses and left, much to Tristan's

satisfaction and the seeming relief of their host. Prudence's manner was strained and unhappy, and Tristan could only suppose her head truly was bothering her.

Silence reigned in the carriage. Prudence looked steadily out the window, her mouth pressed in a mutinous line. Tristan watched her from where he sat in his corner. He supposed he shouldn't have acted so strongly. But he couldn't help it. The doctor had been all but pawing Prudence. As for the others, by Neptune, it had been too much to be borne. Tristan was just a man and he could only take so much.

In fact, considering what he *could* have done but hadn't, he thought he'd handled the situation rather well.

Prudence looked at him. "I cannot believe you threatened poor Dr. Barrow."

"That bastard wants to bed you, in case you haven't noticed."

She flushed. "We were merely talking. I see him quite frequently at my house as he loves Mrs. Fieldings's cooking."

Tristan crossed his arms. "That's not all he loves. He was annoyingly present, leering over you, staring at you. I've never seen such behavior—"

"Haven't you? In all the taverns you've frequented, all the houses of ill repute, you've never seen anything so tawdry?"

"I would not wish *my* behavior to be compared to that of someone who frequents a house of ill repute," he retorted, and then paused. Good God, was that really him, sounding so priggish? What the hell was wrong with him?

Prudence sniffed. "*I* would not wish to have such double standards of good and evil. I am not a green girl who needs rescuing. I am over thirty and well capable of taking care of myself."

"That man was importuning you."

"No, he was paying attention to me. There is a difference, you know." Her chin firmed mutinously. "Either way, 'tis none of your concern. I am well able to deal with my own suitors, thank you."

Tristan clamped his teeth over the things he wanted to say, none of which would help his case now. Damn it, he was an earl now. Surely earls could do things that sea captains could not.

But no; he would not think like his father. There were rules and there were laws. Since Tristan was no gentleman, he didn't have to worry about the rules. But laws—not even an earl should be above them.

He leaned his head against the high squab of the carriage, regarding Prudence for a long moment. She sat fuming in the opposite corner, her jaw set mutinously, her eyes sparkling with ire.

She looked...beautiful. Without another thought, Tristan leaned across the carriage, picked her up and set her on the seat opposite his. "Now we can talk."

She gasped. "What do you think you are doing?"

"Bringing you to a more amenable distance."

"For whom?"

He managed a grin. "For us both. I cannot hear you from the opposite corner."

She planted her palms on the seat and scooted even further away than before. "I can hear you just fine from here. If any of those men at the party tonight had treated me the way you are treating me right now, it might well have been within reason to wish to challenge them for their horrid and inconsiderate behavior. But tossing about threats merely because someone said a nice word—I won't stand for it. Not now. Not ever."

Tristan raked a hand through his hair, wishing he could explain his feelings. The problem was, he wasn't sure if he knew exactly what they were himself. "Prudence—"

"That is another thing. When we are in public, it will not do for you to call me Prudence. It is Mrs. Thistlewaite."

He stared down at his boots, his irritation fading with each moment. Perhaps he had reacted a little too strongly. He sighed. "Did I embarrass you?"

"Drastically!"

He winced. "I apologize. That was not my intent. But I don't like seeing other men treat you with disrespect."

"And I don't like it when you barge in where you are not wanted. I am not one of your crew members injured in the war and in need of rescuing!"

That galled him. A flame of something other than irritation spiked through him. "Prudence, I have apologized. I cannot do more."

"I do not accept your apology."

"No?"

"No." She turned from him, flipping up one corner of the leather curtain that covered the window and staring stonily into the night.

Damn it! This was not how he wanted their night to end. His gaze flickered over her, noting the curve of her breasts through the low-cut neckline, the delicate hollows of her shoulders, the elegant line of her neck. His fingers itched and curled into his palms, his head swirling a bit from the wine and brandy.

Before he knew what he was about, he'd reached across the carriage and picked her up once again, only this time, he placed her firmly in his lap.

She sat still for a stunned moment, her skirts trailing over his knees. "You—you cannot do that!"

"I just did," he said smugly, placing a kiss on her jaw right where it touched her neck.

She gasped, her eyes widening.

"I'm sorry if I embarrassed you this evening, love," he murmured against her neck.

She scrambled as if to get out of his lap, but he held her tighter, trailing his lips from her jaw to just below her ear.

"My lord, you—"

"Tristan," he murmured, nibbling softly on the sensitive lobe of her ear.

Prudence grit her teeth, clinging desperately to her anger. She was furious, and with good reason, she told herself, even as a sensuous shiver traced down her back. His mouth traveled down her neck to her collarbone and, despite her intentions, she caught herself lifting her chin just a bit so he could continue his ministrations.

Waves of delight shivered through her, her breasts peaking. He'd been horrid this evening, she reminded herself, fisting her hands in an effort to maintain coherent thought. But...he had apologized, too. She needed to remember that though she and Reeves had taught the earl manners, they hadn't managed to civilize him. This was a man who would never be civilized, no matter the circumstances.

His lips brushed her outer ear, then her temple, his breath warm and delicious. A bit more of her previous irritation melted, little by little. His hands were warm on her through the thin silk of her gown, his lips doing magical things to her. She should fight him, she told herself. She should fight him and demand that he return her to her seat. But she couldn't. She couldn't because her traitorous body was refusing to pay her any heed. The ability to think and thus frame a reasonable argument was rapidly leaving her. In the place of reason came a flood of emotions so potent, so powerful, that she was enthralled, caught in a net of heat and lust. Drowning in the silken honey of desire. She'd thought giving into her desire once would have slaked her fires. Instead, she wanted him all the more.

What did it matter, anyway? He had embarrassed her this evening, although a little part of her was thrilled at the attention. Truth be known, when she'd caught Tristan glowering at her dinner partners, she'd flirted a good bit more than she usually did.

It was odd how she both enjoyed and detested such behavior. She enjoyed it because for that moment— when he was staring at her with such focused desire— she'd felt powerful and even beautiful. Both were rare emotions, and she'd treasure them. But at the same time, she disliked being so affected by such things.

Tristan's large, warm hands slid down her back to her waist. His hands tightened and he pulled her closer, settling her against the hard ridge forming in his breeches. Desire tightened her throat, sent her senses careening. Surely he wouldn't do this, wouldn't take this any further...

He threaded his hand through her hair, dislodging her pins and scattering them over the floor as her curls tumbled to her shoulders. His other hand slid down her leg and closed about her ankle, his fingers warm through her thin silk stocking. The sight of his large, masculine hand about her ankle was oddly erotic, especially when he slid his hand up beneath her skirt to cup her calf, then her knee.

Prudence quivered, her breasts tightened and she wished with all her heart that his touch would linger. Endure. Grow bolder.

She wanted him, but... she thought of his expression at the dinner party, of how possessive he'd been. Wouldn't this just make matters worse? Or would it release yet more of the pressure that steamed between them, that pulse of awareness that had been growing since the first time she'd marched to his house ready for battle?

The thoughts chilled her and she caught his hand just as he readied to slide it up to her thigh. "There is one thing we must understand if we are to progress any further."

His gaze narrowed and Prudence's heart beat even harder. There was a menace to this man, a dark power that attracted her almost as much as it caught at her senses. But she refused to be cowed.

Ignoring the pounding of her heart, she straightened her shoulders and pushed free of his hold, sliding across the seat to a safer distance. She needed the space—and the time—to gather herself. When he was near, she had to fight to remember who she was, who *he* was.

Not that such a thing kept her from wanting him. Hardly that. But it was important that neither of them have any doubts as to what their relationship was. She cleared her throat. "I believe we both need to understand that this... dalliance is nothing more than that." Though her face burned with embarrassment, she managed to meet his gaze levelly. "Do you understand?"

Amusement touched his lips. "You are a conundrum, my lovely Prudence. I thought ladies never—"

"I am no lady." For the first time since she'd left London, Prudence was unabashedly glad for that fact. And it was true, according to the dictates of polite society.

His brows drew down. "You are a lady. One of the finest I've ever met." He reached over and threaded a lock of her hair through his fingers, lifting the strand to his lips. "But you are also a woman, and therein lays the difference between you and those mewling cats society bows and scrapes before. They are not real, nor do they wish to be."

Her stomach tightened as he rubbed the strand of her hair over his cheek, his eyes never leaving her. "Prudence, I want you."

The words washed over her, his voice so deep it drew her toward him. She shivered, a trace of heated passion that rippled over her, across her, inside her. Her breasts peaked and crested, her knees grew weak and unstable. She wanted him, too. And why shouldn't she? She was no innocent, never before touched. She had been touched. By Phillip.

At one time, the thought of Phillip might have turned her from this moment, made her feel guilty and alone. But now, all it did was send her forth. Phillip would not have wanted her to stop living merely because he'd died.

But now, she faced a choice of a more complex sort. Unlike her relationship with Phillip, there was no future for her with Tristan. No matter the physical attraction between them, it could not be. He was an earl, required by the trustees to be socially acceptable. She, meanwhile, was anything but. They would never approve of her, especially as the trustees were well aware of her public disgrace.

Which left her with what? Over the weeks, she had come to know the sailors in Tristan's household, and they had become important to her in their own right. There was Toggle, who was a bit confused, but always sweet natured. Gibbons with his missing arm; she worried about him for he was so despondent. Adkins who was horribly scarred, but always found something to laugh at. And Stevens, who always made her feel welcome. She'd come to care for them all. If she encouraged Tristan to pursue their relationship, it would easily jeopardize his chances of winning the fortune. She refused to be the cause of more distress to those who had already suffered.

What she had to do was admit to herself that this attraction was only temporary. A short-term indulgence, one brought on by the yearning this wonderful, intelligent man aroused within her. And once the trustees arrived, it would end, as suddenly and as seriously as it had begun.

Her heart ached as she looked at him in the flickering light of the carriage lamp, admiring his eyes, his fine nose, the cut of his jaw.

He raised a hand to his own cheek. "What is it? You look as if you've found something horribly wrong."

She smiled somewhat mirthlessly, the carriage swaying a little as they rounded a corner of the narrow road. "Perhaps I've merely found something terribly right."

Tristan picked up her hand and held it to his lips. "Prudence, I was a fool this evening. Can you forgive me? I cannot promise I will never again be jealous, but I will at least contain my actions to a more proper time and place." His breath warmed the skin on the back of her hand. "I can tell I upset you. Let me make it up to you."

"I might," she said, smiling a little at the huskiness of her own voice. "But only on my terms."

His expression darkened, the smile still in place. "You are a warrior at heart, aren't you, my dear? You'd sooner fight than breathe."

"I do not like to lose," she said, the carriage bumping slightly over the uneven road. "Who does?"

"And making love with me would be losing?" A deep chuckle escaped him. "I think you need to redefine what you think 'losing' is. Or perhaps..." His gaze dropped to her lips, his eyes darkening, "...perhaps I need to redefine the word for you."

Her heart sped up a bit at that, her breasts swelling a little. She met his gaze boldly, though she had to fight not to keep her breathlessness from showing. "What do you intend to do?"

His green eyes sparkled then, the thick black lashes

lowering. Ever so slowly, he reached over and undid her cloak, his fingers warm against her throat, her shoulders. He caressed every inch of skin as he exposed it, lightly brushing his fingertips over her. His movements were slow, languorous, sensual.

They were going to make love. She knew it with a certainty that held her in thrall. A wave of anticipation clasped her, the intensity of it astounding her. Just the thought of being with this man was a torture and a pleasure unlike any she'd ever had.

Tristan freed the cloak from her and then slid her to his side. Suddenly bereft of his warmth, as well as her cloak, she shivered a little, crossing her arms before her. She watched as Tristan rolled the cloak into a long thick rope.

"What are you doing?"

He flashed a grin that set her heart pounding. "I am marking the line of battle, m'lady."

The line of battle. She rather thought she liked that.

He moved down the bench a bit and pushed one end of the 'rope' over the top of the seat, then slid it down the back of the cushion to tuck it between the cushions. The remainder of the rope he let trail over the seat to the carriage floor.

"There," he said when he'd finished, leaning back to observe his handiwork.

She looked at the thickly cushioned seat, at the line of her cloak against the plush red velvet. "So...this side of the seat is mine."

"And this side is mine," he answered, patting the seat by his thigh.

She really wished he hadn't done that, drawn her

gaze to his thigh. He had the most incredible muscles there, outlined in sharp relief by his breeches. She had to swallow before she could continue. "And we are to wage war? On this carriage seat?"

"I'd prefer to think of it as wrestle. For control."

Well. That sounded rather promising. Despite her misgivings, Prudence smiled a little. "I don't believe it would be a fair match. After all, you are quite a bit larger than me."

"Perhaps 'wrestle' is the wrong word. The more correct term would be... 'entice.'" His dark, smoldering gaze raked across her. "The game is to see who can entice whom to cross the line first."

*Entice.* Such a tiny word. And yet it held so much promise. Prudence's heart rang loudly in her ears. "What exactly do you mean when you say 'entice'? That could mean a lot of different—"

He untied his cravat.

"Oh!" she said breathlessly. She glanced at the carriage windows where the leather curtains were latched into place. "I don't know if we should—"

He tossed his cravat to one side. He was out of his waistcoat in equal time, tossing it to the opposite seat. "Whoever crosses the line first of their own free will, loses. Although..." His teeth flashed in a grin as he pulled his shirt free from the waistband and pulled it over his head. "In this war, my love, we both win."

# Chapter 16

Even the most cautious of servants will find that surprises happen. The question becomes whether they take you—or you take them.

*A Compleat Guide for*
*Being a Most Proper Butler*
by Richard Robert Reeves

$\mathcal{I}$t was silliness. It really was. And Prudence knew that. But she was fascinated. Fascinated with the thought of lovemaking in a carriage.

And even more fascinated with the man who sat within arm's reach, his shirt gone. "What if we get caught?"

"My love, they will have to stop the carriage before they come to open the door. Besides, it is a long ride."

That was true. It had taken them almost an hour to reach the squire's. Prudence watched as Tristan's shirt joined the other articles of clothing on the seat across from them.

He paused, eyeing her up and down. "Well?"

She suddenly realized she hadn't moved an inch, but was sitting on the edge of her half of the seat, watching Tristan disrobe. Every movement he made fanned the fires banked deep within her.

If *she* wished to entice *him,* she had to do something. But what? Almost of their own volition, her fingers found the ribbon at the neckline of her gown. She had just begun to untie it when she caught Tristan's gaze.

He sat so still as to appear to be a statue, his lips firmly together, his eyes bright and hard. He looked so...tense. As if he was only barely in control.

Ah! He was struggling to maintain his composure. That was interesting, indeed. Perhaps if she slowed things down a bit and made the anticipation work *for* her...

She dropped her hands back into her lap. "I think I will wait."

His brows lowered. "Wait?"

"For you to finish disrobing." She sat back in her corner, watching him from beneath her lashes. "Pray continue. I am vastly enjoying this."

He eyed her a moment, disbelief in every line of his expression. "I don't believe that's fair."

"Fair?" She smiled. "Who said we had to be fair? I rather thought the purpose was to test one another's ability to withstand temptation."

"It is," he said, though his tone was somewhat grim, which made Prudence's smile widen.

"Hm. Then perhaps you are just afraid..." She looked at him from beneath her lashes. "Of losing."

That seemed to goad him enough, for he snapped his mouth closed and yanked off his boots.

Prudence was mesmerized by the site of his broad back, of the muscles that rippled beneath his skin, of the narrowness of his waist and the sinew of his arms. God, but he was a lovely man.

And for this moment, all hers.

The thought buoyed her a bit and she was able to keep her composure even when he tossed aside his boots, and began to undo his breeches. The next moment was one Prudence would remember all of her life. One moment he was before her, resplendent in his black breeches—and then he was naked, every tightly chiseled, sinewy inch of him exposed.

The scar on his leg gleamed white against his muscled sinew. She remembered that she had kissed it, a delicious shiver rippling over her.

Prudence's pulse pounded behind her ears and eyes. Her skin tightened and tingled.

Tristan turned on the seat to face her, his muscular legs slightly splayed so she could see—

She closed her eyes, hands clenched at her sides, before taking a deep breath. Perhaps this was a dream, a wonderful dream. Slowly, she opened her eyes...he was still there. And still magnificent, every inch of him. She was awash in longing simply by looking at him.

Had there been no line down the center of the seat, she might well have disrobed, slid to his side, and pulled him to her. But this was no longer a moment of sharing, but of winning.

And she refused to do anything else.

Forcing herself to appear calm, Prudence smiled ever so slightly, hoping her lips weren't trembling as much as her legs. "Well..." She let her breath smooth the word and linger in the smoky darkness of the rocking carriage.

She traced the neckline of her gown with her fingers, noting how his gaze seemed locked on her hands. She slid one hand down her front, over the curve of her breast, to her stomach, and lower.

His expression tightened. "What are you doing?"

She smiled. "Undressing." This was power, she realized. Real power. He was watching her every move, unable to look away.

Prudence lifted her foot and placed it on the opposite seat. She pulled off her slipper and let it fall to the carriage floor. Then she gathered the hem of her dress in one hand.

She never once looked away from Tristan's face, from the flash of heat that darkened his eyes when she pulled the hem across her knee and exposed her calf and foot. "My stockings must come off."

She slid the gown a bit higher, exposing now her thigh all the way to the top. Her chemise hid the top of her stocking ties, but she pulled it aside and began to slowly unlace the satin strings.

Tristan's gaze never left her leg. Indeed, he seemed mesmerized, his gaze captured by the movement of her hands, his breathing harsh in the silence.

She undid the ties and then began to slowly roll her stocking down her leg. As she did so, she allowed her hands to linger on her own skin, brushing here, touching there.

The sound of his breathing filled the narrow space. Prudence watched Tristan from under her lashes, her own body heating at the sight of his obvious arousal, at the tension that marked his expression, at the desire that burned in his gaze.

She removed the stocking and then took off her other shoe, careful to keep the hem of her skirt on her thigh, high but not too high. Not yet, anyway.

She took her time taking this stocking off as well, lingering on her own curves, using Tristan's expression to gauge her movements. He seemed particularly heated when she touched her skin, and so she cupped her calf and trailed her fingers up it to the hollow behind her knee.

Tristan leaned forward, his hands touching the cloak line but not moving it. His eyes burned tightly, his body taut. "If you will cross the line, I will kiss you where your fingers touch."

Prudence found that her own breath was unsteady, her own body burning beneath her fingers. "Everywhere?"

"Everywhere."

She threw the stocking to the floor and pulled her gown back to her ankles. His gaze was riveted to her. "Tristan, if *you* cross the line, I will allow you to do more than merely kiss me."

A white line appeared beside his mouth.

Smiling, Prudence undid the ribbon at her neck. It opened and released her gown. She loosened the shoulders, and pushed it down, off her arms, past her waist. She lifted her hips from the seat and pushed the gown to the floor, where it lay, a puddle of satin and lace.

Tristan had never seen anything so beautiful. She was brazen and yet of a rare and beautiful quality. A respectable woman, and yet a woman of passion and longing that made him want her all the more.

He'd never met anyone who so completely tantalized him, challenged him. Watching her undress was torture and pleasure, both.

She sat now in nothing but her chemise. The thin material clung to the tops of her breasts, casting curious shadows between and beneath them. Pert bows rested at the crest of each breast, begging to be untied.

Tristan was so aroused he ached. Yet still he did not move. He grasped the edge of the seat, totally engaged in watching the woman before him. He regretted the challenge he'd made in drawing a line down the seat.

She undid one of the ties of her chemise. The top draped down over one breast, clinging to the delectable slope. She reached up for the other tie, her fingers hovering.

Her rich brown eyes met his. "What if you *invite* me to cross the line?"

He set his jaw. "I would lose."

"I see."

Tristan heard the desire in her voice, her fascination with her own longing. He felt the same way. But he could not allow her to win this contretemps. He could not.

She undid the other tie and the chemise fell from her breasts, exposing the creamy mounds to his hungry gaze. They were beautiful, full, with rose-kissed nipples that drew his attention and made him even more painfully aware of her.

With a graceful lift of her hips, the chemise went the

way of her gown and she was completely nude, her eyes shining, her lips curled in a secret smile, as if she knew very well what she was doing to him.

It was the most arousing, sensual moment of his life.

She lifted her arms and began pulling pins from her hair. "What if we should change the rule?"

Tristan found he could not look away from her breasts. "Yes?"

"It is not crossing the line unless your hips touch the cloak. But hands and else . . ." Her eyes sparkled. "Hands and else may roam wherever they will go."

Tristan's blood roared anew. "Hands and else?"

"Anything but hips."

"I accept the change in rules."

Her lips curled into a small smile. "I thought you might." She withdrew two last pins. Her deep brown hair fell to her shoulders in a silky swath.

Tristan caught his breath. She was glorious.

She leaned back, her legs slightly parting as she did so, the dim light touching her body with intriguing shades. Her hair streamed over her shoulders, covering one breast and leaving the other for his hungry gaze. "What now?"

He reached over the line and placed his hands on her knees, his fingers lingering on her delicate skin. "What now, indeed?"

Her bare skin burned him through the pads of his fingers. His body reacted immediately. Already hard, his erection leaped with the touch.

His mind and imagination was already inflamed, fanned by her tempting disrobing. Now, his skin tingled with delicious sensation, and his body yearned for more. "May I kiss you?"

Her eyes darkened, her chest rising and falling in a way that let him know she was as affected as he. "I suppose we could meet at the line."

"Indeed we could."

Prudence leaned forward. Tristan found himself watching her full breasts as she leaned, the sight enrapturing.

And then...she was there. And he was kissing her, his mouth covering hers, his tongue gently slipping through her lips.

The kiss heated, expanded, exploded. Suddenly, kissing was not enough. His hands were everywhere, as were hers.

This was madness. Lovely, sweet, joy-inspired madness. Tomorrow he'd think about the consequences. For right now, he just wanted to get lost in her loveliness.

It seemed to him that Prudence felt the same. He could feel the tumultuous pounding of her heart, smell the clove-scented passion of her breath. She was his. All he had to do was slide forward, pull her into his lap, make her his and—

Something caught at his leg. Tristan looked down at the cloak bundled against his hip.

She moaned and tugged at him.

With the most incredible control he'd ever exhibited, Tristan put a bit more space between himself and the line. "I can't, sweetheart. I can't cross the line. Not unless you invite me..." He waited, praying she'd give in, hoping she'd allow him to—

"No." She leaned toward him, sliding her fingers through his hair, and pulling him forward until his lips were against hers. Her lashes lifted, and her eyes met his as she said against his lips, "Take me."

He trembled with the need to plunge into her, to bury himself to his loins, and take her over and over and over. But every time he slid in her direction, the cloak stopped him. Reminded him of their game. If she was too proud to lose, he was too stubborn.

He placed his hands on her arms and pushed her from him. "I will not forfeit myself."

A slow smile curled her lips and she leaned back against the squab, the red velvet making her skin milky white, her breasts begging for his touch. She stretched her arms over her head and shrugged. "Then do not."

Tristan realized she was being deliberately provocative. And doing a damned fine job of it, too. As if she could read his thoughts, she reached down and cupped her breasts, her lashes low over her eyes, her lips pursed invitingly.

God, but she was delicious. He could not hold out much longer. This called for extreme measures. He reached over the line of battle and placed his hand on her knee.

Her lashes lifted, her eyes such a warm, cinnamon brown. He leaned over the cloak line and placed a kiss on her cheek, the corner of her mouth, her neck... With each progressive kiss, he slid his hand higher. Higher still. When his lips found her shoulder, his hand rested on her thigh. He lightly brushed his fingers over her skin, trailing them up...up...He allowed his fingertips to trace the tight curls that enticed him beyond measure.

He bent to clasp her nipple in his mouth the same

moment his fingers found her secret folds. Prudence gasped and arched, bringing herself even more within his reach.

"Say it," Tristan murmured as she writhed against the seat. "Say you want me to join you."

"No," she gasped. "I—Oh, God!"

"Say it," he ground out. He slipped a finger deep into her wetness, curling it just so. "Say you want me to cross the line."

"*No,*" she repeated, shaking her head vehemently, her dark hair spilling over the back of the velvet seat.

Damn, but the woman was determined. She was also intriguing and erotic, and he ached with the desperate need to taste her. He couldn't remember ever wanting a woman this badly. Ever working this hard to win his way into any woman's graces. But there was something about Prudence that was just...different. She was more than most women—more caring, more honest, more sensual.

She moaned as his fingers moved in her. She reached down and clutched his wrist, writhing against him.

He could feel the moisture that slipped from her, the fullness of her causing him an agony of need. "Prudence, let me—"

"No," she gasped and then squirmed, her want growing, the finger tormenting but not satisfying. "Tristan, I want—" She bit her lip, twisting her head this way and that.

He leaned forward and whispered in her ear, "Indeed I can, my love. But you have to ask first. Ask me to cross the line and you will stop wanting, stop needing."

His entire body was taut with the effort to control his responses. He wanted her, badly. So badly. But he would not be the one to give in. He increased his ministrations, now brushing the pad of his thumb over her most sensitive spot.

She arched almost instantly, growing hotter, more insistent. *"Tristan!"* It was a cry and a plea.

"Damn it, Prudence," he said through gritted teeth. "I can't—" He tried to pull his hand away from her, but she grabbed his wrist and held him fast.

Damn it all. She could neither stop nor leave her pride behind, and neither could he. What in the hell had he been thinking, to suggest the damn line to begin with?

Prudence placed her hands on either side of his face, drawing him near. "Tristan, move with me."

"What?"

"Move *with* me. We'll cross the line at the same time. We'll make love on top of it."

He just looked at her. Then, ever so slowly, a smile broke through his lust-clouded mind. "We will both win," he heard his astonished voice say aloud.

He had to laugh. His Prudence was always the most practical of all women, even in the heat of passion. He reached over and cupped her bottom in his hands and in one smooth movement, slid her beneath him even as he moved over her. She helped, too, her legs splaying to engulf him, welcome him, her feet on the edge of the opposite seat.

The cloak line ran directly beneath her back. "Will this bother you—" He got no further. With a blissful smile, Prudence clasped her legs about his waist and impaled herself on him.

All thought left Tristan's mind. All he could do was feel. Feel her heat and tightness, feel the warm band that encircled him like a hot, wet glove. He was enthralled, engrossed, and enrapt, all by a woman whose head did not even reach his shoulder.

She wiggled slightly, her breathing as harsh as his. "Tristan," she managed to say through panting gasps. *"More."*

More. What a powerful word. And if it was more she wanted it, it was more she would get. Tristan obligingly began to move, pressing into her, increasing the pressure, the rhythm.

The feelings increased, multiplied. The rocking motion of the carriage pushed them further, adding to the moment. Tristan twisted slightly in an effort to get even better angle, but his bad leg hit the seat behind him.

He winced, gasping in pain.

"What is it?" Prudence asked.

"My leg," he groaned. "This damned carriage."

Prudence's gaze met his, a wicked smile playing about her lush mouth. "Tristan, let me on top."

For a moment, he could just look into the warm brown of her eyes. Then an answering smile tickled his mouth. "Very well, sweetheart. Hold on to me."

She clasped her arms about his neck. Tristan put his hands on her waist and then, with a smooth movement, he rolled to one side.

Her gasp filled the air and for a moment, she held completely still, her head thrown back as she savored the feeling of him buried truly deeply in her. Tristan grasped her hips and helped her move, sliding her forward and then backward, rocking her against him. Prudence was soon setting the pace, a hand on each of his shoulders, her hair raking across his neck and chest. The sensations built and grew. Tristan had to fight for control, but fight he did. And he was amply rewarded when suddenly, she stiffened and gasped his name.

Waves of pleasure tightened about his shaft as she fell forward across him. Tristan clasped Prudence to him, holding her tightly as his own desires exploded along with hers.

Moments later, his arms still tight about her, their hearts still thundering loudly, Prudence pushed herself upright. She still encased him in her velvet sheath, the motion making him groan.

She paused, pushed her hair from her eyes, a concerned expression on her face. "Are you—did that hurt?"

He chuckled and pulled her back to his shoulder, then held her in his arms as he returned to his seat. "No, my sweet." He tugged the cloak free from where it was partially pinned beneath them and spread it over her. "That did not hurt at all. In fact, it felt—" He kissed her nose. "—magnificent—" He kissed her cheek. "—and absolutely wondrous."

A shy smile touched her lips, her eyes sparkling gently. "I think I have a slight problem."

He twined a strand of her hair about his finger. He couldn't seem to stop touching her, stroking her, exploring her softness. "What problem is that?"

"I think I might like this too much."

He laughed softly. "There is no 'too much' where this is concerned."

"No?"

"No. Indeed, that is the beauty of the thing; there are few limits."

"Hmmm." She traced a finger along his jaw. "I suppose neither of us won the war."

He smiled, sleepily satisfied and content somehow. "We both won, sweetheart. We both won."

Prudence rested her cheek on his shoulder. Had they both won? She was not sorry they'd made love again—it was destined to happen. She knew that with every beat of her heart. This moment was meant to be. What she wasn't so sure about was what would happen now. Some of the glow left at the thought. "We should get dressed."

He sighed. "Must we?"

"Yes. As much as I love Stevens, if he came out to meet the carriage and found me like this, I don't think I could bear to ever face him again."

"That would be a problem. Very well, my sweet. Let us dress."

They gathered their clothes and began to dress, though Tristan slowed things down considerably by passionately kissing her while she was attempting to put on her stockings.

It was as she was adjusting her dress and smoothing it back into place that the truth dawned on Prudence with the clarity of the ring of a church bell; she loved him.

The thought sucked all of the strength from her legs and made her sink weakly to the seat. Surely not. Perhaps it was just a warm flicker of enjoyment from their passionate embrace. Or a response to being touched after such a long, long time. Surely it was nothing more...

But it was true. She, Prudence Thistlewaite, loved Tristan Llevanth, the dangerously uncivilized earl of Rochester.

She placed a hand over her mouth, more to still her trembling lips than any other reason. There had to be some mistake. Some lapse in judgment or consideration. Some...error.

"Done," Tristan said, his cravat once again about his throat, though only knotted this time. "That is much better. Now we will be able to maintain our dignity when Stevens opens the carriage door."

Prudence managed a faint smile. "That is very important."

"Keeping one's dignity? At times, yes." His teeth flashed in a smile. "And then there are times when it can be quite cumbersome." Without any more warning than that, he reached over and picked up Prudence and set her back in his lap.

"What are you doing?"

"Staying warm." He wrapped the cloak about them both and leaned back in the corner.

Enclosed in his arms, Prudence pressed her cheek against his chest. Once the trustees gave their approval, he would be London-bound where the women of the ton would make it their business to match him with someone of his own station.

And that would not be her. She never again wished to return to the heart-rending emptiness that she now felt was London. Never again did she want to walk the halls of the great houses and hear the stirrings of whispers, the cruel mocking laughter, or worse, the superior stares of those who never really cared.

Tristan brushed a strand of hair from her cheek. "I always knew you were a passionate woman. But until tonight, I didn't really know what passion was."

Prudence tried to smile, snuggling deeper against him as the coach swayed down the road. "It was wonderful."

And it had been. And would be. At least, it would be until the realities of their life intruded. For now, at least, she wouldn't think of that.

She listened to the steady beat of his heart, her cheek resting against the crisp linen of his shirt. His breathing deepened, his body relaxed and she wondered if he slept.

She'd never thought to love again, not after Phillip. But she'd been wrong.

Tristan shifted a little and moved his shoulders, his arm tightening about Prudence as if he wished to hold her closer. The warmth of his embrace soothed her.

Prudence didn't move. She blinked back tears even as she snuggled against him. The trustees would be coming soon and the reason she was in his life would disappear the second they agreed to grant him the title and funds. It would be time for her to go, soon enough.

Meanwhile, she'd take what she could from this moment, savor it as much as she could, and then, let it go, just as she would let him go. Just as she'd had to let Phillip go—

The carriage lurched to one side, sliding them both against the door. Tristan's arms tightened and he took the brunt of the force on his shoulder.

"What is that blasted coachman doing?" Tristan muttered as they swayed wildly to the other side.

The coach lurched again, even more wildly this time.

Tristan was thrown forward. He grasped Prudence to him with one arm and used the other to catch his weight, his bad leg hitting the edge of the seat opposite. He grunted with pain.

The carriage careened side to side as if the hounds of hell were at its rear wheels, the single lantern swaying on the ceiling hook and flickering madly.

A shot rang out, the sound reverberating in the silence of the night.

Through the uncertain light, Tristan cursed. "Damn it all! It's a highwayman!" He pushed Prudence to the floor and reached behind her for a box. Inside were two pistols. He pulled them out and glinted a cold smile. "Do not fear, my love. This is one highwayman who will never again see the light of day."

# Chapter 17

You may discover that your employer's cantankerous nature hides a true love for a good fight. Do not be surprised. Even the gentry find a scrape or two an amusement.

*A Compleat Guide for*
*Being a Most Proper Butler*
by Richard Robert Reeves

Tristan blew out the lamp, sending the inside of the carriage into darkness. He reached farther back beneath the seat, searching until he found another box, this one longer than the other. He opened it and removed a sword.

Prudence grabbed his knee. "Tristan, give me one of the pistols."

Though he could not see her face now, he could imagine the calm bravery in her brown eyes. "Can you shoot it?"

"Of course. My father taught me when I was a child."

He shoved the pistol into her hand just as the carriage pulled to a sliding halt, the horses neighing madly. "Hide it in your skirt and don't—"

The door was wrenched open. Tristan cursed when no figure appeared. With the brightness of the moonlight, it would have been child's play to shoot their attackers. But whoever planned this was too experienced, and no one appeared in the gap.

"Come out with yer nabbers on yer head!"

Bloody hell, the man sounded huge.

Tristan moved to the door, but just as he reached it, Prudence threw her arms about him and pressed her body to his. He hugged her back, resting his cheek briefly against her hair.

His mind whirled with thoughts and emotions. He remembered how black his life had seemed only a few short weeks ago, so black that he would have welcomed tonight's fight with a blood thirst unalleviated by thoughts of a future or desires of the present. Now, things had changed. He would fight this fight, and he would win. If he did not, Prudence's life could well be forfeited.

The thought both invigorated him and frightened him. He had to find a way through this mire. He *had* to. There were no other options.

With one last look at Prudence, Tristan gathered himself and climbed out of the carriage. A huge, hulking man stood to the right of the door, the moonlight gleaming off his blunderbuss.

"My lord!" the coachman said. He stood beside the coach holding a strip of broken reins. John was one of Reeves's men and a magician with horses, though not, apparently, with a blunderbuss. "I am sorry, my lord. I didn't see them until it was too late. I tried to give them the slip and outrun them, but the leathers broke and I couldn't—"

"I am sure you did the best you could." Tristan glanced around, trying to discern the number of their attackers. So far, except for the large man, no one else was in sight.

John leaned forward to say in a low voice, "Both of our outriders escaped, my lord, though one was injured. Surely they will reach the cottage and bring the others to help—"

"'Ere now, enough yabbering! Out with yer goods so we can all go home early this evening. 'Tis cold, ye know. I've no wish to take an ague."

"Of course. That would be most distressing." Tristan whipped out his pistol and pointed it directly at the man's heart.

"I wouldn't do that," came a cultured voice behind Tristan. Something pressed through his coat, a sharp point resting between his shoulder blades.

The coachman gulped loudly. "They's two of them, my lord. I meant to tell ye that, but I didn't have time."

The sword pressed a bit more painfully into Tristan's back. "Drop the pistol."

Tristan grimaced and dropped his pistol to the ground.

"That is right, my good friend," said the man behind him. "A very wise decision, one that will let you live another day."

The big ruffian came forward, waving his pistol. "Empty yer pockets, guv'nor. And make it quick-like. We've two more culls to tend to this evenin'."

Fury built inside Tristan's temples. He emptied his pockets, throwing a watch and some coins onto the ground.

"That's all ye have?" the giant said, disgust in his voice.

"Easy, my friend," came the more cultured gentleman from behind Tristan. "I daresay there's more in the carriage. I thought I heard a woman's voice after they stopped." The thief's voice dripped with amusement. "Perhaps we shall have two prizes this night, instead of one."

Tristan waited no more. He threw himself forward and out of reach of the sword pressed into his back. With every ounce of force he possessed, he lunged toward the large ruffian, knocking the pistol aside and landing squarely on his attacker.

The huge man crashed to the ground with a startled "oof!", his pistol skittering beneath the coach, the metal clacking on the stones that paved the road. Without giving anyone time to do more than blink, Tristan raised his fist and slammed it into the man's jaw.

The man grunted and shook his head, but he did not lose consciousness. Tristan cursed loudly. He had large fists and normally one of his blows would black the lights on any man. But not the behemoth. The huge ruffian lifted meaty hands to grab Tristan about the neck.

Breathing suddenly became a luxury. Tristan clawed at the thick fingers, but they remained in place, tightening and tightening. Spots danced before Tristan's eyes and he struggled for breath. God help him, but was this it? Was he to die on the side of the road in the black of night, in sight of Prudence?

The thought of Prudence gave him new strength. He drew up a knee to hit his attacker in a more exposed area, but the man was too quick, drawing up his own knee to block the blow.

Tristan blinked, struggling to stay conscious. His hands were wrapped around his attacker's wrists, keeping the grip from being truly lethal.

"I vow," said the cultured thief, "you have mud all over your clothing. That is a great pity, for I wished to have that coat for myself."

There was a faint noise and then Prudence materialized out of nowhere.

*"Mon dieu!"* the thief said, stepping forward, his sword drawn.

But Prudence was not interested in swords. She stood with her pistol leveled at the huge man attacking Tristan. In two short steps, she had the muzzle leveled at his temple. "Let him go."

The man froze. The huge oaf shot a surprised glance toward the other thief. "Jack?"

"Easy, my lady," the thief said, all laughter gone from his voice. "Willie, do not move. She looks deadly intent."

"I am," Prudence said. "Release him."

The behemoth slowly loosened his hold on Tristan's neck. Tristan balled up his fist, lifted up and hit the man in the temple with every ounce of strength he possessed. The last blow hadn't had the luxury of being so well placed. This time, the man's eyes rolled back, and then closed as he slumped, unconscious.

Tristan pushed himself to his knees. "Prudence, get back in—"

The tip of a blade flashed to the side of Prudence's throat. Her eyes widened as a black-clothed arm snaked about her waist. The thief regarded Tristan over her head.

Tristan's ears rang. All he could do was look at Prudence.

"Drop the pistol, my dear," the thief said softly into Prudence's ear. "It looks so unwieldy in those lovely hands."

Tristan caught her gaze, his heart pounding in his throat. "Do as he says."

He thought for a moment she would disagree with him, but instead she very, very slowly laid the pistol on the ground. As soon as she stood, the thief kicked the pistol beneath the coach and pulled her flush against him.

Tristan's vision flamed red. The bastard was holding Prudence, his arm insolently around her waist. No one was allowed to do such a thing. *No one.*

"Don't look so glum, man of the ham-like fists," the thief said, amusement in his voice. "And do not move. Or the lady here will never again smell the sweet scent of jasmine that is so prevalent in this part of the country."

Tristan grit his teeth. He was halfway up, his weight on his bad leg. He didn't know how long it would hold. "What if I do move?"

"Then you had best kiss the lovely lady goodbye. Or better yet, watch me do it for you."

"Bastard," Tristan snarled. "If you touch her—"

"You will what?" the man said. His teeth flashed whitely in the moonlight, his half mask hiding only the color and shape of his eyes. "Fortunately for you, I am not a man given to violence against the gentle sex. In fact," the thief used his free hand to lift one of Prudence's curls, "I rather enjoy women. All of them."

Fury bolted through Tristan, hot and cold, furious and pounding. "If you harm her, I will kill you."

"Alas, you cannot. Not only is there your health to consider, but there is that of the lady's. Now, slowly empty your pockets. And this time, do it all of the way. I will be watching. First the right one, then the left one."

Tristan's jaw tightened. The sheer effrontery of the man. Tristan found himself looking at Prudence. She met his gaze steadily before casting her eyes toward the ground.

He frowned. She was trying to tell him something. Tristan slowly removed the remaining funds from his pockets, though in truth, there was lamentably little. Still, it gave him time to try and comprehend Prudence's minute gestures.

She looked at him again, then down at the ground, only this time, she closed her eyes and let her head fall forward ever so slightly.

Tristan nodded. As he emptied the last bit of coinage in his pocket, he managed to reassure himself that the short sword was still tucked in his waistband.

Prudence gave a gasp and then slumped forward, her body a dead weight. The thief tried to catch her, the sword forgotten a moment as he tried to keep his balance. Prudence collapsed on the ground as if unconscious.

Tristan lunged forward, his sword at the ready. The highwayman stepped back, bringing up his rapier in answer. There was a clang as the two weapons met.

"A short sword against a rapier." Tristan smiled, though he did not feel like it at all. "I believe I have the advantage."

"It depends upon your skill, my friend. And mine." The highwayman lunged forward, his eyes shimmering in the holes in his mask as his blade flashed wickedly in the bright moonlight.

Tristan parried the man's moves. The short sword was the stronger weapon, for one solid blow above the hilt line could break the rapier in half. But the rapier was faster, more deadly. One slip of his defense, and his opponent would have him skewered on the tip.

The trick was to keep the man moving, which was not easy, especially as the fall with the behemoth had stiffened Tristan's leg. Every move was painful and growing more so by the second.

The thief made a sudden feint, which Tristan parried, though it carried him back a few steps. To regain ground, Tristan charged, careful to use his good leg for balance. Each step was an agony.

Just one hit, that's all he needed. Yet as he fought, it became apparent that his opponent was something out of the ordinary with the rapier.

Tristan grimly settled in to defend himself, parrying lunges and feints with such rapidity that it was all he could do to keep abreast. His leg ached and cold sweat beaded on his forehead. He could not spin and leap like his opponent. But he could stand his ground and fight like a demon.

During an especially brutal onslaught, the rapier sliced through Tristan's coat, leaving a bloody sting to his arm. From the corner of his eyes, Tristan caught movement. Prudence stepped forward as if to stop the fight. "No!" Tristan snapped, his gaze on his attacker.

Prudence stepped back, and he could hear a low murmur as the coachman caught her arm. "Don't distract him, madam!"

Tristan fought on, his body drenched now with his efforts. The thief's breath rasped harshly in the cold night air. The light from the moon outlined him in full form, the line of his shoulders, the creases of his greatcoat, the dark hair flowing to his shoulders.

"Look, you," Tristan growled as he brought the short sword up to catch the sweep of the rapier once again. "Give, and I will let you breathe another day."

The man chuckled, the sound sending a trigger of alarm through him. That chuckle… Tristan's brows lowered. He knew it, recognized it from somewhere long ago.

He frowned, knocking away the rapier when his opponent once more stepped forward, the tip of the blade slicing across Tristan's chin. "Ow!" He touched his chin, the slick wetness of his own blood dripping onto his hand and down his neck. "You little devil!"

His opponent laughed delightedly. "So I am. Let us finish this once and for all."

A horse sounded down the road. "Ah!" Tristan said, flourishing his sword once more, "my men come. You are a dead man."

The stranger approached with lightning quickness, his blade whipping in and out. "If I die, then so will you."

Tristan twisted away, bringing up his own sword in retaliation. Onward they fought, silent but for their labored breathing and the clank of their weapons.

They were evenly matched and it became more a question of who would tire first. Tristan began to think perhaps he had the advantage over his slighter opponent, but just as he stepped to one side to avoid an especially vicious attack, his good foot slipped on a loose rock. He caught himself with his other leg and pain exploded behind his eyes.

Teeth grinding together, Tristan forced himself to remain standing. No. He could not fall. Prudence needed him. She—

A shot rang out, so close it made Tristan start. The thief paused, his eyes widening behind his mask. He wavered on his feet a long moment, looking down at his shirt.

Prudence stepped forward. She held a smoking pistol, the front of her dress covered in mud where she'd crawled beneath the carriage. From where he stood, Tristan could see her pale face, her pulse beating wildly in her throat.

The thief touched a hand to his shirt. It came away black in the moonlight. *"Mon dieu,"* he said in an oddly detached voice. "I think you have killed me."

With that, he fell to his knees, the rapier dropping into the mud. A weak laugh bubbled from his lips. "Our last run. We thought it would—" He faltered, his eyes sliding closed as he fell to the ground.

Tristan's knee buckled at the exact moment and he

fell beside the man. Prudence was there in a trice. She threw the pistol to one side and reached for him. "Oh Tristan, can you—"

The horse burst into sight. But it wasn't MacGrady or Toggle, or even Stevens who'd come at the call to action. It was Reeves. He dismounted and threw the reins to the coachman, and then ran forward, pausing only to remove the lantern from the side of the carriage.

But instead of coming to Tristan's side, he went to the thief's and knelt. He pressed his fingers to the man's throat. "He's still breathing. Thank the lord!"

Tristan allowed Prudence to help him to his feet, her warm hands holding him in place. He hugged her to him, enveloping her completely. Oh God, to have almost lost her. He didn't dare think what might have happened if—

The thief moaned softly. Reeves undid the muffler around his neck and pressed it to the man's wounds. "He will live," the butler said, relief evident in his quiet voice. "It's not a deep wound, but it must be cleaned."

"I am not cleaning the wounds of a man who tried to kill us all."

Reeves sent Tristan a sharp look. "He didn't try to kill you, just wound you."

"He seemed in dead earnest," Prudence offered.

"Aye," Tristan said with a sarcastic note in his voice. "It certainly *felt* as if he was trying to kill me."

Reeves tied his muffler into place about the man's side. "He has never killed anyone. Not once in his entire career as a highwayman, and there were plenty of opportunities."

The thief stirred, then lifted a hand to his head. "What the hell happened?"

Reeves bent over him. "You were wounded. Lie still and I will take you to the cottage."

"*My* cottage?" Tristan said, scowling. What the hell was wrong with Reeves? "Surely not—"

The thief pushed himself up on one elbow, pressing a hand to his side. "Reeves?"

From where she stood beneath Tristan's arm, Prudence gave a start. Her wide brown eyes found his. "He knows Reeves?"

Tristan frowned at the thief. "How do you know Reeves?"

Reeves finished his ministrations and stood, picking up his lamp. "That is quite simple, my lord. I visited him last week."

"You visited a highwayman? What for—" Tristan looked at the highwayman. "*No.* It...it cannot be."

The man managed a weak smile, his mouth barely visible beneath the edge of his mask.

Tristan reached down, wincing when his leg protested, and slowly removed his opponent's mask.

Reeves lifted the lamp. Light spilled over the thief's face. Dark hair spilled over his brow; his eyes shimmered a hard green. "I cannot believe it," Tristan said. "Christian?"

# Chapter 18

To properly starch a cravat, place the linen smooth side down on a marble-top table. Heat is, of course, the crucial element. Without it, all would be a damp, wrinkled mess.

*A Compleat Guide for*
*Being a Most Proper Butler*
by Richard Robert Reeves

Reeves took Prudence's arm and led her to one side. "This is his lordship's long lost brother."

Prudence could only stare in wonder. "He is…he was a highwayman."

"Yes, a dangerous career, one we can only hope he will abandon."

Prudence found herself nodding absently. She couldn't seem to get her mind wrapped about that fact. And neither, from the look on his face, could Tristan.

Quietly, Prudence slipped aside, watching as the two brothers regarded each other, amazement and joy warring for expression. For an odd moment, she felt alone, outside.

It was where she belonged, she decided. This was not her home, not her family. Her family was her mother, who would be waiting to hear how the evening went.

Prudence wasn't sure what she would say, but none of it had to do with what had occurred in the carriage.

The memory of that burned in her mind. The passion she'd felt, the love that even now warmed her in the chill evening—it was all real.

But that did not make it possible.

No, she would end this relationship gracefully. Easily. He need never know her feelings, especially as he did not share them.

_Or did he?_ Her heart leaped at the thought. Was it possible Tristan cared for her? He had been very attentive lately and his reaction to the men at the dinner party had been quite odd, though she'd originally attributed that to his pride. But perhaps...perhaps it was something more.

But did that really resolve the issue? Did it change the fact that he was who he was? She tried to imagine him more settled. Yet all she could remember was his expression when he stared out at the sea, the bitter, intense longing.

What future could their relationship have if Tristan's main wish was to leave, to sail the seas...away from her? She knew he could not do so because of his injuries. But that did not alter the fact that his heart was already somewhere else. She would not accept being second place in his life. If being with Phillip had taught her one thing, it was that a relationship only worked if both people involved were committed. To each other *and* their relationship.

She pulled her cloak tighter, watching his face in the light of the lantern. A cut marred his chin and his face was flushed from the cold and the fight.

He looked incredibly dear in that moment and it made Prudence's heart ache.

Christian struggled to his feet, swaying slightly as he did so. Tristan was there instantly, his strong arm about his brother's shoulders. It suddenly dawned on her that she had *shot* Tristan's brother.

She pressed a shaking hand to her forehead. "Tristan, I did not mean to shoot your brother! I mean, I did, but had I known who he was—"

"Nonsense," Christian said, flashing her a smile. "You were protecting Tristan. I am glad to see that he fell into such good hands."

Prudence's cheeks heated. "You are mistaken. Your brother and I are not—"

"Madam?" Reeves took her arm. "Do not feel badly about shooting Master Christian. The bullet barely grazed him."

"But... I shot him dead on."

Tristan grinned, lifting something in his hand. "You hit him squarely in the pocket watch."

Prudence stared at the mangled watch in Tristan's palm.

Christian laughed, then winced. "I shall be bloodied and bruised, but I will not die. Besides, you did nothing you should not have. Indeed, I salute you for your bravery, madam."

He coughed a bit, groaning as he did so. Tristan

called for John the coachman to come and assist him in getting his brother on his horse.

Prudence watched them, feeling more miserable by the moment.

"Madam?"

She looked up at Reeves. "Yes?"

"Shall I escort you home? His lordship may be a while. Master Christian wishes to return to his home and not the cottage."

"Yes. Thank you. That would be very nice."

Tristan returned to them, wincing with each limping step. "Prudence, I want to talk to you."

Her heart tight, she managed a smile. "You need to be with your brother now. I will see you tomorrow."

Tristan took her hand and pulled her close, oblivious to Reeves's presence. "Do you promise?"

Prudence gently disentangled her hand. "Of course."

He looked at her a moment, but nodded. "Reeves, please see Mrs. Thistlewaite home. Take the carriage; I shall take your horse."

"Yes, my lord."

Smiling, Tristan cupped Prudence's cheek with a warm hand. "We will talk tomorrow."

John the coachman asked a question from where he held Christian's horse; something about the other high-wayman. Tristan gave Prudence one last smile, then he was gone, limping off to help John awaken the huge thief.

"Are you ready, madam?"

She straightened. "Yes, I am." She would go home to Mother and they'd work on their plan to start a school. Mother should hear from her friend in Scotland any day now, and perhaps that would get their endeavors off to a good start.

Yes. That was what she should be thinking about and not the earl next door. She was silent in the carriage on the ride home, wrapped in her own thoughts. Reeves made no effort to engage her attention, though he gave her a long look when he finally escorted her to the door.

Mother was waiting. Prudence brushed off the barrage of questions and hurried to her room, closing the door with a heartfelt sigh. Now, inside the silence of her bedchamber, Prudence threw herself on her bed and cried.

Tristan looked over his mug of ale at his brother. They'd been drinking since the doctor had left.

It had been a bit awkward, calling the doctor to attend his brother after the incident at the party, but it had to be done. Tristan was not about to lose his brother after finally finding him.

The doctor refused to look at Tristan, which was fine with everyone concerned. Still, though Tristan despised the man for flirting with Prudence, he was glad the competent physician took the time to make certain Christian was fine.

Tristan stared into his mug of ale. Prudence had looked at him rather oddly when she'd left. Rather sad, as if...he frowned. *As if she meant to say goodbye.*

He put the tankard back on the table.

"Tristan?"

He looked up to find Christian regarding him over the rim of his own drink.

Christian set down his own mug. "You've developed a dour disposition over the years."

"You just found me at an ill time."

Christian's mouth flickered into a smile. "Not as ill as it was for me."

Tristan managed a grin. "Perhaps not." He lifted his mug. "I propose a toast."

"To what?"

"To the women in our lives."

"There is not enough ale in this tavern for such an endeavor."

Tristan managed a painful smile. There had been women before Prudence. He just could not remember any of them. Not a one. His ale tasted suddenly bitter and he set it aside. "All these years and you are still a damn fool."

Christian grinned, a wicked flicker of humor that made Tristan's heart tighten.

Damn, but he had missed his brother. All the agony of those painful days and nights following their separation seemed far, far away.

Of course, there were some differences. This Christian was harder, sharper, with an edge beneath a seemingly charming veneer. Tristan could not forget the black-cloaked figure that had lunged across the road at him, the one who had held Prudence at sword point.

That still rankled. "You are fortunate you did not hurt anyone tonight."

Christian didn't pretend to misunderstand him. "You are speaking of the lady."

"Yes."

"A lovely woman. Is she yours?"

Tristan wished he could answer that. He grabbed the mug and took a drink.

"Ah," Christian said.

"What do you mean by that?" Tristan snapped.

"Nothing. I only meant...she is lovely. And if she lives nearby—"

"She is a widow." Tristan wasn't sure why he'd added that, but it seemed important to tell Christian.

"She looked far too young to be a widow."

"The light was poor. She is older than she looks."

"Those are the best kind," Christian said with a considering nod, not seeming to notice Tristan's rising ire. "Not too young and a widow. They have enough experience to have lost that shy demeanor I find so annoying. And yet, if they are young enough, they still retain an attractiveness that can be just as enthralling."

"We should discuss something else."

"Why?"

"Because I don't wish to discuss her with you."

"Hm," Christian said, his lips pursed thoughtfully. "Do you find her interesting?"

"She annoys the hell out of me." That, at least, was truthful. When she wasn't making him lust after her in a most distracting fashion, she was indeed inciting his ire. It was one of her greatest skills. "I went with her to a dinner party this evening. We were on our way back when you found us."

"How delightful. Did they have dancing? I know the quadrille."

"How would you know that?"

Christian smiled slyly, reminding Tristan of a million other sly smiles covering everything from putting frogs in their tutor's bed to suggesting that they slip away from their mother's watchful eye to play with the village boys.

But that had been far away and long ago. Now Tristan wondered who his brother really was. "There were moments this evening I thought you were determined to kill me."

Christian's gaze met his steadily. "I am not a murderer."

"So Reeves would have me believe."

"I have not killed anyone...yet." A secret smile touched Christian's face. "But there will come a day. I am certain of it."

Tristan shrugged, moving his leg a bit to one side so that the back of the chair did not press against it. "I cannot make that claim. I've fought many sea battles and killed more men than I can count."

Christian's green eyes darkened. "Does it bother you?"

"A little. Some were fighting for their country, as was I. Those were more difficult."

"I can imagine." Christian raised his hand to garner the attention of the serving maid to his empty tankard, wincing as he did so.

Tristan frowned. "You should be in bed."

"Nonsense. A mere flesh wound."

"It was enough to knock you off of your feet." Just knowing Prudence had been enough to knock Tristan off of his. Tristan raked a hand through his hair, wondering why he felt so hollow, so empty.

Christian's eyes glowed with admiration. "You wield a sharp sword, my brother. It is not often I am bested."

"I wasn't besting anyone. I was struggling to outlast you and failing. Thank goodness Prudence found that pistol—why in the hell are you laughing?"

"Prudence? The lady's name is Prudence?"

"Indeed it is."

"That is amusing."

It was indeed. "A less prudent woman I have yet to know."

"She charged in not once, but twice, all in an effort to save you. And succeeded, too." Christian eyed his brother a moment. "She seemed to think you quite worthwhile. But then, so do I. Tristan…I am glad to see you."

The faintest hint of thickness touched Christian's voice.

Tristan reached across the table and grasped Christian's arm. "I never forgot you. Never. When I had to push you from that window—" He couldn't finish.

Christian squeezed his brother's arm so hard it hurt them both. Then, grinning sheepishly, he released Tristan and wiped his eyes with his sleeve. "Sand in my eyes," he mumbled.

"Yes. Me, too." Tristan cleared his throat. "Did you injure yourself when I pushed you? I always worried about that."

"I thought I'd broken my arm, but it was just bruised. Tris, our good fortune is amazing. The late earl was a horrible father, but we have finally gained something from the connection."

"I wonder." Tristan slid his mug to the center of the

table. "Did you know I was at Trafalgar with Nelson? It's where I injured my leg."

"So Reeves told me."

"After the war, I was ordered to London to meet the king. Everyone in society wanted to meet me, as Nelson... Christian, he died in my arms."

"I didn't know that. I am sorry."

"Yes. It was difficult. When I arrived in London, I was treated like a... like a..."

"A war hero?"

"No. Like a curiosity. They wanted to hear about Nelson's death, but not about the man himself." Disgust sat heavy on Tristan's tongue. "They wanted tidbits of gore, hints of weakness, it was as if they wished to pick him to death even though he'd already died." He met Christian's gaze. "I never wish to go back. The title will mean nothing to me here. But the funds... That is another story. I need them to help my men."

"You will get the funds."

"I hope so, though if what Reeves has told me is true, the trustees are the most shallow, most self-important fops to walk the earth."

"So? Show them a bit of silk and they will leave you be."

"Silk is not so easy for me," Tristan said grumpily. He eyed his brother for a moment. "You always did know how to dress, even as a child."

"Both Mother and I liked pretty things." Christian sighed. "I still dream of her, you know."

"So do I."

They were silent a moment. Christian leaned back in his chair, careful not to put any pressure on his side. A smile touched his mouth. "You know, I still cannot believe you are here."

"Nor I."

They sat a moment in silence, grinning foolishly at each other.

"Christian, I intend on using the funds for my men. What will you do with your portion?"

All levity left Christian's face and he said in a quiet tone, "I will do the one thing I've wished to do since I was ten; find who was responsible for Mother's imprisonment." He paused, his green eyes almost luminous in the smoky tavern. "Tristan, I am close to discovering who betrayed Mother."

Tristan put down his tankard. "Yes?"

"I must go to London. The answers are there." Christian sighed. "I suppose Father did help us."

"Twenty years too late."

Christian caught the serving wench's eye and winked. "More ale, love."

She winked back and sashayed off, Christian watching her go with appreciation.

"A skirt chaser, eh?"

Christian pretended to be hurt. "I am not a 'skirt chaser.'"

"No?"

"No. I am, however, a 'skirt *catcher.*'"

Tristan shook his head. "You were never shy."

"And you were never slow. I've loved women from the time I could appreciate them. The fascination never wanes."

"It appears you have inherited some tendencies from our father after all."

Christian's smile faded. "Never say that again."

Tristan grinned. "Make me."

Christian's eyes narrowed even as he smiled in delight. "Don't tempt me."

It was an old game, one they'd played countless times before, a right of passage for most males, Tristan supposed. Suddenly, his heart felt full. Had it not been for the nagging worry over Prudence's farewell look, he would have been an incredibly happy man.

Christian tilted his head to one side. "Do you sail at all?"

"I cannot keep my balance. A captain who cannot keep his feet when the ship rolls is as useful as an oyster with a cart."

"I like to eat oysters. I get them from the street vendors in London all of the time."

"Wonderful. I am reduced to street vendors' fare."

Christian flashed a white smile. "It's your job to develop into an ogre and my job to remind you that you are all too human."

"Thank you. I don't know how I lived without you all these years."

"Poorly, from the sound of it."

Tristan nodded, though he wondered if perhaps Christian was right. Tristan had been well fed. His house was snug and warm. He'd had the companionship of his men. And when the urge had demanded it, he'd been welcomed by the tavern wenches in town.

Had he more coin to assist the lads, he'd have had a perfect life. Except for one thing... Prudence.

All throughout his home now, there were little touches of Prudence here and there; the chair remained ridiculously close to the settee, the breakfast table was now a permanent fixture in his library, and Stevens had hung a special hook in the front closet for her cloak. Small things and yet they gave the place a sense of something. Of home, perhaps.

His heart tightened. He'd lived in many places. Been to many countries. And lain with many women. But none had the ability to make him feel that one thing—the warmth of home. He set his jaw. He'd had a home once. And it had been ripped from him when his mother had been arrested. The pain of it haunted him still. He did not need another "home." He needed—

Hell, he didn't know what he needed any more. At one time, he'd have sworn that being able to sail once more would have completed him. Now...now he was not so sure. His entire life felt empty, useless even. Damn it. What was wrong with him? Could it be...was it Prudence? Was the mere thought of never seeing her again making him feel so wretched?

A strange hollowness filled his chest, stretched his heart. She'd snuck into his life and changed it without him even realizing what had happened.

"Tristan?"

He looked up.

His brother had pulled his chair closer and now sat facing him. "Tristan, what ails you? You keep fading away as if something is on your mind."

"Prudence." The word hung between them.

Christian sighed. "You are smitten."

"I am not. I just... I care for her."

"You are smitten."

"Damn it—"

"I can see the signs. You, my dearest brother, are in deep smit. Very deep smit, indeed."

Tristan raked a hand through his hair. "I care for her, but—"

Christian leaned forward and suddenly, the merriment was lost from his eyes. "There are no buts when love is involved. Tristan, if you love her, you must do something about it." He slowly stood, rubbing his chest and wincing as he did so. "Life is never certain. If you want the lady, then make her yours. Otherwise..." Christian shrugged. "She will leave and you will be left alone. Again."

The surety of the words cut Tristan like a knife. But they also built his resolve. Christian was right; there was no reason to tarry. Tomorrow he would call on Prudence and set all of this straight. He grabbed his cane and hefted himself to his feet. "Thank you, Christian. I will do as you say."

It was wonderful to have his brother back in his life. Now, all he needed to do was convince Prudence that she belonged there, as well.

# Chapter 19

In an emergency, no proper butler will turn from a course of action that might, under normal circumstances, be repugnant to a man of breeding and class. Extreme instances call for extreme measures.

*A Compleat Guide for*
*Being a Most Proper Butler*
by Richard Robert Reeves

$\mathcal{P}$rudence blinked. "I beg your pardon. What did you say?"

Mrs. Fieldings sniffed. "I said 'tis the captain—or the earl—or whatever he is. He's here. In the sittin' room."

"But—but—" Prudence sat in her own bedchamber, before the mirror, a brush in one hand. She looked down at her nightrail. "He's here *now?*"

Mrs. Fieldings crossed her arms. "The cat as chases the yarn best beware the hidden tangles."

"I don't care about cats and tangles. It's only seven thirty in the morning!" Prudence dropped the brush and hurried to twist her hair into a neat knot at the back of her head. With the housekeeper's help, Prudence was soon dressed and running down the stairs.

What could he want? Perhaps...a faint leap of hope lifted her heart. Perhaps he came to tell her that he loved her.

Her heart thundered at the barely whispered thought. *What if he did?* Would that mean that he'd given up his dream of going back to sea, of living a free and unfettered life? Could he be happy with such a decision?

Morning light streamed through the windows as Prudence opened the door to the sitting room.

Tristan turned from where he stood beside the fireplace, staring down into the flickering flames. He was dressed in one of the new coats Reeves had ordered for him, his hair neatly tied back, his riding boots so shiny they gleamed like a mirror.

He looked so handsome that Prudence's step faltered ever so slightly, though she quickly hid it under a bright greeting. "Good morning, my lord. I trust you are feeling no ill effects from last night's excitement?"

His gaze darkened on seeing her. "Prudence."

She dipped a curtsy. "Good morning," she repeated in her firmest tone, praying he would follow her lead and make this easier for both of them. Prudence took a chair by the fire and gestured to the opposite one. "Pray have a seat."

He paused, his brows lowered as he looked at her.

"Please," she repeated, a faint rush of desperation

tinting her voice. She did not want to cry—*would not* cry.

Tristan took the seat, setting his cane to one side, his gaze never wavering. He appeared tired this morning, too. Only that and the cut on his chin proved last night's events.

She touched her own chin. "You might have a scar there."

"Scars are nothing new."

Prudence nodded. "How is your arm?"

"Fine, fine. Prudence, we must—"

"And your brother?"

Christian's expression softened. "I spent over an hour with him last night. I had missed him."

A million emotions were hidden behind those words. Prudence's throat tightened. "I am glad you found him."

"Thank you. But that is not what I came to speak to you about. Last night, we did not have the time to discuss what happened between us. Prudence, I have made a decision. We must marry."

Prudence didn't think she was breathing. It certainly felt as if her heart had frozen in place. *"Must?"*

He straightened his shoulders as if the weight of the world pressed them down. "It is only right."

She looked at him. There was nothing light or happy in his expression, just the grim determination of a man doing his duty.

Her heart sank. Duty. He merely felt guilty for—"No."

Tristan scowled. "No?"

"No." It was a pity love did not solve all problems.

Oh, it made them bearable, but only if both people loved equally.

"Damn it, why not?"

"I was married once. Phillip and I had love, respect, common interests, an understanding of each other—Tristan, we have none of those."

His brows lowered. "We enjoy being together and—"

"We have passion and nothing more. That is not enough." She drew a shaky breath and stood. He did the same, leaning on his cane, his brows low.

"It's enough for me," he said, his voice low. "I never before had any wish to marry. But now, I can think of no reason not to. Surely that is enough."

"Is that all you can say?"

Tristan's jaw worked. "I find your company entertaining."

How lovely. She thought she would explode from her feelings and he thought she was "entertaining." Tears welled in her eyes. "Tristan, you should know something. Two of the trustees were harmed by Phillip's investments. When I left London, it was under a cloud of scandal. Phillip had already died, but the furor over the financial losses was still raging. Tristan, if those two members of the board—Lords Ware and Southerland—see us together, they will not be happy. They will demand you never see me again."

She waited but after a moment, Tristan just shrugged. "We won't tell them then. I shall say you've been my tutor. Once the funds are mine, I may do as I wish. It would serve them well if I did such a thing."

She stiffened, her gaze meeting his. "I will not hide from those men. Not now, not ever."

"I wasn't suggesting you hide, just—" He rubbed a hand over his face as if struggling with the words.

Prudence didn't know what to say. It was worse than she thought. He wished to keep their relationship a secret and then, when it no longer mattered, parade it forth like a beacon of rebellion. "I am flattered," she managed to snap, unable to disguise the hurt.

His brow lowered, puzzlement on his face. "Prudence, I truly mean this."

"I don't believe that. Tristan Llevanth, I will not marry you. Not today. Not tomorrow. Not ever."

He blinked. "What?"

"You heard me. I want no part of such a farce. Now, if you don't mind, I have things to do. Please do not return. We have nothing more to say to each other." Heart thudding sickly, she turned on her heel and left, shutting the door behind her. As soon as the latch clicked, she picked up her skirts and ran up the stairs for her room, her feet flying. The tears began before she reached her room, but at least she was spared the embarrassment of weeping before the man she loved.

"Hmm," Reeves said thoughtfully. He pursed his lips for a long moment, then shook his head. "I can think of no answer, my lord. I would suggest you forget about Mrs. Thistlewaite."

Tristan blinked. "Forget about her?"

"Yes, my lord. It sounds as though Mrs. Thistlewaite does not care for you as you thought." Reeves waved a hand. "I would forget about her and find another. With the earldom secured and the fortune in your pocket, you should have your pick of any woman around. In fact, you can have your pick of any woman in the country, I daresay." Reeves's blue gaze met Tristan's. "Why settle for the widow? You can do far, far better."

Tristan grit his teeth. "I do not wish for another."

Reeves shrugged, then picked up the tray. "I would suggest you think it through a day or two and then decide. There really is no hurry, for as you told Mrs. Thistlewaite, you cannot claim her until after the trustees leave, anyway. Perhaps the doctor will be available to console her in the meantime." The butler turned toward the door.

"Reeves."

"Yes, my lord."

"I did not mean to insult Prudence when I suggested we not tell the trustees."

"No, my lord. I am certain you did not. But I cannot but think the words must have been rather...hurtful."

Tristan rubbed his forehead. "I shall apologize to her. I—I wish her to be in my life."

"May I ask why, my lord?"

Why? Because he could not imagine life without her? Because it seemed that his happiness was completely bound up in hers? Somehow the words would not come. Tristan looked over at the untouched breakfast table. "I do not like taking breakfast alone."

Reeves followed Tristan's gaze. "Indeed, my lord. It is quite unpleasant, having breakfast alone. It is a dilemma, my lord."

"Damn it, I know that!"

"Yes, my lord. If you see Mrs. Thistlewaite and declare yourself to her now, then you risk losing the fortune. If you wait until after the trustees leave, then you risk making it seem as if you didn't really care for her so much as you cared for the funds."

"Exactly."

"My lord?"

"Yes?"

"I am quite certain you will think of something." The butler turned, and let himself out of the door.

"Bloody hell!" Tristan muttered. "What good is having a butler if they don't have better answers than that?"

Tristan leaned back, staring into the fire, feeling completely lost and alone. Good God, he'd made such a muddle of it all. What was he to do now?

The clock ticked loudly in the library. Tristan didn't notice. The breakfast table had been removed and a luncheon tray had arrived, followed several hours later by a dinner tray. Tristan had not touched either, instead preferring liquid sustenance in the form of his brandy.

Drinking would not solve his problems. He knew that. But it dulled his pain so he could think more clearly. He stood, stretching a bit and then fumbling for his cane. God, but he was stiff and sore from his adventure last night.

Wincing, he took his glass to the sideboard, grumbling when he found the brandy decanter empty. "Blast it all! *Stevens!*"

There was no answer.

Tristan cursed loudly, then went to the door and out into the hallway. *"Damn you, Stevens! Where are you?"*

Still no answer.

*"Reeves!"* Tristan bellowed.

Almost immediately a measured tread could be heard approaching. Reeves entered the hallway, pausing when he saw Tristan. "My lord?"

"I need more brandy, and Stevens is nowhere to be found."

"He is in the kitchen with some of the men, fixing one of the table legs for the chef." Reeves came forward and took the decanter. "Will there be anything else, my lord?"

Yes. The starched-up butler could fetch him Prudence. That would be nice. But it was also an impossibility. Tristan knew how stubborn Prudence was. If there was one thing a day and evening of deep thought had made him realize, it was that it would take a significant act to win her attention now that he had made such a mess of things. "Just fetch the damn brandy."

"Yes, my lord." Reeves bowed with dignity, then turned and walked down the hallway.

Tristan watched the butler leave, a faint feeling of guilt plaguing him. He was in a foul mood and he knew it. There had to be something he could do to prove himself to Prudence. He sighed and turned back to the library. He entered the room, coming to a halt within two steps. There, sitting by the fire, booted feet stretched out to the flames, was Christian.

He caught Tristan's shocked expression and grinned. "Good evening, brother."

Tristan looked at the terrace doors. "How in the hell did you get in here? Those doors were locked."

"And I opened them."

"How?"

Christian waved a hand. "I cannot tell you. It would break my oath to the brotherhood of highwaymen."

Tristan limped to a chair near Christian. "A brotherhood of thieves. Lovely." He sat heavily. "I would offer you some brandy, but I am out at the moment."

Christian reached into his pocket and took out a flask. He reached over and took Tristan's glass from a small table, unscrewed the top of the flask, and poured a generous amount into the cup. "Here. I daresay this is better than what you have, anyway."

Tristan took a sip. The brandy was rich and smoky. "Where did you get this?"

"A benefit from being in the brotherhood," Christian said, taking a long pull of the flask, before sighing with satisfaction. "There. 'Tis damnably cold, you know."

"Yes," Tristan answered, his mind mulling over his situation with Prudence once again.

Silence flooded the room for a short time.

Finally, Christian sighed. "As cozy as this is I must ask why you sent for me?"

"I didn't."

"But I received a missive. It said you needed me."

Tristan scowled. "Reeves and his damn interfering."

Christian's brows rose. "So you don't need me?"

"I can handle my own problems."

"Hm." Christian's gaze flickered over Tristan's rather mussed clothing. "What problems are we talking about?"

"Prudence."

"Ah." Christian reached over and took Tristan's empty glass. "I fear I can be of little help there. But I can, at least, share your misery." He poured some more brandy into the glass and handed it back to Tristan. "What happened?"

"I made a mull of it. I asked her to marry me."

"Good God! I didn't know it was so serious."

"Well, it is. Or so I thought. But when I asked her to marry me, she refused."

"Did she tell you why she said no?"

"I don't think so."

"She didn't say a word? Not a hint? Nothing at all?" Tristan's face heated. "No. I told her I wished to marry her, but not until the trustees had left."

Christian picked up the flask and replaced the lid.

"What are you doing?"

"I do not share my brandy with fools."

"She agreed with me! She said herself that the trustees would not approve of the marriage. Her husband died amid some scandal and she left London in a hotbed of rumor. Some of the trustees were involved and they were not kind to her."

" 'Kind' is not a word I'd apply to Father's friends. What did you reply to all of this?"

"That we didn't have to tell the trustees anything. We could keep it secret."

"Good God!" Christian put the flask on the floor on the far side, away from Tristan. "I will never bring you another dram for the rest of your life."

"Then don't!" Tristan snarled.

"Did you at least mention to her that you loved her? That you could not live another day without her? That the stars ride in her eyes, and the silky wind is blessed by the tumble of her hair?"

Tristan scowled. "That is nonsense."

"It is poetry," Christian said smugly. "Women love it."

"I didn't get the chance to say much of anything to Prudence, though if I had said that, she would have laughed in my face and then thrown me out, rather than simply thrown me out."

Christian shook his head sadly. "You, my own brother! To be so foolish in the ways of women."

"I don't know why my actions were so horrid! She knows I must care for her to ask to marry her. Why else would I do it?"

"Tristan, put yourself in her slippers a moment. Here comes a man to ask you to marry him. But instead of telling you he loves you, he explains that while he wishes to marry you, he cannot just yet because he fears retribution from the very men who laughed her out of London. Therefore, if she doesn't mind, he'll just keep her in the closet until the trustees leave. Then, once there is no price to pay, no fury to face, he will bring her out, dust her off, and plan a marriage."

Tristan sighed. "You make it sound much worse than it was."

Christian raised his brows.

Tristan gulped his brandy. "I didn't mean it to sound so poorly. I just thought I could win the fortune and still have Prudence. She seems to think I will regret marrying her. I won't of course, but she thinks it's so."

"That's because you didn't tell her you loved her, you ass." Christian tilted his head to one side, regarding his brother through narrowed eyes. "You *do* love her, don't you?" he asked quietly.

"Yes." The word rushed through Tristan's lips as if

they'd been just waiting for such a question. An odd pressure tightened his chest. "I love her madly. I once thought I would never again find happiness without the sea. But now that I've known Prudence...Christian, something has changed. I will always miss not being able to sail, but if I had the sea and not Prudence, it would not satisfy me. But if I had Prudence, but not the sea..." Tristan shrugged. "I would be the happiest man alive."

"Why did you not tell her that?"

"Because I didn't think it would matter. I thought I would marry her and then let her know how I felt."

Christian sighed. "Men!"

"Hold it right there. You are a man."

"Yes, but I am exceptional. Unlike you, who have spent your entire life at sea with a group of male companions, I have surrounded myself with females. It has opened my eyes to many things."

Tristan scowled. "I worry about you sometimes."

"You are lucky I am here. We must put our minds together and find a way out of this fix."

"I wish we could. Christian, if I declare myself to her now, I will lose the funds for the men. If I don't, she won't ever truly believe I care more for her than the money, which I do. Without her, I don't want the funds."

"This is a quandary then." Christian frowned. "First things first. You must see her and apologize."

"I already tried."

"Do it again. And again. And again. Eventually she will see you."

"Only to tell me nay. She is not the type of woman to forgive lightly. I vow but I did not mean to insult her, though...I can see where it did sound ill. Horrid, even."

Christian nodded. "Even as a child, you were never very good at expressing yourself."

Tristan gave his brother a flat stare. "Thank you."

Christian waved a hand. "It's what I'm here for. In my life, women are quite different from your Prudence. The bad ones won't leave and the good ones won't stay. Usually because of that...what is it called? Ah yes. The need for 'steady employment.' Really! Don't they know I am the son of an earl? Steady employment, indeed."

Tristan smiled absently. "If you do not enjoy being a viscount, you could always try your hand at life on the stage. You've always been—" A distant thought itched. He sat a little straighter. Was there a way to *show* Prudence how much he loved her? "I wonder..."

"What?" Christian asked absently, retrieving his flask and taking a sip.

Tristan's mind rang with sudden clarity. A thought began to form, a plan of such scope—could he?

He put down his glass. He needed to think clearly. Very clearly, if this was to work. Slowly, he looked over at his brother. "Christian?" The first real smile of the evening touched his lips. "I need your help. I know just what must be done."

Christian paused, the flask halfway to his lips. "Do as you will, oh Captain Brother. I am yours to command.

Just know this: If your plan does not work, I claim the right to pursue the lovely widow on my own."

Tristan's smile faded. "Not while I'm alive. Now stop your posturing, you scurvy cod. We've work to do."

# Chapter 20

I have often heard it said that "man does not live by bread alone." I find myself in full agreement. After all, what is bread without a little wine?

*A Compleat Guide for*
*Being a Most Proper Butler*
by Richard Robert Reeves

$\mathcal{P}$rudence threw back the covers and kicked impatiently at the sheets. She hadn't spoken to Tristan in an entire week. Though he came every day and asked to speak to her, she refused to see him. Which was a very good thing, she told herself repeatedly, as it allowed her time to pace obsessively and mull Tristan's last words over and over and over.

When she was not pacing, she was either avoiding Mother's regretful looks and deep sighs, or lying in bed, pretending to sleep. Like now.

"They will consign me to bedlam if I don't stop this," she told the chilly air in her bedchamber.

Sighing, she rose and wrapped a shawl about her shoulders, slid her feet back into her shoes, and walked aimlessly to the window. It was actually frightfully early to be in bed. But four hours of listening to Mother wonder aloud yet again why the earl had called today and why her daughter would not receive him had proven too much for Prudence to bear.

Sleep was, of course, an impossibility. And not just because of the early hour. She didn't think she'd slept more than two hours at a time since the last time she'd seen Tristan.

She leaned against the window frame and pulled the curtain open, then looked out, resting her elbows on the sill. The sun had already set on the horizon, the tree branches etched in dim relief against the moon-flooded sky.

Restless, she hugged herself, pressing her forehead to the glass and stared sightlessly out the window.

How was Tristan? The trustees were to have visited today. Prudence hoped he'd remembered his manners, how to address each of the trustees, how to greet them in his library—all the things that would mark him as a gentleman in the trustees' rather shallow books.

Of course, they would never see the real Tristan, the one who cared about his men, though he barked at them constantly. The one whose eyes darkened with pain when he spoke of his mother. The one who'd looked at her with so much tenderness...

She moved restlessly. What was she doing, thinking of Tristan? There was no future in it, she told herself miserably. He'd asked her to marry him out of a sense of duty and nothing else. Worse, if the trustees discovered their connection, they could well cut off his income.

She sighed, huddling beneath her shawl. She hadn't lit any lamps, and all about her was black and still, silent except for the tick of the ormolu clock that rested on the mantel.

The thin sliver of moonlight illuminated the garden below, and she rested her head against the window frame, absently noting the sway of the plants in the night breeze. As she watched, the gate slowly opened...

She blinked. But it was still there, a solitary figure in a cloak backing through the gate, pulling...something tethered on a rope. She leaned forward, squinting against the dark and...she gasped. Tied to the end of the rope was *a sheep*!

Prudence whirled and grabbed her morning gown from the wardrobe. She changed and ran from her room, passing Mrs. Fieldings on the stairs.

"Where are ye goin'?" the housekeeper asked, her shriveled face pulled into a look of suspicion.

"Someone is in the garden!"

The housekeeper followed. "I just brushed yer cloak. 'Tis on the peg by the front door."

Prudence reached the bottom stair. "I don't need a cloak. I am going to find out once and for all who is putting that sheep into our garden!"

"'Tis a wise man as heeds the hiss of the snake."

"Yes, well, this snake is wearing a cloak."

Mrs. Fieldings sniffed. "No thief I know would wear a cloak."

Prudence stopped by the front door and grabbed her cloak, tossing her shawl to a side table. "Not only was the snake wearing a cloak, but it appeared to be trimmed."

That gave Mrs. Fieldings pause. She eyed Prudence warily. "Did ye say it was trimmed? How?"

"I only saw it from the upper window for a few seconds, but it looked as if there was trim around the hood—" Prudence's gaze locked onto the hooks by the door. Mother's cloak was gone. The red one. The one trimmed in ermine.

Prudence turned to look at Mrs. Fieldings, who had turned a curious shade of red. "Do you know anything about this?"

The housekeeper crossed her arms over her gaunt breast. "A prudent man keeps his knowledge under lock and key, least it fall to the wayside in disarray."

Homilies. Prudence didn't have time for homilies. "I suppose I shall just have to find out for myself." She reached for the doorknob, but Mrs. Fieldings was quicker.

The housekeeper planted herself against the door, arms crossed, chin in the air. "Now, Madam. Better to control your temper than let fly an arrow of harm."

"Move."

"The heart of the angry shall—"

"Mrs. Fieldings, do you see my fist? The one inside my glove?"

The woman's eyes widened. "Are you threatening me?"

Prudence leaned forward. "Yes."

That seemed to flummox the housekeeper completely. While she was busy searching for a proper homily, Prudence reached past the woman and pulled the door open. The panel hit Mrs. Fieldings soundly in the rump, causing her to gasp and move quickly out of the way. "Well, I never!" she said, huffing as she went.

"I daresay you haven't, which is a great pity." Prudence ignored the housekeeper's shocked protests and entered into the garden.

Walking quietly, Prudence made her way to the gate and crossed her arms. "Good evening, Mother."

Mother whirled, gasping. On seeing Prudence, she sagged against the garden gate, one hand to her chest, the other still tightly wound about a rope. "Goodness! You frightened me to death!"

"*I* frightened *you?* I'm not the one skulking around, leading sheep into the garden!"

Mother glanced over her shoulder. The rope in her hand led to a very fat, very slow-moving, and very disinterested sheep.

"I recognize that sheep," Prudence said.

The sheep seemed to realize she was the topic of discussion, for she opened her mouth, revealing large, yellowed teeth, and *baa'd* loudly.

Prudence shook her head. "Mother, *you* were the one who put the captain's sheep in our garden all this time. Why would you do such a thing?"

Mother made a helpless gesture. "I know this looks bad, but I didn't— That is to say, I never thought— I really didn't want—"

Prudence held up a hand. "We are going inside

before we freeze to death. Maybe you can make a coherent sentence then."

"Yes, but I ... I have to feed Daffodil first."

Prudence raised her brows. "Daffodil?"

"Our sheep. I mean, the earl's sheep." Mother had the grace to look slightly shamefaced. "I always feed her a little when she arrives. It's the only way I can get her to follow me. Usually I just open the gate and she trots in. But for some reason, she has been very, very difficult tonight." Mother frowned at the sheep that now stood munching on the shrubbery beside the gate. "I wonder if she's feeling quite the thing. I have not brought her to visit lately, and she has very tender feelings."

"Sheep do not have feelings."

Mother looked affronted. "They do, too!"

"Oh for the love of—I cannot believe you!" Prudence shook her head. "I cannot wait to hear your explanation for all of this. Feed your silly sheep and come inside. I'll have Mrs. Fieldings make us some tea." With that, Prudence returned to the house, where she found the housekeeper standing glumly in the hallway.

"I warned the missus, I did! 'Secrets are best kept in the open.' That's what I told her all along."

"You knew Mother was putting the sheep in our garden."

"Not at first. She was too sly for me then. But the third time, I noticed her cloak was damp and I knew she'd been out." Mrs. Fieldings smiled with a certain moribund satisfaction. "Didn't take me long to figure out which way the wind blew then."

"Mrs. Fieldings, would you please make some tea. Mother and I must talk."

"It's already on. I figured ye'd be wanting some tea to calm yer nerves. I started up the fire in the sittin' room, too, I did. Ye can have yer talk in there, just no yellin'. As soon as yer tea is done, I'm goin' back to bed."

With that unsympathetic caveat, Mrs. Fieldings trudged back to the kitchen. Prudence made her way into the sitting room. Her own mother... How could she have done it?

When Prudence thought of all the times she'd stormed over to the captain's and berated him about his sheep, it was almost more than she could stand. Goodness, what he must have thought of her then. What he must think of her now... She closed her eyes, tears beginning to well.

Mother entered the room, taking off her cloak as she did so. The hem of her gown was damp and bits of straw clung to one of her sleeves. "Prudence, I—I don't know what to say."

"Just explain why you went to such trouble."

Mother wrung her hands. "Oh dear! Do not look at me like that! I didn't mean any harm. Indeed, I had the best of intentions. I really did!"

"You misled me."

"Well... a little. I didn't lure Daffodil through the fence the first time. She appeared on her own."

Prudence raised her brows.

"Do not look at me as if you think I am lying! I am telling the truth!" Mother took Prudence's hand and led her to the settee. "Prudence, you must understand."

"I think I do."

"No, you don't." Mother sat, then pulled Prudence down beside her. "When we moved here, it dawned on me that while this was indeed a new beginning for me, for you it was . . . well, it was an exile of a sort."

"I was perfectly happy with my lot." Or she had been until she'd discovered the magic of being in Tristan's arms. Arms she'd never again feel clasped about her. A horrid lump grew in her throat.

"Prudence," Mother said gently, patting her hand, "I knew we were moving to an out-of-the-way place, but when we arrived, it was so desolate. So isolated. It's not what I wanted for you. But then I saw the earl—well, he wasn't an earl then, but he seemed so perfect for you."

"Perfect? He was rude and arrogant and refused to have anything to do with us!"

"Except for that, he was perfect," Mother amended hastily. "He is not an easy man, is he? But I knew he had to be quite kind to allow all of those wounded sailors into his home. There is something honorable and brave about him. I don't know what it is, but . . ." Mother shrugged helplessly.

Prudence knew what it was that made Tristan the one and only person you wanted to be with when things were wretched; it was his heart. He was steadfast and loving, capable of immeasurable caring. And she loved him dearly.

Mother sighed. "I am so sorry to mislead you about the sheep. But I had to do something. The earl is stubborn and wouldn't visit us. But he was the only man around, except for the doctor, who would not do for you at all—"

"I thought you liked the doctor."

"Oh, I do. But he is far too weak for you. You'd monopolize the relationship within the hour and that would be that."

"Mother!"

Mother pinkened. "Well, it's true. You have a good bit of me in you, and that was ever my problem. Although, to be honest, I was never as outspoken as you, but that is only because I was raised so differently."

"I am not sure if you're complimenting me or disparaging me."

"It is a compliment. Only, it does not lead to a providential marriage unless your partner is of equal strength."

Prudence had to smile a little at that. "Like Father."

"Exactly. Thank goodness he was who he was, or the marriage would have been a disaster." Mother's eyes grew misty. "I still miss him, you know."

Prudence nodded. "Sometimes, I think of Phillip, but... Mother, it doesn't matter. None of this matters. Tristan— I mean, the earl—and I are no longer speaking."

"That was another thing that made me certain I'd done the right thing, when the captain became an earl! What could have been more perfect then?"

"Mother, I don't care if he's an earl."

"I do. You deserve an earl. Even a duke." Mother considered this a moment. "I could even see you with a prince, although having witnessed one prince up close when I was in my youth and being thoroughly disgusted—some are monstrously fat—I wouldn't wish that on anyone."

Prudence managed a pained sigh. "Thank you for

that, at least. I cannot believe you were so secretive. I never knew you to be so."

"I never had any reason to be before. It is amazing what you will do for your children. I felt badly at first, though poor Daffodil is usually quite docile. All I had to do was tuck a bit of apple into my pocket and let her smell it. She'll follow you for miles for just one bite, greedy creature."

Prudence squeezed Mother's hand. "I am certain Daffodil is a good sheep. Mother, about the earl—our relationship will never be more than it is now. Please, promise me, no more tricks."

Mother sniffed. "You may have given up on him, but I have not."

"Mother, one of the trustees is Lord Ware."

Mother paled. "The one who told everyone you—" Mother's lips clamped into a white line. After a moment of visible struggle, she said in a clipped voice, "I have a few choice words to tell that man."

"I am certain he didn't mean what he said. He lost almost three hundred thousand pounds to Phillips's scheme and was angry. Still, he would never countenance a connection between Tristan and myself."

"What does the earl have to say about that?"

"Nothing. I will not let him."

"Oh, Prudence! You shouldn't—"

The door opened and Mrs. Fieldings came in with their tea. She plopped the tray on the table. "Well, didn't hear no screamin'. I suppose ye got things settled, eh?"

Mother smiled gratefully. "Almost. Thank you so much for the tea. We need something warm—"

A knock sounded on the outside door. Prudence and Mother exchanged surprised glances.

"Who'd come at this hour of the night?" muttered Mrs. Fieldings, leaving the room. "No good Christian would come to visit after dark."

The knock sounded again. Mother stood and crossed to the window. She squinted down into the night, trying to see the front door. "Oh, I can't see a thing!"

"Mother, come and sit down. Mrs. Fieldings has already let our visitor in. I can hear him in the hallway." It was not Tristan's deep voice, but another familiar one. Prudence bit her lip as the door opened.

Mrs. Fieldings entered the room, her usual sour expression gone. Reeves followed closely, smiling a little when the housekeeper announced in a rather impressed voice, "Mr. Reeves to see Mrs. Thistlewaite."

Reeves bowed. "His lordship sent me. He wishes your attendance at his cottage."

"Wonderful!" Mother said, clasping her hands together. She turned to her daughter. "Prudence, go and get your cloak—"

"I am not going anywhere."

Reeves nodded gravely. "Madam, his lordship has made me privy to your disagreement. May I say I am gravely disappointed in him, as he is in himself."

"I don't ever want to see him again."

"Madam, I cannot blame you, but I don't think you understand. I was sent to fetch you, no matter what it takes."

Mother gave an excited hop. Reeves turned his head in her direction, his brows raised inquiringly.

Mother colored and smoothed her hair. "Oh dear,

but the fire gets a bit warm. I'll just stand over here." . She moved to the other side of the fire, slightly behind the butler.

Reeves bowed, then turned back to Prudence. "Madam? It would mean a lot to his lordship if you would attend him."

Prudence wished her heart would stop galloping so. "Did he tell you that?"

"Yes, madam. He was most fervent."

Fervent. That sounded rather nice. From behind Reeves, Mother waved her hands wildly, gesturing from Prudence to the door, urging her to go. Prudence sent her a quick frown, then said to Reeves, "Did his lordship say *why* he wished to speak to me?"

From her vantage point behind Reeves, Mother leaned forward, agog.

Reeves nodded. "The trustees, madam. They arrived today. I believe his lordship wishes to tell you the outcome himself, as well as pay you for your efforts."

Prudence's shoulders slumped. He wished to pay her. The impersonality of it all weighed her down. "I see. Please thank him for me, but I believe it would be better if his lordship just sent his payment here. I don't wish to see him."

*"Oh!"*

Mother's cry of outrage made both Reeves and Prudence turn.

"Prudence, I have had enough."

Prudence blinked at her mother's stern tone. "What—"

"Take your cloak and go with Reeves."

"But I don't wish—"

"This is not for you, but for me. Prudence, I know you and the earl had a disagreement, but it is rather selfish of you to let such a paltry thing stand in the way of such a kind invitation."

Prudence flushed. "It is neither paltry nor selfish."

"I am dying to know how the visit with the trustees went. If you do not go, it will be a week before we find out. I simply cannot wait that long. So fetch your cloak and go with Mr. Reeves."

Prudence was on her feet without realizing it. "Mother! I already went to bed once this evening! At least I had until you brought that sheep into the garden."

"You were not sleeping. You were merely lying abed, tossing and turning. Don't pretend otherwise." She crossed the room to her daughter's side, placed her hands on Prudence's shoulders and turned her toward the door. "At least this will get you out of the house and stop your moping about."

Prudence's cheeks pinkened. "Mother, I don't think I want to—"

"Nonsense. Of course you do."

"But—"

"Prudence." Mother looked directly into her eyes. "If you don't go, you will spend the rest of your life *wondering*."

"Mrs. Crumpton," Reeves said softly. "His lordship requested your attendance as well."

Mother exploded into a wreath of smiles. "Well!

There you go! Prudence, it looks as if we have an invitation to the earl's cottage!" Before Prudence could protest again, Mother was off to the front entryway to collect their cloaks.

# Chapter 21

Ah, the joys to be had in a job well done! Has there ever been a more pure, more satisfying euphoria?

*A Compleat Guide for*
*Being a Most Proper Butler*
by Richard Robert Reeves

*T*he ride to Tristan's was filled with Mother's incessant talking as she tried, at first gently and then with increasing force, to talk Reeves out of some vital tidbits of information. The butler was amazingly reticent, merely smiling now and then and quietly saying that his lordship would soon reveal all.

What there was to reveal, Prudence could not begin to know. Why did Tristan wish her to attend him? And why had he asked Mother, as well? Whatever he had to say, she could only hope she kept her composure. The closer they were to the earl's cottage, the less certain she was of her ability to remain calm.

They arrived at a house filled with light. Stevens opened the door before they'd even climbed down from the carriage.

"Right this way, madam!" he said, beaming pleasantly.

Mother bustled right by, anxious to get into the house, but Prudence lingered on the front step. "Stevens? Where is your new coat?"

He was dressed as he used to be, in an ill-fitted sea coat and a rather faded striped shirt. "Ah, that," he said. He cast a wild gaze at Reeves.

"Yes, that," Reeves said. "Master Stevens has stopped wearing his new coat because of, ah, the silver buttons."

"What of them?"

Reeves exchanged a look with Stevens.

"Weel now, missus," Stevens said, swallowing rather loudly. "Those buttons were ah, bright and shiny." A thought seemed to occur, for he clapped his hands together and said with increasing enthusiasm, "Yes, that's what they were! Bright and shiny! And they made all the men envious. Afore ye knew it, fights was breakin' out and the men wouldn't hardly speak to me, sayin' I was a changed man because of those buttons and all."

Prudence eyed first him, then Reeves.

Reeves gave her a pale smile. "Shall we retire to the library? Your mother is in the hallway and looks quite impatient."

"I suppose we should go, then."

Stevens winked broadly at her. "Forge ahead, missus! Forge ahead!"

Reeves bowed and soon Prudence was following Mother down the narrow hallway. Along the way they ran into not one, but four of the other men, all equally mussed and beaming so brightly they almost tripped over their own smiles. Prudence's steps faltered a bit, though Mother hurried on.

The entire household was awash in happiness. Prudence's chest ached the tiniest bit. Obviously the trustees' visit had gone well.

That was good; she could be happy for Tristan, if not for herself. She only wished things had been different. For both of them.

She reached the library just in time to see her mother curtsy to a tall figure dressed in impeccable black breeches and waistcoat. The man looked every inch an earl. Only . . . he wasn't. What he was, was a highwayman. Or rather, a viscount/highwayman.

"Viscount Westerville," Prudence murmured as Stevens shut the door behind her. She curtsied as he bowed in her direction, his green eyes sweeping over her with appreciation.

Tall and lean, he was dressed head to toe in unrelenting black, which on another man would look far too somber. But on the black-haired, green-eyed viscount, it did nothing but emphasize his devastating charm. He was a handsome man, of lithe grace and an elegance that was difficult to describe. "Society will like you very well," Prudence said, wondering what this all meant.

Christian smiled, a rakish, devil-may-care smile that crinkled his eyes and made him look instantly younger. "Society may like me, but I have no intentions of liking it."

Tristan's voice rumbled from beside the fireplace. "My brother makes a fine coxcomb, does he not?"

Prudence had to collect herself before she turned. But even then, she was not prepared for what she saw. Tristan was dressed head to foot like...a pirate. He wore tight black breeches and leather boots that rose to his thighs. A flowing white shirt was tucked into a broad black belt from whence hung an assortment of pistols, knives, and one very large cutlass. Even more astonishing was the small gold ring that hung from one of his ears.

If the trustees had seen him dressed thusly—"Good heavens," she sputtered. "Tristan...what have you done?"

He threw her the lopsided smile that always sent her heart tumbling in place. "My brother and I decided it was time to show the trustees our true colors."

"But—but—"

"But before you say another word," Christian said, taking her by the hand. "Come and sit with your lovely sister on the settee."

Mother flushed bright red and giggled. "Oh, Lord Westerville! Don't begin with me! I'm old enough to be your...aunt."

Prudence sank onto the settee. "I don't understand. The fortune—what happened?"

Christian threw himself into the red chair. He grinned lazily. "My lady, do not look to Tristan. It was I who won the fortune." He waved a hand. "Of course, I shall have to spend a season in London and prove myself, but that is just a formality. The trustees were quite adamant that I should get the fortune and not my barbaric brother."

Silence met this announcement.

"I beg your pardon?" Mother said, her smile fading. She blinked rapidly as if trying to read something that was written in too small of letters. "Lord Westerville, did you say that *you* have won the earl's fortune?"

Christian sighed, placing his head against the high back of the chair. *"Veni, vidi, vici."*

"I came, I saw, I conquered," Prudence translated without thinking. Her mind worked furiously. "Christian charmed the trustees."

Mother's brows shot up. *"You* charmed the trustees?"

"All of them," Christian said with a dramatic wave of his arm. "Every last panty-laced one."

"Goodness!" She looked uncomprehendingly at Tristan. "But—"

He nodded. "I have the title, but no money. They flatly refused."

"And no wonder," Mother burst out, gesturing toward Tristan's clothing. "What else could they think after seeing you dressed like that?"

Tristan's grin looked amazingly like his brother's. "I did more than dress like a sailor."

"Oh?" Mother said, her eyes wide, uncomprehending.

Christian nodded. "He also cursed like one. Didn't he, Reeves?" he said as the butler entered the room with a tray bearing a teapot and some cups.

"Indeed he did," Reeves said pleasantly. "I fear I had not had the pleasure of hearing many sailor curses until I arrived here, but I must admit, few have their way with such an array of phrases and words as his lordship."

Prudence put her hand to her forehead. "I—I don't understand. Tristan—don't you *want* the funds?"

"Yes. But more than that, I want you."

Silence met this. Deep, abiding silence. Tristan took his cane from where it leaned against the wall by the fireplace and limped to Prudence's side. He took her hand in his and placed a kiss to her numb fingers. "Prudence, my love." His green eyes smiled down at her. "I am not a wealthy man. I have but what you see here. Still, I love you with all of my heart."

"Oh." It was all she could manage to say over the harsh pounding of her heart and the ringing in her ears. She struggled to comprehend what he was saying, what had happened, why Christian looked so smug and Reeves so pleased. But most of all, she struggled to absorb Tristan's words.

"Prudence," Tristan said, "will you listen to me? I once thought I would never be happy unless I was at sea. But now, I realize that you are the real adventure." He put a hand to her cheek and looked tenderly into her eyes. "I desire nothing more than having you by my side now and forever."

He loved her. Prudence's lips quivered. She couldn't say a word, but merely stared up at him. Slowly, she reached for his hand where it cupped her cheek. She wrapped her fingers around his wrist and turned the palm to her lips and kissed him.

His eyes darkened. "Prudence! Do you mean— You will marry me?"

Still unable to speak, she nodded. She was enveloped in a bone-crushing hug that lifted her off her feet and stole her breath. In that instant she knew she was right where she belonged—in Tristan's arms.

When Prudence was finally placed back on the floor,

the room was spinning and the beginning of a smile tickled her lips. He loved her. And he'd asked her to marry him for that reason and no other.

Mother dropped back against the settee, staring straight ahead, a dazed expression on her face. "I don't understand. I just don't understand. All that money. Gone. Just…gone! And *now* you ask Prudence to marry you?"

Reeves cleared his throat. "My lord? If I may?"

Tristan took a seat, pulling Prudence into his lap. "Reeves, please do. I am too busy right now to explain things."

Prudence put her hands on his face and turned him toward her. "Just one thing…if you cannot provide for the men, I don't wish you to regret being with me—"

"Ah, love. I will provide for the men. I was already working on some plans before Reeves came with this damnable inheritance. I would have solved the issue myself eventually." He placed his finger beneath her chin and lifted her face to his. "I am not a man to quit. When I want something, I get it."

Prudence had to grin then. Whatever happened, so long as he was happy… What more could she ask for? She smiled warmly into his eyes and wrapped her arms about his neck.

Tristan held her more tightly. He was so blessed. So very, very blessed.

"But—But… I don't understand," Mother wailed.

"Madam," Reeves said, "it was like this. Lord Rochester realized he cared for your daughter, but because of her unfortunate standing in the ton, he could not have the money and marry her. At least, not until the trustees released him from the provisions of the will, which they would not do if they knew he loved her. Which he does."

"No money? None at all?" Mother repeated.

"None. Lord Rochester, having at least one trait in common with his father, was not willing to wait. Nor was he willing to deny his lady love in public. At least, he wasn't after he'd thought about it." Reeves sent his master a rather stern look.

Tristan sighed against Prudence's hair. "I'm sorry about that, love. I should never have suggested such a thing. I was a cad to do so."

"Yes, you were," she said, snuggling against him. She turned sparkling brown eyes his way. "I shall exact my revenge another time."

He chuckled. "I look forward to it." He took her hand and placed a kiss upon it, pausing when his thumb brushed her ring finger. "Prudence. One more thing. About Phillip."

"Yes?"

"You loved him."

She threaded her fingers through Tristan's. "I loved him. Phillip was my best friend and a wonderful companion and I will never regret being with him. But you, Tristan, are more than that. You are the love of my life."

His heart swelled and he pressed a kiss to each of her fingers.

Reeves cleared his throat. "As I was saying to Mrs. Crumpton, upon reflection, his lordship came up with a new plan. He did the next best thing to winning the fortune himself."

"Which is?" Mother said, rubbing her temples.

"He made certain that though the trustees would not award him the money, they would definitely award it to his brother."

Mother looked at Christian. "But...he is a highway-man!"

"Not all of the time," Christian said with a deprecating flick of his hand, the lace at his cuffs draped delicately from his muscled wrist. "The trustees do not know of my little, ah, hobby. You are not aware of this, but I become a highwayman only when my funding grows short."

"Only when..." Mrs. Crumpton blinked.

"Yes. Other times, I live in my manor house in Dorset, where I plant all sorts of things and sponsor some bloody good hunting. I won the estate at cards, yet another fact the trustees do not need to know. They merely think me a gentleman farmer and that is all I intend to let them think me."

"A gentleman farmer," she said blankly.

Christian nodded. "One of the trustees is, in fact, a very close neighbor of mine, though he did not know it until today. I am regarded as something of a recluse, you see."

Prudence looked up at Tristan, a question in her brown eyes. "But...what of your men?"

"My brother...my soon to be *very* wealthy brother, has offered to purchase my old ship, the *Victory,* and pay for the initial establishment of a home for wounded sailors."

Prudence gave a pleased laugh. "That is wonderful!" she said, and looked at Christian through a suddenly shy smile. "Thank you so much. You are every bit as generous as your brother."

"I wish that were true," Christian said, standing, a startlingly fashionable figure, his green eyes burning with something beyond excitement of the moment. "This bargain does many things for me, none of which are charitable in nature. With, perhaps, the exception of seeing to my brother's happiness. I would pay three times what I have to secure that."

Tristan smiled at Christian over Prudence's head. "And I would do the same for you."

They looked at each other for a long, long moment. And then Christian bowed. "I would love to stay and savor the moment, but I must go. Poor Willie is still at the inn with a pained head. He will not be happy until he is back in Dorset, presiding over my stables. He really had no stomach for the road, you know. He is a much better head groom."

Reeves looked up from where he was handing Mrs. Crumpton a cup of tea. "A good servant will do many things in the name of his master. I hope you are compensating him for his large imagination while under your command."

"Of course," Christian said. "I believe in compensation. In all forms."

Christian took Prudence's hand and glanced over it to Tristan. "Strange how she does not seem quite so old as you described."

Prudence twisted to look at Tristan. "Old? Did you tell him I was—"

"Chris, I am so sorry you cannot stay," Tristan said, pulling Prudence even closer. "But I know you must leave. *Now.*"

"Sad, but true. Very true." Christian made his way to the door, pausing only a second to look back at Reeves. "I assume you will be visiting me next? I still have to win the final approval of the trustees, though it should not be too difficult of a task."

"I shall come the instant Lord Rochester is married."

"Excellent! I shall return for that. But I do think I shall need your help in London. I plan to reopen Rochester House. Tristan has kindly allowed me the use of it in exchange for funding his charity."

Reeves bowed, his blue eyes narrowing slightly. "I shall look forward to it. It has been a while since I had the joy of dressing someone who appreciates it."

Tristan chuckled. "Reeves, do not set your hopes too high. Christian won't wear puce, only black."

Christian nodded. "Color seems so...tawdry."

Reeves gave a small sigh. "I can see I have my work cut out for me."

"You always do," Tristan said. He looked down at Prudence, who sat upon his knee, her eyes warm with love.

Theirs would be a union of spirit and fervor. They would clash and argue with the same passion they shared beneath the sheets.

He would never leave her, nor she him. Together, he would help the sailors and she would run her school. And together, they would live a life blessed with love.

What more could anyone wish for?

Prudence leaned forward and placed her arms around his neck. "God bless Reeves," she whispered, placing her forehead against his.

He smiled in return. "God bless Reeves," he agreed.

# MEN ARE LIKE A BOX OF CHOCOLATES . . .

**You never know what you're going to get, but they're all tasty!**

There are over six billion people on this planet and half of them are men (yeah!). But how is a gal to choose among so many? Are you drawn to the quiet and sensitive bespectacled gentleman next door? Or are you just dying to tame that bad boy with the tattoo? Are you a fan of Russell Crowe or Tobey Maguire? Perhaps you like them all . . .

In these four Avon Romance Superleaders, we've compiled a little sampling of the yummiest men around to tempt even the pickiest heroine. Turn the pages and meet four irresistible heroes—a sexy cop, a debonair billionaire, a rakish reformed pirate and a scandalous dark lord . . .

*If you like the smooth
sophistication of a mousse-filled
chocolate, then you'll love*

# DON'T LOOK DOWN
### by Suzanne Enoch
### Coming January 2006

Ex-thief Samantha Jellicoe and British billionaire Richard
Addison are back for another sexy, twisted escapade of
romance, stolen jewels and male escorts in sizzling Palm
Beach. Sam is trying to set up a legitimate security business,
but when her first client ends up dead, Sam can't rest until
she figures out whodunit—a task complicated by Rick's
heated scrutiny.

"I caught you red-handed in Florida three months ago, and
now here in Devon. It's probably a good thing you did retire
from the cat burglary business."

Oh, that was enough of that, the superior British ass.
Samantha leaned up to kiss Rick, feeling the surprise of his
mouth and then his arms slipping across her shoulders as his
body relaxed. She slid the rope off her arm and twisted it
around his hands, ducking from beneath his grip.

"Sam—"

She whipped the free end of the rope around him, pulling
it tight and knotting his hands across the front of his ribs.
"Who's slipping now?" she asked.

"Take this off," he snapped, the gloating humor leaving his voice and his expression.

"Nope. You've disparaged my abilities." She pushed against his chest, and he sat down heavily in one of his Georgian reading chairs. "Apologize."

"Untie me."

Ooh, he was mad. Even if she'd been inclined to do so, letting him loose now seemed a supremely bad idea. Besides, she'd been working on a healthy adrenaline high that he'd managed to wreck. Before he could push to his feet, she tied him to the chair with the rest of the rope. "Maybe this'll convince you not to confront people breaking into your house unless you have something more substantial than charm to defend yourself with."

"You're the only one who breaks into my house, and I'm beginning to find it less amusing."

"Of course you are," she mused, stepping back to admire her handiwork. "I'm in charge."

Dark blue eyes met hers. "And apparently into bondage. Naughty, naughty."

"Apologize, Rick, and I'll let you go."

His jaw twitched, his gaze lowering to her mouth. "Let's say I'm calling your bluff. Do your worst."

"Ah." This was getting interesting. "My worst is pretty bad," she commented, her adrenaline beginning to recover. Tying up Rick Addison. Why hadn't she thought of this before? "Are you sure you're up for it?"

"Definitely," he returned, pushing toward her against the rope.

Slowly, Samantha leaned in and licked the curve of his left ear. "Good."

He turned his head, catching her mouth in a hard kiss. "So

is this what I should expect every time you meet with a client?"

Samantha pulled her pruners from her back pocket, amused at the sudden wariness in his eyes. "Apparently," she returned, snipping the neck of his sweatshirt and then opening up the front of the material to expose his chest and washboard abs. The first time she'd set eyes on him she'd thought he looked more like a professional soccer player than a businessman, and she still couldn't quite control the way his body affected her.

"Then I definitely encourage you to expand this business of yours."

"I don't want to talk about business right now."

*If you enjoy the seemingly
innocent surface of a cherry cordial
hiding a sinfully sweet center,
then you'll love*

## SEX, LIES, AND ONLINE DATING
**by Rachel Gibson**
**Coming February 2006**

Hardluvnman. Bigdaddy 182. Welcome to the world of online dating. Lucy has gone on a series of blind dates—and has pretty much given up—when she meets Quinn. At first he seems promising, but then he tells her his tales of woe, and she figures she's dating another loser. Except this time, Lucy doesn't realize she's dating a cop—one who is after a female killer—and, though she doesn't know it, Lucy may be a suspect. Is Quinn out to protect her or to get her?

Lucy pushed back the sleeve of her jacket and looked at her watch. Ten after seven. Ten minutes late. She'd give hardluvnman another five, and then she was leaving.

She'd learned her lessons about dysfunctional men. She wanted a nice, normal guy who didn't drink too much, wasn't into extremes of any kind, and didn't have mommy/daddy issues. A man who wasn't a compulsive liar or serial cheater. Who wasn't emotionally retarded or physically repugnant. She didn't think it was too much to ask that he have sufficient verbal skills, either. A mature man who knew that grunting an answer did not pass for conversation.

Lucy took a drink of her coffee as the door to Starbucks swung open. She glanced up from the bottom of her cup to the man filling up the doorway as if he'd been blown in from a "mad, bad and dangerous to know" convention. The bill of his red ball cap was pulled low on his forehead and cast a shadow over his eyes and nose. His tanned cheeks were flushed from the cold, and the ends of his black hair curled up like fish hooks around the edge of the hat. Rain soaked the wide shoulders of his black leather bomber's jacket. The jacket's zipper lay open, and Lucy's gaze slid down a bright strip of white T-shirt to the worn waistband of faded Levi's. As he stood there, his gaze moving from table to table, he shoved his fingers into the front pockets of the worn denim, his thumbs pointing to his button fly.

Mr. hardluvnman had finally arrived.

Like his photo on the Internet site, Lucy could not see him clearly, but she knew the second his gaze focused on her. She could feel it pinning her to her chair. She slowly lowered her cup as he pulled his hands from his pockets and moved toward her. He walked from his hips, all long and lean, with a purpose to each step. He navigated his way through chairs and coffee drinkers but kept his gaze on her until he stood across the small table.

The shadow of his cap rested just above the deep bow of his top lip. He raised a hand and slowly pushed up the brim of his cap with one finger. By degrees, the shadow slid up the bridge of his nose and past thick black brows. He looked down through eyes the color of a smoldering Colombian blend.

Lucy was a writer. She worked with words. She filled each of her books with a hundred thousand of them. But only two words came to mind. *Holy crap!* Not eloquent, but fitting.

"Are you Lucy?"

"Yeah."

"Sorry I'm late," he said. His voice was deep, testosterone rough. "My dog got into the garbage just as I was leaving, and I had to clean up after her."

Which Lucy supposed could be true but, she reminded herself, probably wasn't. Not that it mattered. After tonight, she would never see this hunk of hardluvnman again. Which was kind of too bad, since he was the best-looking thing she'd seen outside of a men's magazine.

"I'm Quinn." He held his hand toward her, and the sides of his jacket fell open across his chest to reveal hard pecs and abs of steel all wrapped up in his tight T-shirt. The kind of pecs and abs that begged the question: Why did a guy like him have to go online to find a date? It didn't take her long to come up with the answer. Inside that hard body, there was something wrong with him. Had to be.

Lucy took his hand in hers. His warm palm pressed into hers. Calloused. Strong. The kind that actually might belong to a plumber. She took her hand back and wrapped it around her cup. "Aren't you going to get a coffee?"

"I'm good." As he sat, his dark scrutiny touched her face, her hair, and cheeks, then slid to her mouth. His voice dropped a little lower when he asked, "Are you good?"

*If you're a fan of the nutty,*
*rough-around-the-edges taste of a*
*chocolate nut cluster,*
*then you'll love*

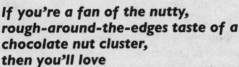

# HER MASTER AND COMMANDER
**by Karen Hawkins**
**Coming March 2006**

The Duke of Rochester's oldest illegitimate son, wounded war hero and one-time pirate Tristan Llevanth, has no idea that he's about to become "legitimized." Under the guidance of the duke's butler Reeves, his bothersome yet delectable neighbor Prudence Thistlewaite molds a reluctant Tristan into a real lord. Lessons turn into kisses, which quickly turn into hot, searing passion . . .

Prudence met his gaze without flinching. "I am here to see to it that you stop running from your responsibilities. I want the issue of the sheep resolved. I came here to see to it that you do something about it."

"I rather thought you came here because you enjoyed my company. My wit."

Her gaze narrowed. "I have asked you time and again to keep your sheep out of my garden."

"And I've said it before and again; shut the blasted gate—*firmly*."

She stamped her foot, her boot landing in a puddle and

splashing mud upon the edges of the moss green skirts barely visible beneath the voluminous blue cloak. "Captain, the gate *was* shut. *Firmly.*"

"Are you saying my sheep are jumping the fence into your garden?"

"Yes. The white one with the black face."

Tristan looked over his shoulder. "Stevens!"

The first mate appeared as if by magic. "Aye, Cap'n?"

"Do I have a white sheep with a black face?"

Stevens scratched his chin, his brow furrowed. "Hmm. Seems I seen one of that cut not too long ago."

"Is it possible that this particular sheep can jump a fence the height of the one surrounding Mrs. Thistlewaite's garden?"

"By Peter's watery grave, no!" the first mate said, chuckling at the thought.

Mrs. Thistlewaite's full lips pursed into a scowl. "Captain, I do not appreciate your levity. I do not know how your sheep manages to creep past my fence, but he does. And then he grazes through my spice bed like a great scythe, eating all of my herbs and trampling the flower beds."

"Hmm." Tristan noted the rising color in the widow's face. He stifled a grin. Perhaps he enjoyed teasing her so much because she looked so very prim and perfect, her hair so severely bound, her cloak buttoned to her throat, her mouth a determined line that almost dared to be invaded. Plundered. *Tasted.*

He found himself staring at her mouth. The bottom lip was fuller than the top and gently rounded underneath. He wondered if it was as sensitive as it looked, how she would react if he kissed her and then gently—

Startled at the direction his thoughts were taking, he pulled himself back into the present. "Mrs. Thistlewaite, as you can see, sheep do not jump good fences, nor do they crawl beneath closed gates, nor do they fly through the air to land in the midst of a garden. I, myself, have a garden, and the sheep never bother it, so I feel there are no grounds for your complaints. You will have to deal with the sheep issue on your own."

"Captain," Mrs. Thistlewaite said, her voice frigidly perfect, "I can see that I wasted my time coming here."

"You not only wasted it, but you have made yourself unwelcome. If you keep pestering me with this sheep nonsense, I shall train my dogs to herd those bloody animals onto your land every blasted morning."

"Oh! I cannot believe you'd— How dare you?" She drew herself up, her eyes flashing fire, her mouth set. "You, sir, are no gentleman."

*No gentleman.* The words flamed across his mind. His father had been a gentleman. "Fortunately for us all, I've never wanted to be a gentleman. Not now. Not ever."

*If you crave the complexity and*
*full flavor of a dark chocolate truffle,*
*then you'll love*

# SWORD OF DARKNESS
**by Kinley MacGregor**
**Coming April 2006**

The first in a dazzling new series, Lords of Avalon, intro-
duces Seren, a lovely young apprentice destiny has chosen
as the future mother of one of the most powerful
Merlins . . . Kerrigan is a Lord of Darkness sent by the evil
Morgen le Fey to capture and hold Seren until the Lords of
Avalon give Morgen what she needs to rule the world of
man and demon. But, recognizing her purity, Seren is what
Kerrigan has yearned for throughout time—yet can he save
her in the face of evil?

"Thank you, my lord," Seren said to the knight holding her.
"You have truly saved my life this day. I can never repay you
for your kindness."

The chase didn't seem to concern him at all as he guided
his horse with expert hand through the town. "And how is it
I have saved your life?"

"Those men who were after me. They were mad."

"How so?"

"They claimed that I was to be the mother of the wizard
Merlin. Mayhap they were only drunk, but . . ." She shivered

as she considered what had almost befallen her. "Thank the Lord and all his saints that you came when you did. I shudder to think what they would have done to me had I gone with them."

He gave her a knowing look. "Aye, there was a higher power that brought me to you this day. Of that I have no doubt."

Seren had just started to relax when she heard the sound of hooves behind them.

The knight turned to look.

"It's them!" she breathed, her panic returning as she saw the two knights again in pursuit. "Why won't they let me go?"

"Have no fear. I won't let them take you."

His words thrilled her. Who would have believed that such a handsome knight would defend a simple peasant maid? "You are truly a kind and noble knight, sir."

But as he looked down at her, Seren could have sworn that his eyes flashed red before he spurred his horse to an even greater speed. The other two knights continued to give chase. They raced through town until they flew over the bridge that took them out into the countryside.

Seren cringed. "I'm not to leave the town," she told the knight. "My master will have me beaten for leaving without his permission."

"There is nothing I can do. Should we return, they will take you. Is that what you want?"

"Nay."

"Then hold tight until we lose them."

Seren did as he said. She wrapped her arms about his waist and inhaled the scent of leather, man, and beast. His horse flew over the open meadow, racing toward the dense woods that lay before them.

All of a sudden, something exploded by their side.

*"Accero, accero domini doyan,"* the knight said in his deep, resonant voice.

Seren gasped in terror as the gargoyle decorations on the horse's bridle lifted themselves off and took flight. They screeched like banshees before they headed toward the men pursuing them.

"What is this?" she asked.

"You're lost in a dream." His voice was inside her head. "Sleep, little one. Sleep." Seren blinked her eyes as exhaustion overtook her. She tried desperately to remain awake but couldn't.

Before she knew what was happening, darkness consumed her.

In an eerie black mist, the visible world faded. The veil that separated the two realms mingled until Kerrigan found himself once more on the black soil of Camelot.

# Bestselling author
# KINLEY MACGREGOR

**Seren** is a lovely young apprentice who has simple dreams.
She doesn't know that destiny has chosen her as the future
mother of one of the most powerful Merlins...

**Kerrigan** is a Lord of Darkness who has been sent by the evil and power-hungry Morgen le Fey to capture Seren and hold her until the Lords of
Avalon agree to hand over the Round Table and several other sacred objects
that Morgen needs to rule the world of man and demon.

Charged with killing Seren once she's no longer useful, Kerrigan never expects to
fall in love. She's the heart he has yearned for throughout time, but can he save her
when all the demons in his realm need her to die in order for them to live?

Buy and enjoy *SWORD OF DARKNESS* (available March 28, 2006),
then send the coupon below along with your proof of purchase to Avon Books,
and we'll send you a check for $2.00.

- - - - - - - - - - - - - - - - - - - - - - - - - - - - - - - - - - - - - - -

Mail receipt and coupon for *Sword of Darkness* (0-06-056544-6) to:

AVON BOOKS/HarperCollins*Publishers* Inc., P.O. Box 767, Dresden, TN 38225.

NAME

ADDRESS

CITY

STATE/ZIP

*Offer valid only for residents of the United States and Canada. Offer expires 6/30/06.

◆ **Avon** Books
*An Imprint of* HarperCollins*Publishers*
www.harpercollins.com

SOD 0306

The seductive allure of *USA Today*
bestselling author

# Karen Hawkins

## CONFESSIONS OF A SCOUNDREL

0-380-82080-3•$5.99 US•$7.99 Can

Brandon St. John suspects the lovely Lady Verena
Westforth of hiding a valuable missive. With a sensuous
kiss and a passionate caress he intends to lower Verena's
guard and find the item in question.

## HOW TO TREAT A LADY

0-06-051405-1•$5.99 US•$7.99 Can

To save her family from ruin, Harriet Ward invented a wealthy
fiance. But now the bank wants proof of the man's existence.

## AND THE BRIDE WORE PLAID

0-06-051408-6•$6.99 US•$9.99 Can

Devon St. John vows he will never give up his beloved
freedom—even when a temptress's impulsive kiss casts a
tantalizing spell . . .

## LADY IN RED

0-06-058406-8•$6.99 US•$9.99 Can

Marcus St. John must recover a lost family heirloom from the
irritatingly beautiful Miss Honoria Baker-Sneed.

## HER MASTER AND COMMANDER

0-06-058408-4•$6.99 US•$9.99 Can

Prudence Thistlewaite wants nothing to do with her wickedly
handsome, ill-tempered neighbor Captain Tristan Llevanth.

Visit www.AuthorTracker.com for exclusive
information on your favorite HarperCollins authors.

HAW 1205